OF SKY & EMBERS

CLAIRE BUTLER

Cover by 100Covers

Editing by Phoenix Rising Literary Services

CONTENTS

For all the readers who saw the one camel trope and thought
"I have to read this book!"

And for Humphrey, the original camel.

CONTENT WARNING

Please note: This series contains explicit content and elements that may be triggering to some. It includes explicit sexual scenes, mature language, and violence. It is not intended for anyone under the age of 16. For a full list of triggers, please visit www.clairebutlerauthor.com

NOTE TO THE READER

The Divine Tapestry Series takes place in a Middle Eastern inspired world. The landscape, the food, and other elements were inspired by various places and cultures that I have been fortunate enough to travel to and fall in love with. Having said that, Merovia is a fantasy world and this is a work of fiction. It is my sincere hope that nothing in this book is offensive to people from the Middle East. I have tried to ensure that this is avoided, however, if it does occur, please know that it was not intentional on my part.

x Claire

GODDESSES AND GODS OF MEROVIA

Water Goddess: The deity who holds power over the essence of water in all its forms.

Sun God: The deity who commands the sun and light. Artists often depict him wearing a fiery crown that symbolizes the sun's rays.

Moon God: The deity who governs the moon and lunar forces. He is sometimes shown holding the lunar phases on a string.

Goddess of Endings and Beginnings: The deity who embodies the cycle of endings and beginnings. She often holds a silver hourglass of sand.

God of Justice and Kingship: The deity of justice, kingship and cosmic order. He upholds the principles of fairness and righteousness. He is depicted as holding a balanced scale in one hand and a crown in the other.

God of Beauty and Fertility: The deity who grants the birth of children. He is known for his admiration and collection of beautiful women. He is sometimes shown holding a mirror in one hand and a rose in the other.

God of Fire and Ash: The deity who wields fire. He receives the sacrifices that are cast into the fire and is responsible for bringing them to the gods. He is represented by holding a staff of flame.

God of Earth and Salt: The deity who shapes the earth. He receives the lesser sacrifices that are buried and is responsible for bringing them to the gods. He is typically portrayed holding a fist full of soil in one hand and a fist full of salt in the other.

God of War and Valor: The deity embodying strength, courage, honor and the spirit of battle. He is often depicted as holding a shamshir or spear.

CHAPTER ONE

HENRI

Henri gripped the hilt of his sword and maintained a defensive stance as he watched the desert warriors slowly surround them. Each step they took was slow and provocative, almost mocking. The sheer size of their frames was enough to be intimidating without the solid muscle that gleamed everywhere he looked. The way they moved and held their spears and shields told Henri they were well trained. There were only a dozen Naiab warriors, but that was enough to put the odds heavily in the Naiab's favor. Henri was confident that he and Malik could hold their own in a fight, but Tahlia lacked training, and Ele and Kala would be easy prey. If swords clashed, someone would not survive.

Hopefully, Ele and Kala remained hidden under the tent tarp. Knowing Ele, though, he had probably emerged, keen to defend his king. Kala wasn't exactly one to sit on the sidelines of a fight, either. Her aim with a slingshot was impressive.

Henri risked a glance over at Tahlia to see that she was yet to draw her hidden dagger. She was simply standing there, limp, staring at one of the Naiab who was directly in front of her. As Henri's eyes darted between them, he could see why. The man was a beast. He was easily the largest out of all the warriors, his golden chest a broad expanse of muscle and his arms thick with corded strength. Like the other Naiab, his body was covered in turquoise tattoos that seemed to shimmer in the sunlight and move beneath the surface of his skin.

The warrior held a spear in his hand formed from sand, but that was not what made Henri's instincts pull taut in warning. It was the way the man's eyes were fixed on Tahlia, his focus both ravenous and analytical, as if she were a beautiful mystery that he wanted to unravel before devouring her whole. When the warrior took a predatory step toward her, Henri swiftly moved to stand between them, shielding her with his body and forcing the warrior to look at him instead.

The Naiab halted and pierced him with a severe expression, but Henri matched it with his own ruthless glare, daring him to take another step. If the man thought he was going to put his hands on Tahlia, he was dead wrong. As if to reinforce the message, Malik flanked Tahlia's side, a sword in one hand and a dagger in the other.

"If you have something to say, Naiab, you will say it to me." Henri's words rumbled low in his throat.

The warrior's gaze sharpened before it drifted over Henri's shoulder. "A king, a murderer, a goddess, and two children. Strange convoy."

"We are traveling to the Old City for the summit," Malik interjected, his tone that of a calm, confident diplomat. "We were refused passage through the other kingdoms and had no choice but to go through your desert. We mean no disrespect."

"Did you mean disrespect when you killed one of us?"

Henri didn't dare take his eyes off the warrior, but he could feel Malik stiffen beside him at the mention of the Naiab warrior who had breached the palace walls only to die at Malik's hands.

"Your comrade tried to kill my king," Malik said.

"Careful," the warrior replied, his tone dangerously low. "In the Idris, if a tongue lies, we cut it out."

Henri's features instantly darkened at the threat. It took all his self-control to keep his blade in its sheath, but he couldn't quite keep the snarl from his voice. "You know who we are and why we are here. Now, what do you want from us?"

The Naiab considered him for a moment as if sizing up his worth. "What we have wanted from the beginning. To talk."

Talk.

Validation washed over Henri like a cool ocean breeze. He had been right to think that the Naiab warrior was not trying to assassinate him. He had wanted to talk. But then Maik had killed him, an innocent man. The validation quickly evaporated.

"So talk," Henri said flatly.

"Not me, not here. You will come with us to speak to our Shahri."

Henri wasn't sure what a Shahri was, but he could guess. No one knew anything about the Naiab, including how they governed themselves or how they managed to survive in the Idris desert. The attacks on the northern wall were the first time anyone had laid eyes on them in centuries. Their sand wielding magic was unheard of, its origins unknown.

"Fine," Henri agreed.

"Kafei." Malik shot Henri a warning look.

The use of the term sounded foreign on Malik's lips after he had moaned Henri's name several times last night in pleasure. He was clearly trying to maintain formal appearances in front of a suspected enemy. Except, Henri wasn't so sure the Naiab were the enemy.

Malik clearly did not share his skepticism. He had never trusted the Naiab. He had killed the supposed assassin without hesitation. Which could be excused as blind loyalty, except for the fact that everyone Henri wanted kept alive for questioning had met their deaths at Malik's hands. Malik had also deliberately withheld information from Henri about the attacks on the northern wall. Perhaps it was nothing more than a series of coincidences, but the alternative was that Malik had done everything in his power to keep Henri away from the Naiab. Which made Henri even more determined to go with them.

Henri held Malik's uneasy stare and drawled, "I'm sure if we're late to the summit, they will wait for me. I am the main event, after all."

Malik's features tightened in disapproval.

Henri ignored him and turned back to the warrior. "We will follow you."

Henri slowly sheathed his sword and angled his body so that he could see behind him without having to turn his back on the

Naiab. Just because he had doubts about them being the enemy did not mean he was going to take foolish chances. Henri was surprised to find Tahlia taking up a defensive stance to protect their backs. She held the dagger in her hand as if she might actually use it. Ele was also armed and leveling a serious scowl at the Naiab warriors, despite the fact that they towered over him like giants. Kala remained at Ele's side, their hands firmly clasped together in determination.

"Ele, you ride with Kala. Tahlia, you ride with me," Henri ordered.

Tahlia glanced over her shoulder at him and he nodded slightly in reassurance before everyone reluctantly put their weapons away. The Naiab let their spears and shields dissolve into sand at their feet. Ele's mouth gaped in fascination at the sight while Kala's eyes widened in fright.

"Are you gods?" Kala spluttered.

"No," the warrior deadpanned. His tone broached no further discussion on the topic.

Ele tugged at Kala's hand to lead her away while Malik strolled over to the tent and began repacking it. Tahlia came to stand at Henri's side but her focus remained on the Naiab warrior.

"Where are you taking us?" Tahlia asked.

"To the Citadel." The warrior said it as if it should mean something to them.

Tahlia inhaled a shallow breath as her eyes roamed his body unashamedly. "You're going to lead us by walking there? Naked?"

All of the Naiab were naked. Their skin had an odd coloring to it, like a golden hue. Henri supposed there was no point in wearing clothes or shoes if they were only going to disperse into sand.

"The sun does not burn us like it does you," the Naiab explained.

Interesting.

"Tell your men to return to the Citadel and you can ride with us. I'm sure Henri can find you some clothes to wear."

Henri blinked, surprised at Tahlia's brazenness in issuing the warrior orders. The Naiab surrounding them also seemed to shift with unease. It was possible that she was trying to increase their chances of escape by convincing the warrior to send his men away. Though, surely, she realized that as long as they were traveling across the desert, there was no way to escape warriors that could move through sand. Maybe she was genuinely concerned about the warrior's welfare. Or perhaps she was trying to feel out the limits of their magic.

Tahlia stared at Henri pointedly before he realized he hadn't moved. He strolled over to one of the camels to retrieve a clean kurta from his saddlebag before he returned and held it out to the Naiab. The warrior considered it before flicking his gaze to Tahlia. Evidently, he was suspicious of her intentions as well.

"You have my word that we will follow you," Henri offered.

"Do I have your word, goddess?"

Henri's brows narrowed. Not only was the Naiab ignoring him in deference to Tahlia, but he had called her a goddess twice now. Tahlia was without a doubt the most beautiful woman he had ever laid eyes on, however he had a feeling the warrior was not using the word in an attempt at flattery.

Her voice was uneven as she replied, "My name is Tahlia. And yes, you have my word."

The warrior tilted his head in a silent signal to his men and they exchanged tense looks with each other before evaporating into sand. A surprised gasp drew from behind Henri, but he couldn't tell if it belonged to Kala or Ele. The Naiab took the kurta and pulled it over his body. Somehow the loose, floor-length, long-sleeved tunic looked tight on him.

"What is your name?" Tahlia enquired innocently.

"Isa."

Tahlia gave a polite, satisfied nod and then looked over at Henri, holding his gaze for a pregnant moment, before she walked in the direction of the camels. Henri sensed that look was meant to convey something to him, but he had no idea what. When he turned to follow her, he noticed that Ele and Kala had already mounted and were waiting for them. Malik was lingering next to his camel, a vicious scowl on his face.

A twinge of guilt twisted his gut for overruling Malik's reservations so swiftly, but Henri promptly pushed it aside. He needed to trust his instincts, now more than ever, and his instincts had always pulled him toward the Naiab. Besides, he didn't really have a choice. He suspected that if he declined their invitation, they would have insisted on escorting them at spear point. Hopefully the Citadel was not too far away and the detour would not take long. He would listen to what the Naiab had to say and then they could continue on to the Old City.

Henri's attention caught on Tahlia as she approached one of the camels only to be confronted by Isa's outstretched hand offering to help her up into the saddle. She stared back at the warrior, stunned at the gesture. Henri quickly moved to intercept but he was too late. Tahlia took Isa's hand, her cheeks warming to a pale shade of rose, as she positioned herself in the front saddle.

Henri cast a warning glare at Isa before pulling himself up into the saddle behind her. To his annoyance, Isa looked completely unrepentant. He simply strolled over to Malik's camel and they both mounted the animal before moving into position to lead the convoy.

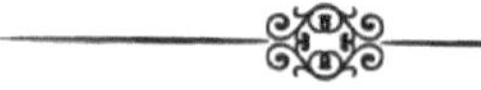

MALIK

Hours later and the blood was still boiling in Malik's veins, wild and hot, as his mind raced with a million thoughts. Most of them murderous. It would be so easy to kill the man in front of him. A blade through the ribs. Strangulation with his own headscarf. Malik probably wouldn't be strong enough to snap the warrior's thick neck with his bare hands, but he was keen to try.

The Naiab's invitation was clearly a trap. The odds of them surviving an attack by a dozen warriors were not great, but they were significantly better than the odds of them surviving the entire Naiab tribe. Once they entered the Citadel, they would be completely outnumbered and at the Naiab's mercy. They might not make it out alive.

Henri's problem was that he was impulsive and reckless and entirely too trusting. He always wanted to give everyone the benefit of a doubt. A chance to prove themselves as allies or adversaries. It was a weakness that would get him killed. If the Naiab only wanted to talk, like they claimed, they wouldn't have attacked the northern wall.

Repeatedly.

Merovian soldiers had died in those attacks. Men and women had sacrificed their lives to protect their people from a foreign enemy. The warriors had materialized out of the sand dunes in broad daylight, making no attempt to hide their bloody intentions before they cast their spears directly at the soldiers on the wall. They had shown no mercy. They had expressed no remorse.

Malik glared at the back of the Naiab's headscarf. The warrior had most likely been there that day, commanding his men to strike, to reap Merovian lives. Doubtless the warrior saw it as restitution for when his people had been cast out into the Idris desert generations ago for refusing to yield to the reign of the Rouhan family. Malik could understand their bitterness at such cruelty, but he would never accept their revenge. He refused to pay the price for the sins of his ancestors, and he would be damned if he let those Merovian soldiers die in vain.

Right now, though, there was nothing he could do to avenge their deaths. Henri had made the foolish decision to accept the invitation, so Malik had no choice but to try to keep Henri alive.

Like always.

It had been this way since the day Henri arrived on Merovian shores, wearing a full ensemble of steel armor despite the blistering desert heat. He had not hesitated to end King Dahane's lucrative slave trade or spared a thought for the consequences of banishing the king's vizier from his kingdom. Nor had he taken precautions before entering the Thaka district. In fact, upon learning that four Merovian kings intended to kill him, he had invited them all to a festival in honor of his reign. Malik had thought him impetuous at best, brazenly arrogant at worst. It was a miracle that Henri had survived the assassination attempts on his life so far. If it wasn't for Tahlia, Henri would be dead.

Malik's thoughts continued to simmer as the hours passed by. The scenery did not change. The dunes rose and fell in sweeping strokes, rolling into each other as the scorching wind blew over them. Beneath a cloudless blue sky, the horizon seemed endless. The heat blasted him like a fueled furnace and dried his eyes to paper. Beneath his cloak and headscarf, Malik's skin was damp with salt and sweat. Having lived in Merovia his whole life, he was used to its arid climate, but the Idris desert was another landscape entirely. It was relentless in its punishing force. The only relief came at nightfall, when the temperature would mildly reduce. Sometimes, though, it was still too hot to sleep.

Not that the heat was responsible for his lack of sleep last night. Malik couldn't recall how many times Henri had made him come, but he had memorized the hardened contours of his body and he still had the taste of him on his tongue. He could still feel

Henri's strong, calloused hands holding him firm as he plunged into him over and over again. Malik shifted uncomfortably in the saddle as his cock stiffened. He was furious at Henri for making yet another reckless decision, and he intended to make his objections very fucking clear when they found a moment alone together. But the second the argument was over, Malik already knew he would be tearing at Henri's clothes with greedy fingers and punishing his lips with bruising kisses before taking him into his mouth like a remedy. The very thought of it made him throb with need.

It was mid-afternoon when the landscape began to change. Striking rock formations emerged before a mountainous terrain came into view. Malik thought he was imagining it, but when he tossed his gaze over his shoulder at the others, they mirrored stark looks of disbelief. This was not on any map of Merovia he had ever seen. Though he supposed there was no reason why it would be. No one, except the Naiab, had entered the Idris desert for generations. Even before the walls were erected in each kingdom, Malik doubted many people would have dared to enter such a wasteland.

As they trekked deeper inside the mountain range, Isa led the convoy into a narrow canyon. Malik looked up in wonder at the towering steep walls of red sedimentary rock surrounding them. The layers in the rock were mesmerizing, each a different shade of red and orange and pink, evidencing just how old these mountains really were. Mercifully, they also blocked the biting rays of the sun, providing a cool, shaded path and welcome respite from the heat. Soft, natural light filtered in from above.

Malik vigilantly scanned their surroundings for threat but he couldn't see anyone. Nor did he get the sense that they were being watched. If the Naiab had sentries, they were well hidden. Which was impossible given that there was nowhere to hide. The walls of the canyon were sheer and void of landings to perch on. There were no boulders or trees from which to take coverage behind.

The sounds of the camels trudging along the path echoed off the sandstone walls like a steady heartbeat. Glancing down, Malik noticed that the sand beneath their feet was gradually changing color. It was fading from a deep, rusty red until it turned a fine, powdery white. As they moved further along the gorge, it became narrow, forcing them to travel single file.

After a few more miles Isa halted the convoy. Malik's senses sharpened as he cast his eyes above and around their surroundings but all he could see was rock and sky.

"Why have we stopped?" Malik demanded.

"We will go the rest of the way on foot." Isa forced the camel to the ground and dismounted.

Malik grit his teeth in irritation but there was nothing he could do except follow suit.

"How much further?" Tahlia asked as she and Henri came to stand with them.

The edge in her voice betrayed her concern for Ele and Kala. Although they would never complain, they looked more than a little weary. Truth be told, the journey across the Idris desert was taking its toll on everyone.

Isa's sharp features softened a little. "Not far."

Tahlia offered a small smile. It seemed to captivate the warrior. There was something happening there. Something that he was missing. Malik used the moment of distraction to covertly check his weapons. His shamshir was resting at his side but he was also carrying two hidden daggers beneath his kurta. It reassured him to feel their steel against his skin. Not that his weapons would be enough to save them against the force of the entire Naiab tribe.

As Malik lifted his gaze, he found Henri staring at him, knowingly. Malik pulled his features taught to emphasize his displeasure at the fact that they were in this situation to begin with. If Henri felt any guilt or remorse at all he didn't show it, which only aggravated Malik more.

He cast his eyes past Henri down the narrow, winding canyon. If the Citadel wasn't far from here, that meant that if they had to escape, they would be fleeing down this ravine. Now that he thought about it, the Citadel was impressively fortified. Surrounded by rugged, mountainous terrain, it was well protected. Any enemy would be forced to approach through the narrow gorge, making it easy to repel them and defend the city.

When Isa began to stride ahead, Henri called after him, "We can't leave the camels and our supplies behind."

The warrior did not stop as he tossed over his shoulder, "They'll be taken care of."

Tahlia exchanged a look with Henri before turning her eyes to Malik in search of an answer.

Ele simply kicked at the white sand beneath his feet. "Sand wielders."

Of course.

There was no need for sentries to hide or position themselves atop the steep sandstone walls because they were quite literally under foot. Malik resisted the urge to stomp his feet like a child. Instead, he fell in line with everyone else as they followed Isa further into the canyon.

They hadn't walked very long before Malik's attention caught on an opening ahead that had been carved into the wall of rock. It was a crude entrance the size of a door. Isa stood beside it and gestured for them to walk inside the pit of darkness.

"Wait." Malik stalked ahead before Henri could walk into yet another trap. "I'll go first."

With his hand resting on the hilt of his shamshir, Malik speared Isa with a charring look before he cautiously stepped into the void.

CHAPTER TWO

TAHLIA

Tahlia stared into the pit of darkness as Malik disappeared inside the entrance. She tried not to shiver but cold fingers crept up her spine in warning. Something about this place felt—wrong. Almost foreboding. Like she shouldn't be here. Like she needed to *run*. Tahlia pressed her feet further into the sand, in defiance of her instincts, and distracted herself by straining her ears to listen for the slightest of sounds. She could no longer hear Malik's footsteps echoing back at her, which was disconcerting, but she also didn't hear any steel clashing or sounds of an ambush.

Tahlia glanced back at Henri in silent question of who should go next, only to find him looking sickly pale and unnerved. It was clearly more than the desert heat or concern for Malik's welfare. It was as if the thought of entering the darkness was paralyzing to him. But before she could open her mouth to question him, Ele stepped forward. He clutched a dagger in one hand and held Kala's hand in the other as she followed a step behind him. Tahlia watched as they strode into the dark void together, their little faces grim with determination. She would never stop being in awe of Ele's loyalty or Kala's bravery.

Returning her gaze to Henri, Tahlia noticed that he hadn't moved an inch and his breathing had become uneven. She moved to his side and gently threaded her fingers through his. The touch seemed to jolt him out of his prison of thoughts. He stared down at her, his eyes rapidly searching hers for something. She offered a curt, reassuring nod. An answer that they would do this together. Henri licked his lips apprehensively and tightened his grip on her hand.

As they stepped inside the sandstone wall, darkness consumed them and the temperature plummeted. Despite not being able to see anything in front of them, they continued to take small, uncertain steps, hoping that the way was clear and that it would eventually lead them somewhere. After a moment, Tahlia's eyes adjusted to the dark. From the edges of her vision, she could just make out that they were inside some kind of tunnel. The silence was profound. It caused her to scuff her feet just to hear the echo of their steps. The air was heavy with the scent of ancient earth but it was not dry. It was laced with moisture.

A faint glimmer of light pierced through the darkness ahead, beckoning them. Tahlia's heart collapsed in relief. Their steps became more certain until they finally emerged from the mouth of the tunnel. The cavernous expanse of a mighty desert cave greeted them, illuminated by the warm glow of sunlight filtering through a natural opening in the ceiling. The others stood in silent wonder at the sight before them and Tahlia and Henri joined them without a word. Because in the heart of the cave, carved into sandstone walls which stretched for miles toward the sky, was a city.

The vertical city was circular in design and seemed to defy gravity itself. Each layer of mineral formation presented a new level. Narrow walkways wound around each level like veins but there were no railings to prevent people from plummeting down the sheer faces of the sandstone cliffs to the ground below. The residents didn't seem to mind though. Each floor was bustling with activity as people went about their daily lives.

Tahlia noted the labyrinth of corridors along each landing, formed from the rock that encased them. They wound through the city, while natural bridges and carved stairs clung precariously to the sandstone walls. The city was a maze. It would be so easy to get lost, but she had a suspicion that every road would eventually lead back to the center and the most astonishing feature of all. At ground level, surrounded by the vertical city, was a field. Tahlia almost couldn't believe her eyes. Despite the harsh desolation of their surroundings, the field was thriving with wheat, vegetables, towering fruit trees, and herbs.

It was inconceivable. There was no hint of water anywhere and the ground remained a fine white sand, not conducive to growing crops. Yet there it was. A testament to the enduring power of nature to thrive in the most unlikely of places.

"Follow me."

Tahlia started at Isa's voice behind her. She had entirely forgotten that he was there and that they should be on guard. This city, while impressive, could trap them. These people, while congenial, could be their enemy. They clearly had an agenda in seeking Henri out, not once but twice.

Tahlia glanced around at the others to find Ele and Kala looking equally sheepish, while Malik remained unimpressed and vigilant. She was relieved to find that some color had returned to Henri's face and he had regained his usual composure. He didn't release her hand, though, which told her that he was fighting to hold the mask in place. So she held it, rubbing her thumb lightly over his skin in a steady rhythm, exchanging what comfort she could give for his strength in return.

Isa led the way into a corridor at ground level. The passageways were so narrow there was barely enough room for two streams of movement. The ceiling was also unnervingly low. Tahlia tried to memorize the sequence of turns should they need to find their way out of this warren later, but she soon gave up. There were too many directions to try to remember and she kept getting distracted. She hoped Malik was having better luck. Knowing him, he was already committing every turn to memory, drawing a literal map in his mind.

As they passed by people in the corridors, Tahlia noticed that no one else had the turquoise tattoos shifting beneath their skin like the warriors. The residents of the Citadel looked ordinary. The only odd thing about them was the unmistakable warmth in their gazes as they greeted them with curious glances and gentle smiles. Excitement charged the air, as if the Naiab had long been anticipating their arrival. Henri inclined his head in polite greeting to the people who looked their way, ever the charming king, but Malik remained distant and stone-faced.

Isa turned down a short private path and they followed him until it opened up into a wide chamber. The sound of trickling water immediately drew Tahlia's gaze to a shallow river which meandered across the floor of the cavern. Along the rugged walls, natural stone formations jutted out at different heights in what looked like smooth waves. Water dribbled down these formations, creating several thin waterfalls that crept along the ground to merge with the shallow river. Patches of green foliage grew among the rocks, a stark contrast to the rustic reds and ochre of the sandstone walls.

It was then that Tahlia noticed a woman standing in front of the shallow river. Her wild long hair was white with age and she wore a teal salwar kameez with no shoes or other adornments. Her skin was dark from the sun and leathery in appearance, but it was not the golden coloring of the warriors, nor did tattoos line her skin.

Isa approached to stand by her side and the woman's lips curved into a proud, secret smile, as if the warrior had been given a task and exceeded expectations. Tahlia's body tensed. Something about the smug, silent exchange made it very clear who was in control of this situation. Tahlia shifted her gaze to Malik and he slid his eyes to meet hers, his jaw tightening in agreement.

At the same moment the woman turned her attention back to them, Isa's gaze snapped to Tahlia. The ferocity of his stare made her limbs lock in place. It held more than appreciation of her beauty or curiosity as to her place beside a king. It was penetrating.

Almost like he could see straight through her, past her skin and bones, to what lay beneath.

He had called her a *goddess*.

Tahlia self-consciously rubbed at the marking inked on the inside of her wrist. Her painted designs were still vibrant. Since that day with Kala, she had been careful not to let the colors fade, not even as they traveled across the Idris desert. Every few days, before the sun rose in the sky, she repainted them. The marking was carefully hidden among the designs. And yet, the way the Naiab looked at her made her feel as if her skin had been stripped bare. Her secret put on display for all to see.

"Welcome to the Citadel." The woman smiled at them in greeting. "We are happy you accepted the invitation to meet with us."

Malik cleared his throat at the implication that they'd had any choice in the matter.

Henri ignored him. "Are you the Shahri of the Naiab?"

"I am. You may call me Lunara."

Tahlia tried but failed to keep the surprise from her face. Women held various high positions, both within the palace and the wider kingdoms, but there were no queens of Merovia. If the Naiab considered the Idris desert to be their kingdom, then Lunara was effectively their queen.

"I'm Henri. This is Malik, Ele, Kala and Tahlia."

Lunara's gaze landed on them one by one, but when it settled on Tahlia, it lingered. Her kind eyes, softened by decades of life and wisdom, suddenly sharpened. Something flickered behind them, something dormant.

It was nothing. It had been a long day and her thoughts were getting carried away. Clearly, she needed to rest. But in a corner of her mind, beneath the surface of her consciousness, a truth began to scream.

Lunara forced her attention back to Henri. "We have much to discuss, but perhaps you would like to rest first."

"We will hear what you have to say and be on our way," Malik interceded abruptly.

Henri shot him a warning glare.

"To the summit." Lunara calmly clasped her aged hands in front of her. "Where your king will die."

The silence was as shrill as a blade. The truth cutting each of them down to slivers.

"But what if you had an ally that could tip the scales of survival in your king's favor?"

"What ally?" Ele's tone was eager but wary.

"I feel this is a discussion best had between leaders. Isa, could you please show our guests to where they will be staying and ensure that they receive everything they need?"

Isa shifted to carry out the command but Ele's swift reply halted him. "No. We're not leaving my king alone with you."

Lunara blinked, affronted. Her gaze pinged between Malik and Tahlia in search of support.

Malik shrugged a shoulder. "I agree with the boy."

The lines around Lunara's mouth tightened and an unmistakable edge crept into her voice. "The children must be tired and hungry."

Ele frowned at the perceived insult. "The children are fine."

"Forgive our mistrust," Henri intercepted, "but all we know of the Naiab is that they repeatedly attacked my northern wall, killed my soldiers, invaded my palace, and can somehow wield sand. I would not be a very good king if I entrusted those in my care to such people."

"You do not trust the Naiab," Lunara stated plainly. "Do you trust me?"

In an instant her eyes shifted from human irises of green to something altogether otherworldly. They became windows into a tempestuous sky, swirling with the dance of storm clouds and the promise of rain. Within their depths were the raw, untamed forces of nature, the electrifying energy of lightning, and the clap of thunder.

Tahlia suffocated a scream as Malik drew his shamshir. Isa crafted a spear of sand and Kala's high-pitched squeal reverberated off the cavernous walls. Henri didn't draw his sword but his body went rigid and his hold on Tahlia's hand became crushing. It was the only thing that was keeping her from collapsing to the floor.

"What are you?" Malik demanded.

"A goddess," Kala said breathlessly.

Kala's wide eyes shot to Tahlia, a look of pure horror on her face. Tahlia's lips trembled, but she lifted her chin and tried to hold herself together piece by shattered piece. If only to show Kala that she was not afraid.

She was fucking terrified.

"I have saved your life more than once, foreign king. And yours as well, child."

Kala's jaw dropped and she went wholly still.

Implications struck Tahlia's mind like arrows raining down on a battlefield. She knew one of the gods had answered her prayers, but she had not realized it was the water goddess. She had assumed the goddess of endings and beginnings had been the one responsible for Henri and Kala's miraculous recoveries. Thinking about it now, though, it was plausible that the water goddess could have turned the tide of their fates. The human body held a lot of water. The poison should have caused Henri's lungs to fill with liquid but they hadn't. The infection in Kala's blood from her injuries should have killed her but it had been flushed clean.

"Who are you?" Henri's brows drew together in puzzlement.

"The water goddess." Malik's words were barely a whisper, as if he couldn't quite believe what he was saying.

There was no denying those eyes, though. They were a portal to the boundless depths of the ocean. Within those liquid orbs, they could see the ebb and flow of the tides, the ceaseless motion of waves, the vast expanse of the sea.

Despite the evidence, Ele slowly appraised her with skepticism. "An actual goddess."

The goddess's expression turned defensive. "Did you think the gods a mere myth, boy?"

"Where we come from, our God is more—invisible," Henri explained.

"This casing is not my true form. This vessel allows me to inhabit her when needed."

Henri faltered for a second, clearly disturbed by the thought of a goddess inhabiting a human body. "You said you saved my life. Why?"

The goddess flicked her gaze to Tahlia, the truth passing between them, but she directed her reply to Henri. "It served me to do so."

"What do you want with Henri?" Malik still hadn't sheathed his shamshir.

It was laughable, really. The goddess could drown them all with half a thought. Make them choke on their own blood and bile until their lungs were fountains of fluid.

"To speak to him in private." She bit out each word with less patience.

"Absolutely not."

"Malik." Tahlia reproached him as the goddess's eyes flashed with lightning. "Isa and I will take Ele and Kala to rest." She steeled her nerve as she faced the goddess again. "Malik will stay to make sure no harm comes to our king."

To her relief, the goddess said nothing, which Tahlia took as assent.

Tahlia turned to Henri and tilted her lips up to his in a farewell kiss, before whispering, "Don't make any deals."

He squeezed her waist in affection and angled his head in silent agreement. Isa led the way out of the cave and Ele and Kala reluctantly followed.

As she walked past Malik, Tahlia leaned in to kiss him lightly on the cheek. "Put your shamshir away and don't anger her."

"No promises."

She returned an unimpressed look but he showed no remorse. It would have to do. Because the chances of them leaving the Citadel alive were getting slimmer by the second.

Tahlia had almost escaped the cavern when the goddess called after her. "You owe the gods a debt. We have not forgotten."

HENRI

"What debt?" Henri's features turned sharp and curious.

"That is not what I wish to discuss with you," the goddess replied dismissively.

Malik sheathed his shamshir but positioned himself closer to Henri so that he would be able to absorb any frontal attack. "You said there was an ally that could tip the scales of survival in Henri's favor. Did you mean yourself?"

"I would be willing to support your king's rule, yes. As would the Naiab, if certain terms are met."

The thought of having a goddess on his side was unfathomable. Henri didn't know much about the deities of Merovia, how they differed from his own God, but he assumed their power would be infinite. Which begged the question why the goddess was even interested in him. What terms could he possibly offer her?

Henri's expression shifted in pensive thought. "How did you come to be with the Naiab?"

The storm in her eyes calmed to a tranquil ocean, as if she were recalling a fond memory. "They discovered my home many moons ago."

"This is your sanctuary." Malik's gaze swept over the cavern again, as if he were seeing it for the first time. At Henri's questioning look, he explained, "All gods have a resting place. They call it their sanctuary."

Henri cast his eyes over the red sandstone walls. Its natural beauty was alluring and reverent, but it was also just a cave. Henri would never have guessed it to be the home of a goddess.

"When your people cast their own out into the Idris desert to die, the banished ones clung to the threads of life for days. They fought with everything they had to survive. That fighting spirit led them here, to me. I was impressed by their obstinacy, so I sheltered them. We have co-existed here for many years."

"You did more than shelter them." A furrowed brow betrayed Malik's thoughts as they began to align. "They are god-touched; the turquoise tattoos, the sand wielding. Is it water that moves beneath their skin?"

The goddess regarded him with thinly veiled irritation. This was clearly not the conversation she wanted to be having. "Subaqueous sand from the bottom of a deep pool. It is laced with my power and dynamic in nature, constantly moving and redistributing. The grains allow the Naiab to move through sand the way that water currents move sediment along the bottom of the ocean."

"That's why their skin is an odd color," Henri mused.

She gave a curt nod. "Such sand can exhibit a range of colors from shades of white to yellow and gray, depending on the mineral composition and organic content of their home."

Malik shook his head in awe and confusion. "Why gift them with such power?"

"The warriors earn it," she replied defensively, before raising her hand to ward off any further questions. "Enough. I did not invite you here for a history lesson. I will give you my terms and then I will leave this vessel so she can give you hers."

Malik's jaw flexed and he shifted his weight between his feet as if he were contemplating how to defeat an opponent. Henri simply waited. He would heed Tahlia's warning not to make any deals with the goddess but there was no reason why he shouldn't hear her out.

Seemingly satisfied by their captive attention, the goddess continued. "The Idris desert is sustained by an underground reservoir of water that has accumulated over hundreds of thousands of years. The aquifer is vital to the preservation of life here. For the past few years, one of the Merovian kings has been depleting it. He has been pumping the water into a dam on his lands and hoarding it."

Henri's features soured in anger as he exchanged a knowing look with Malik. "Nasir."

"The rate of extraction is surpassing the rate of rainfall. The water table has dropped dangerously low. Soon, the land surface will become unstable and every living thing will wither and die."

"So make it rain," Malik said plainly.

"The rain I would need to create in order to recharge the aquifer would change the ecosystem forever; the layers of rock, the slope of the terrain. And it would not stop the Merovian king. He would simply siphon the water away."

"Then kill him."

The goddess narrowed her eyes at Malik as gray clouds swirled dangerously beneath their surface. Malik didn't flinch, as if taunting the wrath of a goddess was not enough to humble him. It was strangely arousing. Henri tried to ignore the involuntary twitch of his cock.

"If I kill him, another will take his place only to continue his enterprise. I would have achieved nothing. The king needs to die, and a new king needs to take his place. One who will return the water to its rightful state."

Henri folded his arms across his chest and considered the information. The high mountains had always held the only source of fresh water in Merovia. It was why, generations ago, an elaborate underground water system had been built to reach from the high mountains all the way to the Merovian kingdoms. The kingdoms relied on the high mountains to provide their lands and people with the water they needed to survive. In return, each kingdom paid a yearly ransom to the high mountain king for water. If he killed Nasir, not only would he be able to repair the water table, but he could ensure that everyone had equal access to water across the country.

"And how will you help me defeat Nasir at the summit?" Henri queried.

"I won't."

Henri arched an eyebrow, prompting her to explain.

"I will not interfere in the realm of the god of justice and kingship."

"The what?"

"The deity of justice, kingship and cosmic order," Malike explained. "He upholds the principles of fairness and righteousness."

"Does he realize the Merovians slaughter their own family at the summit?" Henri's voice rose in barely restrained anger.

The goddess stared back at him, unmoved.

Malik scowled. "You said you could help tip the scales of survival in Henri's favor."

"The Naiab will help your king if you meet their terms."

"Considering we would be saving them from extinction, I would think they would have no terms," Malik drawled.

The water goddess slid her attention back to Henri. "Do this and you will have my support throughout your reign."

"That sounds very vague," Malik muttered.

"I have said what I came to say. I shall leave you to consider my offer."

The woman's eyes immediately transformed back to their human irises and a plain shade of green. They blinked and the elderly woman swayed a little, as if she were reacquainting herself with her body.

"Are you all right?" Henri wasn't sure if he should offer a hand to steady her or if she would find that affronting.

"I am fine. The goddess is quite respectful when she inhabits me."

Henri refrained from asking how many times she had been inhabited and for what purpose. The question seemed too personal.

"Did you hear everything that was discussed?" Malik asked abruptly.

Clearly, Malik did not share Henri's concern about sensitivity.

"I did. We are willing to send a warrior to help you survive the summit."

"One warrior?" Malik spat. "How will one warrior make a difference?"

"The prevailing of injustice is maintained by the apathy of many. One man, one child, one king …," Lunara looked pointedly to Henri, "can alter the outcome of entire worlds. Rest assured that one warrior could change your king's fate."

Malik looked unconvinced, and perhaps a little threatened. If the warrior was Isa, he had good reason to feel intimidated.

"We have one condition," Lunara continued.

"One condition on the plan that sees us save your people?"

Henri ignored Malik's jibe. "What is it?"

"We want to be formally recognized as the sixth kingdom of Merovia. And we want the walls torn down." Lunara landed her gaze on Malik. "All of them."

CHAPTER THREE

MALIK

"Absolutely not." Malik perched his hands on his hips and began pacing.

He knew that Henri would be foolish enough to consider the proposition but under no circumstances would Malik allow it to happen. The walls had been erected for a reason. That reason still held. In fact, now that the Naiab had sand wielding powers and a goddess on their side, that reason really fucking held.

Malik halted abruptly and turned on his heel to face her. "Is that why you attacked our northern wall? You were trying to tear it down?"

"We attacked to get your king's attention."

Malik cocked his head in blatant disbelief. "You could have sent a letter."

"Would it have reached him?" Lunara returned boldly.

Shit.

Somehow, she knew that he had been intercepting Henri's mail. Which meant the Naiab had spies in the palace. If they ever returned home, Malik would dismiss every servant and adopt more rigorous measures for staff selection.

Malik leveled an accusatory finger at her. "You killed Merovian soldiers."

"They fired on us. We simply retaliated."

"You attacked us!"

"Malik." Henri stepped between them and shot him a warning look.

Malik's nostrils flared as he forced himself to turn away. It enraged him that Henri wasn't disputing her on this when he knew the truth. Perhaps the lives of those soldiers didn't mean much to him. But even as he thought it, a small part of Malik knew he was wrong. Henri had been unable to turn a blind eye to the slave trade or the squalid conditions of the Thaka, he would feel responsible for the loss of each one of his soldiers.

"When our attempts to get your attention failed, we sent a warrior to infiltrate the palace."

"How?" Henri prodded. "How did your warrior get through the northern wall?"

"He didn't. He went over it. Sand storms are quite common, so they don't raise suspicion."

Malik's face twisted in self-loathing as he met Henri's gaze, silently conveying their shared recognition that they should have realized it sooner. If the sand in the Naiab's skin could transport them across vast distances, it stood to reason that it could transport them in the air as well. They had seen it for themselves when a narrow whirlwind had formed, stretching up into the sky in a vertical motion, only to soar over the palace wall and land a short distance away from where they were training. It had dissipated, condensing down until it formed the outline of a Naiab warrior. A warrior Malik had killed. Malik also recalled Inaya telling him that the Naiab were capable of whipping up sand storms as high as the northern wall. Perhaps the attacks had been a diversion.

Henri must have come to the same conclusion because he didn't press the topic further. Instead, he asked, "Why do you want to be recognized as the sixth kingdom of Merovia? Your people have been content to live out here in the desert for generations, unaffected by the politics of the Merovians kingdoms."

"And yet even removed from their politics, our very existence has been threatened by one of the kings. Nothing has changed since our ancestors were cast out that day. They do not care if we live or die. But now, there is a chance to create a new order. The arrival of a foreign king on Merovian shores has threatened everything. If you survive the summit, the kingdom of every king you slay shall fall under your rule. The Rouhan family will lose their grip on this country."

Every word the woman said was true. And yet, every word she uttered was a lie. Malik had been playing the game of politics for too long not to notice a carefully curated story when he heard one. If Henri survived the summit, it would undoubtedly detonate centuries of tradition, ushering in an era of potential change. Such moments were ripe for those with ambitions of power to make their move.

Lunara spread her upturned palms wide in humble supplication. "All we want is to ensure the continued survival of our people. It is not unreasonable to want justice."

Malik speared her with an analytical stare. "Justice is the shadow of revenge."

She did not deny it. He wouldn't have believed her if she did.

"I will consider it," Henri replied evenly.

And he would, Malik knew. He needed to talk to Henri before he made a rash decision. He needed to convince him that the Naiab had an ulterior motive and that the goddess couldn't be trusted. Hopefully Tahlia would back him up on that front. As much as it painted him to admit, if Henri was going to listen to anyone, it would be her.

"You are welcome to stay with us for as long as you need," Lunara offered.

"We will be leaving in the morning," Malik replied curtly.

The sooner the better in his opinion.

"Then I will have someone escort you to your chamber."

ELE

The warrior's immense size filled the corridor as he walked ahead of them, leaving little space for others to pass. Even so, Ele was pretty confident he could bring him down. Perhaps slice his ankle tendons. Cut him off at the knees. He wondered what happened to a Naiab when they died. Did they turn to sand?

Out of the corner of his eye, Ele felt Kala's stare burning into him. He glanced over and she rolled her eyes at him, as if she knew exactly what he was thinking. He shrugged. Ele knew that if it came to it, Kala would dive in to help him take down the desert giant. In fact, he suspected that she was more ruthless than he was.

Isa turned down a passageway and stopped outside a door-like entrance that had been carved into the sandstone wall. There was no door, though, only a woven rug that hung down from a frame bolted into the rock.

"How many chambers do you need?" Isa asked.

Tahlia looked at the tapestry with mild interest. "Only two."

Ele couldn't help but smirk as he watched Isa try to do the math in his head. He would probably conclude that the king and his courtesan would share a bed while Malik would guard the children.

He would be wrong.

Ele knew something was changing between Henri and Malik long before he stormed into Malik's room that night, after finding Kala half dead on the streets of the Thaka. He might be young but he wasn't blind. The way they acted around each other, the way they looked at each other. It was the way Nathaniel used to look at Henri when he was sure no one was watching him. Ele didn't really care who Henri shared a bed with, as long as they were loyal to him. The more people who cared about Henri, the safer he would be.

"There is another one just down the passageway." Isa indicated to another tapestry adorning the opposite wall just a little further ahead. "I'll have some food brought to you."

"Thank you."

Despite her polite dismissal, the Naiab's eyes lingered on Tahlia. He made no move to leave at all. It was like he was waiting for something.

Ele cleared his throat and growled, "She belongs to Henri."

The warrior's gaze cut to him. "A goddess belongs to no one. They cannot be claimed, only worshiped."

Kala's mouth gaped open and she released a nervous giggle. Ele glared at the Naiab before he batted the rug aside and strode past it. The room was small, with a low ceiling that felt like it might collapse on top of them. The walls were the rugged surface of the cave's interior, adorned with natural patterns and jutted rocks. No doubt this room had been carved by hand.

A simple bed sat at the very end of the chamber with a blanket and pillows tossed on top of it. There were a few pieces of furniture; a table and two chairs, fashioned from weathered wood. On top of the table, an oil lamp burned brightly, but even so, the room was mostly shadows. An earthy smell filled his nostrils. It smelled like rock and old air.

"People live like this?" Kala's eyes danced around the room.

"I suppose you would get used to it." Tahlia sighed. "Especially if the alternative is dying in the Idris desert."

Ele wondered how long it had taken the Naiab to carve out their home. From what he could see, the Citadel was like a spider's web. There were endless passageways and levels and rooms. It would make his job that much harder.

Ele's features turned serious. "What do you think the goddess and the Naiab want from Henri?"

"I don't know." Tahlia pinched her lips together anxiously.

"The gods are not to be trusted." Kala removed her headscarf and set it on the table, allowing her two braids to escape. "The only joy they feel is from watching us suffer. They crave blood and violence."

"The Naiab seem to trust the water goddess," Ele pointed out.

"If their powers come from her, there would have been a price to pay." Tahlia's voice sounded strained, as if she didn't like talking about them. "The gods don't give anything freely."

"I wonder if they practice human sacrifice here like they do in the Old City," Kala said softly.

Ele's face contorted in horror. "Human sacrifice?"

"Let's not speak of it." Tahlia's eyes flittered between Ele and Kala, suggesting she had something else to say to them but was hesitant.

"You don't have to ask. We were never going to just sleep," Ele said.

Tahlia's features crumpled with guilt. "I know you're both very tired but I don't know how much time we have."

A corner of Kala's mouth tugged up mischievously. "We'll find out what we can about the Naiab and the water goddess."

"Wait until after Isa brings your food," Tahlia reminded them.

"What about you?" Kala's features fell instantly and her voice was a little too gentle as she looked up at Tahlia with concern. "What will you do?"

Ele frowned at the delicate exchange. Clearly, there was something going on here he didn't know about.

"I'll wait in the other chamber for Henri and Malik to return. If they're going to outsmart a goddess, they'll need my help."

Kala didn't look satisfied with the answer but she didn't say anything more.

TAHLIA

Tahlia couldn't stay still. Which was irritating, given how small the room was. There wasn't enough space to walk her emotions out and every time she sat down, she sprung back up again as if propelled by nerves. Every instinct in her body was urging her to run, even if it meant fleeing into the desert at twilight with nothing and no one to ensure her survival.

She had done it once before. She could do it again.

Except last time she hadn't left anyone behind. The other girls were all dead. Her family had betrayed her. She'd had no one. Now it was different. She had a family who cared about her and would defend her, even die for her. And she would give her life for them. Which is why her feet kept going around in circles.

Not that fleeing would save her. The water goddess knew who she was. The painted designs on her skin couldn't hide her from them now. She wondered how the gods would enact their revenge. Kala was right; the only thing the gods enjoyed was pain and suffering. Immortality had a way of blunting emotions. Beauty became dull. Love grew shallow. Against a backdrop of eternity, everything faded to mundane. But pain was immediate and sharp and entertaining. It could pierce through the nothingness and remind them that, once upon a time, they were not so divine.

Perhaps they would not kill her straight away. The torment of not knowing when or how they would come for her might be enough to keep them amused for a little while. She was clutching at stars, she knew, but the alternative was unbearable.

Tahlia had just forced herself to sit down again when the tapestry lifted from the entrance and Henri and Malik stepped inside. She jumped to her feet, relief coursing through her veins at the sight of them both alive. Her distress must have been evident because Henri immediately crossed the room to envelope her within his protective arms. It was embarrassing the way she clung to him, as if his embrace was the only thing sustaining her, but he didn't question it and he didn't let her go.

When she finally forced herself to pull away, she stole a glance at Malik and saw the gravity on his face. "What happened?"

"The water goddess wants Henri to kill Nasir and return the water he's apparently been hoarding so that the Naiab don't wither away and die. In return, she *won't* help Henri survive the summit, but she *will* be eternally grateful." Malik's words dripped with sarcasm.

Tahlia blinked and turned to Henri for his retort but he remained silent as he absorbed their surroundings. His posture drew tight as he surveyed the low ceiling and rugged walls encased in shadows. She couldn't blame him. The room had felt small before, but now with three of them taking up space, it felt like a tomb.

Tahlia returned her focus to Malik. "And the Naiab?"

"They will give us one warrior to improve Henri's chances of survival at the summit. But only if we acknowledge the Idris desert as the sixth kingdom of Merovia and tear down the walls. All of them."

Malik tossed his headscarf onto the table with a little too much force. Henri had removed his as well and was now tugging at the seam of his kurta as if trying to get the garment to breathe.

Earlier, Tahlia had been pleasantly surprised to find that someone, probably Isa, had retrieved their belongings and relocated them to their chamber. She had been able to wipe the sand from her skin with a damp cloth and change into a clean silk dress.

As she attempted to make sense of the unfolding events, Tahlia's brow furrowed in contemplation. "Nasir has yet to challenge Henri and I don't think he will. He'll wait until the outcome of the summit, hoping someone kills Henri for him. If Henri somehow survives the summit, Nasir will surely send another assassin. It will be a race as to who kills who first."

"And if Henri survives the summit and manages to kill Nasir, he will be king of all of Merovia."

"Except the Idris desert," Tahlia pointed out.

Malik's features turned dark. "Until the Naiab kill Henri and take the entire country for themselves. With the walls down, sand magic, and a goddess on their side, what's to stop them?"

Tahlia glanced over at Henri only to find his skin had drained of color and his chest was heaving with shallow breaths. "Henri?"

He didn't respond but his eyes shifted around the room as if scanning it for hidden threats.

"Henri, you can't agree to their terms," Malik said tightly. "The Naiab are trying to use you as a pawn in their game to obtain revenge and make a play for power."

"Henri." Tahlia's voice was firm as she made her way over to him with cautious steps.

He was sweating. Panic was leaking out of every pore and his limbs were shaking.

Tahlia grasped both sides of his face to hold him still and forced him to look at her. "Henri, you're all right. Everything's all right."

"What's wrong?" Malik demanded as he rushed to their side.

Tahlia didn't know exactly, but she was sure it wasn't the talk of the summit and the threats they faced. Right now, he looked as if he were trapped inside a memory. His eyes were distant and drowning in terror. She knew of the nightmares that plagued him most nights. The way he thrashed and called out in his sleep. She had never asked him about them, or the scars on his body, but she didn't need the details to know that the ordeal haunted him.

"Henri, look at me," she urged.

"I-I c-can't breathe."

"Breathe me." Tahlia pressed her forehead against his, locking their gazes together so that she was the only thing he could see.

She inhaled a deep breath, encouraging him to follow her lead. He looked at her desperately, as if he wasn't sure she was real.

"Feel me." Tahlia undid the clips on her shoulders, letting her dress fall to her feet as she guided Henri's hands to cup her breasts.

His palms were clammy but his features shifted in confusion at the soft sensation of her skin.

"You are not there. You are here with me," she said firmly.

"What is happening?" Malik asked urgently.

She didn't dare answer or look away for fear of severing the connection with Henri. Amidst whatever torture he was enduring within the prison of his own mind, she would be his refuge, guiding him safely back to them.

Tahlia closed the breath of distance between them with a kiss and Henri startled before his trembling lips answered hers. His hands slipped to her hips, slowly tracing the curves of her body, like he was trying to navigate his way back to her. Tahlia deepened the kiss, drowning his senses in her, exploring his mouth with her tongue, her fingers still framing his stubble-lined jaw. She could feel his cock hardening as it pressed against her, straining against his pants.

It always amazed her how the body could still respond when the mind was absent. As if humans were nothing more than a collection of nerve endings and primal instincts. Thankfully, it had allowed her to perform while escaping moments she didn't care to remember. For Henri, though, she would use it to anchor him to this moment, to her.

She lifted his kurta and to her surprise Malik helped to pull it over his head, before ridding him of his pants. When she touched

Henri's abdomen, he flinched, his muscles pulling taut as if she had struck him.

"No one is going to hurt you," she murmured against his lips, tracing kisses down his neck to the base of his throat. "You're here with me."

His hands coasted over her ass and squeezed as he pulled her flush against his body. The possessive jolt sparked a warm throbbing between her legs. It had only been a few days since they'd tasted each other but somehow it felt longer.

After Henri's accusations against Malik, Malik had told her to be whatever Henri needed, so she had. They had used each other most nights, finding solace and release tangled up in one another. The sex was great but she knew Henri's mind often drifted to Malik. It didn't make her jealous, though. Her mind often drifted to Malik as well. To them together, with her.

Tahlia gently guided Henri backwards toward the bed, then onto it. His hands gripped her hips as she straddled him, her wet entrance moving tantalizingly over his solid length.

"You're in control Henri." She twisted her wild, dark curls over one shoulder and parted her lips breathlessly at the delicious friction being ignited between her thighs. Henri's eyes focused on her as if he were pulling himself out of a haze. He fixated on the lush swell of her breasts as they tipped forward, the hardened peak of her nipples begging him to suck them between his teeth.

"Ride me," he ordered.

Tahlia palmed his cock and pumped it hard before guiding it inside her entrance. She gasped in pleasure as she sank down onto him, letting him fill her. She began to rock against him, forcing his cock deeper, slamming it against her inner wall. Henri moved with her, lifting his hips to tilt himself further inside her.

Then she felt a hard body pressing at her back. Without breaking stride, Tahlia looked over her shoulder to find Malik naked, his eyes filled with understanding. He guided her face to his and seized her lips in a kiss. She had not expected it, nor the heat of it as he kissed her thoroughly. Malik had never shown a lick of attraction to her, but this kiss was not born from carnal desire. It was gratitude. He had realized what she was doing for the man he loved and he was thankful for it.

Malik gripped a handful of her ass, pushing her forward, while the other hand splayed against her core, holding her firm to intensify the angle of the penetration. Tahlia ripped her mouth from his to let out a string of expletives as she tried to adjust to the piercing depth of it. Henri reached forward to swirl his thumb over her clitoris with every thrusting motion and Tahlia groaned in response as she melted back against the hard planes of Malik's chest. The pain mixed with pleasure in the most delicious way and she couldn't stop herself from pounding into Henri.

It was too much.

It was not enough.

She needed more. She needed both of them, thick and hard and driving into her from every angle until she screamed.

"Tahlia." Henri moaned her name like a prayer.

Her eyes shuttered closed and she arched her back, reaching her arms over her head to wrap themselves around Malik's neck.

Malik's teeth nipped at her earlobe before grazing the slope of her neck. Henri's hands tightened on her hips, stealing control and accelerating the pace, urging her towards release. It came in an earth-shattering combustion, her slick walls pulsating as the waves built and crashed inside her over and over again.

When the orgasm finally dissipated, she shifted off Henri, her legs still trembling, to stretch out beside him. Her body felt like liquid, her limbs numb with euphoria. She could barely lift her head to see Malik licking the wetness from the shaft of Henri's cock. A tingling sensation fluttered inside her at the sight. His tongue stroked and lapped at the glistening head. Then he took him inside his mouth and sucked him hard while fisting him mercilessly.

Despite her exhaustion and the tenderness between her legs, Tahlia could feel her need building again. It was pure eroticism to watch them together. The fusion of two masculine opposing energies, air meeting electricity, sparking a celestial storm. They could paint the heavens with their radiant chemistry.

Henri threaded his fingers through Malik's hair and gripped him as he shattered inside his mouth. Tahlia could almost feel the force of the release as it rippled through his body, leaving him satiated. Malik lifted his head and reared over Henri to capture his lips with his own. It kindled her to know that her taste was still on Malik's tongue, mixed with Henri's cum. The kiss was slow and soft and sensual, conveying what words never could. That no matter what torture Henri had endured, they would never let it happen again.

Because he was their king. Their lover. And they would fight for him until the last drop of blood was spilled.

CHAPTER FOUR

TAHLIA

A coarse hand clamped over Tahlia's mouth, silencing her and jolting her awake at the same time. Fear widened her eyes and sent her heart pounding into her throat. She was completely naked, lying between Malik and Henri who were also naked, their limbs carelessly draped over her in exhaustion. The Naiab warrior lifted a blade to her line of sight and the dull light from the oil lamp glinted off its sharp edge. She blinked in answer to the unspoken warning and he cautiously removed his hand from her face.

Tahlia glanced down at the men sleeping on either side of her and sent up a silent prayer that she would see them again. Though the prayer seemed a little pointless given that it was the gods who wanted her dead. She shifted ever so carefully off the bed and stood up on shaking legs. Isa retrieved her dress from the floor and handed it to her. He did not avert his eyes as she pulled it over her frame. Tahlia stared at him defiantly as she fastened the clips on her shoulders but if he noticed her boldness he didn't care.

Satisfied, Isa gestured for her to leave and she silently slipped outside into the passageway. In the second it took for him to follow,

Tahlia contemplated sprinting down the corridor but she knew she wouldn't get far. At this point, dignity was all she had left.

"She wants to see you," Isa said by way of explanation.

"You mean kill me."

He didn't deny it. Tahlia lifted her chin as if she had stared down worse fates.

She hadn't.

They began walking, retracing the route they had taken earlier, though this time the warrior remained beside her instead of forging ahead. Perhaps he was concerned that she would, in fact, try to run. She doubted his actions were meant to comfort her in any way.

"Your companions, do they know?" Isa asked.

"No."

Her clipped response insinuated that it was none of his business. The only person who knew was Kala, despite Tahlia never speaking about it out loud. Some traumas were better left abandoned in the recesses of time. To talk of them would be to breathe life into their carcass, to acknowledge their mark on her soul.

Entering the dimly lit chamber, Tahlia was surprised to find it empty. The sound of trickling water from the thin waterfalls dribbling down rock formations echoed loudly in her ears. Normally she would find such a sound tranquil, but now it sounded like death creeping up on her.

"Follow the river." Isa indicated to the shallow water which wound across the floor of the cavern. The gentle current kept flowing northward, disappearing further inside the maw of the cave.

Hesitating, Tahlia glanced up at Isa. She didn't know why. It wasn't as if he would save her. His narrow eyes met hers, stern but not unkind.

He was definitely not going to save her.

Tahlia swallowed hard, trying to conceal her fear as she cautiously traced the path. Eventually it led her into a dark cavity where the air smelled ancient and frigid. Stalactites hung from the ceiling like frozen daggers, intermittently releasing drops of icy moisture to the ground. Flowstone formations cascaded down the walls, like ribbons of liquid stone. A rainbow of shimmering light reflected along the surface. It drew her attention to the vast pool a short distance ahead of her.

The pool was surrounded by tall stalagmites which rose from the floor like sentinels. As she approached the edge, she noticed that the water was unusually still. There was no fresh air in the cavern, nor wind to caress the water's surface, but even so, there should have been some movement. Instead, the water was unnaturally stagnant. Like a sheet of glass.

Beyond the edges of the pool was an immediate drop, plunging into a deep chasm. Despite the chilling depth, though, she could see all the way down to the bottom because the floor was illuminated with familiar bright turquoise blue sand.

"Thinking of jumping?"

Tahlia's hand flew to her mouth to stifle a scream as her feet stumbled back from the edge. The goddess in Lunara's body stood a short distance away, her eyes aqueous spheres of the ocean tide.

"No." Tahlia lowered her hand and balled both of them into fists at her sides to stop them from shaking. "I'm very fond of living."

"Evidently." The goddess appraised her with a critical gaze. "The girl who defied the gods. You caused quite an uproar that day. Most mortals consider it an honor to be chosen for divinity."

"For death, you mean."

"A mortal death for eternal life as a divine."

"Liar." Tahlia's voice trembled as she whispered the accusation. Frightened tears sprung behind her eyes, but she forced herself to stand her ground. "Six young girls sacrificed, but only one would have been chosen to ascend."

"Secrets, secrets." The goddess tsked. "Some gods demand more than others."

Like the murder of innocent children. But they were not the only ones to be sacrificed. There were many divines to appease and many rituals to complete. The priests of the Old City took their oaths very seriously. They believed that if they dedicated their lives to the gods and served them diligently, they might be called upon in death and venerated to the spiritual world.

"Except on that day, none of the offerings ascended."

Tahlia's forehead creased in confusion. "What?"

"When we discovered that an offering had fled, the wrath of all the gods was incited, but the rage of one god in particular was unparalleled. You see, you had already been chosen to ascend by the god of beauty and fertility. He refused to choose another. You might say he became obsessed with you." Her lips curved into a malicious smile. "I don't think anyone has ever rejected him before. In his mortal life or his immortal one."

"It wasn't personal."

"Being divine does not change the nature of men. When a woman says no, it's always personal. He will come for you, if the other gods don't get to you first."

A single tear escaped her fortress of control but Tahlia quickly wiped the traitor away. "Does that mean you're not going to kill me?"

"For now. I need you alive to convince your king to agree to my terms."

Tahlia lowered her gaze to the pool as she tried to persuade her scattered thoughts to focus. The turquoise sand shimmered beneath the water. Each grain seemed to glisten with its own inner magic.

"This is the womb of your power."

It was a statement, not a question. An observation and a logical conclusion. The goddess didn't reply but she did move to stand closer to the pool.

"Are you afraid that Nasir's underground system will reach it?"

"No. It is well protected. But the water table is not. Soon it will be depleted beyond restoration and every organism in this desert will wilt and succumb to death."

"And you care about that?" Tahlia's tone was biting. "The sacrifice of innocent children is acceptable but the end of a desert dwelling tribe is not?"

Lightning struck in Lunara's liquid orbs. "I do not ask for sacrifices to be made in my name."

"What do you ask for?" Tahlia's gaze fixed on her in earnest. "What was your price for changing them?"

The goddess considered her for a moment, as if debating whether to answer the question. It was clear that Tahlia was referring to the Naiab's sand wielding abilities, having made the connection between the sediment at the bottom of the pool and the turquoise tattoos that shifted beneath their skin.

"The warriors choose to endure the trial. They earn what I have to offer them."

"Why offer it to them at all?"

"Because it serves me to do so." Her words were sharp and void of patience. "Perhaps you will answer one of my questions now. Who helped you?"

Tahlia pressed her lips together resolutely. The goddess noted the movement and storm clouds churned in the portals of her eyes.

"Someone shared with you the secrets of the spirit world and taught you about *feliq;* the symbols you drew on your skin. It kept you hidden from us for years until you prayed that day, begging us to save your king."

Folding her arms tightly across her chest, Tahlia's voice fell softly. "I couldn't just let him die."

"And now your life will be forfeit."

Tahlia inhaled a steadying breath. She couldn't bring herself to regret her choices. Henri was alive. Kala was alive. That was all that mattered. She was never meant to live a human life. The years that she had stolen from the gods were more than she could have hoped for.

"If there is anyone the gods want to punish more than you, it would be that informant."

Tahlia leveled her with an unyielding stare and a sacred promise. "I will take that secret to my divine existence."

The goddess's mouth pursed in silent disapproval before her features shifted to curiosity. "Then perhaps you will answer me this; why did you flee? Given the choice between death and immortality, most mortals would choose to be divine."

"Was that your choice?"

The question seemed to surprise her. Standing at the edge of the pool, the goddess peered into its depths as if the answer lay somewhere buried beneath the sediment. Perhaps it did. Time seemed to stand still in this place. Like it had been captured within the stone. Each layer was a testament to a distinct chapter of the past, suspended in perpetuity, encapsulating secrets long forgotten yet eternally preserved. An indelible tapestry of history.

Tahlia's gaze drifted to their reflections upon the surface of the water and the strangeness of the moment struck her with aching clarity. To be standing next to a goddess, her fate, and still be drawing breath into human lungs.

The goddess also appeared to be lost in introspection. Tahlia wondered if she even remembered her origins, how she came to be.

Perhaps in her mind she had always existed. But all lesser gods had been human once. A truth they preferred to forget.

"I will tell you a story."

The words were so sudden Tahlia's breath hitched but she waited for the goddess to continue. Her eyes remained fixated on the water, as if she were peering into a pool of memories.

"Many years ago, I lived a human life. I fell deeply in love with a man and I wanted nothing more than to share a mortal life with him. To have a handful of short years. A home built with our own hands. Children. I was so blinded by our love that when he sold our story to the gods for a chance at divinity, I didn't question it. He told me that he wanted our love to live on forever. To transcend time and space."

Tahlia's gut hollowed out in anticipation. "What happened?"

"Soon after my sacrifice and ascension I learned that he had never loved me the way I loved him. He had many lovers, in fact, and many children. He was a connoisseur of beauty, who loved being the object of worship by women. But the thought of aging, of losing his ability to attract the most beautiful of women, was a fate worse than death. He desired to become divine so that he could collect all the beautiful things in the world, so that they may be sacrificed at his altar."

Nauseating dread flooded Tahlia's stomach as her eyes betrayed her shock. "The god of beauty and fertility was your lover?"

The goddess finally looked up at her, her expression eerily empty. "The gods knew. They thought it would be amusing for me to learn the truth. To be doomed to exist for all eternity with his betrayal and my own stupidity."

"I-I'm sorry," Tahlia stammered.

"Don't be. He has had to live with my existence for an eternity as well. There are few things more frightening than a patient woman with endless time."

Tahlia wasn't sure what she meant by that but she wasn't going to ask. The last thing she wanted to do was get involved in the petty squabbles between gods. Instead, she tried to refocus.

"Nasir hasn't challenged Henri at the summit. Henri would need to survive the summit and then find a way to kill him in order to return the water to the Idris desert," Tahlia mused.

"Then it is in his interest to agree to the Naiab's terms."

"Malik will never allow it." Tahlia shook her head in certainty. "He doesn't trust the Naiab."

"The former regent has his own agenda. Whether Henri lives or dies will be up to you."

Tahlia released her folded arms and blew out an exasperated breath. "You're a goddess! Can't you just kill Nasir and replenish the water table?"

"I see your informant did not share all our secrets. Being a divine does not make us all-powerful. There are limits to our domain. We are bound by the rules of our creation. There are makers and destroyers. Those that sustain life and those that end it."

"And what are you?"

"Water sustains life. But it can also drown it."

Tahlia's forehead tensed with worry. She wasn't sure how to interpret that.

"You will learn all of this and more when you ascend."

When. Not *if*.

Because even the Idris desert was not remote enough to escape the reach of the gods. Her fate was inevitable. She had stolen half a life, now she owed them more than her death. She owed them an eternity. But with whatever fleeting time she had left of this mortal life, she intended to use it wisely.

ELE

Ele peered over the precarious edge of the naturally formed stone bridge. Several stories below, he could see a circular carpet of wheat, peppered with occasional tree tops. It was illuminated in the dark by more than a dozen blazing torches. The view was an unusual sight to behold. One that only birds would normally see as they flew overhead. He couldn't stop staring at it. From the ground, Ele knew how impressive and large the field actually was. It was large enough to feed an entire city of people, but looking down on it from this height, it looked small. Perhaps that's why the gods were so dismissive of mortals, as Kala claimed. If he were a god and this was his view of the world, he might be dismissive too.

At the soft sound of steps approaching, Ele looked up to see Kala walking towards him.

"Isn't this place amazing?" Kala's face beamed with excitement.

It was. Like something out of a dream. But it was also a spy's worst nightmare. He had spent several hours exploring the Citadel in an effort to learn as much as he could, but he had barely covered any ground at all. The fact that it was the middle of the night and the city's residents were asleep, had helped him to move about freely and without discovery. However, it had also removed any possibility of overhearing conversation or asking innocent questions. He had hardly seen anyone at all during his exploration. There was no one guarding the field or patrolling the passageways. It was like the Naiab believed that nothing could threaten them out here.

Or perhaps *they* were the only threat out here.

"Amazing but dangerous." Ele cast his gaze over the edge of the bridge. "One wrong move and you're dead."

Kala shrugged. "Sounds like the Thaka."

Ele grimaced in agreement before turning his attention back to her. "What did you manage to find out?"

After waiting for the Naiab warrior to deliver their food, they had both scoffed down what they could and then crafted a plan. It was Kala who suggested that they should part ways to cover more ground. She would find out as much as possible about the water goddess and Ele would find out what he could about the Naiab. Her obsession with the goddess had not escaped his notice, and he was still curious about the strange interaction between her and Tahlia, but he didn't question it. They had agreed to meet in the middle of the high bridge to ensure no one would overhear them.

Looking down at the vertical sleeping city, the precaution seemed unnecessary.

"I couldn't find any evidence of human sacrifices," Kala announced proudly.

It was not what Ele had expected to hear. In fact, he had entirely forgotten about that gruesome possibility.

"What would the evidence look like? A bloody altar?"

"A tophet." At his puzzled look Kala explained, "A large fire pit. The priests conduct the ritual and throw the sacrifice into the fire."

"They burn people alive?!"

"Rumor is they drug them first but yes, the most important sacrifices are burned. The god of fire and ash receives the offerings and brings them to the gods. The less important sacrifices are buried alive. The god of earth and salt acts as a middle man between those offerings and the gods."

Ele stared at her in horror and revulsion as his stomach threatened to hurl its contents over the bridge. The very thought of it turned his blood cold. He had seen lots of violence in his life. From the desperate bloody violence on the streets of his home to the calculated, brutal violence of the battlefield. But this was different.

"What did you find out?" Kala asked.

The question pierced his thoughts and the grisly images faded from his mind. "I think the warriors are the only ones who can wield sand magic. The rest of the Naiab don't seem to have the blue tattoos beneath their skin."

"I saw that too."

"I also think the warriors are the only ones who can leave the city. I watched the entrance for a while. They were the only people who came and went."

"It is the middle of the night," she reminded him. "Not many people would be coming and going."

"True."

"It was likely a changing of the guard."

She was probably right but something about this place just made his skin itch.

"Besides, where would people go?" Kala added. "Even if they did travel across the Idris desert, none of the Merovian kingdoms would let them past their walls."

"I don't know. It just feels like ... we're trapped here." Ele shivered involuntarily.

Kala grabbed his hand. "I want to show you something."

She led the way off the stone bridge and along a slender passage that curved around the level. It led to some carved stairs which took them up another level. To his surprise, Kala navigated the corridors with an unwavering sense of direction. Finally, they arrived at the foot of a rocky cliff, the cavern wall towering above them.

"A dead end." He raised a quizzical eyebrow.

"For some."

Kala surveyed the wall briefly before reaching out for a rock that jutted out of the cliff face.

"What are you doing?" Ele baulked.

"What does it look like?" She hoisted herself up, carefully selecting each handhold and foothold.

Now that he was looking closer, Ele could see cavities had been carved into the wall, marking a clear path for those who dared.

"Are you coming or not?"

Ele looked up as she stared down at him, void of fear of the deadly drop below. He opened his mouth to protest, to point out just how dangerous this was, but then she grinned at him as if daring him to. Ele snapped his mouth shut. If Kala could do it, he could do it. And if he couldn't do it, he had the feeling he would never live it down.

Reluctantly, Ele began to climb. He tried to ignore the crumbling dust that shifted from each hold he grasped onto. He wondered exactly how many people had used these holds and whose dumb idea it was to make holes to climb a sheer rockface. To his relief, it didn't take long before they reached a narrow ledge. Kala smirked at him as she sat there waiting with her legs dangling over the edge.

When he sat down beside her, his legs felt a little wobbly and his fingers hurt. "Why in the world did I just do that?"

"Because I did," she replied smugly. "And because of that."

She pointed up to a hole in the cave's ceiling, wide enough to reveal a glimpse of the starry sky. Unlike with the rough interior of the cave, the sky looked like a luxurious satin sheet upon which thousands of shining jewels had been sewn. They glittered as soft, gentle moonlight filtered through the opening, bathing Ele and Kala in their light. The celestial view was mesmerizing, as was the brave girl who sat beside him.

Noticing his gaze, Kala returned a shy smile. She had many different smiles. A smile for excitement, a smile for mischief. A teasing smile or a relieved smile. But her shy smile was his favorite. It was rare, and that's why he treasured it. Because it took a lot to make her blush.

"You climbed up here for this?"

"No, silly. I climbed up here for that." Kala pointed to the end of the ledge which wound around the cliff face and disappeared.

"Where does it lead?"

"Out of the cave."

It took him a moment to understand what she'd said. "You found another way out?"

"A passageway leading to a dead end is kind of strange, don't you think?" Her tone implied it was the most obvious conclusion in the world.

"It makes sense they would have a second entrance."

"We can leave any time we want," she said proudly.

Kala placed her hands in her lap as she swung her legs back and forth, staring up at the night sky. Sometimes she seemed older than him. Smarter too. Definitely braver. It worried him that maybe one day she would outgrow him. That their friendship wouldn't be enough to keep her by his side.

Ele's voice was small when he asked, "Do you think you ever will? Want to leave Henri's kingdom, I mean."

Her face scrunched up. "And go where?"

He shrugged. "I don't know. Merovia is a big country. And there are countries beyond it. An entire world, really."

"Maybe."

Maybe.

He felt his heart collapse just a little.

She threw a curious look at him. "Would you ever want to leave?"

"Where ever Henri goes, I go."

"Because he's your king."

"Because he's my family."

Kala pursed her lips in thought. "What about your real family?"

Ele leaned back, placing his palms on the ground behind him. "I doubt they're still alive. I used to think about them years ago, but I don't anymore. I know I won't see them again."

It didn't sadden him. He had made peace with it a long time ago. Life could be cruel like that, but it could also be miraculous. Like when a drunken prince tumbled out of a pleasure house and instead of killing the little pickpocket who had tried to steal from him, he smuggled him into the palace and offered him a job.

"What about yours? Would you want to see your family again?"

"No."

Her answer was a little too swift, too certain.

"Don't you miss them?"

"The people who betrayed me and almost beat me to death? No, I don't miss them."

Ele held his silence. He had always suspected who had done it but had never asked her.

"Just because someone gives birth to your or gives you a name does not make them family." Kala's serious features shifted to a teasing smile. "I mean what kind of name is Ele, anyway?"

"It's not my name."

Kala raised a single curious brow.

"At least it's not my full name. It's short for my real name."

"What's your real name?"

A playful gleam danced in his eyes. "A secret."

"Does Henri know?"

Ele shook his head.

"Now you have to tell me!" Kala insisted.

"How about I promise to tell you my name on your twentieth birthday?"

"What! That is way too long to wait! Why then?"

Because it guaranteed him many more years of her by his side.

"Because by then you would have forgotten all about it." He grinned.

"No, I won't."

He knew she wouldn't. He was counting on it.

Kala sighed. "If we even live that long."

Ele's features turned stern. "Of course we will."

Her face seemed to fall a little, as if she wasn't so sure.

"Henri probably won't survive the summit. And Tahlia ... " She wrung her hands in her lap and averted her gaze.

Ele shifted closer and wrapped an arm around her shoulders, pulling her in tight against him. She rested her head against his collarbone and he covered her hands with his.

"We'll find a way to save them. Both of them," he said.

He didn't know what secret she and Tahlia shared but he was going to find out.

After sitting in silence for a while, the lull of sleep gently beckoned them. They carefully climbed down the stone wall and began making their way back to the chamber. As they were about to turn down into the passageway, Ele suddenly yanked Kala flush against the wall, making their bodies as small as possible. She didn't shriek or push him away, her body simply went rigid with silence as if she trusted him implicitly.

But trust was a fragile thing, easily called into question, or broken entirely. Because Ele could think of no good reason why Malik would be returning to the chamber in the dead of night.

CHAPTER FIVE

MALIK

Malik glanced over to the entrance of the chamber as Ele and Kala stepped inside, dressed and ready for the day's journey. They would be leaving as soon as possible and for Malik, that was not soon enough. The enforced detour to the Citadel had cost them an entire day's travel. Time was slipping through their fingers faster than sand. They couldn't afford any further delays.

Even so, Malik knew that Henri would want to speak to Lunara before they left. He wasn't yet sure whether Henri had decided to accept the terms of the goddess or the Naiab. There hadn't really been time to discuss the matter further after last night's exertions. There was a lot about last night Malik wanted to discuss with Henri. Another time, though, when they were alone.

Henri had never spoken to him about the torture he endured at the hands of Heroux and, in truth, Malik was afraid to hear it. He had witnessed what Heroux was capable of inflicting on others many times over. Worse, he had carried out Heroux's orders himself. The thought that, under different circumstances, he may very well have exacted such punishment on Henri at Heroux's command was—there were no words.

He would rather cut off his own hands.

Thankfully, the memories that had plagued Henri last night seemed to have passed. He still appeared ill at ease in the small room, but he was calm and focused. In fact, he was the only one among them who looked well rested.

Kala helped herself to some dates on the table as Ele continued to stand at the entrance, as if he were guarding it. He was staring at Malik shrewdly, studying him. Malik's brow twitched in interest. He wasn't sure what to make of the scrutiny. He held the boy's gaze for a moment, daring him to say something, but he didn't, so Malik looked away.

Tahlia was still readying herself for the journey, tucking her braid neatly beneath her headscarf. Her mood had been unusually somber since waking. She'd hardly said a word. From the way Henri's attention kept shifting to her, he had noticed it as well. But now his eyes were also darting to Kala and Ele and his features contorted in suspicion.

"There are five people in this incredibly cramped space and yet no one is saying anything." Henri narrowed his eyes at them.

They all glanced at each other, the silence growing heavy in the air between them.

"Ele?" Henri prompted.

"Malik?" Ele deflected.

"What?"

"Do you have anything to say?" Ele probed. "Maybe about where you disappeared to last night?"

Fuck.

Fucking little shadow.

Malik could feel Henri watching him carefully as Malik's gaze drifted to Tahlia.

She stilled. "You followed me?"

Ele frowned at Tahlia in confusion. "Where did *you* go?"

"I was only trying to make sure you were safe," Malik insisted. "I didn't trust Isa not to harm you."

"Isa? You went somewhere with Isa?!" Henri's expression turned rageful.

"To see the goddess," Tahlia replied.

Kala coughed as she choked on a date. She hit her chest several times and managed to swallow it before popping another one in her mouth.

Refocusing, Henri prompted, "And?"

Tahlia slowly lifted her eyes to Malik, the question clear. His silence was an answer and an apology. He had felt it straight away when she shifted off the bed in the middle of the night to leave with the warrior. When they slipped out of the chamber, he had quickly dressed and armed himself before following them. At first, he had lingered just outside the cave, but once Isa left, he had trailed Tahlia deeper into the cavern until she reached the pool. And the goddess.

"Someone explain," Henri ordered.

The room flooded with tension as Malik and Tahlia's gazes remained locked on each other, their secrets passing between them.

"Does it have anything to do with the debt you owe the gods?" Henri pressed. "Or why the warrior called you a goddess?"

"I am not a goddess." Tahlia closed her eyes as if it pained her to speak. "Not yet."

Henri's gaze danced between Malik and Tahlia. "What does that mean?"

She inhaled a deep breath, trying to reinforce her composure. "When I was a child, I would travel with my parents into the Old City when they had business to attend to there. One such day, a priest noticed me. He claimed that I had been chosen by the gods to ascend to divinity. My parents were overjoyed that our family had been chosen for the honor. They left me there, with that priest, as if they had received a gift instead of losing a daughter. I was taken to live in a Hara with the other ones chosen by the gods and they gave me the mark of a divine."

Tahlia's fingers trembled as she rolled up the long sleeve of her kaftan and exposed her wrist. The tattoo was woven in with other designs she had painted on her skin, but now that he knew what to look for, Malik could see it clearly.

"What's a Hara?" Ele frowned.

"It's where the chosen ones live until they are sacrificed," Kala explained.

"Most of the other chosen ones were adults, but in the room that I stayed, there were six young girls," Tahlia continued.

"Six," Kala's voice fractured.

Ele paled. "For sacrifice?"

Seeing Kala standing there, Malik couldn't help but wonder how old Tahlia was when she was chosen. Had she been Kala's age or even younger? It made him physically ill to think about. He knew such practices were commonplace in the Old City, but he had never really permitted himself to digest the gruesome reality of it. There was no point in debating the morals of a tradition when he had no power to change it. The kings of Merovia did not interfere with each other's rule, and Ozkan had always been particularly devout.

Tahlia pressed her lips together tightly, holding the words in, but they tumbled out anyway. "I was so young. I knew of the gods but I didn't realize what it was to be chosen by them. One night I snuck out of the room to watch the rain and I stumbled across the priests performing a ritual. I couldn't breathe, I was so scared. I tried to run but I ran straight into an old man who cleaned the Hara. He must have seen the fear in my eyes and took pity on me because he told me everything. All the secrets he had learned in a lifetime spent cleaning the Hara. He showed me what designs to paint on my skin for protection. He said it would hide me from the gods. Then ... he told me to run."

"That's how you ended up at the training house," Malik mused.

Ele shook his head, stunned. "So, because the water goddess knows who you are, the gods now want you dead?"

"The gods will seek their revenge," Malik intervened, "but apparently the god of beauty and fertility is particularly vengeful."

"The god of beauty and fertility." Henri frowned. "Shouldn't that be a goddess?"

"Since when have men not controlled women's bodies and re-production?" Tahlia deadpanned.

No one could argue with that.

"There is nowhere to hide," Kala said in a fearful voice. "The gods don't forget and they don't forgive."

Henri's features turned to steel. "They won't get near her."

"What would happen if … " Ele winced. "You died? Would you become a goddess?"

"Ele." Malik shot him a reproachful look.

Tahlia angled her head slightly, clearly trying to hold on to some measure of dignity which was hanging by a thread. "I don't know."

"Nobody's going to die," Henri growled, silencing the speculation.

Malik hoped Henri was right but he couldn't see a way out of it. Kala had spoken the truth; there was no evading the gods now.

"Does anyone else have any more secrets?" Henri seethed through clenched teeth.

Tahlia cast a covert glance toward Malik while Kala exchanged a knowing look with Ele.

Fuck.

HENRI

Emerging from the dark tunnel into the Idris desert, Henri blinked against the sudden onslaught of light that pierced his eyes. Although the sun had only been in the sky for less than an hour, it was already merciless in its intensity. The heat seared what little skin had been left exposed through his floor length kurta.

When his eyes adjusted, he noticed Isa standing in the middle of the narrow gorge, stroking the ears of one of the camels who was kneeling at his feet. To his surprise, the animals were saddled and readied for the journey. He felt his chest loosen slightly. The sight gave him some reassurance that they would, in fact, be permitted to leave. Malik strolled past Henri to inspect the bags, clearly not trusting the Naiab to have packed them properly. Ele and Kala followed him but Henri lingered by the entrance, waiting for Tahlia.

"You will find more food supplies for your travels," Isa offered before moving away from the animals.

Henri didn't reply. He only maintained a lethal stare that promised violence for what the warrior had dared to do last night. The thought of Isa entering the chamber on silent feet, threatening Tahlia with a blade, and stealing her away from them was mortifying. The fact that Henri had not woken was unforgiveable. He had been caught up in his own head, so exhausted by his own thoughts that he had slept like the dead. Tahlia could have been harmed, or worse, and he had not been there to protect her. It would not happen again. If the warrior so much as looked at her—

Tahlia stepped out of the tunnel into the sunlight and it was as if a desert rose had bloomed in their presence. She offered Henri a small smile as she came to stand by his side, linking her arm casually in his. The Naiab's eyes fastened onto her and his posture grew taut as he breathed in her scent; jasmine, fig blossoms, and rose petals.

He was dead.

The second Henri advanced, Lunara emerged from the mouth of the entrance, causing him to halt. Her eyes were a human shade of green but the knowing look she cast him told him that she didn't have to be a goddess to know that he was about to spill blood. Henri tilted his head slightly in open challenge. After all, it was the goddess's bidding that had sent the warrior to retrieve Tahlia last night.

Clasping her hands in front of her, Lunara offered a tight smile. "I came to bid you farewell and to see if you have considered my terms."

Ele and Kala remained standing by the camels, watching attentively, but Malik moved swiftly to flank Henri's other side. A sense of foreboding shadowed his every step. Henri knew Malik was anxious about what his decision would be. He also knew what Malik would advise him to do. For better or worse, Malik's decisions would always be based on fear and err on the side of caution. But Henri did not care if his decisions placed his own life in danger. He would always put the needs of his people ahead of his own. As king, he was prepared to pay any price, to make whatever sacrifices were necessary to ensure the safety of his people.

Except this one.

To sacrifice the life of someone he cared for, that was a decision he could never make.

"I have considered your terms and I wish to speak to the goddess," Henri said.

Lunara deliberated for a moment, or perhaps she was waiting for the goddess to respond. Then her eyes shifted, like a veil lifting to reveal the otherworldly creature that inhabited her.

The orbs of the water goddess brewed with stormy seas, as if she already knew what he was going to say. "You have an answer for me."

"I have a condition," Henri countered. "If I agree to kill Nasir and return the water, and if I support the Idris desert in becoming the sixth kingdom of Merovia, and if I tear down all the walls, then in return, Tahlia will be free of her debt to the gods."

A sharp breath escaped Tahlia's lips but Henri's attention did not waver from the goddess before him.

Lunara's features remained fixed as stone. Not a trace of humanity lingered. "That is not within my power to grant."

"You are a goddess."

"If her debt was to me alone then I would forfeit, but it is not. She incurred the wrath of all the gods. Her end is inevitable."

"Then I reject your terms."

"Henri." Tahlia's fingernails dug into his arm with urgency. "Don't do this. You can't save me, but you can save yourself. Agree to the Naiab's terms and they will help you survive the summit."

"By sending one warrior?" Malik scoffed. "It is not enough."

"It is something," Tahlia shot back angrily.

Henri lifted a hand to silence them both and Tahlia released his arm petulantly. "I have made my decision."

Without another word, the goddess was gone and Lunara's eyes had returned to their humanly form. The woman swayed a little as she settled back into her skin, but then her attention focused on him.

Her expression soured in bitterness and disbelief. "You would condemn an entire city of people to die."

"Your people. Not ours," Malik returned.

The words were cruel but Henri was grateful that Malik had said them.

Because he never could.

He had promised his reign would be one of equality and fairness and protection. For all people, not just his people. Even if that meant he would live one more day or ninety days. But this was Tahlia. She needed to live so many more days than that.

"That is not the king that we heard whispers about. A king strong enough to slaughter that tyrant Heroux. A king fearless enough to stop the slave trade. A king merciful enough to eradicate the tax on water for the poorest of his people."

Henri could feel his resolve wavering but he reinforced his mask of indifference. He couldn't afford to show any sign of weakness or regret. It was a gamble. Lunara and the goddess needed to believe him capable of such callousness.

"This is your choice, not mine," Henri replied. "I was willing to save your people. If you want them to live, convince the goddess to meet my terms."

"She can't!" Lunara shot back.

Henri shrugged. "Then we will be on our way."

With a decisive turn, he strode purposefully toward the camels where Ele and Kala were staring at him in silent question. A subtle inclination of his head served as a command for them to mount their camel. They obeyed without protest.

Malik moved swiftly to Henri's side and gave him a curt nod to reassure him that he had made the right decision. Whether Malik saw through his performance was beside the point. If Henri survived the summit, he had every intention of killing Nasir. Not only as retribution for trying to kill him but also in vengeance for the way he had treated Tahlia. Controlling her every word, her every breath, her every desire, and then framing her for Henri's assassination attempt. Kareem was right. There were many reasons to kill a man. He had a list a mile long for Nasir. Once he was dead, Henri would be able to redistribute the water and the Naiab would live. Whether he would support their bid to become the sixth kingdom or tear down the walls was another matter.

Henri took a seat behind the second hump and Malik moved into position at the front before he tugged on the reins. Placing a hand against Malik's solid back, Henri braced himself as the camel lurched, violently pitching him forward before righting itself again. It was only at that moment that he realized Tahlia remained standing by the entrance. Lunara was nowhere to be seen. She had likely returned inside the sandstone wall, but the Naiab warrior stood before Tahlia, holding something out to her. He was saying something but his words were pitched low enough to evade Henri's ears. What was evident, though, was the discomfort written all over Tahlia's face.

Henri clenched his jaw and began to calculate how best to jump off the wretched animal without breaking his legs when Tahlia suddenly snatched the offering. Isa caught her fingers and held them for a second too long as their eyes locked in a battle of wills. But just as soon, he released her, and Tahlia turned on her heel to make her way over to her camel. Henri's lethal stare burned into the warrior as his heart pounded to thoughts of bloody carnage. Isa's gaze never strayed from Tahlia, though, as he watched her mount her animal. It was as if he was blind to everything else in the world but her. Henri wasn't sure if the man revered Tahlia for being chosen by the gods or if he was simply under her spell, like most men. Not that it mattered. The warrior would never see her again.

TAHLIA

By the time Malik permitted them to stop and set up camp, the sky had unfolded into a blanket of stars. He had warned them that every day would be longer than the last, in order to make up for the time they had lost in their unexpected diversion to the Citadel. But if they stayed the course, by his calculations, they would arrive at the Old City the day before the summit.

If today was any indication, it would be a grueling few days ahead. The dramatic landscape of rolling dunes, though beautiful, had quickly become monotonous after several miles. The oppressive heat was only disrupted by burning winds that hurled abrasive grains of sand into their faces. Each passing hour felt like an eternity and with absolutely nothing to occupy the mind, Tahlia's thoughts had inevitably lingered on the summit, Henri's impending fight to the death, the ramifications should he not survive, and whether she would even live long enough to see it. No matter how hard she tried to ignore the thoughts, they plagued her. Seizing her heart and mind and refusing to let go. While a part of her longed for the arduous journey to come to an end, another part of her hoped they would never arrive at the Old City. Whatever relief she would feel upon seeing the towering wall on the horizon would undoubtedly be drowned in dread a moment later.

As Henri and Malik pitched the tents, Ele made quick work of creating a campfire thanks to the extra kindle that Isa had packed for them. The flames provided just enough light for Tahlia and Kala to prepare a simple meal of hard cheese, flat bread, olive oil, and dried meat. In truth, Tahlia had little appetite, but she knew she had to fuel her body to endure the remaining trek across the Idris desert. Really, she ought to be savoring every meal, the sensation of taste on her tongue, the basic human need to eat. The divine could only dream about such things, if indeed they dreamed at all. She wasn't sure what was worse; the prospect of becoming a divine or the possibility of not ascending at all.

Tahlia could feel Kala's eyes on her, peeking up from beneath her long eyelashes as she sliced the bread. She was clearly trying to assess if Tahlia was on the brink of unraveling after Henri's failed attempt to negotiate her life with the water goddess. Kala's concern was sweet but Tahlia didn't have the energy to try to convince her that she was accepting of her fate. She wasn't. At the same time, there was little other choice. It was a cruel kind of madness. If she had any privacy at all, she might thrash or rage or cry, but in the end, it would not change anything. It would only serve to entertain the gods. So she held her emotions in a cage of silence.

"I think what you did was very brave."

Kala's whispered words pierced her armor but Tahlia refused to meet the girl's gaze. She couldn't. Her vision was blurred with bitter tears that she refused to let fall. When Henri and Malik approached, Tahlia averted her eyes as she handed them their plates of food. Ele collected his and took a seat around the campfire with Kala. Malik joined them but Henri lingered by Tahlia's side.

"You could have told me, you know," Henri said quietly. "I don't share your beliefs or your gods. I would not have judged you for it."

"I know." Tahlia strained to keep her voice steady. "But even if I had told you, we would still be here. The outcome is the same."

"We'll find a way. I swear to you, I will stand between divinity and death to keep you by my side. You are mine. No force of heaven or earth will take you from me."

Tahlia lifted her eyes to meet his and saw the raw determination engraved on his face. He would do anything to keep his promise. His features shifted, though, as his gaze fell to the brass vial hanging around her neck.

"Is that what the warrior gave you?"

Her fingers instinctively closed around it as she glanced downward. The vial was strung on a silver chain and shaped like a teardrop with a beautiful floral design etched into it.

"Yes."

Taking her plate, Tahlia made her way over to the campfire and Henri followed.

"Why would he give you something like that?"

Tahlia shrugged as she took a seat. "Does it matter?"

After everything that had occurred, the motivations behind a gift was the least of her concerns.

"What did he say to you?"

"Nothing of significance."

Henri's stare bore into her, suggesting that he didn't believe that for a second. Tahlia sighed.

"He said he hoped we had a plan to ensure your survival at the summit. Malik, do we have a plan?"

Even Tahlia was surprised at how her tone changed to a brutal accusation. She was angry, she realized, and not just at the inevitability of her fate. They had been offered an alliance in their hour of need and Henri had blindly rejected it. Because of her. Because he was trying to save her life instead of his own.

"One Naiab warrior would not have made a difference," Malik replied steadily.

"You don't know that. Three kings and who knows how many Rouhan nobles. Do you honestly believe that Henri can defeat them all?"

The words erupted from her mouth, exposing the grim reality that everyone had been refusing to acknowledge for months now. Tahlia was no warrior but even she knew that no amount of training and skill with a shamshir could save a man from odds like that. Malik was deluding himself if he thought it could. They were delivering Henri to his death.

Ele and Kala shared worried expressions while Henri remained quietly pensive.

"What do you suggest we do?" Malik countered.

"Henri has to change his mind. Accept the Naiab's offer."

"Not unless the water goddess meets my terms," Henri replied stubbornly.

Tahlia released a shrieked growl of frustration. "I refuse to be the reason for your stupidity!"

"You are not the only reason for his decision," Malik reminded her. "Destroying the walls would provide the Naiab with an opportunity to seize control of the entire country. Henri is trying to save your life, but he is also protecting Merovia."

"He can protect Merovia *after* he survives the summit," she returned through gritted teeth. "You had no issue with him forming an alliance with Nasir who also desires to claim Merovia for himself. Why are you so threatened by the Naiab?"

"So you did know the details of Nasir's offer of alliance." Wariness crept across Henri's expression.

Shit.

"I told her," Malik intercepted. "After Nasir tried to poison you. I didn't see any point in keeping it from her. I'm sorry if I overstepped."

Henri cast his gaze to Tahlia but she was staring at Malik, her eyes conveying a mix of reproach and gratitude. She would tell Henri the truth, they both would, just not right now. Malik was right when he said that Henri's focus needed to remain on the summit. He couldn't afford to doubt the loyalty of those around him.

"The Naiab are the larger threat because they are unknown to us," Malik explained. "Nasir we can predict. The Naiab have sand magic and a goddess on their side."

"Maybe that's why we should ally with them," Ele interjected carefully. "Better to make them allies than enemies."

Kala shook her head. "You can't trust the gods."

Malik ignored both of them. "I think you are being blinded by the handsome warrior."

Tahlia's eyes flashed with fury. "Don't you dare."

"What makes you think Isa won't try to kill Henri the moment the other kings are defeated?" Malik persisted.

"If he does, you can kill him! You're good at that!"

"Enough." Henri's tone hardened like steel struck with an anvil. "I have made my decision. It is final."

Indignant heat flamed Tahlia's cheeks. There was so much more she wanted to say. She wanted to detonate her feelings across the entire desert. Malik stared at her as if he understood all the reasons why she needed to rage at him. Her emotions were naked—anger, fear, love—interwoven with a powerlessness to change any part of what was to come.

"Henri will survive the summit," Malik asserted confidently.

"If he doesn't, it will be because of you."

Tahlia's words were pure poison and the way Malik's face drained to hear them proved their potency. Leaving her food untouched, Tahlia rose from her seat and walked over to her tent. If she stayed, she would only continue to say things she would regret later.

"Tahlia." Malik seized her elbow lightly and she turned to face him, ready to apologize if he asked her to. "Do you trust me?"

The question was so unexpected it took her a moment to comprehend. Then she saw it, a secret concealed behind his caramel eyes. He was hiding something from her, from all of them.

Her heart somersaulted with hope and anxiety. "What have you done?"

Perhaps he had sent assassins to murder the other Merovian kings against Henri's orders. Or maybe he had made secret deals with the Rouhan nobles in exchange for them not challenging Henri at the summit. Whatever it was, he had kept it to himself, which meant Henri would not condone it.

"Trust me." Malik released her elbow before casually returning to the campfire.

Tahlia stood there, stunned, as a million possibilities battered her mind. Despite the warmth in the air, a shiver ran through her body without warning. She crossed her arms tightly over her chest, as if that would help fortify everything she was trying to keep inside. Her words. Her thoughts. Her tears. That's when she noticed that Kala was looking back at her, her face contorted with concern. Tahlia offered a tight smile that was probably more like a grimace. It was all the reassurance she could manage right now.

Stepping inside her tent, Tahlia found that her things had been laid out for her; her perfume, the oil she used on her hair, her paints. Not that her paints would afford her protection anymore, but she still had to hide her mark from prying eyes. Besides, the ritual of painting designs on her skin had become a comfort over the years. Tahlia didn't know who had done this for her, Malik or Henri, but the thoughtful gesture left her heart heavy. She pressed the heels of her hands to her stinging eyes and forced herself to inhale a deep breath. There was nothing more she could do. Henri had made his decision and Malik had made a plan without them. She had no choice but to accept the role that had been laid out for her, like an echo of fate.

Tahlia undressed and ran a damp cloth over her skin before changing into a thin slip of a nightdress. Exhaustion threatened to pull her down like an undertow and soon she was lying on her bedroll, her wild dark curls splayed out beneath her head. She couldn't remember succumbing to sleep, and she couldn't recall if she dreamed, but she certainly woke when something came for her in the night.

CHAPTER SIX

TAHLIA

Tahlia was going to die; of that she was certain. She didn't even try to scream or fight back as panic flooded her senses, plunging her into a state of paralyzing terror. The darkness enveloped her like death itself, winking out all her senses. She should have left the oil lamp burning beside her bed, or slept with a dagger clutched in her palm, but she hadn't thought about those things and perhaps it didn't matter in the end. Maybe it was a mercy to not see death advancing toward her in the shadows as it reached for her throat.

"Don't scream."

She knew that voice.

Tahlia broke free of her paralysis to shove violently back at the muscled chest looming over her, though her impact was futile because the body was like a sandstone wall. It did not move. Within the shadows, the turquoise tattoos shimmered softly over the planes of his naked form.

"What are you doing here?" She hissed as she righted a thin strap of her chemise which had fallen off her shoulder.

"I came to speak with you."

The shifting glow of Isa's tattoos indicated he had leaned back from her, settling on the edge of the bedroll. Grateful for the space, she sat up a little.

"If Henri finds you here, he will kill you."

"He can try."

Tahlia didn't have to see Isa's face to hear the smirk in his tone. She threw him a withering look, though she knew it was pointless.

"Did the water goddess send you?"

"I came because I believe you don't want your king to die. And I can help save him."

Tahlia's pulse skittered with hope but it was futile. "Henri has made his decision. He's as stubborn as a mule."

"This is *your* decision. You hold the power to decide whether he lives or dies."

Her stomach churned in apprehension. "What exactly are you proposing?"

"Take me with you into the Old City, get me into the summit, and I will ensure your king lives."

"How? One man would hardly make a difference."

"I am no ordinary man." His words made her shiver.

He wasn't lying. Her instincts had told her that the moment she laid eyes on him. It wasn't just that he was god-touched, granting him control over the desert sands. It was in the way he held himself, like he believed himself to be untouchable and impervious to any threat.

"I have no power to meet Lunara's terms, or those of the water goddess," Tahlia said.

"Those are not my terms," he replied dismissively.

"Then what do you want in return?"

"A kiss."

Tahlia's lips parted in astonishment as her eyebrows rose. "A kiss."

"You sound surprised. Most men would be willing to do anything, surrender all they possessed in the world for one kiss from a goddess. Murdering a few kings is a small price to pay."

She wanted to point out that she was not a goddess yet but it was a mute argument. She had been chosen and marked. It was only a matter of time—and fate.

Tahlia fumbled amidst her things to light the oil lamp. The flame softly illuminated Isa's nude form but she kept her eyes trained on his face as she studied him carefully. She had a feeling he was consciously making the same effort.

"Why do you need me to get you into the Old City?"

"There's a wall," he replied flatly.

"That didn't stop your people from getting into Henri's kingdom."

He tilted his head, conceding the point. "I could get inside the Old City but it would be difficult for me to get inside the summit undetected. I wouldn't exactly blend in."

It was true. Besides his golden skin and turquoise tattoos, the man was over six feet tall and looked as if he'd been carved from rock. He might be able to disguise himself in the Old City but he wouldn't be able to conceal himself at the summit.

"Then how do you propose I get you inside?"

"With this."

He reached for the vial around her neck that hung loosely between her breasts. He held it lightly in his fingers, careful not to touch her skin, but the pulse in her throat fluttered all the same.

"I will turn to sand and you will carry me inside it. Just like you will carry me every day until we reach the Old City. Though I would be grateful if you released me at night. It can be quite taxing staying in my sand form."

He released the vial and it settled back against her skin. As he withdrew his hand, she felt the tension in her chest cavity loosen a little.

Tahlia licked her lips self-consciously, trying to maintain some facade of indifference. "That's why you gave this to me. It was your plan if Henri rejected the offer."

He angled his head. "It was my plan to see you again, goddess."

"Don't flirt with me. And don't think I am vain enough to believe that you would be willing to do this in exchange for a kiss. You clearly have an ulterior motive."

"But do you believe I can save your king?" His eyes flared like embers as his expression turned sharp and deadly.

Tahlia's throat constricted but the answer was already on her tongue. She didn't know why. She had no evidence and it made no logical sense. Perhaps it was pure desperation masquerading as truth.

"Yes. I do."

"Then we have a deal?"

Malik's words echoed in her mind with warning; did she trust him? Trust him enough to save Henri's life? She knew his history and what he had done. She protected some of his secrets and he guarded some of hers. He would never betray Henri. His love was undeniable. She would have said that there were no limits to what Malik would be willing to do to save his life. Except that was not true. He was not willing to ally with the Naiab or risk his country. Malik had a plan, but what if that plan failed? What if Tahlia had the opportunity to alter the outcome of Henri's fate and she didn't take it?

Life was a divine tapestry of infinite threads. Each fiber a person, a choice, a moment, a memory. A collection of endless possibilities, experiences, and alternative endings. As each thread intertwined, the story would shift, shaping one's identity and defining the purpose of the design. With each stitch, the pattern would evolve through joy and sorrows, love and loss. The gods loved nothing more than to create tension and tug on threads until they snapped. In this moment, it felt as if she were being given a taste of what it meant to play god.

Tahlia dipped her chin in silent agreement, because she would never be able to forgive herself if Henri died trying to save her life when she had the power to save his. There was no changing any of their decisions now. The dye had been cast.

MALIK

As they approached the Old City, a hush fell over their caravan. The air shimmered with heat, distorting the view in the distance. A great wall emerged from the desert haze, towering majestically from the golden sea of sand. It looked almost identical to the wall along Henri's northern border. Looming several meters high, it would provide the sentries with an unparalleled vantage point for miles. No doubt they would have spotted them already and perhaps even mobilized against their perceived threat. Malik was glad he was seated behind the first hump, with Henri seated behind him. His body would provide at least some shielding from any wayward arrows.

"Do they know to expect us?" Tahlia asked nervously as she brought her camel alongside theirs.

Malik's features pulled tight. "I sent word confirming our attendance at the summit before we left."

"They forced us to go through the Idris desert hoping it would kill me," Henri replied bitterly. "I think the fact that we're still breathing will shock everyone."

They advanced slowly so as to appear less threatening, but when they drew closer, Malik saw that his assumption was correct. The top of the wall was lined with archers and the watchtowers were also manned. The soldiers held their arrows though, awaiting orders from a leader that Malik couldn't quite discern from among the men. Malik halted their caravan a short distance away and tugged down the fabric covering his face. He would have preferred to stay out of range of their arrows but he needed to be close enough so that he might be recognized.

In the course of his duties to Heroux, Malik had traveled to all the kingdoms of Merovia, but none more often than this one. The annual summit had forced him to witness the draconian brutality of kings and men repeatedly, always fueled by the lust for wealth and power, alongside the complete disregard for life. In his bones, he had always detested it, but he had never really questioned it. Until he met Henri. It was a ritual for his people, the same as any other, in the sense that it felt like it had always existed. There was no interrogating its foundations, its purpose or necessity, it simply was. But now he wanted to tear it from the pages of history, reduce its cornerstones to rubble, and burn the entire arena to the ground.

"I am King Henri of Merovia." Henri projected his voice as if he were shouting across the expanse of the Idris desert. "I demand entry into King Ozkan's kingdom to attend the summit."

One of the guards raised his hand in signal and the sentries subsequently lowered their weapons. A moment later, the sound of cogs turning echoed beyond the wall and the gate opened before them. Malik tensed as they slowly entered through the gaping maw of the gate. His instincts took over his mind and body as his eyes vigilantly scanned their surroundings for threat. He would not put it past the Merovian kings to lay a trap or ambush them before they even reached the Old City. They were cowards and Henri had proven himself to be their greatest threat. No one approached their caravan though, not as they kept traveling from the border, nor as they finally reached the streets of the Old City.

Malik cast a glance at Tahlia as they crossed the threshold into the city. He watched her spine go rigid and she sat a little higher in the saddle than she was moments before, but her eyes were fixed ahead in determination. He could only imagine what it would be like for her to return here. What painful memories haunted these streets. To be willing to endure them was testament to how much she truly cared for Henri. Malik's admiration for her grew with every step she took forward.

In some ways, the Old City looked like every other city in Merovia. The buildings were thick, solid square structures, made of mud-bricks with flat roofs. They sat side by side with no space in between, each of them at various heights. The roads were wide and sinuous. Closer to the heart of the city were several plazas where merchants called out, peddling their wares. Except where there would have normally been bubbling water fountains, there were towering statues of the gods. Carved from rock, they had been weathered by centuries of wind and sun, and yet still they stood, a symbol of the enduring devotion of the people.

Within the labyrinth of streets were several temples, each adorned with intricate carvings and mosaics in homage to the divines. Adjoining each temple was a Hara, where the ones chosen by the gods to become divine were housed before their sacrifice. Along with the annual festivals to celebrate the changing seasons and to win the favor of the divines, the priests regularly conducted rituals to invoke blessings upon the city and its people. It was said that beneath the foundations of the Old City were secret passages where the veil between the mortal realm and the divine was thin. Some even claimed that they could hear the echo of celestial voices from beneath the depths of the earth.

The scent of spices and baked bread drew Malik's attention back to the bustling street market around them. His stomach grumbled involuntarily. After days of dried meat and meager rations, he couldn't deny that he was craving a substantial meal. Henri would also need fresh food to replenish his strength if he was going to emerge victorious tomorrow. Malik clenched his jaw in irritation. If they hadn't been forced to detour to the Citadel, they would have arrived in plenty of time to recover from their journey across the Idris desert. Now there would barely be enough time to rest.

King Ozkan's palace, though not as beautiful as Henri's, was still grand. It stood several stories high, with domed rooftops and ornate minarets. The path leading to the palace was lined with date palms. Upon recognizing Malik, the soldiers forming a guard around the exterior divided to let them through. A stony courtyard lay at the entrance, featuring more statues of the gods, their vigilant postures suggesting a watchful presence.

"How many gods are there in Merovia?" Ele asked as he took in the sight.

"Too many," Kala grunted.

Malik pointed to one of the statues. "That one is the god of justice and kingship. He is often shown holding a crown in one hand and a set of scales in the other. That one over there holding a staff of flame is the god of fire and ash."

"The god that accepts the sacrifices that are thrown into the fire and brings them to the gods, right?" Ele muttered under his breath to Kala.

Kala nodded and tossed a careful look over at Tahlia but she appeared to be trying her best to ignore the conversation.

Malik indicated to another statue. "That one is the god of earth and salt, holding soil in one hand and salt in the other."

"He accepts the sacrifices that are buried," Ele recalled.

"And he shapes the earth," Kala added.

"Then there is the sun god and the moon god," Malik continued. "And—"

"Stop, please. I can't possibly remember all of them," Henri groaned.

Malik chuckled but wondered if Henri had put an end to the conversation for Tahlia's sake. As they dismounted their camels, servants approached to take the reins and unload their belongings.

"Inform King Ozkan that King Henri has arrived," Malik announced. "We will need chambers prepared, with supper and hot baths waiting."

The servants dipped their heads in acknowledgement and hurried inside the palace. Henri came to stand at Malik's side, followed by Tahlia who was clutching the vial around her neck as if it were a prayer bead. Curiously, she had filled it with sand from the Idris desert. Malik didn't understand the sentiment but he didn't question it either. Personally, he didn't need a souvenir to remember the past nine torturous days. If he never crossed the Idris desert again, he would be grateful.

"Well, at least there are no stairs," Ele remarked with a grin as he surveyed the palace.

Henri threw him a dirty look.

"Kafei." A male servant rushed out of the palace toward Henri, his cheeks flushed. "Please forgive the delay in receiving you. I will take you to your chambers now."

"It's almost like you weren't expecting us," Malik admonished.

After washing their feet just inside the entrance, they followed the servant through the corridors of the palace. Their attire and general state of disarray earned disapproving glances from the courtiers but Malik met their stares with a defiant glare, prompting them to swiftly avert their eyes. It was diminishing enough that King Ozkan hadn't received Henri in person, or had rooms prepared for his arrival, now they were being paraded through the halls while still smelling like the camels they rode in on. Malik knew Henri wouldn't be bothered by it, but he was. Malik wore clothes and jewelry the way a soldier wore plates of armor. From satin to silk, gold to silver, the more brazen and extravagant the better. It commanded attention and conveyed the message of his status and affluence. Without it, he felt unarmed. Insignificant. Easy prey.

The servant led them to the guest wing of the palace and opened a large set of double doors. "Kafei, this chamber has been prepared for you. It has several adjoining rooms should you wish to use them."

"Thank you," Henri replied.

The servant bowed and walked backwards several steps before turning and retreating. Ele and Kala were the first to step inside and they quickly released noises of impressed delight. Malik could understand why as he joined them. The room was expansive, its walls draped in rich tapestries depicting scenes between the gods and mortals. Tales of benevolence, wrath, violence, and sacrifice. Tahlia's attention drifted over them with cool indifference, but she crossed her arms tightly over her chest, the only hint of her discomfort.

In the center of the room sat an ornate canopy bed, easily large enough to fit three people, adorned with expensive silks and plush cushions. A narrow table was positioned along the wall, featuring a selection of fresh fruits, hot dishes, and fine wine. Malik could already smell the spiced meats, steamed barley, and grilled vegetables.

At the far end of the room, the polished tiled floors opened out to a grand stone balcony. A muscle in Malik's jaw twitched at the view. The room overlooked the arena where the summit would take place. Ozkan had chosen this room for a reason. Henri must have noticed it too because he wandered out onto the balcony to take a closer look. Malik and Tahlia exchanged a heavy look before silently following to stand behind him. A slight perfumed breeze wafted through the billowing curtains, carrying the scents of the orange and fig trees.

The arena was an impressive elliptical structure, standing several stories tall, composed from massive travertine blocks. From the outside it looked ancient and worn, but inside, rows of tiered seating encircled the amphitheater, offering panoramic views of the annual spectacle that unfolded within its walls.

"Is that where I will fight tomorrow?" Henri tossed over his shoulder.

Malik murmured affirmingly. Interest piqued, Ele and Kala approached to linger by the curtains for a better view. Tension filtered through the air. Malik could almost taste it sharp and sour on his tongue. Now that they had survived the Idris desert and arrived safely in Ozkan's palace, there was no avoiding the reality of what they would face tomorrow. Bloodshed was inevitable. Kings would die. And the balance of power would shift. Henri would either emerge victorious, having won several Merovian kingdoms to his name, or he would be dead.

Henri turned from the ominous view. His face was a carefully constructed mask but Malik knew the war that raged beneath it. The tumult of rage and resentment at being coerced to fight in this savage ritual, blended with a determination to survive at all costs, subdued by the sobering truth that this might be the last night of his life, and burdened by the need to maintain a façade of strength for the sake of those around him.

Henri looked to each one of them before saying, "We should get some rest before morning. Ele and Kala, there's an adjoining room you can use. Take some food with you."

With a slight dip of her chin, Kala made her way over to the table along the wall and started piling food on a plate.

Before Ele could join her, Henri laid a hand on his shoulder and lowered his voice. "Don't forget your promise to me."

Ele scowled up at him. "I won't."

Henri's lips twitched in an affectionate smile as he ruffled the boy's hair. Ele quickly ducked out of his reach before joining Kala to heap food on a plate.

"Nor will I," Malik added and Henri gave a curt nod of gratitude.

"What did you make them promise?" Tahlia stepped closer. Her voice was almost too soft, as if she were trying to keep it light but there was still a nervous edge.

"If I die tomorrow, Malik will challenge my successor. He needs to rule my kingdom if I can't."

Tahlia's eyes flared in horror.

"And if we both die, Ele will make sure you and Kala get out of here safely."

"But no one's going to die," Malik said. It was a reflexive response. Like a heart pumping blood or lungs drawing breath.

Henri ignored him, his eyes turning serious as he fixed them on Tahlia. "Either way, you will be safe. I promise you."

His attention momentarily diverted as Ele and Kala walked past and bid everyone goodnight, but once they exited through the adjoining door, his focus returned to her. Not so long ago, Malik would have felt a surge of jealousy to see Henri look at anyone the way he was looking at Tahlia right now. Instead, he felt his heart soften in understanding. The gravity of ensuring everyone's safety weighed heavily on Henri, even when faced with his own death. Tahlia was trying to be brave for both of them but Malik could see her control was fraying at the edges.

"Well then, I had better get some rest," she said.

"Tahlia." Henri grasped her arm as she turned to leave, his brows drawing together in question. "You're staying with us tonight."

It sounded more like a plea than a question.

Tahlia flicked her gaze to Malik before returning it to Henri. "No. You two need this night together."

Because it might be their last. The unspoken words ricochet between them.

"Besides, I'm tired. I'm going to take some food and find a room and enjoy a long bath."

"Are you sure?" Malik pressed. He didn't want to be the reason that she forfeit precious time with Henri.

Tahlia smiled as if she could hear his thoughts and walked over to lightly press her lips to his. He kissed her back, a chaste kiss of tenderness and affection.

"I am sure."

Tahlia turned to Henri and he enveloped her in his strong arms, cradling the back of her head in his hand, as if he could keep her safe by simply never letting go. It was a long moment before they pulled away from each other, only to meet each other's lips with a deep, sensual kiss. It was obvious that Henri wanted her to stay. Not only to find pleasure in the soft curves of her body and comfort from her presence, but also to make sure that she was safe. The knowledge that Isa had taken her from their bed in the middle of the night had unnerved him. Coupled with the gods' quest for vengeance against her, Henri never wanted to let her out of his sight again. It was foolish to believe that he could protect her against them, but Malik empathized with the blind, compelling need to try. There was no enemy, in this mortal world or the immortal realm, that Malik would not cross in order to save Henri's life.

CHAPTER SEVEN

ELE

Ele sat on the cold tiled floor by the balcony, staring out at the wall of the arena. He and Kala had both eaten as much food as their stomachs could handle before Kala claimed the first bath. Now he was alone with his thoughts and they never offered much comfort.

He'd had many nights like this one in his life, where he wondered what the next day would bring. When he was little, all he thought about was whether he would get to eat again or if he would live to see the end of the day. Survival was all he knew. Every day lived was a victory. But since Henri took him into his employ, he hadn't had to worry about those things. He was fed and clothed and sheltered. His life would end in bloody violence if he was caught spying but the risk was worth it. Better to die the king's spy than just another child unwanted on the streets.

"I *still* have sand in my ears."

Kala's words jolted him from his thoughts and he looked up to find her walking over to him, hitting her palm against her ear as if she could shake the sand out of it. She sighed in defeat as she plopped down beside him, folding her legs beneath her. Her hair was a collection of wet strings down her back but her skin was clean enough that he could see the smattering of freckles on her cheeks. He couldn't help but stare at them. They were his favorite constellation.

"So, what's the plan?" Kala asked.

"Plan for what?"

Kala raised an eyebrow at him, as if he were dense. "For saving Henri."

"There isn't one. He made me promise not to leave the room tonight or get involved at the summit tomorrow."

"And you're going to listen to him? We can't just do nothing," Kala insisted.

"Some battles have to be fought alone. It's what makes a man." At Kala's skeptical stare, he explained. "Henri was born a prince but never wanted to be king. When he fought Heroux on the battlefield that day, he was weak and badly injured and armed with only a small axe. He should have died that day but he didn't. He won. Not only did he kill Heroux but he stopped a war. It took that battle for him to want to become a king."

"And now this battle could end his reign."

Ele blew out a long breath. "If he dies, Malik will challenge his successor. If Malik dies, I have to get you and Tahlia back to the coast to board a ship to Sirasinda. There's a queen there who will help us."

"Okay," Kala said slowly, her mind churning over the possibilities. "So, we have a plan for if Henri dies, but what's the plan if he lives?"

Ele took a moment to think. "He'll have to rule over three new kingdoms, deal with the Rouhan's who have just lost all their power, and Nasir won't waste time before sending another assassin to kill him. Except Henri won't give him the chance. He'll kill him the moment the summit's over."

"Nasir's smart. He'll have a plan for if Henri lives or dies. We should too."

Worry creased Ele's forehead. Kala had a point. They were all so focused on whether Henri would survive the summit, no one had thought that the real danger might occur after his victory. Nasir had already tried to kill Henri. Twice. He had been planning Henri's death since before he arrived at Merovia.

"What do you think Nasir's plan is?" Ele asked.

"What would I do if I were an evil king planning to murder all my rivals and take control of an entire country?" Kala tapped her chin as she paused for thought. "I have no idea."

"He'd be pretty stupid to try to kill Henri himself considering Henri would have just killed three kings and a bunch of nobles." Ele said. "Besides, Malik would never let Nasir get close enough."

"He'll run?" Kala suggested. "Get to the safety of his kingdom and then whatever his plan is, he'll go from there."

"Then we have to make sure he doesn't escape tomorrow."

Kala nodded resolutely. But then her features softened and she bit her bottom lip anxiously. "Do you think Henri will survive tomorrow?"

"Yes."

His answer was so swift and sure it prompted Kala to sit up a little straighter. "How do you know?"

Ele stared out at the arena where the blood of countless kings stained the floor. "Because he has to."

TAHLIA

Tahlia placed her plate of food down on the table but her stomach twisted at the sight of it. The thought of eating made her feel physically ill, despite the fact that she hadn't eaten fresh food in days. She walked away from it and steepled her fingers, unsure what to do with herself. Had she made the right decision not to stay with Henri tonight? Would she regret it in the morning? Time was such a precious thing. Once it seemed endless and but now it dissolved with every breath, like sand passing through an hourglass until suddenly there was nothing left.

No, she had made the right decision. There would be other nights because Henri would survive tomorrow. Isa would make sure of it. Whatever the Naiab's agenda was, whatever price they would pay for her deception, at least Henri would be alive.

Reassured in her conviction, Tahlia peeled the clothes from her body and readied a bath, pouring oils into the water to soften her skin and make it fragrant. Tomorrow she would not be pulling on leathers or wielding a shamshir, but she would arrive prepared for battle. By having the silk rose, the most coveted courtesan in all the kingdoms by his side, Henri would appear that much more powerful.

Unclasping the silver chain from around her neck, Tahlia opened the lid to the teardrop vial and poured the sand out onto the tiles. Then she returned the necklace to her throat and sauntered into the bathroom, leaving the door ajar just a little. Steam curled off the surface of the water as she slowly submerged herself in the bath. It felt luxurious after days of washing her skin with a lightly damp cloth so as not to waste drinking water. Her muscles immediately relaxed and her nostrils filled with the scent of jasmine, fig blossoms and rose petals. As she settled into the peaceful quiet, she listened intently for sounds of movement coming from the other room.

A charge electrified her bloodstream when Tahlia detected the softest of footfalls. She couldn't help but wonder if those footfalls would approach the door. If he was tempted to peek through the sliver she had left open for him. It wasn't an invitation to join her. It was a dare. To see what he would do.

For the past few nights, she had poured the sand from the brass vial onto the floor of her tent and Isa had materialized before her. Naked. Glorious. He was too tall to stand upright and his broad frame took up almost the entire tent, but he hadn't complained as he sat beside her bedroll and ate the food she had secreted for him. Apparently, using sand magic depleted a lot of his strength because he ate like he'd been starved for days.

At first, Tahlia had simply watched him. She wasn't sure what else to do, if she was meant to make polite conversation or ignore him entirely. The silence unnerved her though, so she started asking him questions. She had thought she might be able to coax some information from him. Perhaps he would let something slip about the water goddess or the Naiab's plans for wanting to become the sixth kingdom of Merovia. But despite answering every question, Isa's responses were brief and vague.

After several nights, she was no wiser about him or his people. What aggravated her more than his ambiguity, though, was his restraint. Despite their cramped lodgings, he had made sure to maintain a respectful distance between them. His eyes never dipped below her face and though he slept on the ground beside her, he hadn't tried to touch her.

Not once.

Perhaps when she told him to stop flirting with her he had taken it literally. Or worse, perhaps he had been playing with her this whole time, making her believe that he desired her when really all he desired was power for his people. Tahlia shifted her legs in the bath, making the perfumed water slosh around her. Her gaze flicked back to the door and she narrowed her eyes. It hadn't moved an inch. She wasn't sure why his self-control bothered her so much. She wasn't interested in inviting yet another person into her bed. Was she?

This was wrong. The reality of tomorrow slapped her in the face and guilt flamed her cheeks. She shouldn't be thinking about having sex with three devastatingly handsome men when in a handful of hours Henri would be fighting for his life. Tahlia sank beneath the water and her own shame for a few seconds, before she resurfaced to smooth her hands over her long, dark hair. She needed to focus on becoming the silk rose, not trying to seduce the Naiab warrior who may or may not betray them.

Climbing out of the bath, Tahlia retrieved a soft towel and dried her skin before ringing the water from her hair. Then she tied a satin robe loosely around her body and checked her appearance in the misted mirror. No one could deny that she was alluringly beautiful, with her rosebud lips, honeyed complexion, and dark features. She could have any man she desired, and tomorrow she would captivate the entire arena so that Henri could slaughter them all.

Tahlia sashayed out into the room but stumbled a little at the sight of Isa not naked. He was sitting at the table wearing long pants that pulled tight across his hips.

Very tight.

Her lips parted in question, or blatant appreciation, but no words came out of her mouth.

"There were spare clothes in the wardrobe," he explained, motioning a hand to the wardrobe on the far side of the room.

Tahlia forced her eyes away from the impressive bulge in his pants to focus on something, anything, else in the room. The tapestries on the wall thankfully did not feature scenes between gods and mortals like they had in Henri's chamber. Rather, they depicted serene landscapes of golden sand dunes and palm trees standing beneath a setting sun. The plate on the table was empty, she noted with mild interest, but it didn't bother her because she still wasn't hungry.

"Shouldn't you be with your lovers tonight?"

She turned a glare on him at such a presumptuous question. "I had to let *you* out."

"I am free. You can go to them now."

Tahlia ignored the suggestion as she walked over to the saddle-bags a servant had dumped on the floor earlier. She began unpacking her paints and setting them out across the bed. It had been days since she touched up the designs on her skin. If she was going to become the silk rose tomorrow, she would need every inch of her to be desirable.

Taking a seat in the middle of the bed, Tahlia unfolded her collection of brushes and arched a leg, causing the satin robe to fall back around her waist. The delicate floral patterns on her arms, legs, feet, and hands were so faded she could barely see their outlines. In contrast, the tattoo on her wrist was disturbingly visible.

"It's impressive how you hid yourself from the gods all these years. Who taught you those protections you wore on your skin?"

Tahlia kept her eyes fixed and her hands steady as she traced the tip of a brush over the faded design. She had wondered exactly how much Isa knew about her. Apparently, Lunara had told him everything.

"Trying to elicit information from me for your goddess?"

She could see his form out of the corner of her eye, still sitting at the table, but he had shifted to face her. His posture was casual, his long legs spread out in front of him like he was stretching out cramped muscles. Tahlia had to admit she was curious what it felt like to be sand. Hundreds of tiny particles packed into a vial, crushed underfoot, or lifted on a light breeze. Did he have a collective conscious? Or was he void of his senses?

"Just like you have been trying to extract information from me for your king."

"I was making conversation," she returned flatly.

It was a lie but she would rather him underestimate her. She dipped her brush into the paint and concentrated on drawing delicate leaves along the stem.

"And what are you doing now?" Isa asked accusingly.

The question prompted Tahlia to peek up at him from beneath dark eyelashes. The satin robe was loose around her chest, exposing the swell of her breasts and the cavity between them. Her crossed leg afforded some modesty to her sex, but her arched leg completely exposed her right down to her thigh.

"Preparing for tomorrow," she replied innocently. "Henri will fight and I will perform. Besides, I don't exactly want people to see this."

Tahlia flicked her wrist, exposing the mark of the divine for a brief moment. Isa pushed to his feet and wandered over to the bed. Her pulse quickened with every step he took. He lowered himself to sit opposite her and reached for her hand. She almost flinched from the heat of his calloused fingers. Dazed, she didn't resist as he pulled her arm closer so that he could inspect the marking.

Her breath stuttered as she took the opportunity to study his face, taking in the strong set of his stubbled jaw, the straight line of his nose, and the lips that were currently pressed together in careful assessment. Nothing about the man was soft. He was all harsh lines and sharp angles, muscles and brute strength. She couldn't help but wonder what he would be like in bed. Punishing. Relentless. Savage. Her core melted at the thought.

She was so distracted she barely noticed that he had picked up a brush and dipped it in paint until she felt the cold wetness against her skin. He was drawing a design to camouflage her marking. Tahlia's eyelashes fluttered in surprise and confusion, but she didn't say a word or attempt to pull her arm back. She simply resumed painting the leaves on her leg, though her hand was not as steady as it was before.

A tormenting silence ensued. It seemed to heighten her senses because she was keenly aware of his exhales as they brushed against her wrist, the warmth of his touch, and the earthy smell of him. If he was trying to unsettle her, she refused to give him the satisfaction, despite her nerve endings flaring and her insides igniting.

"There will be priests at the summit tomorrow. Are you worried about being recognized?" Isa asked.

Tahlia tried to focus as she shook her head slightly. "I was a child when I ran from them. In any case, I doubt they would have taken much notice of my face. When you kill dozens of children a year, one face looks much the same as the others."

At least that was the logic she was trying to convince herself to believe. In truth, the thought of seeing the priests again, of having their eyes on her, made her want to flee back to the Idris desert. No matter that she was no longer a child but a grown woman. No matter that she had a king by her side to protect her. A part of her still felt like that young girl, standing frozen in the shadows of a temple, watching another chosen one be consumed by flames.

"Does your king think he can save you from your fate?"

Her hand trembled slightly. She thought of Henri and his determination to protect the people he cared about. "He will try."

"Because you belong to him?"

The words stilled her. She was very familiar with the possessiveness of kings, but Henri had never made her feel like property. Something to be bought and put on display, used and then discarded. Or in her case, gifted to someone else. He respected her. Fought for her. Their relationship had evolved into more than just physical attraction and sexual intimacy. It wasn't linear or exclusive. Nor was it defined or conditional. In fact, she was the one who had pushed Henri to explain her place at his side, her purpose in his life, but he had always refused. The choice was hers to stay or go. To set the boundaries between them and claim her own space in his world. The absence of definition or labels did not make her question their bond. For her, he would brave any danger. For him, she would give her life without hesitation. That was the exquisite madness of love. Unspoken yet undeniable.

Isa released her wrist and she pulled her arm back to admire his work. The lines were clean and carefully drawn, her marking all but disappeared amongst them. Then he shifted a little closer, cupping a hand beneath her knee to angle her leg open slightly. Her hysterical heart slammed against her ribs like a caged bird as he dipped the brush into paint and began drawing a design on her inner thigh.

"But does he worship you?" His whisper was a soft growl.

Heat instantly flooded her center and her sex began to pulse. His fingers were so very close to her entrance. His head was practically between her knees. She was suddenly desperate for him to move lower. She needed friction. From his fingers. From his tongue. If he touched her there, he would find her wet and ready for him.

But he didn't move closer.

He trailed the brush lightly over her skin, flaming her desire with every stroke. Tahlia understood the art of seduction. How to entice men by skillfully revealing just enough to keep them spellbound, while withholding parts of herself to maintain an alluring air of mystery. Desire was in the wanting. The fantasy that she created through music and dance. But she, herself, had never been seduced before. Isa's restraint was a cruel and delicious torture, but she was the mistress of temptation.

"They both do," she purred.

Isa's gaze snapped to hers, his eyes smoldering with an unmistakable primal desire and a dark promise that sent shivers down her spine.

"Then they won't mind sharing. Because after tomorrow, I intend to claim my kiss. And I know exactly what part of you I want to taste, goddess."

CHAPTER EIGHT

HENRI

After eating their fill of the assorted dishes and ripe fruits, Henri and Malik washed the sand from their skin and changed into clean clothes. The exchange of mundane words occasionally punctuated the solemn atmosphere, but then the quiet would reclaim its hold again, descending upon the room like a dense fog, suffocating any lingering sound and leaving behind only a hollow vacuum of thoughts.

Henri had faced death many times in his life, and yet it never failed to grip his soul with dread. The worst part about death was the waiting. He had marched for countless miles in his father's army and endured weeks of encampment on the battlefield waiting for the enemy to arrive, only for the war to be over in a matter of minutes. Hundreds of bodies slain around him, having marched to their own slaughter. When he was being tortured by Heroux, death was a silent witness, always hovering by the door waiting to claim him. But he had held on to his life with a desperate grip, buying time for those that needed it, all the while longing for the moment to arrive when he could finally let go.

Tonight, it felt like death was lurking in every shadow. Time was both lingering and vanishing all at once. If this was the last night of his life, he wanted to savor every second of it. Yet another part of him was impatient for the harrowing wait to be over and his fate to be decided. His heart atrophied at the thought. If he died tomorrow, his death would not be swift or dignified. The kings of Merovia would take their revenge in blood. They would tear him apart piece by piece as recompense, as a warning to others, as was their right.

Then their bloodlust would turn to Malik.

"Admiring the tapestry?"

Malik's words cut through his thoughts and Henri blinked the grand tapestry in front of him into focus. It depicted a bloody fight between mortals and kings, which was being overseen by a god; the god of justice and kingship, no doubt.

"It's impressive," Henri said.

Malik gave him a skeptical sideways glance as he came to stand beside him. "There are plenty of them in the Old City."

Henri continued to stare at the tapestry but he couldn't see a thing. He refused to spend what could be the last night of his life being tormented in the prison of his mind. He needed to abandon his thoughts of death and saturate his senses with Malik until all he felt, all he could think about, all he knew was him. The scent of him. The map of hard muscles beneath his clothes. The aftertaste of him.

Henri forced his lips to curl into a wicked smile as he turned to Malik and trapped his face between his palms. "We are in a holy city and all I can think about is doing something unholy to you."

He pulled his lips to his in rough demand. Malik opened his mouth in response, inviting Henri's tongue to explore and suck and take what it wanted. Desire surged through Henri, immediately swelling his cock until it was throbbing and full. Gripping the back of Henri's head, Malik's fingers splayed between the waves of his hair as he deepened the kiss. It was a desperate kind of hunger between them. Feverish and voracious. As if they both wanted to drown themselves in it.

Henri forced them to stumble towards the ornate canopy bed in the middle of the chamber. They broke apart for the seconds it took to rid themselves of their clothes before colliding again in an explosion of hands and tongues and teeth. Henri's body flushed with heat as his mouth shifted to devour the column of Malik's throat. Malik moaned and palmed Henri's balls, drawing a breathy growl from him. Fuck, Henri wanted him so badly. In every cell of his body. In the pores of his skin. Henri pinned Malik's body against the bedpost and their cocks slammed against each other, hard and heavy.

"Do you even know all the things I want to do to you?" Henri ripped his mouth away from Malik's throat to pierce him with a predatory look, drinking in the heady sight of him. His caramel eyes, void of their usual dark kohl lining, were molten against his warm, olive skin. His broad muscular body normally exuded power and control but now his chest was rising and falling with shallow breaths. Somehow, he was both intoxicatingly beautiful and brutally handsome. "A lifetime would never be enough."

"It's yours." Malik's forehead lined in earnest. "All of me. All of my days. Whatever happens tomorrow, no matter where you go, I will find you."

A wave of fear rose up inside him at the words, threatening to pull Henri down like a strong current, but Malik seized him and pushed him onto the bed. He lay back as Malik took control, rearing above him to brand his body with his lips and nips of his teeth. Henri closed his eyes, immersing himself in the sensation. He wanted to lose himself in it. To vanish completely.

Malik slowly descended to his abs, leaving devastating kisses in his wake, and Henri felt a bead of moisture gather at the head of his erection in anticipation. When Malik finally sunk between his legs and rolled his tongue over that bead of moisture, Henri almost released himself then and there. Leashing his pleasure was painful as Malik gripped him at the base and consumed him to the hilt. Henri groaned in carnal ecstasy and fisted the sheets on either side of him.

"Eyes on me, my king."

Henri's lips twitched to a smirk at the order but he opened his eyes. *Fuck.* He had never seen anything as erotic as Malik taking his entire cock down his throat. Henri couldn't resist rocking into him, riding his mouth harder, plunging himself deeper. Malik's grip moved to Henri's hips and he took it all, every thrust, his tongue lapping up the cum that leaked from him. It was intoxicating to watch him, to know the power Henri had over him in this moment. He owned him. He would possess his soul if he could. Mark every inch of him with his hands and his cock and his cum until no one questioned who he belonged to. Who he served.

"You're mine," Henri growled and Malik sucked him tighter. "Fuck."

Henri felt his control slip as his seed flooded his cock.

"Malik." It was the only word he could say as he spilled himself into Malik's mouth.

The release was so powerful it paralyzed him. His vision blurred and his limbs tingled before going limp. His mind emptied of every thought he'd ever had. Malik swallowed before rising up to lean over him and capturing his mouth in a greedy kiss, as if he couldn't get enough of him. Henri could taste his cum in the kiss. Salty. Addictive. He could already feel himself hardening again.

Malik must have noticed it too because he pulled back an inch, a sly grin on his face. "Does my king want me to kneel before him?"

Yes.

"No. If I left this world without feeling you inside me, I would regret it for all eternity."

The grin slid from his face. "Henri, you don't have to. In fact, it's probably not a good idea to do this before the summit."

"We don't have the luxury of time, and I want to make the best of what little is left. I want this. I want all of you. But you're going to have to help me here."

Malik opened his mouth to protest further, but whatever he saw in Henri's face compelled him to close it again. "We need oil."

Malik moved off the bed and walked in the direction of their saddlebags while Henri propped himself up on his elbows, forcing feeling back into his numb extremities. His head was still spinning from the force of the orgasm, and he wasn't exactly thinking clearly, but one thing was certain; he didn't want to stop and he didn't want to have any regrets.

When Malik returned with the vial of oil in his hand, his expression was still concerned. Henri shuffled down to the edge of the bed and placed his hands on either side of Malik's hips as he stood between his legs. Malik's eyes searched Henri's for some kind of hesitation but he wouldn't find it. As if to reinforce his request, Henri moved a hand to leisurely, provocatively, stroke Malik's cock. Malik's face contorted with barely restrained desire. Henri loved watching Malik lose control. It felt like a victory to break through his resistance and push him past the point of caring about rules or strategy. Malik's lips, swollen from the head he'd just taken, parted in breathless craving. Soon Henri would have him screaming his name.

"I promise you. I'll only ask you to go slow once." Henri turned around, exposing himself as he kneeled on the bed.

He thought he heard Malik swear softly behind him but he ignored it and tried to convince his body to relax. He wanted this, but he knew it was going to hurt and it was hard not to tense in anticipation of the pain. Malik parted his cheeks and Henri expected to feel something inserted inside him, so he flinched when Malik's mouth softly kissed his perineum. His instinct was to pull away because he had no idea this would be part of it, but Henri held firm, trusting that Malik knew what he was doing.

Malik's tongue began licking in long, slow strokes. It felt … strange. Wet and rough, like he was discovering every inch of him. Preparing him in some way. Henri tried to concentrate on the sensation, to welcome it. Malik's breath was hot against his sensitive skin and the feeling was surprisingly stimulating. Henri's need only intensified more when Malik caressed and squeezed his balls in tandem.

"Take a deep breath for me."

Henri complied and then felt a gentle pressure against his anus before the penetration of a single oiled finger. His muscles immediately clenched as his body protested the invasion.

"Relax."

"I'm trying to."

"Keep breathing."

Henri concentrated on taking in deep breaths through his nose and out of his mouth. His mind and body screamed at him, but he focused on adjusting to the feeling. After a few moments, gently, slowly, Malik inserted another finger. Henri gritted his teeth against the white-hot pain slicing through him but he forced himself to breathe. Soon, though, the pain changed from being penetrated to being in control. Henri could feel himself gripping Malik's fingers with his muscles.

"That's it." Malik's voice was steady behind him as he gradually worked him, driving in and out.

Henri could feel himself stretching and opening with every movement. After a while, it was almost comfortable. In fact, it felt *good*.

"Malik. Get inside me. Now."

"Are you sure?"

"Yes."

Malik retrieved his fingers and Henri exhaled at the sudden absence of them. He felt empty, somehow, but then he could feel the tip of Malik's cock pressing against his entrance.

Malik braced a hand against his lower back. "Breathe in."

Henri tried not to tense as Malik entered slowly by inserting his oiled, swollen tip. A million nerve endings caught fire and Henri's legs began to quiver. Malik pushed past the head, then retreated, continuing the steady rhythm, easing into him slowly. Henri's muscles gradually began to relax and his body calmed. It felt strange, like he was being filled, but it was no longer unpleasant. He wasn't sure he could handle a faster pace or deeper thrust, but for now, this was enough. Malik didn't seem to mind. He was moaning in abandoned pleasure.

Glancing back, Henri could see his features were molded into a sinful expression as he moved inside him. Henri's arousal turned rigid at the sight.

"I think you like fucking your king."

The whimper that escaped Malik's throat was pure agreement. "You're so tight."

"I want to feel you come inside me."

"Fuck, Henri." It sounded like Malik wanted nothing more.

He plunged inside him, slowing his rhythm to more deliberate thrusts until he finally screamed Henri's name. It was almost enough to make Henri come as well. The warm liquid pooled inside him as Malik gripped his thighs, holding on through the vibrations of the orgasm. When he pulled out, Henri could feel Malik's cum leaking down onto his balls. They both folded onto the bed and lay there spent, soaking in silence for a few minutes as they faced each other, watching their breaths sync.

"Are you all right?" Malik asked, though he didn't look as concerned as he was before.

"I'm fine. I told you, my plans for you always involve oil."

Malik chuckled softly. "You might be a little sore tomorrow."

"I'll live."

Or he wouldn't.

Either way, it didn't matter. Malik's throat worked, hinting at words left unsaid. Henri knew he wanted to talk about tomorrow. His strategy, technique, weaknesses and tactics. But none of that were the words Henri wanted to say.

"I love you. You should know that," Henri whispered.

Malik went unnaturally still as he stared back at him wide eyed. Henri wasn't sure he was breathing, so he lifted his hand to stroke his dark hair with his thumb.

"You're not going to die tomorrow." Malik said it as if he could command their fates.

"Dead or alive, it changes nothing. I love you."

Malik gripped Henri's face between his hands and pressed their foreheads together, breathing him in. "Henri, I am yours. There is no span of time or plane of existence where I do not love you. Love itself is inadequate to describe how I feel about you. You are everything. My whole heart. My one desire. My reason for drawing breath—"

Henri kissed him vehemently. He didn't ever want to let go. If death was lurking in every shadow, then let it witness this and envy the one thing it could not touch.

Love.

A force so strong that it would tether them together no matter what drove them apart.

"I want you again but we need to sleep." Malik groaned against his lips.

"We can sleep when we're—"

Malik pressed his hand over his mouth. "Don't say it. Just let me hold you."

Henri shifted, adjusting his arm beneath Malik's body to draw him close. Malik lay his head against Henri's shoulder, letting his arm drape across his chest and resting his hand against Henri's heart. Henri sensed Malik was finding reassurance and comfort in its steady beat beneath his touch. The coming dawn whispered the grim promise that it would stop beating. That it would be violently torn from his chest, bled dry and impaled on a pike. But even then, his heart would belong to Malik.

Forever bound.

TAHLIA

With every step that Tahlia took, the sound of tiny bells followed. Bands of silver bells were strung around her ankles, wrists and hips. Her arms, legs, hands and feet were decorated with assorted designs, a process that had taken her and Isa several hours to complete last night. She wore a barely there silk dress which only just covered her breasts and sex, leaving her abdomen bare and her legs exposed up to the hip. Her thick dark curls cascaded around her heart-shaped face in a display of wild natural beauty, while several small rings pierced the arcs of her ears. Dark kohl lined her emerald eyes and her skin was perfumed with rose and jasmine. Normally her feet would be bare, to allow her to move freely during dance, but today she wore dainty slippers, to allow her to run in case she needed to flee.

Before she glided into Henri's bedchamber, her fingers clutched at the vial around her neck in an attempt to steady her erratic heartbeat. Its thundering pace escalated, though, at the sight of Henri and Malik already dressed for battle. They weren't wearing armor or leathers. In fact, they looked like they were wearing ordinary clothes, made of a light material that would allow their skin to breathe through the oppressive heat. Except she knew that the clothing was made from a plant fiber that was tough enough to stop arrows. Still, it didn't seem like enough.

Their waists were girded with sword belts and Tahlia noted that Henri still carried his longsword instead of a shamshir. She knew he had been training relentlessly with Malik to learn how to wield Merovian weaponry, but perhaps he still felt more comfortable using a sword from his own country. Or maybe it was a superstitious choice. Perhaps the longsword had saved him countless times before and he didn't want to tempt fate by fighting without it.

Under different circumstances, Tahlia would have admired how sexy and dangerous they both looked with their chiseled physiques and powerful frames. Their bodies had clearly been sculpted for war. Instead, the scene made her stomach sink like a stone.

Her gaze drifted to Ele who was sitting on a divan, sharpening several daggers with a whetstone. Kala sat across the room watching him, her features set in grim determination.

Collecting herself, Tahlia forced a smile as she sauntered over to Henri. "You both look very impressive. If I didn't know any better, I would say you were trying to steal my audience."

Henri returned a charming grin and reached for her hand to place a feather-light kiss on the back of it. "We could never be as breathtaking as you."

"Speak for yourself," Malik scoffed.

So this was the way they wanted to face the summit; by making light of the situation and faking confidence where they had none. She could do that. If it helped them stay alive, she could do anything.

"I am surprised you aren't wearing more jewels," Tahlia directed at Malik.

"I'm saving that outfit for the after party."

Tahlia's laugh was a little too high. Hopefully Malik had used his collection to bribe the Rouhan nobles to forego challenging Henri.

"Are you armed?" Ele furrowed his brow at her.

Tahlia blinked in surprise. "I can barely fit myself into this dress let alone a weapon."

"Ele's right. You need to be able to defend yourself." Kala wandered over, eyes scrunched as she appraised Tahlia's dress for any hidden cavities. She held her hand out expectantly to Ele, palm upturned. "Give me the smallest ones."

Ele surveyed the daggers he had already prepared before passing two to Kala. They were almost comical. Barely the length of her hand and the blades were ridiculously thin. Kala didn't hesitate to pass one to Tahlia to slide down the front of her dress.

She shuddered at the kiss of cold steel against her skin. "That feels precarious."

"Slipper?" Ele suggested.

"Thigh," Henri countered.

Kala rolled her eyes. "Predictable."

She gestured for Tahlia to sit down on the lounge and then she moved behind her, gathering Tahlia's thick hair in both hands. Tahlia couldn't see what Kala was doing but she could feel her pulling the hair into sections before twisting and weaving the strands together.

Malik folded his arms over his chest and cocked an impressed eyebrow. "She's concealing the dagger in your hair with a braid. Clever girl."

Henri nudged Malik's shoulder. "What did I tell you in the Thaka that day?"

"Anyone would think I'm the one going into battle," Tahlia muttered.

"We all are," Kala replied over her shoulder pointedly.

She was right and the knowledge made Tahlia's stomach sour. After a minute of tense silence, her hair was done and Ele had finished sharpening the daggers. Henri and Malik added them to their sword belts, and Ele fixed one to his as well. Kala simply slipped two daggers beneath her kaftan.

"Ele, before we go, I have something for you." Henri retrieved a rolled sheepskin from his saddlebags and handed it to him.

With a frown of curiosity, Ele unraveled it to reveal a beautiful shamshir. His eyes immediately lit up and his jaw slackened in awe. It was smaller than a normal shamshir, probably lighter too. It was encased in a wooden scabbard covered in blue velvet so dark that it almost looked black. As he carefully unsheathed the curved single-edged blade, Tahlia noticed the steel was engraved and decorated. The pommel looked to be made of bone and a short golden tassel hung from it. Ele weighed the blade in both hands as he admired it.

"I had it made for you," Henri said. "It's Pelascene steel, the finest there is."

"It's beautiful," Ele breathed.

Tahlia's heart swelled painfully. It was only natural that Henri would want to give Ele his first sword. It was the kind of proud moment a father would dream about sharing with his son one day. Yet it felt bittersweet, knowing that Henri might not live to watch him wield it.

"It is. But a sword gains its reputation from the one who wields it, not the one who forges it," Henri insisted.

Ele raised the blade high. "Then this sword is going to be renowned across the land for vanquishing your enemies and safeguarding the defenseless."

"I have no doubt." Henri's proud smile dissolved just as quickly as it formed. "Is everyone ready?"

Tahlia had no idea how Henri and Malik could stand there looking so calm and composed when she felt like she was about to burst out of her skin or collapse to the floor in anguish. She didn't, though, and maybe that made her more like them than she realized.

Together, they ventured into the empty corridors of the palace, with Malik leading the way. Every step felt heavy. Like she was forcing her body to move forward while her instincts were screaming at her to run in the opposite direction. The light sound of jingling bells were in stark contrast to her tightly wound insides.

Tahlia gripped the vial around her neck again and wondered if Isa could feel her desperate touch. Henri would *not* die today. The goddess had told her that whether he lived or died would be up to her and she had made her choice. She chose him. Isa would fight for him. Malik would defend him. Together, they would save him. He was going to be all right.

All too soon, they stepped outside the palace into the blistering heat of the morning. The arena loomed a short distance ahead. Tahlia's breath hitched in dread. The structure was ancient, enormous, and foreboding. It cast a long shadow across the barren courtyard, and even that looked ominous. How many kings had walked this path over the years to attend the summit? How many kings had never walked back out again?

As they crossed beneath the stadium's outer wall, Malik halted at the base of a steep incline of stone stairs that reached two stories high.

"Each king has their own entrance into the arena," Malik explained. "This one is yours."

Henri cast his eyes up the stairs but didn't waver for one second before he started climbing. Tahlia counted his every step. As they drew closer to the top, the rumbling chatter from a large crowd echoed in their ears. On the last few steps, Tahlia reached for Henri's arm and folded her own into the crook of his elbow. His eyes fastened on her for a moment and she gave a curt nod. She was ready to go to war for him. He cast his gaze beyond her to Ele and Kala who were bringing up the rear. Then he turned to his other side and reached back for Malik who was a step behind him. Their hands briefly clasped, squeezing tightly, before releasing as they all walked out into the arena.

The sheer scale and vastness of the building's interior stole Tahlia's breath away. Two floors of tiered stone seating wove around the entire elliptical structure, divided into sections by thick columns. The sectors were clearly designed to distinguish between different social classes of spectators. Tahlia could already see that the common people took up the wings of the first-floor seating, whereas the nobles occupied the more central seats. Positioned directly in front of the arena floor, giving them the closest view of the action, were the Rouhan nobles. As the ruling family of

Merovia for hundreds of years, they always maintained a distinct status separate from the rest of nobility.

Down below, the floor of the arena was covered in sand, no doubt to absorb the blood and provide traction for fighting. In the middle of the floor, patiently waiting with his arms folded beneath ruby robes, was a priest. Tahlia's palms began to sweat. It was customary for priests to be involved in such rituals because they represented the gods. In this case, the priest represented the god of justice and kingship. Nevertheless, just knowing that a priest was so near made her feel like the air had been sucked out of her lungs.

Tahlia tore her eyes away from the priest to refocus on the scene in front of them. Standing on the second floor of the arena, they found themselves facing a royal gallery. The Merovian kings were already assembled, all of them dressed for combat. Except one.

"King Henri." Nasir threw his arms wide in greeting, as if he had spotted a dear friend. "Welcome to the summit. We have been waiting for you."

As the kings turned toward them, Tahlia noticed a priest standing by Ozkan's side.

Oh, gods.

It should not have surprised her, given Ozkan's renowned devoutness, but she still froze mid-step. She needed to pull herself together immediately. The priests would not recognize her. Even if they did, they could not touch her. She was the silk rose. Courtesan to King Henri. The gods might have chosen her but Henri had also chosen her and right now his life depended on her.

Ozkan sneered at Henri in open disgust. Dahane's eyes turned predatory, like he had locked gaze with his intended prey and was already imagining himself slitting Henri's throat. Nasir's smile was pure cunning, his attention singularly focused on Henri. It was like she ceased to exist at all, now that she did not belong to him. In contrast, Kareem's gaze was firmly fixed on her. His eyes roamed her body greedily, mapping her flesh as if she were his for the taking.

"Though we didn't quite believe Ozkan when he told us you had somehow survived the Idris desert," Kareem added.

Henri cocked his head to one side. "I did warn you. I am a hard man to kill."

"You are late." Dahane spat.

"That's my fault." Tahlia pressed her breasts against Henri and ran a hand suggestively down his chest as she looked at him with bedroom eyes.

Henri leaned in to place a soft kiss on her exposed shoulder. "What can I say? Kings have nothing on the silk rose. Especially when the silk rose has nothing on her."

Tahlia's insides fluttered, but not from desire or the pretty compliment. Would that be the last time she ever felt Henri's lips on her skin? He held her gaze as he pulled away, the perfect picture of charisma and arrogance. She hoped he couldn't see the cracks forming beneath her mask of seduction.

Henri turned his attention to Dahane. "Are you in a hurry to die?"

The corner of Dahane's mouth lifted in lethal amusement. "Have you noticed the dock? Never has one king drawn so many challengers against him at the summit. You should be flattered."

Tahlia cast her gaze down to a boxed area beside the floor of the arena where at least a dozen Rouhan nobles stood, donned in battle attire, glaring up at Henri with the promise of death. Her head whipped to Malik as her eyes flashed with panic, but his neutral expression remained steady, as if it was of no consequence.

Which made no sense at all.

She had assumed Malik had made efforts to try to dissuade the Rouhan nobles from challenging Henri. Wasn't that his plan? Wasn't that what he had meant when he asked her to trust him? So why didn't he care that his efforts had clearly failed? Tahlia tried to subtly draw his attention but he adamantly refused to look at her.

"All that remains is to decide who gets to kill you," Dahane continued.

"And who gets the spoils of war," Kareem added, his eyes crawling over her skin.

"That is less contentious. We share the silk rose, each one of us plucking her petals until there is nothing left but a broken stem." Dahane shifted his gaze to Ele and Kala who were standing behind them. "The children will fetch a fine price as slaves."

"Enough talk." Henri's voice rumbled dangerously low in his throat. "You think you can kill me? Then come at me!" He lunged for Dahane, but Malik was quicker, darting in front of him, while Tahlia held him firm.

"I intend to," Dahane bit back. "As I was the first to lay a challenge against you, I claim that right."

"Since there are so many challengers," Malik intercepted, "we need an independent authority to make the decision as to the order."

"My priest can assist," Ozkan replied.

"No," Malik countered. "Nasir is the obvious choice. He is the only king here who hasn't challenged Henri. Since he has no stake in the outcome, his decision will be impartial."

No. Fucking. Way.

Tahlia's jaw dropped in shock and she felt Henri stiffen beside her.

"Does anyone oppose?" Malik asked, looking at each king.

Something was wrong. Something was *very* fucking wrong.

Tahlia gripped Henri's arm, urging him to speak, but he remained silent. Ozkan and Kareem murmured their agreement while Dahane begrudgingly huffed his consent. Nasir's features turned serious, as if he were considering the merits of the proposal, but Tahlia knew better. She had spent years in his bed and knew all his tells.

This was planned.

Nasir nodded in acceptance. "I am honored to be entrusted with this task. I will ensure the proceedings are fair."

"Get on with it then." Henri met Nasir's eyes in a silent dare.

Nasir shifted his stance as a vicious grin edged his mouth. "The first challenger is Malik."

CHAPTER NINE

HENRI

"Traitor!" Ele cried.

The word barely registered as Henri's mind struggled to process what was happening right in front of him.

Malik. Was the first challenger.

It couldn't be true. It was *not* possible. Nasir's face glowed with satisfaction as he basked in Henri's shock and confusion.

Malik gripped the hilt of his shamshir as if he were impatient to begin. "Dahane."

"No." Dahane shot back through gritted teeth. "I will kill you after I kill your king."

"Nasir has named me first challenger, which means I get to choose who to kill first. I choose you."

"Did you not know that Malik had sent scorpions to the other Merovian kings?" Nasir enquired innocently.

"You what?" Henri spluttered.

Tahlia fingers flew to her lips in horror. "Oh, gods."

"Fine." Dahane tore away from the group and marched down the aisle to the arena floor.

Malik followed him without a backward glance or a parting word. There was nothing Henri could do but stare after him, paralyzed by a mix of fear, betrayal, and disbelief. On noticing their descent, the crowd erupted in violent shouts and excited applause that reverberated down to Henri's bones. They were thirsty for savagery. But it was meant to be *his* blood they called for, not Malik's.

The priest standing in the arena raised his hands to the cloudless sky and made proclamations, presumably to the god of justice and kingship, but Henri couldn't hear a damn word over the feverish spectators. He disengaged Tahlia from his arm and moved to the edge of the gallery, splaying his fingers along the stone balustrade as he stared down at the arena floor, as if that could somehow bring him closer to the fight. Closer to Malik.

It was happening again. A swelling, vicious crowd, each person vying for the best vantage point, eager to witness the carnage they had been promised. It was more than an execution, it was a performance. Entertainment. But to him, it was someone he loved, and they were about to die. Like Nathaniel. Like his mother. He had been helpless to watch them take their final breaths as steel met skin, ending their lives, and carving out his heart. He had thought if he was king, if he reclaimed his power, he could protect the ones he loved. But now here he was, no longer a boy but a man, a king, and he was still helpless. Would he always be destined to watch the people he loved die?

Tahlia pressed a hand lightly to his back, silently letting him know she was there. Ele moved to his side, with Kala trailing behind him.

"Malik can win," Ele said confidently. "He's one of the best fighters I've ever seen."

Ele was right. Dahane looked to be a formidable warrior but Malik was quick, cautious, and calculating. Henri struggled to beat him on his best days. Malik also had the advantage of knowing Dahane; how he fought, his vulnerabilities. He would have already devised a strategy to defeat him.

Satisfied that the gods were watching, the priest departed and Malik and Dahane stepped into the arena. Dahane drew his shamshir and began circling Malik as if he were the apex predator. Malik unsheathed his shamshir, holding it in one hand while palming a dagger in the other. Henri gritted his teeth as he shifted on restless feet, his body flooding with nervous adrenaline.

Nasir came to stand on his other side as the crowd grew quiet in anticipation. "Keeping secrets is typical for Malik, unfortunately." He sighed, feigning disappointment. "He has a seductive tongue."

"When? When did he issue the challenges?" Henri seethed.

"The day we left your kingdom."

That couldn't be right. They had spent that day together in the royal bath, exploring each other's bodies and ignoring the ever-growing threats around them. At Henri's suggestion, Malik had sent Inaya in his place to escort the Merovian kings to the border. Unless he had asked Inaya to deliver the scorpions on his behalf.

Dahane charged at Malik, shamshir raised, but Malik stepped out of the way, grabbing him by the back of his shirt and shoving him to the side. Dahane recovered swiftly, sweeping his blade in a wide arc at Malik's waist. Steel met steel as Malik deflected the blow while swiping his dagger for Dahane's throat. Dahane leaped backward, clearly surprised by the hair-width escape. He took a few seconds to appraise his opponent anew before lunging again.

"I must say, Henri, I thought you were smarter than this," Nasir taunted. "Malik has always desired to be king. If he kills Dahane, he will become one. If he kills all three Merovian kings, he will rule most of the country. Only you and I will stand between him and complete dominion."

"You snake," Tahlia said sharply. "That is not why Malik did this."

He had done it to try to save Henri's life. He was sacrificing himself to give Henri a better chance at surviving the summit. Right?

Except, if that were true, if he was desperate to the point of martyrdom, he should have accepted the Naiab's offer of a warrior. If he had, things might have never come to this. On the other hand, if his motive was to become king, to make a play for power, the Naiab warrior would have been an obstacle.

Dahane delivered a brutal kick to Malik's gut, causing him to buckle for a split second before he recovered to deflect Dahane's overhead attack. Malik executed each movement with ruthless efficiency, his demeanor unwaveringly composed as he waited for the right moment to unleash a deadly strike. That was, after all, his nature. To be patient. To study his opponent. To lie in wait and attack when least expected.

"Of course, it wouldn't be the first time he has tried to kill a king," Nasir continued, as if Tahlia hadn't spoken.

"And how many kings have you tried to kill?" Henri shot back. "Me. At least twice."

"Oh, I can't take credit for that."

"It was always your plan to murder the other Merovian kings. First in your secret alliance with Heroux and then in your offer of an alliance with me."

"Secret alliance with Heroux," Nasir chuckled as though the idea was absurd. "A mere smokescreen to conceal the real alliance."

Henri's forehead creased before understanding suddenly struck him. "With Malik."

"Unlike you, Malik accepted my offer. He never wanted his brother to rule. He gained Heroux's trust and then convinced him to go on endless foreign war campaigns, expanding his empire and his army. Malik hoped Heroux would die on the battlefield, giving Malik the chance to claim his kingdom without having to challenge him at the summit. A fight he knew he could not win. But then you killed Heroux and claimed the kingdom for yourself."

Malik parried a blow and slashed at Dahane's abdomen, sending blood spattering across the sand. The wound wasn't deep, though, because Dahane's onslaught didn't slow. In fact, it became wild and unrestrained, like he had abandoned all strategy in exchange for a singular focus; to obliterate.

"So, you sent an assassin to kill me."

"Think, Henri. I know Malik is very pretty, but try not to be so blinded by his cock."

Henri rounded on him, his eyes flashing with rage. "What did you say to me?"

"Henri!" Tahlia screamed and Henri's attention flew back to the fight.

Blood seeped through Malik's fingers as he pressed firmly on his upper arm. Fuck, it was his sword arm. The wound looked bad. He was still clutching his shamshir in his hand but would he able to wield it? As if in answer, Malik wiped the blood on his clothes and switched his shamshir to his other hand just in time to defend against a series of rapid strikes.

"Malik gave the order for your assassination that day," Nasir said, his voice like velvet.

Henri's heart stopped as the world around him seemed to fade into the distance. "You're lying."

Even as he said it, somehow, deep down, Henri knew it was true. Hadn't he been sure of Malik's involvement directly after the event? It was too convenient that the assassin had taken his own life, that Malik had cut him to pieces before Henri could inspect the body. It was why Henri had asked Ele to spy on him, to learn everything there was to know about the former regent.

"If you don't believe me, ask your courtesan."

Henri pivoted to Tahlia, whose wide, fearful eyes were also laced with damning guilt.

"She has always known about Malik, the assassination attempt, everything. It was one of the reasons I gifted her to you. So that if you rejected my offer of an alliance, she could kill you."

"The poison." Ele's voice shook with disbelief.

"But I didn't," Tahlia protested as Henri's face drained of color. "I would never. I swear to you."

It didn't make any sense. If Tahlia was the one who had tried to poison him, why was he still alive? Unless they were working together. Perhaps Tahlia and Malik had formed a new alliance, cutting out Nasir. Maybe their agenda had changed and they needed Henri alive. Until now. Had they both seduced him only to deceive him?

"The assassin met with a woman," Kala murmured.

"That wasn't me. It was—" Tahlia swallowed the words, alarmed at her careless slip.

"Who?" Henri demanded as he took a menacing step towards her. "Who?!"

"Inaya."

Henri stared at her blankly, his mind a torrent of rapid-fire thoughts, each conclusion worse than the one before. Inaya. Captain of the Guard. The person he had nominated as regent of his kingdom while he attended the summit. She had been involved in an assassination plot against his life. A plot orchestrated by Malik, his lover. A plot known by Tahlia, the woman whose bravery and loyalty he would have never questioned.

He had been betrayed. By everyone.

Except Ele and Kala.

Henri's gaze swerved to Ele who looked equal parts shocked and crestfallen. Henri knew Ele would blame himself for failing to uncover Malik's treason, thereby endangering his king. Despite his careful investigation, Ele hadn't found anything to suggest that Malik was involved in the assassination attempt. The boy's features shifted to ruthless detachment and steely resolve, as if he planned to murder Malik the first chance he got.

He would have to get in line.

Deafening applause suddenly exploded from the ferocious crowd below.

"Looks like we have a new king," Nasir mused.

Henri turned back to see Malik standing in the middle of the arena holding Dahane's beard up as if it were his head. Dahane's body lay discarded in the sand, blood pooling out from beneath it.

Malik was king. And he was fucking *smiling*.

Henri was a fool. He should have trusted his instincts from the start. He knew Malik was a smooth courtier. He had been playing both sides for years, manipulating everyone around him, observing the game of kings as he waited for his chance to become one. Now that day had finally arrived.

"Henri don't!"

He barely heard Tahlia call after him as he charged down the aisle toward the arena floor. Around him, the crowd continued to rumble, chanting Malik's name, their memory of the slain king already forgotten.

Sadistic animals, all of them.

The salt and copper scent of sweat and blood immediately filled his nostrils as he stepped into the arena. Malik was savoring the moment, reveling in their adoration, even as blood coated his sword arm and droplets fell to the sand at his feet. He was so distracted by the adulating crowd, he didn't notice Henri's approach until his fist met his face.

ELE

Ele felt the blow as if he had been struck himself. It was a powerful punch, the kind that broke bones. Not that he would be able to hear the crunch over all this noise. Malik staggered backward, shock evident in his eyes, but Henri didn't stop his assault. He was murderous, though Ele noted he had yet to draw his sword. Malik moved to defend himself against each blow but refused to fight back, which only provoked outrage from the crowd. Ele couldn't hear what Henri was shouting at Malik or Malik's justifications for what he had done. He didn't have to.

Malik had betrayed Henri. He was a dead man.

"He can't do that!" Ozkan rushed to the balustrade, leaving Kareem standing with his priest.

"No, he cannot," Nasir replied with disapproval. "It seems Henri does not want to abide by the rules of the summit and wait until next year to challenge the new king."

Kareem leisurely strolled over, exchanging a knowing look with Nasir. "He has no respect for Merovian law or the gods."

"Then he deserves to die," Ozkan seethed.

Nasir made a sweeping gesture. "Since Henri has chosen to break the rules, they no longer apply. All challengers are free to enter the arena."

"What?!" Tahlia exclaimed in horror.

Ozkan wasted no time thundering down the steps, drawing his shamshir in anticipation. Ele's eyes darted urgently between Henri and Malik, hoping one of them would notice, but they were so fixated on each other, they weren't paying attention to anything else. Charging into the arena with a fierce battle cry, Ozkan raised his blade at Henri but Malik swiftly shoved Henri aside and met Ozkan's strike with his own steel.

Ele pumped his hands into fists at his sides as relief coursed through him. He wished he were down there, fighting at Henri's side, but he knew Henri didn't need him to defeat Ozkan. It was two against one. Ozkan didn't stand a chance.

Tahlia whirled on Nasir. "This is all your doing!"

Nasir ignored her, instead turning his attention to the boxed area beside the arena where at least a dozen Rouhan nobles were roaring and waiting for their chance to spill royal blood. Catching the eye of one of them, Nasir gave a signal.

Oh no.

Ele's heart hammered as the challengers started vaulting over the barricade. Henri must have noticed them because he swiftly impaled Ozkan on his sword before calling out to Malik in warning. They both retreated to the center of the arena, where they stood back-to-back, bracing themselves to confront their advancing rivals. Ele drew his shamshir.

"No." Kala grabbed his arm. "You made Henri a promise."

"I can't just stand here and do nothing!"

"Aren't you going to join the fray, Kareem?" Nasir asked.

"Don't insult me, Nasir." Kareem rolled his eyes. "I am not as easily manipulated as the others. Thanks to your scheming, Henri and Malik will both die and you and I will get what we came for."

Tahlia ripped the vial from her neck and poured sand out onto the stone floor. The grains began to swirl and shift, creating a whirlwind which stretched upward to the height of a man, before solidifying into the shape of a figure. Kala gasped as Isa materialized in front of them; flesh and blood and bone, completely naked, his chest heaving as if he had exerted himself. In the morning sun his golden skin radiated beneath a mosaic of turquoise tattoos.

"Go!" Tahlia urged him but Isa was already sprinting down the aisle.

"What the fuck was that?" Kareem exclaimed.

"Sand wielder." Ele grinned despite himself.

The instant Isa landed on the arena floor, he conjured up a double-edged spear from the sand and launched into battle, slicing through skin and organ and bone with abandon as he morphed from solid flesh to whirling sand. Ele had never seen anything like it. The man moved like a hurricane, reaping lives and staining the ground with blood. Now Ele understood why the Naiab had only offered them one warrior.

The ferocious cries from the crowd turned into screams of terror as nobles and commoners alike scrambled out of the stands to flee the arena. Despite the sand magic and carnage of bodies falling around them, the Rouhan challengers were relentless in their assault. Henri and Malik remained locked in combat, fighting furiously, refusing to give ground.

"Looks like you might have been outplayed, Nasir." Kareem smiled smugly. "I think I'll take what I came for and leave the rest to you."

A sharp scream snapped Ele's attention back to see Kareem dragging Tahlia, one meaty arm wrapped around her waist while the other locked her throat in a chokehold.

At the same moment, Nasir swore and stalked over to the priest. "You will send me word of the outcome immediately."

The priest nodded and Nasir stalked off toward a stairwell, most likely his private entrance into the arena. Ele shifted his weight in the direction of Tahlia and Nasir, unsure which one to follow or what to do.

"I'll take Nasir, you save Tahlia," Kala ordered.

She didn't hesitate to run after Nasir, only stopping for the brief seconds it took to retrieve her hidden dagger and drive it deep into the priest's kidney. A lethal blow. The priest crumbled to the floor but she kept going, flying down the stairs until she disappeared from sight. Ele smirked, stunned but impressed. He had always suspected that she was more ruthless than him.

But he was just as lethal.

Ele bolted after Kareem who had managed to haul Tahlia to the top of a different set of stairs, despite her kicking and screaming. Ele watched as she sunk her teeth into Kareem's arm, causing him to jolt backward, allowing her precious seconds to retrieve her hidden dagger. Not fast enough though, as Kareem backhanded her across the face sending her sprawling to the stone floor while the dagger clattered down the steps.

Ele released what he hoped was an intimidating roar as he charged at Kareem with his shamshir erect. Surprise flashed across Kareem's face before he quickly unsheathed his own blade in time to deflect Ele's blow. Ele struck again, lunging and striking. He knew he needed to be quick to land a deadly hit. There was no way he could match Kareem in strength. He needed to outwit him, out maneuver him. But Kareem suddenly seemed larger than he was a moment ago. Stronger too. Ele's arm quivered with the reverberations each time their blades met.

Kareem laughed at him but Ele gritted his teeth in renewed determination. He knew the king was probably holding back, taunting him, confident in his own victory, but Ele didn't care. The man had hurt Tahlia. Kareem was going to die at his hands.

Ele tried to remember everything his tutor had taught him these past few weeks about where to step, how to defend, how to move. One day he wouldn't have to think so hard because he would be a grown man and a great warrior, defending Henri from his enemies and protecting his kingdom. Tahlia would be safe. But today Henri was fighting for his life and Tahlia was badly injured and Kala was alone in her pursuit of Nasir.

Kala.

He needed to help her.

Ele didn't feel the blade go in. In fact, he felt no pain at all. His body halted of its own accord as his mind staggered to catch up to what had happened. He was vaguely aware of Tahlia screaming his name, of Kareem grabbing her again and hauling her down the stairs. Ele tried to stop him but he couldn't make his body move. He was suddenly so cold, which was strange given the blistering Merovian heat. The world tilted and he collapsed to the floor. As his vision began to blur and his thoughts faded, he glimpsed a starry constellation through a crevice in a cave's ceiling, and Kala's smile as she sat next to him, bathed in ethereal moonlight.

CHAPTER TEN

KALA

Kala raced down the steps of the arena and burst out into the open courtyard. It was empty. Her eyes darted around but there was no sign of Nasir anywhere. She was only moments behind him, he could not have disappeared into thin air. Kala bounced on the balls of her feet, eager to run but no idea where.

Think.

Nasir would have planned his escape in case things didn't go his way at the summit. If Henri survived the summit he would be king of this kingdom, which meant he could order the guards to stop Nasir from leaving, to kill him on sight if he wanted to. Nasir would need to escape before Henri could issue the command. Horses were faster than camels. He would have headed to the royal stables.

Kala sprinted across the courtyard, unsure if she was even going the right way. The stables could be anywhere. She tried to remember the outline of the palace grounds from what little she had seen yesterday as they passed through the entrance. But they hadn't even gone to the stables. They had left their camels to the attendants and made their way directly inside the palace.

The scenery blurred around her as she skirted around walls, dodged endless statues of gods, and narrowly avoided colliding with passing servants. She briefly glanced inside every building she passed, flittering between them like a wren in search of water. Her feet slapped across the dirt and her breaths came in short gasps as she pushed herself harder, faster. She couldn't think about the possibility of being too late or what her plan was when she finally found the stables. All she knew was that she needed to stop Nasir.

Rounding the corner, her chest sagged in relief as she spotted two rows of date palms in the distance, leading to the palace entrance. She could barely make out the soldiers patrolling it, but it was heavily guarded. Not that their numbers would matter. They would part in seconds for Nasir. He was a king. They would never question his right to come and go as he pleased. Had he already charged through them?

Kala stopped and allowed herself a moment to breathe as she looked around frantically. She had her bearings now but she still didn't know where the stables were. She could ask someone, a servant perhaps. Just then the deafening sound of horse hooves filled her ears and her stomach dropped. Nasir and several guards shot out at speed from the opposite side of the stony yard.

No. No. No!

Her gaze darted from the palace entrance to Nasir and back again. She threw herself into a desperate run. If Nasir made it past the guards, he would flee to the safety of his kingdom and plot his next move against Henri. She refused to let that happen. Her skinny legs pumped, hurtling her forward, as she retrieved what she needed from beneath her kaftan. When she got within range, she took aim and hurled it with all her might, nearly launching her arm from its socket.

The dagger narrowly missed Nasir, slicing the back of his neck.

Nasir jerked his horse to an abrupt halt and his guards mobilized around him as Kala screamed a curse. He reached behind to touch the graze on his neck. She hoped she'd drawn blood. Then his eyes were on her from across the yard, his jaw tightening in fury. Kala's face turned to stone as she pointed a finger at him in a death promise. His horse reared beneath him, mirroring its master's rage.

"Kill her!" Nasir roared.

Panic rose inside her as several soldiers from the palace entrance charged in her direction. Kala bolted. She might not have thought this through. She ran, desperately trying to remember the way back to the arena. If she could just get to Henri, he would be able to call the guards off her, assuming he was still alive. But she hadn't been paying attention to her surroundings in her pursuit of Nasir and now each courtyard looked the same. Behind her, the urgent shouts of the palace guards blended with the pounding of their footsteps as they gained on her. She didn't dare glance over her shoulder, she could already feel them at her back.

Kala had been hunted like this before. By predators within the Thaka. By Dahane's slave traders. By her own family. Some days she had been fast enough to get away but other days she hadn't been. Once caught, there was no way she could defend herself against palace guards. She was armed and fierce but they would overpower her easily.

She could not afford to be caught.

Unlike her, though, the guards knew every inch of the palace grounds. They could easily split up and heard her into a trap. She needed to get out of their line of sight and find somewhere to hide. She might not be able to outrun them or overpower them but she could certainly out-wait them.

As she dashed past a statue of a god, Kala pushed it over, eliciting cries of outrage from the guards as it shattered at their feet. *There.* That building looked vaguely familiar. She remembered it was a warehouse of sorts, filled with crates and carts and various goods. Kala darted inside and immediately ducked at the sound of voices. Crouching down low she crawled in between sacks of grain, barrels of salted fish and meat, and bags of dried legumes. Several carts had already been loaded with textiles and timber, earthenware and tanned skins. Annoyingly, the voices seemed to be following her so she jumped up into a cart, nestling herself between several full bags, and pulled the corner of a tarp over her.

"Did you hear the king is dead?" The man's voice was muffled from beneath the tarp but she could still make it out.

"Yes, but I've heard different tales of who killed him; the foreigner king, his former regent, or a sand wielding jinn."

"Too much wine." The man laughed. "Either way he's dead. But even dead kings have to pay taxes. Is it all loaded?"

"Ready for your escort."

Kala glanced around beneath the stifling tarp but it was pointless, she couldn't see a thing. The voices had stopped but she hadn't heard the men walk away. It was better for her to stay where she was than chance moving. At least she wasn't sharing a cart with spices that would make her sneeze, or butchered livestock that would turn her stomach. Curious, Kala placed a hand against the bag in front of her. It felt solid and weighty but there was no telling what was in it.

The cart abruptly lurched and she braced herself against the wooden panels to keep from falling over. Blinding light pierced through the material of the tarp making her wince. Her heart hammered at the realization that the cart was moving and she was no longer inside the warehouse. From the rhythmic jolt and clatter of hooves, the cart was being pulled forward, but it also sounded like there were more horses than what was necessary to pull a single cart. Perhaps there were other carts filled with trade goods bound for the same destination.

Oh gods.

If she didn't get out of the cart now, she would leave the palace grounds and never be able to get back in. But she couldn't just hop out. There was no way she would go unnoticed. Even worse, the cart might be searched by the guards upon leaving the palace and she would be discovered. Kala retrieved her second hidden dagger and sat poised, ready to attack the hands that reached for her. It might not be enough to save her life but at least she could slice off a couple of fingers.

After a few tense minutes the terrain beneath the wheels shifted from smooth to coarse. Did that mean she was outside the palace? The cart continued to roll on and soon the bustling noises of a city surrounded her. Relief washed over her at the knowledge that the cart was not going to be searched and she wouldn't be discovered by palace guards, but her relief was short lived as her mind calculated the situation she had found herself in. Best case scenario, the cart held a local delivery of goods. Worst case scenario, she could end up on the other side of the country.

She had to do something. Her mind raced with a million thoughts until she recalled the men had said something about taxes and an escort. Which was strange because king's collected taxes, they didn't pay them. Unless—

Kala stabbed the bag in front of her and yanked the blade down until gold coins poured into her lap. She clasped a hand over her mouth to stifle her gasp. The cart was filled with bags of gold. The horses surrounding her were an escort. There was only one person the king's paid taxes to every year; Nasir. This payment was his annual ransom for water.

She was going to the kingdom of the high mountains and she would be delivered right inside its palace walls.

TAHLIA

"We leave now!" Kareem ordered as he dragged Tahlia to the stables.

His guards quickly moved toward their horses which were saddled and ready. Kareem threw her to the ground and dirt skinned the flesh from her hands and knees but she barely felt it. She had been hysterical as Kareem dragged her down the stairs and out of the arena. Now she was numb. Empty.

Ele. Was dead.

Only a soft whimper escaped her throat as she remembered the sound of steel tearing flesh, how Ele had stilled as if he wasn't quite sure what had felled him, the rivulets of blood that had leaked out of him. She had left him there to die. Alone. No one to hold his hand or soothe him with calm words in his final moments. He would never draw breath again and she would never forgive herself because it was all her fault. If Ele hadn't tried to defend her, he would still be alive. He had been so brave and gallant and foolish and now he was dead.

Kala was probably dead too. It wasn't like her to leave Ele's side and she wasn't afraid to fight, yet Tahlia hadn't seen her when Ele charged at Kareem. Nasir could have killed her but he had no reason to. The girl was nothing to him. If the priest had taken her—

Tahlia sobbed. She could only hope that Henri and Malik would survive the summit. They would look for Kala and rescue her. But if Henri lived, he would find Ele's lifeless body crumpled on that stone floor. She couldn't imagine it. Didn't want to. It would destroy him.

Rough hands threw her onto her back and grasped at her wrists, binding them tightly with crude rope. She didn't fight back, though a part of her knew she should. It wouldn't matter anyway. Clawing and kicking hadn't brought anyone to her aid as Kareem dragged her through the palace courtyard to the royal stables. They had passed dozens of servants and nobles but no one dared question the abuse of a woman by a man, let alone by a king. Kareem could rape her right now, out in the open in broad daylight, and no one would stop him. In fact, they would probably watch, wishing they were him. Anything was justifiable to blind eyes, deaf ears, and stiff cocks.

"My two favorite things in the world; a woman's cries—" Kareem sniffed the air appreciatively as he loomed over her— "and the smell of blood."

Tahlia knew she should be terrified but even fear didn't stir in her veins. Ele was dead. She no longer cared what happened to her. Kareem could violate her body, it was nothing that hadn't been done before. He could try to break her but she had already shattered into a million shards of glass. All that remained was not her. Her mind had somehow disconnected from her body and her surroundings because all she could feel and see and know was Ele getting stabbed over and over again. The experience was both familiar and foreign. Like remembering a dream she once had.

Calloused fingers shoved beneath her silk dress, grabbing at every inch of her skin. Tahlia stared up at the sun even as bile rose in her throat.

"No more hidden daggers?" Kareem searched her body before ripping the slippers from her feet. "I must admit, you surprised me before. I didn't think you had that kind of fight in you."

She didn't. Not anymore.

He seized her chin, gripping it painfully as he brought his face to within an inch of hers. His breath was hot and foul against her cheek. It infected her senses as she was forced to breathe him in. Still, she refused to meet his eye. Not out of defiance, she simply didn't care. It didn't stop him from inspecting her though. His gaze trailed over her face like he was assessing the shine on polished silverware. She knew he was probably scenting the perfume on her neck, the oils she had used in her hair that morning. Dark kohl lined her emerald eyes, though it was probably smudged by now. Her bottom lip was split, the blood dried and caked to a scab. Her cheek was swollen and bruising from where he had struck her.

"The silk rose," he crooned. "Flawless. Mesmerizing. Untouchable. And yet so many hands have touched you. You enter a room and weave your spell to create an illusion that you are every man's fantasy, but in reality you are every man's whore. Still, they want you. Not even the gods can resist you. It's pathetic really. But you are mine now and I intend to ruin you. He can have what's left of you when I'm done."

The words drifted through the fog of her mind until they snagged on her consciousness. Her gaze finally snapped to his but it wasn't Kareem's eyes that stared back at her. A scream tore from her throat.

HENRI

Henri sliced and parried, severing tissue and limbs as blood sprayed his skin and clothes. His muscles screamed from exhaustion and he had a gruesome, gaping wound to his thigh but he refused to yield. Adrenaline flooded his veins, keeping him moving, dulling the pain, and sharpening his senses. He didn't dare lose focus to check on Malik but somehow he knew he was still fighting, defending his back as if he hadn't stabbed it himself. But the only reason both of them were still alive was Isa.

Henri didn't know where the Naiab warrior had come from but he had annihilated most of the Rouhan nobles in a blur of wind and sand and blood. The floor of the arena looked like a battlefield, as if the challengers had been ambushed by a small army rather than one sand wielder. In his peripheral vision, Henri could see that Isa was no longer shifting between sand and human form, but he continued to slaughter with effortless ease, wielding a double tipped spear. If this was the devastation one warrior could wreck, no militia would ever stand a chance against the Naiab.

The thought both comforted and troubled him.

Yanking his blade from the guts of a noble, Henri scanned his surroundings for the next opponent only to find that there were none left. Over a dozen Rouhan nobles lay dead at his feet, their bodies butchered, their eyes lifeless. The stench was almost unbearable as the sun beat down on their corpses. A heavy silence filled the arena. The hollow echo of death. Less than a hundred spectators remained in the stands, those brave enough or perhaps foolish enough to stay and watch history be written, but even they could not muster a sound for what they had witnessed.

"Henri, you're hurt." Malik rushed toward him.

Henri hissed as the pain of his thigh suddenly pierced his consciousness but he held up a hand in warning. "Touch me and I'll kill you."

"That wound is deep," Malik urged. "You could bleed to death."

"Then you won't have to assassinate me," Henri shot back.

Malik stood across from him, stunned, as his chest heaved from exertion. His face was glistening with blood and sweat and his sword arm lay limp at his side as if it were broken as well as drained of blood. It was a miracle Malik was still alive. Henri couldn't decide if he was grateful or disappointed. Either way, he couldn't stand to look at him.

Henri limped to where he had slain Ozkan, the pious prick, and started shoving the other bodies off his carcass. He was vaguely aware of Isa lingering nearby, taking up a protective stance as if he was ready to hurl his spear into the crowd.

"Why would you say something like that?" Malik pressed.

The bastard was choosing his words so carefully. It made Henri want to rip him apart limb from limb. Even when confronted with his betrayal, he was still walking the edge between truth and lies. Henri gripped Ozkan's hair and yanked his head back, sawing his beard off with his dagger.

He held it up to what was left of the crowd and projected his voice until it echoed off the stone walls. "I have cut off the beard of Ozkan and removed his claim to kingship. I hereby claim his lands for myself."

Turning to Malik, Henri tossed Ozkan's beard to the ground between them. "If you want it, you're going to have to kill me for it."

"Henri, what are you talking about?" Malik demanded.

"For once just tell me the fucking truth! Did you order my assassination?"

Malik recoiled as if he'd been struck. They stared at each other, a million unspoken words passing between them, with one notable absence.

He didn't deny it.

Henri felt his heart crack beneath his ribs. He had known, but to have it confirmed made the pain even sharper. He felt like he couldn't breathe.

Malik swallowed hard. "I ordered it before we met. Before I knew you."

"And then you lied to my face."

"Of course I lied." Malik's voice held a note of exasperation. "You would have killed me. You were my enemy."

"And what am I now?"

Malik gaped at him. "How can you even ask me that? I was willing to die for you today!"

"Instead, you became a king."

Malik made a noise that sounded like a strangled scoff. "You want Dahane's lands? Have them." He turned to the crowd and shouted, "I hereby renounce my claim to kingship!"

"Because you lost," Henri spat. "Because you chose the wrong side."

"I chose your side!" Malik jabbed a finger into the air. "Since the day I swore myself to you in front of everyone, I have only ever been on your side. Henri, I was trying to save your life."

"You had a secret alliance with Nasir," Henri countered.

"*Had*. Before you. Before us."

"And what about Tahlia? Did you know about her secret with Nasir? Because she certainly knew about yours."

"I ... " Malik expelled a long breath. "Yes, I knew."

"And neither of you told me about the other. How should I interpret that, Malik?"

"You should trust that every decision we made has been to protect you!"

Henri made a scornful sound.

Malik's jaw tightened. "This is all Nasir's doing. He's gotten inside your head. He wants us to turn on each other."

Malik cast his furious gaze up to the king's gallery but his face quickly fell. Henri followed his line of sight. The gallery had been abandoned. There was no one on the second floor at all. Isa was the first to sprint up the aisle and Henri and Malik quickly followed.

"Nasir would have fled like a coward," Malik muttered.

"Ele would have gotten Tahlia and Kala to safety," Henri panted, trying to ignore the stabbing pain in his thigh at every step.

When they landed at the top of the aisle, they both halted. Ele's body lay crumpled on the stone floor, his shirt stained crimson, his shamshir gripped in his small lifeless hand.

"No."

Henri wasn't sure who had spoken or if what he was seeing was real because it couldn't be, it just couldn't. There was no version of today in which this happened. Ele couldn't be dead. He was supposed to escape and lead the others to safety across the sea. He was supposed to grow up and become a man. He had so many more days ahead of him. He couldn't be dead.

"Ele." Malik rushed to his side and scooped up his limp hand in his.

Isa simply stood over him, assessing his small body, his face grave.

Henri jolted from his frozen stupor and stumbled over to collapse beside him. He lifted Ele's head carefully to cradle it in his lap, brushing his curls back from his forehead. His skin was pale and cold.

"Not Ele. *Not Ele.*" Henri chanted as if his words could turn back time. "Someone do something!"

He wasn't sure who he was pleading with.

Malik pressed his fingers under Ele's jaw and then held his fingers in front of Ele's lips. "He's still alive."

Henri sucked in air as if he could breathe for him.

"His heartbeat is faint but it's still there," Malik said.

"Save him," Henri demanded.

Malik gently peeled back Ele's blood-soaked kurta to reveal a deep stab wound. Isa swore at the sight of it.

Malik shook his head and tried to speak but choked on the words. "Even if I was a healer—"

"That wound is not survivable," Isa said quietly.

They were wrong.

Henri refused to believe it. Ele was a fighter. He had survived so much already in his short life, he could survive this. Death couldn't have him. Henri would never surrender him.

"He's *mine*," Henri growled.

An idea stilled his thoughts. He tore his gaze away to meet Isa's, his eyes alight with intensity.

"The water goddess. She saved my life and Kala's. She can save Ele's." Isa opened his mouth to protest but Henri cut him off. "I'll do anything. Tear down the walls, restore the water table, make the Idris desert the sixth kingdom, you can have all of Merovia, whatever you want, just save him."

"Ele won't survive the journey to the Citadel," Malik pointed out.

"How do I pray to her? Tell me how you pray!"

Isa sighed but then closed his eyes. They seemed to shift beneath his eyelids, as if he were searching for something inside his soul. When he opened them again, his orbs were a portal to the limitless expanse of the ocean, the ceaseless tides, and the ancient seas. The water goddess was inhabiting him. Isa must have prayed to her and was now allowing her to use him as a vessel. The water goddess stared down at Ele but Isa's expression remained impassive.

"Save him." Henri's words were both a desperate plea and a blatant command.

"I can't," the goddess replied simply.

"What do you mean you can't? You're a goddess! You're all powerful!"

"I am not. We are limited by the rules of our creation. I am bound to water in all its forms. I cannot mend organs or bone."

"You saved me! You saved Kala!"

"I did what was within my power to do. There was never any guarantee. This is not within my power and I will not interfere in another god's realm."

"Another god," Henri repeated, latching on to her words. "Which god? What god could save him?"

"The goddess of endings and beginnings," Malik murmured and Isa dipped his chin in silent confirmation.

"Fine. Summon her right now," Henri commanded.

"Henri," Malik warned.

"You can't just summon a goddess," Isa said blandly. "People are born and die every day, why should she care about this one?"

"She'll care." Henri's voice lowered to a dangerous tone. "I have something she wants."

Malik's expression tightened. "Henri, don't."

Isa cocked his head with interest. "Very well. But if you wish to speak with her, she will need to occupy someone."

They both turned to Malik who went unnaturally still.

"Do it," Henri ordered.

"A vessel cannot be forced to host a god. They must give of themselves, willingly," the goddess warned.

"I do." Malik stood up, bracing himself and curling his hands into fists as if he were preparing for combat.

He cut a final look to Henri, which was probably meant to convey a strong warning, but Henri didn't care. Then Malik closed his eyes and submitted himself. Henri waited, counting the seconds as he absentmindedly stroked Ele's cheek with his thumb. When Malik's eyes tore open, they reflected endless cycles of birth and rebirth, the perpetual motion of creation and dissolution, the lightness of hope and the darkness of inevitability.

Malik slowly turned his head to Isa, the movement disturbingly stiff, and blinked. "This is unpleasant."

"I want to make a deal with you," Henri interrupted before the water goddess could reply.

Malik's gaze drifted toward Henri and stared down at him as if he were nothing but a speck of lint. The goddess hadn't even acknowledged the boy dying right in front of her.

"My life for his," Henri said.

Malik's brows creased as if it were the most ridiculous thing he had ever heard. "You brought me here for this?"

Isa lifted his shoulders in a delicate shrug that looked unnatural on such a masculine frame. "A little entertainment makes eternity pass quicker."

It was strange to see them interact as if they were old friends and he was somehow on the outside.

Malik waved his hand dismissively. "Keep your life, mortal."

"But I am a Merovian king!" Henri protested. "Surely, my life is worth more to you than a young boy's!"

"Life is life. Death is death. It's all just stardust," the goddess of endings and beginnings replied.

Henri's features hardened in desperation. "I will give you anything. Anything you ask for."

Malik flicked a glance back to Isa and they exchanged an all-knowing look before he returned his attention to Henri. "If I save the boy's life, the balance of fates must be restored. Are you willing to accept that burden?"

"Yes." He had no idea what that meant but he was willing to do anything to save Ele.

"An ending that was not fated. A beginning that will never come to pass."

An exchange. The goddess was talking about an exchange. Ele's ending for someone else's ending or beginning.

"You do not get to choose the price or who pays it, but it will be because of you. Your choice on this day."

Chilling unease seeped into his bloodstream but he refused to change his mind. Ele would not die today.

"I accept."

A feline smile parted Malik's lips. He crouched down gracefully beside Ele and leaned in close, hovering his face inches above Ele's. Then he exhaled. It was a chorus of breath, a whisper of life, the sigh of a beating heart.

As Malik leaned back, Henri cupped both hands around the boys' cheeks. His skin still felt cold, his body lifeless.

"Ele."

"He will need a healer," Malik said and somehow Henri knew it was Malik speaking, not the goddess of endings and beginnings. "She repaired his organ and saved his life but he's still wounded. He will need time to recover."

"He's not waking up," Henri's voice trembled with panic.

If the goddess had somehow tricked them and not held up her end of the bargain, there was nothing more that could be done to save him.

"The boy will live," Isa placed a steady hand on Henri's shoulder.

"Whoever did this to him will not," Henri vowed.

It had to be Nasir or Kareem. Ele must have been trying to defend Tahlia and Kala, it was the only explanation. Which meant Tahlia and Kala were not safe.

"We have to find them."

Malik must have followed Henri's train of thought, because he said, "They could have fled to safety."

He sounded like he didn't believe his own words.

"No. They would have never left Ele." Henri noticed Malik's mouth tighten as his posture tensed. "What? What are you thinking?"

"That Kareem likely seized the opportunity to take Tahlia."

Henri's features darkened in a violent rage.

"What does the king of the black sands want with her?" Isa's voice was dangerously low.

"She is the silk rose. He has always wanted her. But that doesn't explain what happened to Kala." Malik frowned. "Kareem would have no use for a young girl. Neither would Nasir."

"When the boy wakes, he can tell us what happened. If they have come to any harm, I will find the man responsible and inflict such pain that even the gods will feel it. Right now, though, we have more immediate concerns. You are king of this kingdom, Henri, ruler of the Old City. But the people may not respond favorably to you."

Isa had a point. No matter how hard he had tried to get to know his people and immerse himself in Merovian culture, he was still considered to be a foreign king. They had barely tolerated him, and only because they knew he would soon die at the summit.

Except he had lived.

And killed a second Merovian king.

And expanded his empire.

"Henri's claim to this kingdom is indisputable," Malik countered. "They saw him kill Ozkan and remove his beard with their own eyes. They will respect Merovian laws."

"Like you did when I arrived?" Henri retorted.

Malik clamped his mouth shut.

Henri wasn't an idiot. The only reason his people hadn't rioted in the streets was because Malik, a Merovian, a Rouhan noble and former regent, recognized him as king.

"By now, word would have also spread through the streets about me and my sand magic," Isa said. "The guards will try to kill me."

Henri's mind catapulted into thought. "We need to get somewhere safe until I can send for my army."

"And Dahane's," Malik added.

"Dahane's army is now your army," Isa corrected him. "You are king of the salt plains."

Malik shook his head. "I renounced my claim to kingship."

"Merovian kings do not renounce their claims. They rule or they die."

"Isa's right." Henri's jaw flexed as he locked eyes with Malik. "So be a king. Be my ally. These people may not want to accept me but they will if you do."

Malik's expression shifted from surprise to resignation. "I will do whatever you ask me to. King or not, I am still sworn to you."

Henri returned a curt nod and carefully gathered Ele's body into his arms, but his injured thigh rendered him unable to stand.

"Give the boy to me." Isa leaned down and Henri reluctantly transferred Ele to him.

Malik extended his left hand as his right dangled uselessly at his side. Henri begrudgingly took it to help him stand.

"We need to find a healer and somewhere safe for Ele to recover. Then we'll send word to our armies," Henri ordered.

Isa released a long breath. "Your army will take days to arrive. Malik's will take weeks. If these people reject you or if Kareem or Nasir attack the city, you will die."

"That's why you're going to send for your army," Henri replied. "How fast can the Naiab travel through sand?"

Isa's mouth twisted into a wolfish smile. "They could be here by sundown tomorrow."

"Henri," Malik warned, his eyes darting between them.

"Do it. Nasir started this war. It's time to gather our forces."

CHAPTER ELEVEN

HENRI

"Are you sure about this?" Henri grunted as they cautiously stalked inside the palace.

Or in his case hobbled. His leg was getting worse with every step he forced himself to take but he would walk until it fell off if it meant getting Ele to safety. Malik led the way through the maze of corridors and Isa followed closely behind them, cradling Ele against his chest. Malik still gripped his shamshir in his left hand and Henri held his longsword at the ready but despite being covered in blood and gore, he doubted they looked all that formidable.

"You are king of this kingdom," Malik replied sternly. "If you want them to recognize you as such, you need to act like it."

It was great in theory but a deadly gamble in reality. If his own guards did not recognize his authority, Malik would not be able to stop them from running him through.

"Besides, there's no place we could go that they wouldn't find us. Especially when we need a healer. This is the fastest way to confront the issue of succession and get Ele the help he needs."

Henri couldn't argue with that. Every minute they wasted was another minute Ele's condition could deteriorate. The goddess had saved his life by repairing the ruptured organ, but he still needed the wound to be stitched. It would take time for him to recover. He could develop an infection or the wound might not heal properly.

They rounded the corner and Henri tensed at the sight of the guards ahead, patrolling what was presumably the entrance to the king's chamber. The guards straightened as they approached, forming a tight, defensive line. Their numbers were fewer than he'd expected but even so, they were more than enough to outmatch them.

"King Ozkan is dead, slain by King Henri," Malik announced with cool authority. "Let your new king through and fetch a healer immediately."

The guards didn't move. They simply sneered at Henri with blatant disdain, the violent threat simmering just beneath the surface. He knew what they were thinking. They were trying to calculate whether they could finish what Ozkan started. A few of them glanced warily in Isa's direction, clearly unsure what to make of a large naked man with golden hued skin and turquoise tattoos.

Malik closed the distance with a menacing stride until he was nose to nose with the largest of the guards. "Are you deaf? Or are you refusing an order?"

"Kafei." The guard replied with deference and Malik's frame stiffened at the word that was clearly directed at him. "With all due respect, we have heard conflicting accounts of what happened at the summit. There is much confusion. Some say you killed King Ozkan as well as King Dahane."

Henri's nostrils flared in barely contained anger. They were giving Malik an opportunity to claim the kingdom for himself. One word from Malik and the guards would slaughter Henri and every other witness that swore a different account. The record would be set straight. The Rouhan family would be restored to power.

Malik's brows furrowed. "You do seem confused."

In the hitch of a breath Malik's shamshir shot through the guard's torso. He stumbled forward, spitting blood onto the tiled floor, and grasping at the sword as if he desired to pull himself free from it. His comrades hesitated to reach for their blades, their eyes rapidly assessing the threat in front of them and the likely consequences should they act. They had no issue killing Henri, a naked stranger, and a wounded boy, but they would never harm one of their own, especially not a Merovian king. The guard slumped to the floor, dead.

"Is anyone else confused?" Malik looked to each of the guards, letting the tension hang heavy in the air. "Henri is now king of these lands. Anyone who fails to recognize that will die a traitor's death. Now let us through and fetch a healer."

The guards gradually parted and Henri hobbled through with as much dignity as he could muster, though his leg was now starting to shake. "I want this palace and the Old City shut down. No one leaves or enters without my permission. Find King Kareem and King Nasir and bring them to me. They failed to abide by Merovian law at the summit and must pay for it with their lives."

"We are expecting allies to arrive at the wall at sundown tomorrow, let them through," Malik added.

Henri glanced at him, surprised by his words, though he could tell they tasted bitter on his tongue.

"And bring our things from the guest wing into the king's chamber."

"Just mine." Henri countered. "King Malik will require a room in the guest wing."

Hurt flashed across Malik's face but it vanished in an instant.

"And I require writing equipment," Henri added. "I need to send a message."

Two of the guards bowed and walked backward several steps before marching down the hallway to carry out their orders. Henri continued toward the double doors at the end of the passage, which a servant opened as he drew near.

The king's chamber was vast but minimalistic, void of the usual grandeur he would expect from a king, but befitting the life of a devout man. The walls were covered in rich tapestries bearing ancient prayers and illustrations of tales of divinity. In the far corner of the chamber was a monument. A carved pedestal made of rosewood sat beneath a gleaming silver fire urn, its surface etched with elaborate patterns. The flame flickered gently, casting a warm glow that filled the chamber with a strangely tranquil ambiance. Surrounding the fire urn were several small crafted statues of divines.

"Lay him down there." Malik gestured to the bed in the center of the room before he disappeared behind two large intricately carved wooden screens.

The screens offered a sense of privacy for what Henri guessed was a washroom. Isa unspooled Ele from his arms, placing him gently across the sheets.

"There will be clothes here somewhere, take what you need," Henri offered.

As Isa walked away to look for a wardrobe, Henri sat on the bed next to Ele, bracing one arm over his body as if he might shield him. But he was too late. The damage had already been done. Malik returned and put a bowl of water with a washcloth on a nearby table. He moved to peel off Ele's blood-soaked kurta.

Henri's hand shot out and grabbed his wrist. "What are you doing? We should wait for the healer."

"If the healer sees all this blood and then finds the wound is less severe than expected, they will ask questions we can't answer."

Henri reluctantly released Malik's wrist but couldn't bring himself to help clean the blood. Ele's skin was still so pale and cold, like marbled stone. The angry wound stretched from his chest to his ribs. It would leave a sizeable scar. Henri's lips twitched to think that Ele would probably bear the scar with pride. He would consider it a mark of his allegiance and a testament to his bravery.

At the sound of a soft knock, Henri turned to see a servant standing in the doorway with parchment, ink and a quill in hand. Isa, now clothed in a kurta that looked uncomfortably small on him, directed the servant to set the materials down on a table before dismissing him. Henri would send for his army tonight. Though whether he could trust Inaya to follow his command he wasn't sure. Maybe upon hearing about his unexpected survival at the summit she would plan a rebellion.

By the time the healer arrived, Malik had managed to strip Ele of his clothes and wash most of the blood from his body. The healer was younger than Henri expected but she entered the room with a quiet confidence and immediately set about examining Ele. Henri moved to stand by the end of the bed to give her space while Malik lingered on the other side.

Upon inspecting the wound, the healer looked up at Henri with an empty expression, as if she was used to delivering bad news. "The puncture isn't deep. No organs have ruptured. He's a very lucky young man. I'll clean the wound and stitch it. He shouldn't get out of bed or physically exert himself for at least a week, but he will recover just fine."

"Why isn't he awake?" Henri pressed.

"The body processes trauma in different ways," the healer replied. "He will wake when he is ready."

Relief buckled his knees and dizziness threatened to bring him down entirely, compelling Henri to lean heavily against the bedpost for support.

"Henri, you need to sit down." Malik swiftly reached his side but held back from touching him. "Let me look at your leg."

"The healer will look at it when she's done with Ele," Henri growled. "You've done enough. In fact, you can leave now."

"What?" Malik's concern quickly switched to anger.

"Ele almost died today because of you."

"Me?"

"You made me a promise, Malik."

"I promised you I would do whatever needed to be done," Malik countered.

"I needed you to protect the people most precious to me!"

"If you had just stayed in the king's gallery you could have protected them yourself! But your pride got the better of you. Instead of trusting me, you let Nasir manipulate you into seeing me as a threat!"

"Get out!" Henri pointed sharply toward the door, his eyes ablaze with fury.

Malik's throat worked as if he were holding back a hurricane of words. "You once told me your father saw betrayal around every corner and it ruined him and everyone he loved. Do not let that happen to you."

How. Fucking. Dare. He.

But Malik didn't wait for a reply before stalking out of the room. Henri clenched his jaw so hard he was shocked it didn't break. He forced his attention back to Ele. The healer discreetly pretended that she hadn't heard a word as she prepared a needle and thread. It was unfathomable that Malik could stand in front of him, after all he had done, after all the lies, and still deflect blame for what had happened.

What was worse was that he was right. Partially, at least. Henri had a duty to protect Ele, to protect all of them, and he had failed. He didn't know where Tahlia and Kala were, but he was sure they weren't safe. They were in danger. Because of him. Even if he did know where they were, he wouldn't be able to tear himself away from Ele's side long enough to save them. Especially not while the kingdom was so volatile.

Until the Naiab arrived, followed by his army in a few days, his reign over this new kingdom was precarious at best. If the people revolted against him, or if Kareem or Nasir attacked his border, he would be defenseless. War didn't seem to be Nasir's style, though. He preferred clandestine tactics to overt ones. And if Kareem had taken Tahlia, he would be too preoccupied with claiming her to wage a war against him. Henri's body trembled with wrath at the thought.

Both kings would die screaming.

Days from now or weeks from now. In a war or at the edge of his blade. The pain they had caused him would be nothing compared to the suffering they would endure at his hands. Sweet retribution for everything they had tried to take from him.

"The boy is done," the healer announced before gesturing toward a divan. "Sit, Kafei. Let me look at your leg."

Henri obeyed and allowed her to assess and clean the wound. When she pushed the needle through his skin, he hissed in pain but fortified himself to bear it. A year ago, he would have guzzled wine to dull his senses, but he doubted he would find any in Ozkan's chamber. Not that he would partake even if there was any to find. He was acutely aware of the need to stay alert.

The healer worked quietly, but she didn't need to tell him that he would require several days to heal. He could barely walk, let alone fight. If the Naiab wanted to kill him or take his kingdom, this would be the perfect opportunity. He was completely at their mercy.

Henri's gaze drifted to Isa who was standing across the room, his arms folded across his chest in guarded vigilance. How the man had managed to get inside the summit, Henri still didn't know, but he suspected Tahlia was involved. If he was right, it meant that the warrior had gotten to her twice now without his knowledge. A fact that made Henri want to kill him, despite Isa being the only reason he was still alive.

Tahlia had betrayed him by not being honest, by not telling him about Malik, and by going behind his back to make a deal with the Naiab warrior, but at least she hadn't tried to kill him. That he knew of.

"All done, Kafei," the healer said as she began to pack her things. "You need to stay off the leg for several days if you can. I will be back to look at it tomorrow."

"Thank you."

"King Malik is in the guest wing. His arm will need tending to," Isa instructed as he opened the door for her.

The healer bowed and walked backward several steps before leaving. Henri hadn't even considered Malik's arm. Until it healed, he was vulnerable as well, though he had still managed to hold his own well enough in the arena. Ironically, the only person uninjured among them was Isa. Probably because it was impossible to strike a target that dispersed into sand.

Isa returned to his spot across the room as if it were his sentry post. Now would be the moment to try to kill Henri if that was his plan. There were no witnesses. There would be no repercussions. Henri would fight back of course but, though he was loathe to admit it, the odds were not in his favor. Though neither of them moved, their eyes locked in a silent standoff, each attempting to decipher the other's intentions.

It was Isa who broke the silence first. "We suspected Malik was behind the assassination attempt when you first arrived in Merovia. We thought he was playing you, that he would challenge you at the summit, but we never could have predicted this. He actually loves you."

"Don't," Henri warned.

"If he wanted to take Merovia he could have, several times now. He could have killed you in that arena. He could have had the guards kill you here in the palace. We were both wrong about him."

Henri shook his head stubbornly. "He lied to me."

"And saved your life."

It was Isa who had saved him, but Henri refused to admit that out loud. "I don't need anyone fighting my battles for me."

"We all need people in our lives willing to fight for us. Against our enemies but sometimes against ourselves. But we need to be somebody worth the fight."

Henri considered his words for a moment. They were surprising coming from a seemingly invincible sand wielding warrior.

"Why did you fight for me today?" Henri asked.

"Tahlia." Isa's response was simple, as if there could never be any alternative explanation. "We came to an arrangement."

Henri narrowed his eyes. "What arrangement?"

"You can ask her that yourself."

A muscle ticked in Henri's jaw. "I've seen the way you look at her."

"It's hard to look away."

"You know what she is and who hunts her."

It wasn't a question but Isa answered anyway. "I do."

"Is that why you want her?"

"My reasons are my own. But it's clear that she loves you. Both of you. It's an interesting dynamic you all have."

Interesting.

It wasn't that long ago Henri would have agreed with him. He had never been monogamous but he had always assumed he would follow that path one day. Get married and have children, live his life within the lines he had been taught. The thought of loving more than one person, of being committed to both equally, had been foreign to him. The idea of being intimate with a man, let alone falling for him, had been beyond comprehension. But then everything changed. It was like his world had become less definitive, more fluid. He had given up trying to explain what was happening to him, what he was feeling, and instead surrendered himself to it because love had the power to go beyond the physical. That was just skin and bones. And even now that it had all turned to ash, the remnants of love still remained.

"You think you can save her." Isa watched him carefully.

"She doesn't deserve to be sacrificed to satisfy some god's whim. I will go to war with the heavens themselves if I have to."

"You can't kill a god."

"I'll find a way."

Isa returned his stare, the uncomfortable truth settling between them. Henri didn't know how he was going to save Tahlia or even if he was already too late, but he refused to give her up. Not without a fight.

"Tahlia isn't the only thing you want," Henri challenged. "Malik thinks the Naiab wish to take Merovia."

"We seek to change Merovia, just as you have tried to bring about change in your kingdom. This country has been ruled far too long by rampant brutality and the self-interest of kings. We wish to tip the scales in the favor of the people, and we want our people to be recognized and accepted."

"Then we can be allies," Henri said decisively. "Help me stabilize my kingdom and I will honor your terms."

"My men will be yours to command. As for me, I will stay only as long as it takes to learn what happened to Tahlia. We both know you are in no condition to save her."

Henri pressed his lips into a tight line, but he was in no position to argue the point. "Make no mistake, Tahlia is ours. You will find her and bring her back to us."

ISA

The king's bedchamber was dark enough to swallow shadows. Normally Isa would have expected an oil lamp to be burning or candles to be lit but there was nothing. He didn't need light, though. He had made sure to memorize the layout of the room when he brought the boy here to be mended. Now it was the middle of the night but he doubted Henri would have rearranged the furniture. It was more likely he had hidden weapons around the room. In the few minutes Isa had to search the chamber under the guise of looking for clothes, he hadn't discovered any weaponry, but that didn't mean there weren't any now.

Henri was a shrewd king. He knew the dangerous position he was in. It was inevitable that his enemies would come for him. It was only a matter of which enemy would come for him first. There would be no better opportunity than tonight. Having fallen out with his lover, Henri was unprotected. Wounded. An immobilized target. It would be effortless to kill him.

Despite not being able to see his outline beneath the sheets, Isa knew the boy slept soundly in the bed. Henri would not risk moving him. Isa also knew that Henri would never leave the boy's side. His devotion was clear for everyone to see, which made his whereabouts predictable.

Earlier, Isa had shifted into sand to gradually maneuver past the guards before collecting himself to pour silently through the keyhole of the king's bedchamber. Now he stood just beyond the door within the room, fully materialized in the shade of night, except for the kard made of sand that he gripped in his hand. Still, he didn't move.

He waited.

For so long, the only sound that hit his ears was the breath filling his lungs. The only thought that occupied his mind was the knowledge that Henri was somewhere in this room. No doubt that was why there were no candles burning. He didn't want to make it easy for his enemies to find him.

It was a feeble defense.

Eventually, the sound Isa was waiting to hear filtered through the air. The scrape of wood. The pad of feet. He let the sounds saturate his senses until his instincts took over and he moved toward it in the dark. In one swift motion, his arm locked around a broad chest and his kard pressed viciously against a pulsing throat.

"Don't kill him." A flame flickered to life from an oil lamp, revealing Henri lounging across a divan.

The assassin tried to struggle free but Isa tightened his grip and sunk his blade into his skin, just enough to draw blood. The man immediately halted. Satisfied, Henri stood slowly, lifting the lamp to appraise their quarry better.

"One of my own guards." Henri's tone was bland, as if he had expected as much. "I guess that explains how you got past them. The real question is are you patriotic or do you work for Nasir?"

Tense silence filled the space between them, so Henri closed it with deliberate, ominous steps.

"You will tell me. Because until you do, I will break every bone in your body. I will carve into your skin all the pain I have endured since coming to this foreign country. I will make you scream until your vocal cords snap and I will make you pray for the goddess of endings and beginnings to end you."

The assassin spat at his feet and Henri smiled, even as his eyes narrowed with the promise of death.

CHAPTER TWELVE

KALA

Kala waited until the camp fell silent and the only sound left was the crackling of the fire. Then she waited some more, her thoughts battling each other; should she stay hidden or try to leave? The truth was there was no way of knowing if it was safe for her to leave her hiding place, but she had no choice. She could not stay hidden for days on end. She needed food. And water. And to pee.

Steeling herself, Kala slowly pulled back the tarp to reveal the night sky sparkling above her. Fresh, cool air filled her lungs and swept over her sweat-soaked skin. It was stifling beneath the tarp, like being inside a clay oven. At the height of the day, she could have sworn her organs were swelling like dough.

Kala rotated her limbs, forcing feeling into them, before she shifted to a kneeling position and looked out over the lip of the wagon. Her assumption was correct. The guards had set up camp surrounding the wagon in order to fend off marauders. There was a single fire but no tents. The men slept on bedrolls laid out on the hard ground, their shamshirs clutched in their hands, ready to respond to whatever threat awoke them. Her eyes traveled further until they landed on two sentries; one positioned on either side of the camp.

This was going to be tricky.

Fortunately, the sentries were facing outward and paying no heed to anything that was happening inside the camp. Kala hesitated, her mind and limbs at war with one another, debating the foolishness of her plan but eager to spring into action. Snapping up the courage, she leaped over the side of the wagon. Her feet hit the ground with a thud, which sounded loud to her ears but didn't appear to rouse anyone else.

Kala wasn't sure how long it would take before they arrived in Nasir's kingdom. She had never seen a map of Merovia before. Not that she would be able to read a map if she saw one. She hadn't received any form of education in the Thaka, except for the lessons that came at the end of a fist. But she had sharp ears for listening, keen eyes for observing, and a quick mind for remembering. She recalled that Ele once told her Nasir's and Ozkan's kingdoms were neighbors. That had to mean they were close. Maybe two days travel. Surely no more than ten days.

It didn't matter. She would need water and food if she was going to make it. An entire day had almost passed since her last meal and she was beginning to feel a little light-headed. Kala was used to the pains of hunger. Until Ele took her to the palace, it had been the one thing that never changed in her life. She woke up to it. She went to sleep with it. Her body was used to running on the lick of scraps and beads of water. Whatever she could find in this camp, she would make it last the journey. But she would need to find *something*.

Hidden in the shadows of the wagon, Kala's eyes darted between the sentries. They walked the edge of the camp, changing direction now and then, but at no point did they turn their gazes inward. She could do this. Once she left the shadows of the wagon she would be completely exposed, with nowhere to run or hide if she was spotted. Which meant she needed to be quick and quiet. The perfect thief.

Good thing she had years of practice.

Kala shot out from her hiding place and raced to her sleeping target. Sure enough, the guard had a waterskin strapped to his side. Her fingers deftly loosened the strap until it fell into her hands. The skin felt reasonably full. It would be easy to make it last for several days. Her gaze darted around for signs of food but she couldn't see any. No pots sat by the fire. There were no plates abandoned on the ground. She supposed the guards wouldn't be likely to leave food lying around, but there had to be supplies somewhere. Perhaps near the horses.

Out of the corner of her eye, one of the sentries changed direction and Kala hurtled herself back into the shadows of the wagon. She clutched the skin against her pounding chest and counted her heartbeats until she was sure she had not been seen. The horses were across the other side of the camp, roped together, making it difficult to see if there were any saddlebags near them. It would be a risk to run that far and back. Maybe she could survive another day without food. She could try again tomorrow night. With any luck, the horses might be tied up closer to the wagon or perhaps the guards would leave some food out.

Unlikely.

Kala fastened the waterskin to her belt while her eyes pinged between the sentries with determination. She needed to do this tonight. The jittery pulse of adrenaline reminded her of another night not too long ago when she had darted across the street to meet a boy hiding in the darkness. She had been terrified of being seen that night but the promise of gold coins lured her. In one fleeting moment, one daring sprint, her life had changed.

When one of the sentries turned in the opposite direction and the other began to relieve himself where he stood, Kala dashed across the camp toward the horses. She didn't much like horses but thankfully the feeling wasn't mutual. Her sudden presence didn't seem to spook the animals, they just turned their heads to stare at her. Kala tried to ignore them as she searched the ground for saddlebags. At last, she caught sight of them a short distance away, safely beyond the horse's reach. Casting a quick look over her shoulder to make sure the sentries were still occupied, she scrambled.

Crouching down beside the bags, her hands swiftly opened them to rifle through the contents. She could hardly see a thing but she could feel the texture and she recognized the smells; dried meat, dried fruit, nuts and seeds, and legumes. Kala started to fill the pockets of her tunic and pants. It wouldn't be much but perhaps that was for the best. If she took any more it might be noticed.

With her pockets full and the waterskin strapped to her side, Kala relieved herself and got ready to sprint back across the camp to her hiding spot in the cart. The horses huffed as if amused by her audacity but she would prove them wrong. She had survived the Thaka, abduction into slavery, and the savage reprisal of her family. Being a stowaway surrounded by her enemies was nothing compared to that. She was, after all, more than a talented thief. She was a royal spy.

ELE

He was warm. That was the first thing Ele noticed. He had been so very cold. The kind of cold that cracked teeth and froze bones. But now he was warm. And comfortable. He could feel the soft pillow cushioning his cheek and the smooth texture of the linen beneath him. Which was strange because he shouldn't be comfortable. He should be somewhere else.

At the summit.

In the arena.

Fighting.

Ele's eyes tore open as his body lurched to sit up but he immediately cried out in pain. His hand flew to his chest. Something was tugging inside his skin. Before he could inspect it, though, he saw Henri emerge from behind two wooden screens at the far end of the room. Henri's eyes were wide with what looked like fear and disbelief, but it was the blood splattered across his kurta and face that had Ele's brows lifting in question.

"Who died?"

"Ele." Henri stumbled to his side, smearing blood all over the sheets. "You're all right."

"Of course I'm all right. Are you?"

"Yes," Henri laughed. "This isn't my blood."

"You survived the summit," Ele murmured as his memories began to come back to him. "Which means you killed the other Merovian kings. Is that their blood?"

Henri's grin dimmed. "No. Ozkan is dead but Kareem and Nasir still live. Are you sure you're all right?"

Kareem. He had fought Kareem when the king tried to take—

"Tahlia! Where's Tahlia?"

"We don't know," Henri admitted. "We've been waiting for you to wake, hoping you might be able to tell us. What do you remember?"

"Kareem grabbed her and tried to force her to go with him but I defended her," Ele said eagerly before his features crumpled in puzzlement. "Did I lose?"

Henri squeezed his shoulder lightly. "You fought bravely."

"But he ... took her?"

"We think so." Malik's voice cut across the room as he strolled inside. He was dressed immaculately in a deep purple kurta with several silver rings adorning his fingers. Kohl lined his eyes and a relieved smile tugged at the corner of his lips. "It's good to see you again, little shadow."

"You both survived." Ele's chest eased in relief.

Malik's expression hardened in an instant as he turned to Henri and beheld the blood. Henri didn't even look at him. Clearly, things were still bad between them. And Malik was a king now. The realization parted his lips but Ele swallowed the words, unsure if it was a touchy subject. Malik was still here, and from the way he was looking at Henri he still loved him, was still loyal to him. That was all that mattered.

"It's not his blood," Ele offered.

"Whose is it?"

"An assassin," Henri replied curtly, still not looking at Malik. "I've been questioning him."

Malik's eyes turned wild. "You what?"

"You captured an assassin?" Ele tried to sit up but grimaced at the sharp pain in his chest.

"Try not to move." Henri pressed a hand firmly against his shoulder, forcing him to lie back against the pillows. "The healer said you shouldn't get out of bed for several days."

"Why?" Ele winced.

Henri hesitated, as if he didn't want to explain. "Kareem wounded you. Deeply. You have sutures."

Ele's hand dived beneath his kurta, his fingers exploring the rough bumps where the fibers wove into his skin. There were so many of them.

Because he had lost.

Ele's stomach dropped. "I failed her."

"No," Henri said firmly. "I failed you. I never should have left your side."

"You're a king. You had to fight in the summit. You trusted me to protect her and I failed."

"No one has failed. We're all still alive," Malik pointed out sternly. "We will get her back. Tahlia is strong. She will outlast Kareem until we find her."

"Kala." Fear suddenly gripped Ele and his eyes darted between Malik and Henri in desperation. "Where's Kala? She went after Nasir. She was going to stop him!"

"We don't know where she is," Henri said softly.

"I have ordered the guards to search the palace grounds for her but so far there's been no word," Malik added.

Ele thought for a moment. "She would have followed him." He was sure of it.

Malik's frown implied that he doubted it, but Ele didn't need to know the details of *how* because he knew *her*. She was stubborn and clever. She would follow her enemies to the ends of the earth for a chance to destroy them.

"Henri closed down the Old City and no one is allowed to leave the borders of his kingdom without his permission. We might still detain them." Malik sounded mildly hopeful.

Henri finally lifted his gaze to deliver Malik a withering look. "Almost two days have passed. They would have crossed my borders by now. My guards would have let them through against my orders."

"Then we need to go after them," Ele insisted.

"You can't leave this bed and I'm not leaving you," Henri replied sternly.

"Henri is also wounded," Malik said. "He can hardly walk, let alone fight."

"You are wounded too," Henri shot back.

"None of us are in condition to fight. Henri has summoned his army and I have called for mine. The Naiab should arrive tonight."

"The Naiab." Ele suddenly remembered Isa materializing from sand and racing toward the arena floor. "Do we have an alliance with them now because Isa saved you?"

"Something like that." The words betrayed everything Henri was not saying.

"You need to tell him," Malik urged gently. "He deserves to know."

Henri speared Malik with a look that would cut most men in half but Malik bore it without flinching.

"Know what?" Ele prompted.

Turning back to Ele, Henri took a moment to organize his words. "I made an alliance with the Naiab in exchange for their help in communing with a goddess. Ele, you ... died. Your wound was too severe. When we found you, I made a deal with the goddess of endings and beginnings. Your end for someone else's ending or beginning."

Ele's jaw slackened in open shock. He had died. The cold he felt, that was *death*. A goddess had saved him. Henri had made a deal with a goddess. Kala would be horrified. Her voice echoed in his head like a warning; the gods were not to be trusted. He was alive, but at what cost?

"Whose ending or beginning?" Ele asked quietly.

"We don't know," Malik admitted. "The goddess can choose at her whim whenever she likes."

It could be a stranger. In which case, they would never know. It could happen now or five, ten, twenty years from now. Either way, he had cost someone their life. Or their beginning. He had stolen their fate.

"Do you feel any different?" Malik asked.

Henri glared at Malik. "Why would he feel different?"

"He is god-touched now. It might have changed him in some way. The gods enjoy their games."

Ele shrugged, still reeling from everything he'd just learned. "I feel fine, just sore."

"Good." Malik forced a smile but it looked uneasy.

"So, what happens when the Naiab get here?" Ele glanced between them.

"If the Naiab truly are our allies," Malik said cautiously, "they can help stabilize the Old City under Henri's rule until our armies arrive. Then we plan for war."

"What about Tahlia and Kala?"

"Isa will go after Tahlia and bring her home to us," Henri replied. "If Kala has followed Nasir, we will find her when we breach his kingdom."

"I'm coming with you," Ele insisted.

"I know," Henri sighed. "Right now, we have to focus on regaining our strength. We're no good to anyone like this."

Ele relaxed slightly against the pillows. He already knew the next few days would crawl by. But he would do whatever it took to get better so he could fight by Henri's side and save Kala. He had been given a second chance at life, and the next fight he had he was determined not to lose.

MALIK

The wall was almost identical to the northern wall of Henri's kingdom. It stood at least sixty feet high and spanned a great distance in both directions. Parapets punctuated the wall at regular intervals while guards maintained constant vigilance on the battlements. If only they knew what was out there.

They were about to find out.

Malik cast his eyes out over the great expanse of desert. The sun hung low over the horizon, disappearing between shimmering waves of heat, as if it were melting into the dunes and spilling itself into the sky. For now, the sands were still, but it was only a matter of time before they would shift, signaling the arrival of the Naiab. Tonight, Henri's newly acquired kingdom would either be secured or seized.

He leaned over the wall, resting his forearms on its edge. His rings clinked against each other as he clasped his hands together. Since the summit, all he seemed to do was wait. Wait for Nasir to make his next move. Wait for the Naiab to arrive to either save or condemn them. Wait for Henri to come to his chamber and apologize for ever doubting him, to savor the fact that against all odds they were both still alive, to fuck him senseless because he could. Because he still loved him.

He had hardly slept last night, the adrenaline and emotions of the day still pulsating in his system, but when he did sleep, his dreams tortured him with the ghost of Henri's hands and mouth. Meanwhile, Henri was actually torturing someone. Malik scowled. He couldn't believe Henri hadn't bothered to tell him there had been another attempt on his life. He knew Nasir would try again soon, but he had hoped they would be given at least one night's grace from fighting for their lives. It had been naïve of him.

Guilt twisted his gut. He should have been there. It was a mistake to leave Henri's side, even though he had ordered him to go. He should have known better but his anger had clouded his judgment. If the assassin had been successful—Malik clenched his jaw. He didn't want to think about it. There was no world he wanted to live in if Henri didn't also live.

Malik wouldn't make that mistake again. Henri could try to order him away but Malik no longer had to follow his orders. He was a king now, and he would do whatever it took to keep Henri safe. Except in this moment, he might be making the biggest mistake of all by letting the Naiab into the kingdom. Malik understood Henri's reasoning for the alliance and the imminent need to protect himself. Malik just didn't like it. There was so much he didn't know about the Naiab. It made them far too unpredictable.

They were the unknown player on the board, but what he did know about them changed the entire game.

If they survived this, if the walls came down and the Idris desert became the sixth kingdom, Merovia would be a new world. There would be no summits, no fights to the death for succession. New territory lines would be drawn. People would be able to travel freely across what was once restricted borders. The god-touched would walk among them, wielding their power for various intentions. It filled him with apprehension.

"They're close."

At Isa's voice, Malik immediately straightened, but Isa's attention was fixed on the horizon as he stepped out onto the parapet.

"You can feel them?" Malik asked curiously.

"I feel the vibrations in the sand."

Of course he did. Tension pulled Malik's features tight as he turned back to observe the desert. "Henri tells me you're going after Tahlia."

"As soon as my warriors get here. But I will need to take a few of them with me. Don't worry, you will have enough to protect Henri until his army arrives."

Malik's throat worked. He wanted so badly to believe him, to trust that the Naiab were true allies coming to their aid. Despite what he had said to Ele earlier, he feared for Tahlia. He knew exactly what Kareem was capable of, and his fixation with Tahlia only amplified Malik's concern. The truth was, they were at the mercy of the Naiab from all sides. If Isa's true intentions were to make a play for Kareem's kingdom, while his men seized control of Henri's, there was no way to stop any of them.

"If you betray us—"

"You'll be dead. Don't make threats you can't execute."

Rage flooded his system. He was going to throw the bastard off this damn wall.

Just then the wind swept across the desert plain like a lover's caress, rustling the fringes of Malik's kurta and tussling his hair. But then the wind quickly turned wild, building to a terrifying intensity. On the horizon, a faint haze grew and darkened as the sandstorm came alive. It roared across the dunes, heading straight toward them. The guards scrambled along the wall, shouting warnings and taking cover, but Malik and Isa didn't move. They stood steadfast on the battlement as the air swirled around them and visibility plummeted. Bracing himself, Malik closed his eyes and held his breath. The sandstorm hit with force, almost sweeping his feet out from underneath him, as thousands of grains stung his exposed skin like tiny knives. He withstood it, determined to hold his ground.

After several thundering heartbeats, the air began to ease and his muscles unclenched. When he opened his eyes, Malik immediately turned to the opposite wall and looked down onto the ground below. Dozens of Naiab warriors were standing in the yard, their golden naked skin shimmering in the sunlight. They held no weapons but stood in battle formation, clearly not trusting that they would be welcomed. And they were right. The guards emerged from the various places they had sought cover and gaped at the warriors who were twice their size.

"Stand down!" Malik yelled, just in case any of them were overcome by what they had just witnessed and stupid enough to try to attack. "Nobody moves."

Malik turned toward the narrow stone stairs to find that Isa was already halfway down them. He took the stairs two at a time to try to catch up. Stepping out into the yard, Malik followed on Isa's heels as he strode over to stand in front of his men. Isa crossed his arms over his broad chest and looked back at Malik as if he were waiting for him to speak.

"Thank you for coming." The words surprised Malik when they tumbled out of his mouth, but he supposed they were true. If the Naiab really had come to their aid, he was grateful. "Henri is now the king of this kingdom, having defeated Ozkan at the summit. But a change in power is always a perilous time. Until his army arrives, Henri will need his allies to help protect and stabilize this new order. In exchange, we will defeat Nasir and repair the water table. The Idris desert will become the sixth kingdom of Merovia and all the walls will be torn down. You have Henri's word on this. And mine."

Malik studied every one of them, searching for signs of animosity or treachery, but all he saw was warriors awaiting orders.

"Ten of you will come with me," Isa decreed. "The rest of you will carry out any orders that Henri or Malik command."

Malik's lungs fully expanded in response. Their eyes met and Malik dipped his chin in silent acknowledgement. Perhaps they would live to see the new world after all.

HENRI

Henri stood at the entrance to the palace as the soldiers who formed a guard around the grounds stepped aside to allow the Naiab through. The warriors had been outfitted with clothes and horses at the wall and now proceeded to ride cautiously, and somewhat awkwardly, down the pathway. Their astute gazes took in the details of their surroundings as if they were assessing it for hidden threats, but their expressions also held a hint of wonder.

Henri supposed the whole experience would be quite foreign to them; traveling on horseback, making their way through a large populated city, arriving at a grand palace. He doubted if any of them had ever left the Citadel, and he was pretty sure they had never ridden a horse before.

The warrior's attention appeared to linger on the statues of gods that littered the stony courtyard. Though, curiously, some of the statues appeared to have been knocked over and lay in shattered pieces at the base. Henri would not be replacing them.

Dressed in his fine attire and jewels, Malik led the group of warriors, looking regal as he sat high in the saddle. Yet, as he got closer, Henri detected a hint of disarray to his usually immaculate presentation. And it looked like there was sand in his hair. Malik dismounted from his horse as the Naiab assembled in front of Henri. Their number was small but Henri knew what they were capable of. If Isa could take out an entire arena, these men could hold a city and secure a kingdom.

"Isa?" Henri asked as Malik approached.

"Gone after Tahlia."

Henri nodded and a small measure of relief washed over him. He wished he were the one going after her but even if he wasn't wounded, he would never be able to reach Kareem's kingdom as fast as Isa could traveling through sand. Isa would find her and his revenge on Kareem would be brutal. Henri only wished he could be there to witness it.

"The Naiab are ours to command." Malik surveyed the men.

"Bring them inside and let them rest for a bit. Tomorrow, I will send them out into the Old City to begin enforcing my reign. There will be no more human sacrifices to the gods. All the Hara's are to be searched and the chosen ones returned to their families. Anyone who resists my orders will be committing high treason."

Henri waited for Malik's reaction, anticipating shock and alarm to cross his face, but his features betrayed no emotion. He didn't say a word.

"You're silent. Aren't you going to counsel me against this?" Henri challenged. "Point out that mere days after taking a pious kingdom is not a good time to change the order of things so drastically. That I should act more tactically to ensure I can survive the backlash from my people. That I shouldn't be inviting the wrath of the gods on top of everything else."

"No," Malik replied simply. "You are king of these lands. Merovian kings don't interfere with each other's reign."

Right. Malik was no longer his advisor. He was a king. If they survived the war to come, Malik would leave to govern his own kingdom and Henri would return to rule his. There would be no reason to see each other except to negotiate trade agreements, and even those could be settled through correspondence or viziers. They would go their separate ways, to opposite ends of the country, and lead separate lives. Perhaps Malik would send for Aras to join him in his new kingdom as king consort. The thought had Henri clenching his jaw as violent urges flooded his veins.

"Besides, you're right. There is never a wrong time for justice. And Tahlia would want us to stop the sacrifices."

Henri slightly softened at the mention of Tahlia. If they survived the war, she would be forced to choose between them; stay with Henri or follow Malik to his new kingdom. She would feel torn, but selfishly Henri hoped she stayed with him. If he lost them both, he wasn't sure he would ever recover.

Henri's expression quickly hardened. "Good."

As he turned to depart, Malik grabbed his arm firmly. "I meant what I said when I declared myself for you. No matter what decisions you make, I will stand by your side. And when your enemies come for you, be them gods or kings or mortals, I will fight for you."

Henri held his gaze hostage, their faces so near he could feel Malik's breath on his skin. "And I meant what I said. I don't need you to fight my battles for me."

"I'm not."

"What do you call going behind my back and challenging the other Merovian kings?"

"Strategic. You wouldn't have survived three kings and dozens of Rouhan nobles and we both know it. I was trying to give you a chance."

"You should have been honest with me," Henri growled.

"You never would have let me."

"Let you sacrifice your life for mine? You're damn right I wouldn't have!"

An awkward cough drew their attention to the Naiab warriors still assembled in the courtyard, awaiting orders.

Henri winced inwardly. "This is not the time or the place to discuss this."

"Agreed. I will come to your chamber tonight." Malik released his arm.

"No. What's done is done. There is nothing to discuss," Henri said dismissively.

"Fine, we won't talk, but I'm not leaving you alone while Nasir is still sending his assassins."

"I am well protected. I have no need of you."

Malik leaned in until their noses were almost touching and Henri found his gaze automatically drawn to his lips. "I will be in your chamber tonight, even if I have to break down the door."

Indignant anger simmered just beneath the surface as Henri tried to ignore the desire that vaulted through him. Because the words held something far stronger than a threat, they held a promise.

CHAPTER THIRTEEN

KALA

When the wagon finally came to a stop, Kala felt like she was nothing more than a sack of crushed bones. In the past day, the terrain beneath the wheels had changed from level and smooth to steep elevations and rocky ground. Hidden under the tarp, she had felt every single jolt reverberate through her body as the wagon rattled over uneven roads and trudged up what Kala presumed to be rugged mountain passes. She knew very little of Nasir's kingdom but she did know that it was situated in the high mountain region.

The temperature was slightly cooler the higher they climbed. Still, the endless jostling combined with the suffocating stale air beneath the tarp had made every breath a shallow struggle. She had tried to distract herself by wondering just how much further they had to travel. Surely the change in terrain meant they were close to their destination. Last night she had run out of food and she only had a few drops of water left in the waterskin. If they didn't arrive at Nasir's kingdom by sundown, she would need to venture out into the camp again for supplies.

Thankfully, the wagon had stopped not long after nightfall and from what she had managed to overhear from the guards, they had arrived at Nasir's palace. Kala waited until everything around her went quiet before she slowly pulled the tarp down. Fresh air filled her lungs and she gulped it down greedily. Even though darkness surrounded her, she could tell that there was a high ceiling above her instead of sky.

Kala silently stretched out her limbs before she crouched and peered over the edge of the wagon. She was in a warehouse filled with various goods. Lit sconces on the wall provided a dull glow over the crates, carts, and barrels. She couldn't see any guards patrolling but that didn't mean they weren't there. They would hardly leave a king's ransom unguarded. She would need to be careful.

Jumping from the wagon, Kala landed on the ground in a low squat but her legs trembled beneath her, weak from the lack of movement over the past few days. She cautiously wove in between the crates and wagons, keeping her eyes alert for movement in the shadows and her ears trained for the smallest of sounds. Finally, she came to the end of the warehouse and what looked to be a large set of double doors. Kala frowned. There were no soldiers standing guard by the doors. Their absence suggested they were most likely posted on the other side of it. Which meant there was every chance she was locked in.

Kala straightened and scanned her surroundings. If she was right about the guards, it meant she was alone in the warehouse. She wandered over to the large doors and placed her hands lightly against the rough wooden surface, laying her ear against it.

Silence.

She tried to peek through the keyhole but all she saw was darkness. Kala perched her hands on her hips, huffed out a breath and resisted the urge to shove the door just to test whether it was locked or not. If there were guards on the other side, she shouldn't draw attention to herself. If the door was not locked, she wouldn't exactly be able to slip past them. She turned on her heel and began exploring the warehouse, looking for another solution. A door or perhaps a window.

Nothing.

Kala chewed on the inside of her mouth as she tried to think. She needed a distraction, something to draw the guards away from their post so she could escape. She could stack up some barrels of wine and then push them over, making a large crash, but would that be enough to draw all the guards? An unexpected noise might lure one to investigate but most likely the others would stay at their post. It needed to be something bigger.

Her gaze landed on the sconces. She could set a fire. There were silks and carpets stacked on one of the wagons that would burn nicely. The room would soon fill with smoke and surely the threat of the warehouse going up in flames would be enough to draw the attention of all the guards. But what if she was wrong? What if there were no guards posted on the other side of the door and it was simply locked? The smoke might kill her before anyone noticed the warehouse was on fire. Or worse, the smoke wouldn't kill her, the flames would.

Kala tried to think of other ideas but the sinking feeling in her gut told her this was her best chance. She stacked some boxes on top of each other so that she could climb up to reach the sconce. After lifting it carefully out of its cradle, she walked back to the wagon filled with carpets and silks. Holding the sconce aloft, she hesitated a second. This was either a bold idea that would work brilliantly or a stupid idea that would get her killed. But she had never been one to back down. Kala lowered the flame onto the corner of the carpets and watched as it took hold. Then she threw it into the wagon for good measure.

It didn't take long before the whole wagon was ablaze and black smoke was choking the air. Kala ripped the hem of her kurta and wrapped it around her face, leaving only her eyes exposed. Then she quickly moved to the front of the warehouse where she crouched down low beside the door and waited. Tendrils of smoke escaped beneath the doorway, leaking to freedom. Her eyes burned and her lungs protested with every breath she took.

Precious seconds passed. Then a shout sounded and the large doors rattled as if someone was desperately trying to open them. Kala readied herself, bracing her fingers on the ground. As soon as the door opened and the guards rushed inside, she bolted. The path was surprisingly clear, with everyone too busy scrambling to fill buckets of water to pay much attention to her. She ran, trying to get her bearings, but everywhere she turned was just another brick wall leading into another stone corridor. She had thought she would escape out into the open, somewhere on the palace grounds, but now she was beginning to realize she might actually be inside the palace itself.

If that was true, it would only be a matter of time before she was discovered. With her ripped kurta, disheveled hair, and several days old stench, she wouldn't exactly go unnoticed. She would need to find a way to blend in. Something that would let her explore the palace freely until she found Nasir.

He would have only arrived a day or two before her but that was enough time for him to have already made his next move, whatever that was. Another assassination attempt? Possibly, but with at least one failure to his name, he might be looking to try something else. If Henri had survived the summit, he would now be king of every kingdom in Merovia except Nasir's, and that meant he had several armies at his command. Nasir was no longer facing a single enemy. He was facing a war.

Kala needed to find Nasir and discover what his plan was. As for what she would do with the information, she didn't know yet, but she would worry about that later. Right now, she needed a disguise.

ISA

It was weightless to travel through sand. Almost like he didn't exist at all and yet it felt like he was connected to everything. A million granules. The ancient earth. The wind. The world. He was conscious and yet not in the way he was in his human form. His thoughts were not trapped beneath skull and skin. He could feel everything, except pain. The sun did not scorch him. Gravity did not break him. He did not inhale. There was only movement, a perpetual state of transformation.

Isa propelled himself forward through the waves of the dunes, allowing himself to be shaped and molded by the elements. Because he could feel everything around him, the everlasting pulse of creation, he knew exactly where he was and where he was going. It was the ultimate freedom but at the same time it grounded him. Normally he would give himself over to it and let the elements take him where they may, but this time there was a focus to his transience, an urgency.

It had been days since Tahlia was taken. Isa did not know the king who stole her away, but he didn't have to. It was clear what any man, let alone a man of power, would want from her. Her beauty was rare. Like hearing a melody in a lifetime of silence. In a world parched and desolate, she was sweet flowing nectar. It was why she had drawn the attention of the gods. No being, mortal or immortal, could ever be indifferent once they beheld her.

But she did not belong to any of them.

She was a goddess. To be worshiped and revered, not claimed or conquered. He would find her, and whatever the king had done to her would pale in comparison to what Isa would do to him. Any man in Tahlia's presence should be brought to his knees before her. Isa would ensure that the king kneeled in pieces.

When the time came, he gathered himself, hundreds of thousands of particles swelling and churning like a reckoning. His comrades joined to form a great sandstorm, providing him with the cover he needed to fly over the wall that separated Kareem's kingdom from the Idris desert.

The instant he landed, though, everything felt very wrong. He tried to move, to drift along the wind, but he was too heavy. Each grain felt as though it was a weight sinking to the bottom of the ocean. An ocean of molten lava. The heat from the sun seared into him, scorching his surface while opposing magnetic forces took hold of him, tearing him apart.

Isa fought to keep himself together while he crawled forward along the ground. It was like swimming against a tide, he was relentlessly being pushed back again. Eventually he made it to the far side of a building where he sensed, through the vibrations of the sand, that he was alone. He collected himself, embracing the metamorphosis as his bones solidified, his skin stretched, and his body came into being. It was not fast and fluid, like normal, but sluggish and dense. Shifting into sand usually depleted him of energy and triggered a voracious hunger, but this time he felt sick. He looked down at his bare chest and arms, studying the tattoos of water that flowed just beneath his skin and the shifting sand encased within them.

Black sand.

Isa stilled. He was aware that Kareem's kingdom was known for its black sand, but he hadn't thought anything of it. He had been able to move freely through all other types of sand, there was no reason to suspect black sand would be any different. Yet, it clearly was. He sensed an insidious infection spreading within him, as if a darkness was infiltrating his veins, taking root in his soul. His emotions felt heightened. Mutinous. Dangerous.

He had come for revenge and justice, to kill Kareem, but now it didn't feel like enough. He wanted more. To obliterate every man and woman who had ever looked at Tahlia the wrong way. Who had touched her skin without her consent. Whose words had caused her to hurt or fear. They didn't deserve to live in a world where she breathed. He would end them all. Slowly. Their pleas for mercy, their feeble excuses, would be shallow echoes on the wind. The streets of the city would turn red with their blood. He would pile the bones of their carcasses like treasure at her feet.

Isa threw up.

The reflex broke through his addled mind, interrupting the dark thoughts that had seized him. He felt his awareness snap back into place. The black sand was doing more than infecting his body, it was altering his mind. Isa wondered if the water goddess knew about the black sand. The effect it had on his sand wielding abilities. The way it polluted him. The idea of her not knowing was nearly impossible. If he had learned anything in his short life living amongst a goddess, it was that there was very little she did not know, and everything had a history.

His questions about the black sand would have to wait, though. He refused to retreat into the Idris desert and there was no time to change plan. He needed to find Tahlia and kill Kareem. If that meant injecting himself with obsidian poison then so be it. He would resist the dark urges that were seeping into his soul and maintain a hold of himself until he could rid his system of the black sand. He would only be exposed to it for a day or two at the most. With any luck, the affliction would leave him when he left the kingdom and he would never have cause to return.

KALA

Kala held the carafe of wine in both hands as she walked down another endless corridor. The wine sloshed inside the clay vessel and her arms grew weary from carrying it, but at least no one questioned her as they walked past. Dressed as a servant, she was too unimportant for courtiers to take note of, and most of the other servants were too busy to care about what she was doing.

She had managed to steal a tunic from the kitchens, where she hurriedly washed her face and arms before swiping the carafe to complete her disguise. She had even taken care to re-braid her hair in an effort to neaten her appearance, though it still smelled like smoke. It couldn't be helped. If anyone questioned her, she could simply say she had been tending to the fires in the kitchen. Lying came easily when her life depended on it.

As Kala navigated through the maze of chambers and halls, she noted the differences between Nasir's palace and Henri's. Henri's was open, like the desert that surrounded it. Most rooms and hallways were not enclosed, but rather led out onto spacious balconies or wrap-around terraces. Some rooms simply lacked walls, offering panoramic views of the landscape. There were beautiful thick marble pillars, mosaic tiled floors, countless courtyards, and tranquil bubbling fountains.

Nasir's palace was all stone walls and a network of steep staircases connecting multiple levels. From what she could tell, when she glanced out of the only window she had been able to find, the palace was built on the towering peak of a mountain. The city was sprawled at its base, in a valley surrounded by other mountains. Inside, the palace lacked beauty and ornaments, but there was something about it that intrigued her. Perhaps it was its unusual design. The way it sat like a beacon, lording itself over the land below.

Certainly, it suited Nasir's aspirations to rise above everyone else. Which was the very reason Kala decided to climb every staircase she found. She would bet her last coin that Nasir's chamber would be on the highest level of the palace. It was simply a matter of learning which level was the highest. Her legs were burning by the time she rounded a corner to find herself face to face with several guards. She froze, despite her instinct to run, but then she realized so many guards were likely protecting the king's quarter.

Her steps were shaky as she forced herself to keep walking. The guards didn't stop her but she felt their eyes watching her every move. The problem was, she had no idea where she was going. There were several doors on either side of the hallway to choose from. She did not want to look like a fool, or worse, like she didn't belong there. Her cheeks heated, knowing she was being watched, but she had no time to second guess herself; she chose a door and opened it.

"The king is not in his bedchamber."

Kala halted in the doorway and glanced back at the guards. They were smirking at her. Evidently, they were bored and she was providing entertainment. She immediately hated every single one of them.

"Where is he?" Kala knew she should keep her voice meek and her eyes trained on the floor but instead her tone was clipped and her stare a blatant challenge.

"Give me a swig of that wine, girl, and I'll tell you."

Kala narrowed her eyes at the guard, as if he were simple. "This is the king's wine."

"And you're just a servant. For now. Who knows what will become of you if you fail to deliver the king his wine?"

"Probably the same thing that will become of you if I tell the king you polluted his wine with your stupid mouth."

Too far.

The guard's face turned molten as his comrades burst into laughter at his expense. "You little shit."

He took a menacing step toward her but then another man rounded the corner, his movements rushed as he headed straight for them. The man's appearance signaled that he was not a servant or a courtier.

"The king sent for me?" he asked, his voice nervous.

The guard gritted his teeth at the man's interruption. "You're the messenger?"

The man nodded nervously as he brushed his tunic down with his hands.

The guard waved in the direction of a door opposite her. "He's in the assembly room."

The messenger strode past her as if she did not exist and gave a shallow knock on the door before entering. Kala smiled with poisoned sweetness at the guard before following directly behind the messenger.

The moment she stepped inside the room, her eyes locked onto Nasir. He stood bent over a large table, studying a map spread out in front of him. She couldn't make out any details of the map. It was a collection of lines and symbols and words.

Another man stood a short distance behind Nasir, an advisor perhaps. "The messenger is here, Kafei."

Nasir lifted his head and Kala shrunk further behind the messenger. It was unlikely that Nasir would recognize her, but she couldn't chance it. She needed to get close enough to learn whatever he was planning but be invisible enough for him not to care about spilling secrets in her presence. At the sound of crinkling parchment, Kala peeked out from behind the messenger. Nasir was busy tending to something, so she took the chance to dart over to the nearest table. She placed the carafe down and tried to look busy. In truth, there was nothing for her hands to do, which made her feel awkward and exposed.

"You will ensure that these letters are delivered to the kings of Merovia at once."

Kala glanced over her shoulder to see Nasir hand three scroll tubes to the messenger. *Three.* Sweat broke out beneath her clothes as she considered which three kings had survived the summit. She had witnessed Malik kill Dahane, making Malik king by conquest, but what if Ozkan and Kareem had also survived? That would mean Henri was dead. Or perhaps Malik had fallen and Henri had survived. She refused to believe it. Henri and Malik would have defended each other to their dying breath. They wouldn't have stopped until they defeated their enemies, which meant one of the kings had escaped. Perhaps Ele had failed to stop Kareem from taking Tahlia. Anxiety pricked at her skin as the thought festered in her mind.

"By the end of the week, they will all be dead," Nasir said.

Kala's spine locked.

"Yes, Kafei." The messenger began walking backward.

Her pulse spiked, sending her heart racing. She didn't know what to do. Leave would be the obvious choice. With the carafe delivered, she no longer had a reason to be in the room. But if she left, there was no guarantee she would get another chance to come back. She might never find out what Nasir was plotting. The only other choice was to quickly hide somewhere. Perhaps they would not notice her and she could overhear more of Nasir's plans. Kala chanced a look over her shoulder at Nasir who had already refocused on the map in front of him, but the man standing behind him was eyeing her with suspicion.

Damn it.

Kala almost knocked the carafe over as she stumbled into an awkward bow before walking backward out the door. She tried to ignore the bitter taste of failure and the sneer of the guards as she trailed behind the messenger, eyeing the scrolls in his hand with envy. If Ele were here, he would find a way to steal one of the scrolls and learn Nasir's plan. But Ele wasn't here. And Kala couldn't read. Which meant she would just have to find another way to disrupt Nasir's plot.

TAHLIA

The journey to Kareem's kingdom was a haze of sand and sun and terror. His soldiers had escorted them on horseback as they fled across the border. The guards made no attempt to stop them from leaving, which doused Tahlia's hope of rescue and made her doubt whether Henri had in fact survived the summit. If he lived, he would have come for her by now. But if he lived, he would have found Ele's lifeless body and perhaps there was no saving any of them after that.

Kareem had forced Tahlia to share a saddle with him. Now that he finally had her in his possession, it was like he couldn't bear to let her out of his grasp. His foul breath on her neck and his wandering hands were the only things that provoked her out of her deep despair, if only momentarily. She didn't fight him. There was nothing she could do to stop him, so she did nothing. They continued riding for days. She had thought Kareem would take pleasure in violating her the first night they set up camp but apart from pawing at her during the day, with his stiff cock pressed against her backside, he hadn't forced himself inside her. Now, standing in his bedchamber, she realized why.

The silk dress was barely more than a strip of material. It lay sprawled across a large round bed alongside bands of small bells for her ankles and wrists. The irony was that she was still wearing the bells she had adorned herself with on the morning of the summit, though they were now tarnished by the desert salt and sand. Paints had also been set out on a tray across the bed, next to various oils and perfumes.

Tahlia felt Kareem at her back as he stepped up behind her. He took a fistful of her dark, thick hair and she braced for him to yank it out of her scalp but instead she heard him sniff it.

"You don't smell like a rose. You smell like a horse; sweaty and well ridden."

The taunt was like a blunt blade. Tahlia simply stared straight ahead into nothingness. Men like Kareem were pitifully simple. The line between carnal desire and the violent urge to destroy blurred until it melded into a single intense craving; power. To control. The need to dominate, subjugate and humiliate. It was a high unlike any other. An orgasm for the ego. An addiction for the depraved. Kareem knew that there were infinite ways to break someone. Whether one well-placed blow or a thousand tiny cuts, the result would be the same; she would bleed out eventually. Sometimes the soul was easier to drain than the body or the mind.

"A servant will attend to you and I expect you to clean yourself up and present yourself to me as the silk rose. You are not worthy of me in the state you're in. I will have nothing less than what I was promised."

The words pricked at the edge of her senses and crawled through the fog of her detachment. The memory of Kareem's eyes shifting into something otherworldly made her lungs suck in a shattered breath. The orbs of the gods' eyes had been both captivating and terrifying as they stared back at her. They had gleamed with an irresistible beauty that concealed a dark, calculated intent.

"You made a deal with a god." Tahlia's voice sounded rough after remaining silent for several days. "Why does he need you?"

Tahlia whimpered as Kareem yanked her back by the hair to sneer down at her. "I am a king."

"He is a god," Tahlia protested feebly.

Kareem snickered, his eyes roaming down her throat to the cleft between her breasts. "For all their power, the gods cannot experience the pleasures of the flesh. He proposed a bargain; I would be his vessel so we could both enjoy you, and then I would sacrifice you to the god of fire and ash so he could claim you for all eternity."

Kareem shoved her to the ground at his feet and she landed hard on the marble floor. It was more than she could bear. The thought of seeing those eyes again, hovering over her as he penetrated her soul, sent violent shivers through her body.

"In return, I will have a god for an ally. Nasir thinks he's so clever with his aqueduct and his schemes. For years he's been plotting to kill us kings and take Merovia for himself, but I won't need an army or a war or a summit to take this country because I'll have a god."

Tahlia sat on her heels, her spine curving beneath the weight of her fate. It was fitting, really. She had stolen her life from the altar of the gods and she had traded her dignity for the wealth and protection of kings. Now both would take their revenge. She had never really had the power to change anything in the tapestry of her life, she had only managed to delay the stitches. Still, she couldn't bring herself to regret the choices she'd made. There had been moments of pure joy; dancing in the street of a festival, feeling true freedom, witnessing unconditional love, and being part of something greater than herself. It didn't make it right but nor did it take away from those moments. They were as precious as jewels, crystalized forever in her memory.

An urgent knock at the door did not spur Tahlia to turn around but she was vaguely aware of someone entering the room.

"Apologies, Kafei, but there has been a disturbance."

"What kind of disturbance?" Kareem demanded.

"An assault on the wall. It's hard to explain. You must come see for yourself."

Tahlia's shoulders lifted slightly as she tilted her head to the side, hoping to hear more. An assault on the wall. Had Henri come for her after all? But if he had, the man would have said so and not been so cryptic about the threat. As for Henri, he would not have come from the Idris desert. He would have marched his army across the border.

Isa.

The Naiab were attacking the wall.

"When I return, I expect to see the silk rose." The words were laced with warning.

She heard Kareem's sandals slap against the floor until he left the room. Rising unsteadily to her feet, Tahlia turned to stare at the door behind her. It was most likely locked and heavily guarded. There was no escape. Despite the possibility of the Naiab attacking the wall, Tahlia couldn't quite convince herself to have hope. She had lost all remnants of it days ago. Even if she managed to survive Kareem, she would not survive the gods. It was all pointless. Isa should never have come.

But he had.

He had crossed the Idris desert for her, even though he knew her fate. The Naiab would be grossly outnumbered and now Kareem had a god on his side. If Isa was prepared to fight for her, she needed to fight for herself.

Tahlia clenched her hands into determined fists. Isa would not find her trembling and defenseless. She may not be a soldier or a warrior. She didn't know how to wield a shamshir and she had never taken a life before. But she was a woman with nothing left to lose, which made her the most dangerous predator in the kingdom.

She owed it to Ele to fight. He had died trying to protect her and she refused for his death to go unavenged. Tahlia swore, before all the gods and goddesses that hunted her, that before she left this human life, she would hold Kareem's bloody heart in her hands.

CHAPTER FOURTEEN

HENRI

The sight of Henri's army marching into his new kingdom resembled a mirage. He couldn't quite believe his eyes and yet it looked so real. Up until that moment, Henri still thought Inaya would defy his order and take the opportunity to seize his kingdom for herself. Instead, she had sent a message along with his army that she remained as regent and was managing his affairs to ensure his reign was secure. Malik's reaction to seeing the missive told Henri he had never doubted her for a second. It had eased some of his own tension, though. It was enough that he was facing a battle with two Merovian kings. He didn't need to be dealing with a coup as well.

The grounds of the palace now resembled a war camp. Henri's army, combined with his newly acquired militia, and bolstered by the small but powerful force of the Naiab warriors, was formidable. The last time he had commanded a military this large was in the Red Wood after he killed their leader, King Heroux. Unable to fit in the barracks, Henri's soldiers had erected their tents in the courtyards surrounding the palace. Everywhere he looked, as he prowled the perimeter of his balcony, were the tops of black tents. Henri could already see there was not enough space left to house Malik's army which was expected to arrive in the next few days. They would need to be accommodated in the Old City. Perhaps the newly vacant Hara's were the perfect lodgings.

On his orders, Malik and the Naiab had raided the Hara's and decreed an end to human sacrifice. The people had been outraged, as had most of his guards, but no one more so than the priests. They had called endless curses down upon him and invited the gods to unleash their wrath in revenge.

Henri was still waiting.

He had allowed the priests to continue all their other duties and rituals. As if trying to make up for the lack of human blood being spilled, they had increased their other offerings and sacrifices of animals. The people of the Old City were unnerved, not only by the decree, but the lack of response from the gods to Henri's blatant sacrilege. But they hadn't risen up against him. They seemed to be waiting for a sign from the gods to render judgment. The chosen ones, however, had not been willing to wait. They resisted being returned to their mortal origins and some even tried to slit their own throats in an attempt to ascend to divinity. Henri hoped they would find a new purpose for their lives that didn't involve their deaths.

"You're hardly limping anymore."

Henri turned to find Malik standing a respectable distance behind him. It was true, his leg was improving, but according to the healer the stitches would need to remain for at least another week. He could sympathize with Ele's irritable mood at being confined to resting in bed. Being restricted in movement grated on him as well, and he had to resist the daily urge to pull the stitches out himself.

From all appearances, Malik's arm had healed completely. He never showed any signs that it was bothering him. When Malik had come to his bedchamber as promised, Henri had stolen a glimpse of the wound through the sliver of space between the two wooden screens of the washroom. It was just wide enough to see the angry gash stitched up across his bicep. Henri's eyes had lingered on his muscular frame as Malik bathed, but then he quickly looked away, annoyed at his own weakness.

Nothing had happened between them that night or any other night. Malik had slept on the divan and Henri had shared his bed with Ele. Last night, though, Malik had not come to his bedchamber at all. Henri assumed it was because his army had arrived and Malik had concluded that he was well protected and had no need of him anymore. Still, his wordless absence grated on Henri. In fact, they hadn't really spoken in days. At least not about what had happened at the summit, or the fact that Malik was now king, or his plans for when the war was over. Their brief exchanges had been restricted to information regarding their forces and resources, preparations for war, and Nasir's likely next move.

To Henri's surprise, there had been no more assassination attempts. The interrogation of the assassin he had caught proved largely futile, if not enjoyable. The man had denied knowledge of Nasir's plans and acquaintances with any other spies in Nasir's employ, but Henri knew there had to be more lurking nearby. Among his servants. His guards. No one could be trusted and nowhere was safe until he killed Nasir.

"I'll be able to ride out with our armies in a week," Henri informed him.

"And Ele?"

"He still insists on coming with us. He's convinced Kala followed Nasir back to his kingdom."

"What do you think?"

Henri considered the scrappy girl he had met that day in the Thaka, holding a slingshot. "I think Kala shouldn't be underestimated. Did you need something?"

If Henri's tone sounded brash, Malik didn't even flinch. "No."

Malik made to leave and Henri's heart stuttered, but then Malik hesitated as a servant approached them with two scrolls in his hand. The servant lowered his eyes demurely as he delivered a scroll to each of them before retreating backward and then bowing low. Henri and Malik exchanged wary glances before Henri began to open the tube.

"Wait. Stop." Malik rushed at him, snatching the scroll from his hand. "If it's from Nasir the parchment could be poisoned."

"What?"

"The page could be laced with poison, ingested through touch."

"Then why are you opening it?" Henri challenged as Malik emptied the tube and unfolded the parchment in his hands.

"Because one of us has to read it."

Henri's nostrils flared as his eyes blazed with fury. "Stop doing that! Stop thinking my life is more important than yours."

"I can't," Malik returned simply. "That is what it is to love someone, Henri."

Henri clenched his mouth closed to stop angry words from bursting forth. He knew damned well what it was to love. He had been willing to sacrifice his life several times over to protect those he cared about.

"And what is love without trust?" Henri shot back.

Malik met his stare with infuriating composure. "Do you want me to apologize for trying to save your life?"

"I want you to be honest with me. Always. No matter the cost."

They regarded each other for a heavy moment. It felt like it stretched on for an eternity. Malik was the first to look away, his gaze lowering to the parchment that evidently was not poisoned. Henri moved a step closer until they stood shoulder to shoulder, their eyes screening the words and then re-reading them, absorbing them. It was an ultimatum. Nasir demanded that Henri abdicate his claim to kingship and surrender his lands. If he refused, Nasir would cut off the water supply to his people in two days. Malik shoved the parchment under the crook of his arm to allow him to open the second tube and unfurl the scroll.

After a moment of reading, Malik announced, "It's exactly the same, only addressed to me. Which means Kareem would have received one as well."

"We thought Nasir's next move would be against me but it's against Merovia." Henri's voice was flat as his mind calculated the devastating implications.

To deny access to water across all of Merovia, except his own kingdom, was catastrophic. Hundreds of thousands of people would die if the kings of Merovia did not submit to Nasir's will.

"People can survive without water for two days, maybe three," Malik said.

Their gazes locked, the disturbing truth passing between them. If they relinquished their claims to kingship, Nasir would execute them and become the sole king of Merovia. All that they had fought for would have been for nothing. But if they didn't relinquish their claims, their people would be dead within the week. There would be no war because their armies would dead.

Malik swore angrily. "We should have foreseen this."

"There was no way we could have known he would do this."

"I should have known." Malik shook his head at himself. "Nasir has held this card the whole time. He'd be a fool not to use it."

"I wouldn't call a man unwilling to commit mass genocide a fool."

"That's why you're a better king than all of us," Malik returned gravely.

Henri's forehead creased with tension. If it were anyone else, he might consider that they were bluffing but this was Nasir. He was capable of anything, especially if it meant he didn't have to get his hands dirty. It would be so easy to wipe out all his rivals from the safety of his palace. To impose his reign on the entire country through one act. Water was life. There was no alternative.

"You have that same look on your face when you learned that the kings of Merovia intended to kill you in three months so you invited them all to dinner," Malik said warily.

"I will send word to Inaya and instruct my people to store as much water as they can over the next two days. You should do the same for your people."

"We'll be buying them days at best. It won't be enough."

"Nasir's kingdom is a three day ride from here. I will have my army assembled and ready to move out at dawn. Send word to yours to meet us there. If Nasir wants what's mine, he's going to have to fight me for it."

TAHLIA

When Kareem returned, he was greeted by the silk rose. Tahlia had bathed in scented water and lathered her long dark hair in oils. She had slipped on the silk dress that had been laid out for her, letting the fabric hug the swell of her breasts and the width of her hips, leaving her abdomen, arms and legs tantalizingly exposed. Bands of tiny bells tinkled lightly at her every movement, providing stark contrast to the heavy fear that coiled in her gut. Kohl lined her emerald eyes and her lips were stained blood red. It had been hard mastering a steady hand to paint the delicate floral designs over her body but she had managed it through sheer determination.

At any other time, the familiar routine would have brought her a sense of comfort and even a twinge of excitement at the opportunity to perform for an audience. When Tahlia became the silk rose, she became powerful. Commanding the attention of influential men, manipulating their desires, but always staying just out of reach. Except this time was different. She knew why Kareem had insisted she present herself as the silk rose. He wished to strip her of her power, disintegrate the identity she had carefully crafted for herself, until she was nothing and no one of value. Only then would he be satisfied. And once he was satisfied, he would kill her.

"Kafei." Her voice was like honey, smooth and sweet.

Kareem looked angry enough to drive his shamshir right through her soft belly. Whatever had happened on the wall had perturbed him. Tahlia tried to ignore the tremble of panic beneath her perfumed skin.

"You've been making friends it seems." He stalked toward her, every step filled with malice. "But if you think your sand wielders will be able to save you, you're wrong. Not even Nasir with his threats and his underground water system can win against me now. I'll drown his entire kingdom before I give in to his demands."

Tahlia wasn't sure what he was talking about but she didn't have time to ponder it before his meaty hands reached out to seize her.

She ducked out of the way. "Kafei, you wanted the silk rose. Let me dance for you."

Kareem hesitated, his posture and expression strained with anger as he considered her proposal.

She was terrified his threadbare control might snap, so she added, "There is no need to send for a musician. My bells are enough. Please, sit. Let me show you."

Kareem slowly circled her, as if he were still fighting his baser instinct, but he forced himself to sink down on the edge of the round bed. Tahlia breathed. His eyes roamed her smooth skin greedily, no doubt imagining which part of her flesh he would devour first. Dread surged through her limbs, locking them in place, but she consciously soothed her body to relax. Then, when she was ready, she began to move.

The pulse of a drum echoed in her mind along with the plucked strings of a sitar. She could almost hear the melody filling the room, compelling her to dance. Her body rolled like liquid and yet each movement was precise. From the turn of her wrist to the arch of her hip, she punctuated the beat, holding the king captive. She could feel Kareem's stare on her like a wine stain on a fine garment. Still, she did not let him tarnish her performance. Her fingers were long and soft as she weaved them above her head, as if calling forth an enchantment. Then she folded forwards, elongating her limbs like they weren't bound by bones. Her dark curls fell like a curtain on either side of her head but drew back when she lifted her chin in a sultry gaze.

Usually, she took pleasure from seeing the looks on men's faces as she weaved her spell, but though she was sure her dance was holding Kareem spellbound, she avoided looking at him. Instead, she lost herself to the movement. She deserted her mind and embraced the freedom of motion until she disappeared within it completely. This had always been her touchstone, her sanctuary. Her body told a story that no words ever could. It conveyed every emotion. It revealed every truth.

When she came back to herself, her gaze found the dark orbs of a god watching her. Tahlia's grace faltered but she quickly recovered it. The spheres seemed to flicker as if Kareem was trying to wrestle back control of his body. Amusement tugged at his otherwise tight lips. Tahlia wasn't sure whether the god of beauty and fertility was enjoying her performance or the internal wrestling match with Kareem but either way, he was entertained. Because he was in control. Kareem was his puppet just as much as she was and they would both dance to his strings.

Her heart throbbed in quiet terror. Since the day she fled the Hara as a child, Tahlia had feared drawing the attention of the gods. Now she was openly performing for one. The god who had chosen her as his personal sacrifice, who wished to cage her soul for all eternity. Her nightmare had manifested and it was so much worse than she could have imagined. She could feel her panic rising, her composure breaking as her thoughts began spiraling. Tahlia latched on to another memory. Ele drawing his shamshir, brandishing the blade as if he were full grown. Ele charging a man twice his size, a king, with not an ounce of fear or hesitation. Ele collapsing to the floor, his small hand clutching at the gaping wound in his chest.

Tahlia's fear melted like ice held over a flame. Revenge forged her bones. The music faded from her mind only to be replaced by the rush of blood in her ears. If she was going to die tonight at the hands of a god, if these were the moments of her human life, her last breaths, she would make them worth more than any other moment in her life. Tahlia swept into a series of tight circles, spinning with precision and captivating beauty. Faster and faster she twirled, getting closer and closer to Kareem. Her hand was a blur as it reached for the blade still hidden within the dark waves of her hair and plunged it deep into Kareem's chest.

Crimson blood spurted from an artery and the vile taste of copper hit her lips. Tahlia was so close that she saw the moment the god abandoned Kareem to his body and his human irises returned. In that split second, Kareem's expression morphed from blatant disbelief to a torrent of anger but Tahlia's face remained impassive, even as she yanked the blade out of his flesh and then plunged it back in. She didn't think about what she was doing as she mangled his flesh, cutting into his muscle, and hacking away at his insides. She only saw Ele, the blade run through his small chest, staggering backward from the unexpected blow. And then she was cutting it free, tearing it out of the cavity, and holding it in her hands.

Kareem's heart.

She had thought her hands would shake but they didn't. She had thought she would feel so many things but she felt nothing. It shouldn't have been this easy to take a life. If Kareem had been in control of his body, perhaps her surprise attack would not have been successful. But the god, being immortal, had not seen it coming. He would have spared no thought for his vessel's vulnerability. The gods were eternally complacent in all things. Their existence was assured. They were not used to defending their lives. It shouldn't have been that easy and yet it was done and she had no regrets. She simply stared at the slippery, bleeding organ in her hand.

"Goddess."

Tahlia whirled around, brandishing the blade in one hand and the heart in the other. Isa stood before her, his chest heaving as if he had run across the entire expanse of the Idris desert to get to her. His corded muscles pulled tight around his wide frame in obvious exhaustion and his skin, usually glowing with a golden hue, looked pale and gray. Immediately her gaze was drawn to the tattoos that normally shimmered turquoise beneath his skin. They were black as ink.

"I came to rescue you but I see you have no need of me." His voice was strained, as if he were in pain.

"I ...," Tahlia stammered as the adrenaline and detachment drained from her veins. She dropped the heart and it landed on the floor with a wet slap. Somewhere in the back of her mind she knew she didn't need to justify her actions but now that someone else had seen what she had done, the horror of how far she had gone, she felt vulnerable. "I avenged Ele."

"He'll be disappointed to know that. You have robbed him of his chance for revenge." Isa forced a brittle smile as Tahlia's eyes widened and her mouth gaped in disbelief. "The boy lives."

Tahlia's legs buckled but Isa moved swiftly to reach her side, steadying her within his solid embrace.

"How?" She choked. "I saw him. I saw the blade run him through."

"It was a fatal wound," Isa conceded. "Your king prayed to the goddess of endings and beginnings."

"Henri's alive?"

"Both your lovers live."

Tahlia released a broken sob as her bloody fingernails clutched into the flesh of his forearms.

"Your king made a deal with the goddess; the boy's ending for someone else's ending or beginning."

"He what?" Tahlia's mind felt like it was swimming, her thoughts bobbing to the surface then drowning again. "No. The gods cannot be trusted."

"The boy lives," Isa repeated.

He said it as if it solved everything. Ele was alive. Wasn't that all that mattered? It was and yet Tahlia couldn't help the feeling that something terrible had been set in motion. She forced herself to ignore it. What was done was done. She felt her limbs solidify again but she didn't rush to move out of Isa's arms. He was warm and firm and somehow gave her the illusion of feeling safe.

She wasn't.

"Kareem also made a deal with the god of beauty and fertility. In exchange for his support, Kareem let the god inhabit him to ..." She couldn't say the words.

Isa didn't press. He simply swept a wave of dark hair back from her tear-filled eyes. The gesture was so soft and gentle that she hardly felt it at all. Yet she felt every second of it.

"Gods cannot be killed but mortals can be," he murmured.

"I killed his vessel. He's probably more enraged at me than ever before." Tahlia stepped out of Isa's embrace and crossed her arms tightly over her chest, trying to hold herself together. "He will come for me soon. There is no changing my fate."

"Maybe. But there is something you can do to change your mortal one." Satisfaction edged his mouth. "Cut off the bastard's beard."

Tahlia's lips parted in shock. He couldn't be serious. She cast her eyes back at Kareem to find that his body had slumped to the floor at the end of the bed like a child's doll whose straw had been plucked out.

Tahlia tried to speak but the words caught in her throat. She forced them out anyway. "There has never been a queen of Merovia."

"You will be the first. Queen of the black sands."

Tahlia blinked at the title, how smoothly it rolled off his tongue. She had been chosen by the gods. She had become the infamous silk rose. Was she now to become a queen of Merovia?

"No one will accept me," her voice quivered.

"I will. My people will. Henri's kingdom will, as will Malik's. Together, we can usher in a new age for Merovia. An age of prosperity and equality and freedom."

It was madness. And yet she felt something shift inside her, like a puzzle piece locking into place. Tahlia tentatively walked over to Kareem's lifeless body. It sounded odd, after cutting his heart out of his chest, but she didn't want to touch him. There was no avoiding it, though. Isa didn't offer to help, he simply waited. This was her choice. If she chose to claim Kareem's kingship, she would need to do it with her own two hands. Tahlia laid the king's head on the ground and tilted his head back. She sawed off the blood-stained beard, hacking at it with grim determination. Because she was no longer the plaything of kings.

She was queen.

CHAPTER FIFTEEN

ISA

Isa had instructed Tahlia to barricade herself inside the former king's bedchamber until he could gather his men. By the time they all breached the wall and assembled near the palace, it was dawn. The black sand swirled beneath their skin, spreading like a slow poison. From the looks on their faces, they all felt its sinister power. It was changing them. Isa knew his men were trying to remain calm and focused, but the unspoken questions lingered between them. Isa had no answers for them. He only hoped that once they left the kingdom, the black sand would filter out of their systems and they would return to normal. In the meantime, though, they would need to adapt as best they could to its noxious effects.

Isa could ignore the toxic sickness in his gut, the heaviness seeping into his bones, but it was the heightened emotions that were threatening his self-control. The vicious mood swings were proving almost uncontainable. When he saw Kareem choking on his own blood, he had wanted to tear him apart until the marble floor was littered with pieces of him. He wished he could have arrived minutes earlier so he could have stayed Tahlia's hand only to prolong Kareem's death over several luxurious hours. He would have taken his eyes first. Then his tongue. He would have sliced off ears, nails and limbs until eventually directing his ministrations to the internal organs.

When his focus shifted to Tahlia, Isa had almost lost control entirely. Lust had flooded his senses, blinding him like a feral beast in heat. He had wanted to take her there and then, while Kareem watched as he lay dying. He had wanted to fuck her until she forgot every man who had ever touched her. His claiming would have been so deep, so thorough, that her body would never respond to anyone else for the rest of her days. She would only open herself to him. She would only come at his touch.

The strength it took to resist the carnal urge was inhuman. His body, coiled tight from repression, was spoiling for a fight when Isa and his men stormed the palace to seize control. It was not as easy as it should have been. Shifting between skin and sand was usually effortless, but the black sand made their movements sluggish and heavy. The transformation was punishing. Still, they forced themselves to fight, shifting where necessary, and remaining in their human form as much as they could. With every life Isa took, he felt like he was feeding a rabid creature. One that starved for fear and blood and destruction. He had never relished killing before but now he enjoyed every second of it like some high he couldn't come down from. The power. The brutality.

It took every last shred of will power not to slaughter them all. With the palace guards butchered or brought to heel, they had announced Kareem's death to the people, quite unceremoniously, by hanging his body in the market square. His beard was sawn off and his chest was cracked wide open, the gaping absence of his heart drawing gasps from the crowd. The rumors had started before they even strung him up; their king had been murdered by his courtesan who was really a sorceress who ate human hearts and led an army of magical sandmen. The silk rose was really Nasir's assassin and Kareem, having been spellbound by her, had unwittingly fallen for one of Nasir's plots to take his kingdom. Or Isa's personal favorite; the king had died by accident during a particularly depraved romp and the courtesan had merely taken advantage of his untimely death by claiming his kingship for herself. And his heart for sentimental purposes.

Isa didn't correct them. As long as they recognized Tahlia as queen, that was all that mattered. Once the palace was secured and Kareem's body was rotting under the morning sun, Isa stationed his men among the guard to ensure that they would not revolt against their new queen. Anyone who showed the slightest sign of dissent was swiftly dealt with. He wished he had more men to send into the streets to test the mood of the people and curtail any plans for dissent. He hoped seeing Kareem's mutilated body would be enough proof of the change in leadership but there would always be those who challenged a claim. Especially if the claimant was a woman.

When Isa returned to the former king's bedchamber, he found Tahlia unraveling. Her face was almost white with shock and cold tears stained her cheeks. Seeing her distress somehow soothed the venomous creature within him, redirecting his every instinct to care for her.

"You're safe," he assured her. "The palace is secured. Your kingdom soon will be as well."

Her chest heaved with relief and another tear escaped down her cheek. Isa chided himself for his thoughtlessness. He hadn't considered what it would be like for her to be locked away in this chamber, waiting to know if her people would accept her as queen or if she would be dragged out and murdered on the palace steps.

"You should eat something," he urged.

"I have no appetite."

"You should get some rest then."

Tahlia nodded stiffly. "Not here. I can't be in this room a moment longer."

It was understandable. The room still bore the evidence of what had taken place. The bed sheets were stained in dried blood and Kareem's heart still sat on the floor, abandoned. Isa escorted her out into the hallway and ordered the guards to empty the entire floor of the guest's quarters.

When they were done, Isa gestured down the corridor. "Choose whichever room you like."

Tahlia quietly went from room to room until she chose one that suited her. Isa called for servants to draw a bath and deliver food, despite what she had said earlier. She looked exhausted and fragile and it made him wonder when she last ate or slept. Tahlia bathed as Isa stood guard outside, and when she finally emerged, she collapsed onto the bed and succumbed to sleep. Isa pulled a divan closer to the bed and watched over her until he couldn't keep his eyes open any longer.

When he woke, he found Tahlia's emerald eyes staring at him. She was still stretched out on her stomach across the bed, her hands curled comfortably around her face, her face framed with wild, dark hair. She was so beautiful he wasn't sure if she was real. If he could spend the rest of his life reliving one single moment, he would choose this. Now. Her.

They held each other's gaze. Tahlia didn't say anything, so neither did he. He wondered what thoughts were passing through her mind. Perhaps she couldn't speak after everything that she had endured. It made him want to charge down into the market square and defile Kareem's corpse.

"You are safe."

He knew he was repeating himself but he said it anyway, in case it was fear that paralyzed her. Her people would not rise against her. Her guards would be loyal to her. Isa would wipe them all from the face of the desert if they didn't. Tahlia blinked, as if she had heard his thoughts.

He shifted uncomfortably in his chair. "Do you need anything? You can sleep longer if you like."

Isa felt like he could sleep for an entire week. He had never pushed his abilities this far before. Traveling across the Idris desert was arduous enough, but then to lay siege to a palace and stabilize a kingdom when being poisoned from within was positively self-destructive. Ironically, he suspected the only reason he was still functioning was because of the black sand. It was noxious and sinister but it was also strangely fueling.

Tahlia didn't answer for a moment but then she rolled onto her side, propping her face up beneath her hands. "I didn't think I'd wake up."

"What?" Isa's brows furrowed in concern.

"I thought somebody would surely end me. If not my people, then the gods."

Isa's expression darkened. "Nobody will harm you as long as I'm with you."

Tahlia searched his face as if looking for the truth in his words. When she was satisfied, she asked, "What are they saying about me?"

"That you killed their king. That you are a beautiful, fearsome creature. I would have to agree with them."

"Don't lie to me."

"I'm not allowed to lie to you. I'm not allowed to flirt with you. What *can* I do with you?"

The blush in her cheeks made his pulse race. His lips spread into a satisfied smile.

"Tell me the truth," Tahlia replied, though her voice was a little unsteady.

"It doesn't matter what they're saying. You are queen."

Tahlia averted her gaze. "For how long?"

Isa leaned forward to rest his elbows on his knees, clasping his hands together in serious thought. She was right. He wasn't sure why the god of beauty and fertility hadn't come for her yet, but it was only a matter of time. Perhaps the god was enjoying watching her squirm, waiting for her impending death. Or maybe he was looking for another vessel to inhabit so he could continue to taunt her.

"I should name an heir now." Tahlia scoffed dryly. "Mine will be the shortest reign in history."

"You outsmarted the gods once."

She slid a withering gaze to him. "I can't just paint *feliq* on my skin and vanish from their notice. I will never be able to hide from them again."

"So don't hide."

"Are you suggesting I try to fight them? Gods cannot be killed."

"No," he agreed. "But they can be trapped."

Tahlia went unnaturally still as her eyes locked onto his. "What did you say?"

"The gods have few vulnerabilities but many secrets. Just like the symbol you used to hide yourself from their sight, there is a symbol that can trap them."

Her mouth fell open in disbelief. "How do you know this?"

"How did you know about *feliq*?"

Tahlia pressed her lips together in stubborn silence.

"The same person who helped you as a child, who taught you the secrets of the gods, taught me as well," he said.

Her expression told him that she didn't believe him. "Describe them to me."

"They have taken many forms over the years," his voice trailed off but he held her gaze. He hoped she heard what neither of them could say. "We have to be careful. The gods may be listening."

"That's not possible." Tahlia straightened into a seated position.

The strap of her simple white night dress slipped off her shoulder. Isa desperately wanted to right it for her. To reach out and glide his rough fingers over the silk of her skin, to trace it up over the arc of her shoulder and align it over her collarbone.

And then he wanted to rip it off with his teeth.

"Isa." Her voice demanded his refocus.

"Think about it. Think about what they told you."

Isa knew the water goddess had told Tahlia about how she came to be a divine. Her love story with the god of beauty and fertility was a tragic, cautionary tale. Though she had been naïve and soft-hearted in her mortal life, the goddess had become devious and unforgiving in her eternal existence. When she found out that her ex-lover was still collecting young beautiful girls, demanding they be sacrificed to him, she became enraged. It was she who had made it rain that night. It had woken Tahlia from her sleep and enticed her outside. She had witnessed the priests performing a sacrifice. It was no coincidence. When she tried to run from the horror of it, the water goddess was there, having taken the vessel of an old man who cleaned the Hara.

"His eyes were milky white, like sea foam," Tahlia muttered as if to herself. "I thought it was just old age."

The goddess had told Tahlia the secrets of the gods and painted *feliq* on her skin for protection before urging her to run. By setting free what her ex-lover coveted the most, she had obtained sweet revenge. Not only against him, but the other gods as well. Their wrath at the audacity of a young mortal girl defying them was like a balm to her everlasting regret. It had brought her satisfaction over the years, just knowing that Tahlia lived somewhere, free of what the gods had planned for her.

But then all of that changed when Tahlia had called out to the gods for help to save her king's life. The water goddess had been furious that day. She considered that Tahlia had wasted her gift of life. Though she never admitted it out loud, she was also concerned that Tahlia would expose the role she had played in events. Gods did not interfere with each other's realms. If there was anyone the gods wanted to punish more than Tahlia, it was the informant who shared their secrets. The water goddess had told him everything then, in case she found herself exposed.

Tahlia's features tightened in anger. "If you knew about this symbol that can trap a god, why didn't you say anything about it until now?"

"I had to save your lovers first. I made you a promise." It was obvious his answer did not please her so he tried again. "I gave you what you needed when you left the Citadel. I made it for you."

Tahlia's fingers lifted to the brass vial hanging around her neck and she studied the floral design, her eyes alighting with a new-found understanding. "Tell me what you know."

KALA

Two days had passed since she last laid eyes on Nasir. Kala had tried every excuse to gain access to the kings chamber but the guards would not let her pass. Having embarrassed one of them with her sharp tongue, she was marked. They didn't care if the king missed out on wine or fruit or fresh linen. They hoped he would kill her for her tardiness.

So she stopped trying to gain access to his chamber and instead began lingering near the stairwell leading up to the king's floor. It was hard to blend in when standing out in the open corridor but she did her best to go unnoticed, whilst paying close attention to who was coming and going. The messenger attended the king's chamber on a daily basis. Sometimes courtiers would also be summoned. It all felt a little pointless, though, if she couldn't find out what exactly was being said. But then something unexpected happened.

Nasir came down the stairs.

Kala was rooted to the spot in disbelief. His stride was purposeful, his expression serious. She wasn't sure if he was angry or simply focused. Either way, he was going somewhere to do something important. Shaking off her stupor, Kala ducked behind a corner to avoid his notice. She counted the seconds before peeking around the wall and following him at a cautious distance.

Nasir descended every floor of the palace and then kept going. Every time she thought they had reached the bottom floor he would go down another stairwell. It was difficult to get her bearings and after a while it felt like they were no longer inside the palace. If she had to guess, she would say they were within the actual mountain, perhaps even underneath it. The air was heavy and wet. It smelled of earth and decay. The only light was from a sconce that Nasir held aloft. Kala trailed its fading light as she followed him down the passageway. She had to move carefully so that her footsteps would not echo off the stone.

With every shallow heartbeat, Kala became more certain that she was about to uncover something vital. She would learn Nasir's secrets, perhaps even his entire plan. Though what she was going to do with it once when she discovered it, she didn't know. It wasn't like she could write it down and send a message to Henri. She would just have to stop Nasir some other way.

Nasir had boasted that Henri and Malik would both be dead within the week, but from what Kala had been able to observe, he was not readying his army. She had not seen generals coming and going. The palace was not a hive of activity like it would be if they were preparing for war. Clearly, Nasir had a different plan to kill Henri and Malik.

If he thought Henri or Malik would bend to his will, though, Nasir was sorely mistaken. She had seen little loyalty in her life. Her own family had turned against her, gold coins proving worthless in the face of injured pride. Kinship had quickly turned to betrayal and murder had been sold as justice. Henri and Malik were different. They were fiercely loyal to one another. They fought for each other, even when they should be enemies. They were from opposite worlds and yet they came together to create their own. Blood did not bind them. They were bound by their hearts.

It reminded her of Ele.

Boys from the Thaka were rough and mean. They respected violence and strength. Ele was different. She knew that from the first moment they met. She had thought him naïve at first but he wasn't. He was smart but he was also gentle and kind. He cared for her.

Henri had asked him to look out for her and he had. He saved her life. Tahlia had saved her life too, even though it exposed her to the eye of the gods. These strangers had become like a family to her. Not by blood or duty but by choice. By deeds. So she would follow this passageway wherever it led and she would fight to ensure that her family survived.

Eventually, the passageway morphed into a stone tunnel which opened up into an underground chamber. The entrance was manned by two guards but they seemed to relax from their positions when they saw Nasir.

"Kafei, how may we serve you?"

"I came to inspect my aqueduct."

"Of course, Kafei."

One of the guards began leading Nasir further into the chamber but the other guard remained at his post. Without Nasir's sconce, Kala was left standing in the dark. The chamber was dimly lit by torches but there was not enough shadow for her to move about without being seen. She needed to distract the remaining guard so she could slip past.

Kala looked around helplessly but all she saw was darkness. She sank to the ground, her hands desperately searching the floor for something, anything. Then she found it. It was small, only the size of a pebble, but if she threw it right it should make enough noise to echo down the passageway. Kala threw it back the way she came and it hit the wall, sending a faint reverberation down the path. The guard stirred, his interest piqued. Kala held her breath. She thought she might have to look for another stone but the guard reluctantly left his post to investigate. He walked straight past her as she flattened herself against the wall and the moment he did, Kala ran.

It didn't take long for her to catch up to where Nasir had gone. She tried to stay hidden in the shadows as much as possible and kept a safe distance to remain out of sight. The guard had led him into an antechamber featuring several large clay pipes that branched off into a system of tunnels. Kala had never seen anything like it. There was a loud rushing sound that filled her ears but she couldn't quite discern where it was coming from or what was making it.

"It is one of the finest aqueducts ever built, Kafei. The water enters from the dam through conduits and is regulated by gates into the pipes, passing through screens to clear the debris. The water is then channeled into these conduits, one for each kingdom. An ingenious underground canal system. The slope from the terrain helps carry the water over long distances and because it travels underground, not much is sacrificed to the sun."

Kala's eyes widened at the realization of where she was standing; Nasir's underground water system. This complicated structure of tunnels and pipes was how Nasir delivered water to the kingdoms across Merovia.

"I am aware of how it works," Nasir chided impatiently. "Turn it off."

"Kafei?" The guard's voice was hesitant.

"The kings of Merovia have not met my demands to abdicate their thrones and surrender their lands," Nasir's voice feigned grave disappointment. "It pains me that so many people will die because of their stubbornness, but I am a man of my word. Turn the water off. I want to make sure it is done."

The guard wavered for a second before relenting. "As you command, Kafei. When the gates are closed, the water flow in the conduits will be cut off."

Kala stared in horror at what was unfolding. The guard moved closer to one of the pipes where a worn lever jutted out from the wall. He took hold of it and wound it around with all his strength, causing a stone gate to slowly descend. The gate groaned as it gradually settled into place. The guard repeated the same action for the remaining pipes and every time he did, the rushing sound dissipated until there was nothing left but eerie silence.

She could hardly believe it. Nasir had just turned off the water supply to everyone in Merovia except his own kingdom.

By the end of the week, they will all be dead.

Kala had thought he meant the kings of Merovia, but he had meant everyone who did not reside in his kingdom. Hundreds of thousands of people.

"See that it stays that way. Permit no one entry down here except for me," Nasir ordered.

"Yes, Kafei."

Kala watched from the shadows, dumbstruck, as Nasir and the guard made their way back to the entrance of the tunnel. Her attention drifted to the conduits and the unsettling quiet that now filled the cavernous space because there was no water rushing through the pipes. She knew what it was like to have little access to water, to save every bead of moisture for her tongue just to keep her body from collapsing. Washing the dirt from her skin and clothes was a luxury she could never afford. Drinking until satiated was an unattainable dream. Water was the lifeblood of everything. Without it, everything and everyone would perish in a matter of days.

The urge to walk over and raise the gates was strong. But surely if she did, the guards would hear the rushing sound of water and come to investigate. She would be caught. She couldn't think of anything else to do, though. If she did nothing, very soon people would start to die. Her family would die.

Kala stepped out of the shadows and quietly made her way to the nearest pipe. It lay silent, like a sleeping beast that she did not want to wake. The lever looked old and worn. She would need all her strength just to turn it one round. And there were several levers to turn. She didn't know which pipe led to which kingdom but she supposed it didn't matter. She would need to turn all of them. Just as Kala made to reach for the lever, hands closed around her arms.

CHAPTER SIXTEEN

TAHLIA

This was a bad idea. All of her senses screamed at her, warning against it, but she had no choice. Her heart pounded so hard it felt like it might fall out of her chest. Perhaps it would be easier if it did. A quick death suddenly sounded tempting and peaceful. Tahlia shook the thought from her mind and forced her eyes to close. Then she prayed.

To *him*.

She wasn't sure how to begin or what to say. She hadn't rehearsed any words, but she figured she didn't need a speech or lengthy explanation for her decision. The god of beauty and fertility had hunted her for long enough. She was tired of running, tired of not knowing which day would be her last. If he wanted her, she was ready to give herself to him. She was ready to end her torment. This is what she said in silent prayer.

When Tahlia opened her eyes, nothing had changed. There was no evidence that he had even heard her. She stood alone in the guest bedroom she had chosen for herself yesterday. Having made the decision to give herself up, she had changed into a simple kaftan and brushed her hair one last time. She wondered if it was these mundane daily rituals the gods missed the most from their human lives. Then again, they probably didn't spare a thought for their mortal history.

Tahlia hoped she would never forget it.

Across the room, a tall mirror reflected her appearance back at her. If the god of beauty and fertility was hoping to find the silk rose, he would be sourly disappointed. Infamous courtesan for years. Queen for a day. A goddess for all eternity. She would offer herself to him as simply Tahlia. He would not reject her, of that she was certain. He had chosen her as a child, before her beauty had fully blossomed.

Tahlia anxiously pressed her fingers to the brass vial around her neck. It brought her some comfort to trace the beautiful floral design etched into it while she waited. She wondered if it would melt in the sacrificial fire that consumed her body to ashes. It was odd to think that trinkets could hold so much meaning in the span of a human life. They were, after all, nothing but objects. What gave them value was the memories attached to them. The people who had crafted them or gifted them. The symbolism they held. The promise they declared.

She wore nothing else of significance except the marking inked on the inside of her wrist, the mark of the divine. It was camouflaged within the other designs she had painted on her skin yesterday to become the silk rose. Though they wouldn't fade for several days, Isa had transferred the paints to her room this morning. They sat on the table ready for use, a sign of his confidence that she would in fact live to use them. Tahlia wandered over to the table, mindlessly running her hands over the small clay pots.

A knock at the door startled her and she looked up to see a servant enter, his head bent modestly. Isa had stationed some of his men outside her door and yet this servant had entered without any announcement from them or invitation from her. He carried nothing in his hands, no reason to be there, and he was yet to speak. Tahlia studied him warily. He was young but not too young. He was muscular, as if he had only known hard labor in his life. And he was good looking.

"I wasn't sure you heard me," Tahlia said, trying to keep her voice light and even.

The servant lifted his head and his dark orbs seized her soul. "I hear and see everything."

Tahlia swallowed hard at the veiled warning. Had he heard her earlier conversation with Isa? Did he know that the water goddess was the one who had helped her all those years ago?

"Not everything," she countered smoothly. "You lost sight of me for years."

"Years for a god is the blink of an eye." He clicked his fingers pointedly. "I found you again."

"And still, you have yet to claim me. Every day I have wondered why you haven't taken your revenge. I thought perhaps you were enjoying my suffering but then it occurred to me; gods can kill mortals but they cannot sacrifice them. That has to be done by human hands. Am I right?"

The god moved toward her, his stride slow and deliberate and dangerous. It took all of Tahlia's willpower not to move. He was trying to intimidate her and though fear was crawling up her spine, she would hold her ground.

"Did your informant tell you that?" the god challenged.

"No. I am quite skilled at reading the behavior of men. Why should gods be any different? I wondered why you needed Kareem. You didn't just want to enjoy me, you needed him to sacrifice me. You need, whoever this is that you are occupying, to sacrifice me to the god of fire and ash or else you can't receive me as a divine. I'll simply be dead."

The god came to stand a breath away from her and lifted a knuckle to graze her cheek. Her instinct was to flinch away from his touch but she allowed it. He drew the knuckle out along the bone as if coaxing her fear from within her, savoring its taste in the air.

"Now wouldn't that be a shame?" he crooned.

She hated him. Detested having his hands on her but she endured it, the practice almost second nature after years of serving as a courtesan. The difference was, she no longer had to hide her feelings. She let her repulsion permeate her entire demeanor as she stared him down.

"I offered you my life, not my body."

"Both have always been mine." His hand suddenly seized her wrist. She tried to pull away but he held her firm and turned her palm outwards. "See? I am seared into your flesh. Even the *feliq* that you painted on your skin every day to try to keep us apart is just further proof that you have never lived one day free of me."

Tahlia grit her teeth. "And your existence for the past decade has been consumed by the hunt for me."

"What a pair we make."

He released her hand and Tahlia yanked it back.

"You're right. We are bound together. It's only fitting that I mark you in return," Tahlia purred.

She collected a paintbrush from the table and dipped it into an inkpot. Then she took his wrist and turned it over to expose the veined skin. The design she painted was simple enough, the strokes neat and elegant. The god had the audacity to smirk at her as she worked, his gaze never lowering to see what she was doing. Such was the arrogance of the divine. But the moment the symbol was complete he stiffened.

Tahlia's eyes fixed on his face as she watched him try to fight it. He clenched his teeth and spluttered, his face deepening to the color of crimson as the veins in his neck bulged. His body went rigid and trembled as his eyes began to water. Yet he remained there. Standing. Whole.

It wasn't working.

He was resisting it and he was too powerful. Tahlia panicked, unsure what else to do. Suddenly his hand launched for her throat and she screamed before it gripped her in a relentless vice. He was trying to kill her. No, wait. He was trying to destroy the vial. If he managed to tear it off her, to break it, there was nothing else that could hold him. Tahlia clawed at his hand around her neck and was surprised to find that she was strong enough to pry his fingers off, one by one. He was weakening. She could see it.

Tahlia watched as the god of beauty and fertility drained from the mortal body he occupied. The irises returned to their human form and the servant crumpled to the floor unconscious while the air above him shimmered with a faint, ethereal luminescence, a blend of radiant light and shifting shadows. Tahlia didn't know how but she sensed the god was still fighting, resisting the call of his prison. Despite his power, though, the god was drawn into the brass vial around her neck. When the last wisp of light and shadow slinked inside, Tahlia snapped the lid closed and held it tight.

Her heart was lodged in her throat. Her body frozen in terror. She had just trapped a god.

In her peripheral vision, she saw Isa materializing from dispersed particles of sand on the floor. Tahlia turned to him but she could barely speak. Hanging around her neck, secured in the palm of her hand, was the god who had hunted her for years. The god of beauty and fertility.

Her captive.

Her prisoner.

The symbol that Isa taught her to paint on the mortal's skin had expelled the god from his chosen vessel. The symbol etched into the brass vial imprisoned him within it. There was no way for the god to escape unless the symbol was broken or the vial was destroyed.

"I can't believe I just did that," Tahlia choked the words out.

"I can. You are a goddess."

"No, I'm not. And I never will be." Tahlia laughed maniacally as she let that truth sink in.

She would no longer be sacrificed to the gods. Now or ever. She was free to live a mortal life without the shadow of her past hanging over her. And she was queen.

Isa just stood there, silently giving her time and space to absorb what this meant. He had been confident in her ability to execute the plan but she had thought it impossible. In her mind, it could only ever end one way; with her dead.

"I owe you my life," Tahlia said in disbelief. "Everything."

"No. You owe me a kiss."

A kiss.

Fireflies launched in Tahlia's stomach. All of a sudden, she felt incredibly self-conscious. It was senseless how the idea of a single kiss could reduce her to feeling like an innocent girl, not a woman skilled in the art of seduction. Isa was just a man and yet he was unlike any man she had ever met. He was a mystery. There was so much about him she didn't know, but what parts of him she had seen only drew her closer. He was loyal to his tribe. He was a leader among men. He had shown her more respect and restraint than any other man in her life. Infuriatingly so. It was clear from the moment they met that he desired her and still he had waited all this time.

She wanted to kiss him. Desperately. She wanted to wind her arms around his neck and press her breasts flush against his taut chest and feel his heart racing beneath hers. There wasn't an inch of his body she hadn't seen and there was nothing about him that was disappointing. His imposing figure and muscular frame exuded strength and intensity. His abdominal muscles formed the shape of an arrowhead, tempting her gaze to travel lower and linger on what he had to offer. It was intimidating. Her hands twitched with the need to touch him. To explore the length of him, to feel him hot and heavy in her palm. She wondered if he would taste like the desert sands that birthed him; all salt and warmth.

She *needed* to know.

"Goddess." Isa's voice was strained, like he was barely holding himself back.

The hunger in his stare was undeniable. His muscles flexed as his tattoos writhed beneath the surface of his skin.

Pounding. On the door.

"Not now," Isa yelled and Tahlia couldn't agree more.

The voice was muffled through the wood. "It's urgent."

Isa swore repeatedly. He retrieved a kurta and pulled it over his enormous body but it did little to hide his obvious arousal. When the Naiab warrior entered, his gaze snagged on the unconscious body at Tahlia's feet, a body she had quite forgotten about, and then flicked between them both. Tahlia was certain her cheeks were flushed. Her core was still pulsing.

Tahlia tried to sound composed as she asked, "What is it?"

"Apologies for the intrusion, Kafei, but the city is in crisis. We have no water."

Isa edged closer to Tahlia and she felt every inch of it.

"What do you mean?" Isa probed.

"There is no water running to the wells or anywhere in the kingdom. One of the guards gave me this." He handed Tahlia a rolled parchment. "He said he delivered this message to the former king and it infuriated him. He spoke of Nasir threatening to cut off the water supply."

Tahlia frowned. "He said something about that to me too."

She read the letter, her eyes widening in horror at every word.

"He's turned it off?" Isa prompted.

"To the entire country except for his kingdom. Isa" —her pleading eyes found his and his expression turned severe— "We can't let these people die."

"Henri and Malik would have also received a letter. They would have mobilized their armies immediately. They'd likely be at Nasir's border by now."

The thought of Henri and Malik marching into battle made her stomach tie up in knots.

"We have to help them," she insisted.

"It would take days to ready your army and even longer to travel to Nasir's kingdom. The war would be over by the time we arrived. Besides, their combined army would be almost three times the size of Nasir's. They won't need reinforcements."

"It's Nasir," Tahlia countered, because that single fact changed everything. Only a fool would underestimate him. "My army can stay but I'm going."

She took a step toward the door but Isa moved swiftly to block her path. "Your kingdom is volatile right now. If you leave, you risk losing it."

Tahlia huffed, exasperated, but then her mind caught on an idea. "Fine. First, I will establish myself as the undeniable queen of the black sands. Then we go to war, just you and me."

"I will fight in any war you ask me to, goddess. But what's your plan for winning your people to your side?"

Tahlia's features shifted to calm determination. "I'm going to make it rain."

KALA

Kala tried to wrestle free of the hands that seized her. She flung her arms and kicked her legs and tossed her head back. She jerked and twisted and bit down on an arm that was wrapped around her shoulders. The guard swore and released her for a precious second of freedom but she didn't make it more than two steps before slamming into the body of the second guard. He gripped her skinny arms as if he might snap them like twigs.

"I thought I heard something."

"Bitch bit me!"

The guard held her firm even as he spun her around but she didn't see the blow coming until she was doubled over, her stomach caving in from the brutal punch. She choked on air but couldn't breathe. The strike to her face that followed was almost nothing compared to the pain in her stomach. She tried to discern if her organs had burst because it certainly felt like something had split open. Or perhaps she had just become soft, used to palace life where no one ever raised a hand to her, compared to the Thaka where violence was as regular as taking a shit. Either way, she was no stranger to pain and she knew how to survive it. She reminded herself not to panic, to relax her bruised muscles and let the air in. It hurt but slowly air began to seep back into her lungs.

"What are you doing down here, girl?"

The question came from the guard who still held her in his grip, which she was strangely thankful for because it was the only thing keeping her from crumpling to the ground. The other guard just glared at her with the promise of more violence.

"I got lost," Kala replied. It wasn't even a good lie.

"Do you know what we do with liars?" the guard taunted. "We break their fingers. One for each lie."

The guard grinned and lunged for her hand. Kala squirmed, thrashing her body around, but it was no use. He clutched at her wrist, trying to pull her hand free. She balled her fingers into fists but knowing that wouldn't be enough to save them, she spat at him. The guard reared backward, wiping a gratifyingly big glob from his eye.

"You little shit!"

The next blow made her vision blink out. She wasn't sure what happened next. Kala was vaguely aware of the sensation of being carried, then dragged. The world came in and out of focus, visions and darkness. Then she was dumped on a tiled floor like a sack of grain. Forcing her eyes to open and her mind to concentrate, Kala saw that they were no longer underneath the mountain. This room was full of light. Her head was dizzy and her body hurt. She thought she might be sick but that sounded too painful for her stomach to endure.

"What's this?"

Oh gods. She knew that voice.

"We found her sneaking around in the aqueduct, Kafei."

"A servant?" Nasir asked curiously.

Kala considered playing dead but her pride wouldn't allow it. Trespasser or spy, they were going to kill her, and if this was to be her final moments, she refused to cower before her enemy. Kala braced her elbows on the tiled floor and pushed herself up into a seated position. She did a mental check for broken bones but she didn't think she had any. A small miracle. The assault must have stopped after she lost consciousness. She supposed it was less fun to beat someone when they couldn't watch her suffer.

"We found her straight after you left. We think she followed you."

Standing was painful. Kala's muscles protested being stretched out and she swayed a little on her feet, the blow to her head still affecting her balance. She raised her gaze until it met with the casually cruel eyes of Nasir. They were standing in the assembly room. She recognized the furnishings from when she had delivered his carafe of wine. In hindsight, she should have poisoned the wine.

Nasir assessed her for a moment. "I know you. The girl at the summit. You threw a dagger at me."

Kala scowled. "My aim will be better next time."

Nasir swiftly raised a hand but it was to ward off a blow from behind that Kala didn't see, a warning to the guard not to harm her. Kala snorted. It was too late for that.

"You followed me all the way into my kingdom, found your way inside my palace, and then trailed me to discover my aqueduct."

Her chest swelled with pride.

"You're one of Henri's spies then."

"His best."

An amused smile broke out across Nasir's face and he chuckled. "I doubt that. You failed."

"So did your assassins."

He spread his arms wide, conceding the point. "You can see why I had to take matters into my own hands. Without water, your king will die, as will his people. Only those loyal to me will live. I suppose I could use someone with your ... potential, though you will need training. I will give you this one chance; pledge your loyalty to me, or die a common girl who thought too highly of herself."

Kala fumed. She wanted to scream at him, to spit and fight and list all the terrible things that Henri was going to do to him. She wished she could live to see it, but it was enough to know that Henri would make sure he died in agony. Hopefully, she could still watch from her place in the sky.

"Tahlia told me about you, you know."

Nasir's expression soured a little, his smile turning brittle on his face. "I care little for what the wilted rose had to say."

"She said you were limper than a rotten cucumber and twice as foul."

Kala smirked with satisfaction as Nasir's cheeks turned red. Tahlia hadn't spoken a word about Nasir to her but it was a truth universally known that insulting a boy's penis was just as effective as kicking them in the balls.

"Kill her," Nasir sneered. "And dump her body outside the city's entrance so that the sun will scorch the flesh from her bones."

"Henri will kill you!" Kala cursed as she was dragged out of the room and down the corridor.

She screamed every insult and profanity she had ever learned, but the private guards only smirked at her downfall and wriggled their fingers in mocking farewell.

ISA

Isa surveyed the swelling crowd with growing unease. Thousands of people flooded the streets, roofs were lined with onlookers, and heads hung out of second-story windows, desperate to hear news of when the water supply would be restored. Babies wailed and children clutched at their parent's sides, their young faces gaunt with fear. At their queen's request, the people carried empty clay plots and ceramic jars, waterskins and earthenware.

Tahlia sat atop a camel in the center of the market square, surrounded by the Naiab for protection. Isa had suggested that she gather her people inside the palace grounds to address them from the safety of a balcony, but she had refused. She insisted on meeting them in the streets, to show them that while she was their queen, she was also one of them. Such a move would endear her to her people, but it also put her in grave danger. If the crowd turned hostile, the Naiab would not discriminate in their efforts to protect her. A lot of blood would be spilled. Some of it would inevitably be innocent. But while he and his men might be able to hold the line of a ground assault, Isa couldn't defend her from arrows or spears. Sitting atop a camel, she was an easy target.

It made his blood surge to know how vulnerable she really was. If anyone so much as harmed a hair on her head, he would level this entire market square to the ground until no one was left standing. He would slaughter them without blinking, and then he would search for more. Isa shook his head, trying to dislodge the urge from his system. He could feel his control slipping through his fingers. He wiped the sweat from his brow but the roaring inside him was building to a crescendo.

Isa looked back at Tahlia and forced himself to focus on her. She was perched high in the saddle but she did not look like a queen. Instead of expensive silks and jewels, she wore a simple beige kaftan and light blue headscarf. The only adornment was the brass vial secured around her neck. She could have been a merchant's wife or a woman from a nearby village. Except the camel she sat on was decorated with brightly colored embroidered regalia and strings of black beads. It signified her wealth and power, her authority as queen.

If Tahlia was afraid, she didn't show it. She held the crowd's attention with effortless ease, somehow subduing them into patient silence. Isa supposed there was an element of the unknown in having a queen as ruler, and perhaps the rumors of her being a sorceress gave people pause for thought. Feeling somewhat calmer and in control, he turned his attention back to the crowd. Fresh adrenaline flooded his senses. He would be ready to carve a path through these people at the slightest hint of dissent.

"Thank you all for assembling here today at my request." Tahlia raised her voice so that it carried across the square. "You would have heard many rumors about me. This much is true; your former king took me from my family against my will and brought me here to destroy me. So I killed him and removed his beard and in doing so, became your undeniable queen."

The crowd murmured restlessly, exchanging wide eyed glances and words of judgment. Isa braced himself to massacre them all.

"It is also true that our enemy, Nasir of the high mountain region, has cut off the water supply to all of Merovia except his own kingdom. He has done this in retaliation against those who oppose his ambition to become the sole king of Merovia. He does not care if you and your children and hundreds of thousands of our countrymen die, as long as he is king."

A new energy rippled through the gathering as people raised their fists and shouted in outrage. Faces turned hard with anger while the air crackled with violent tension.

"But I care. And so do the other Merovian kings, who are now, as we speak, marching to bravely wage war on Nasir and restore the water supply to Merovia. The gods are with them and will grant them victory, but the gods are also with us. As your queen, I will never allow my people to be treated this way. Your lives forfeit for one man's desire. All life is precious. Water is what sustains us. So I call on the water goddess; let it rain."

The crowd shifted with unease at her bold summons to the goddess but above them clouds began to form in a vacant blue sky. Everyone's eyes drew skyward to watch as the clouds emerged, swirling in the atmosphere, growing heavy and dark and full. Gasps escaped as people pointed above, their jaws slack with awe and disbelief. Isa didn't dare take his eyes off the crowd but he could already smell the sweet change in the air. Then, with a flash of lightning and a deep rumble of thunder, the heavens opened up.

Rain poured down like a heavy monsoon, drenching the crowd and soaking the black earth beneath their feet. The people cheered and called out praises to the water goddess but they were muffled amid the sounds of the storm. Children danced in the streets as the people raised their earthenware and waterskins to capture every last drop.

Isa felt his tension wash away as he scanned the elated faces around him. They were joyful and grateful. Their new queen had the favor of the gods. There would no longer be depraved rumors about her or questions of allegiance. Tales of this day would live on in legend, passed down through generations, as the day a queen of Merovia commanded the water goddess to make it rain.

Isa cast a glance over his shoulder at Tahlia. It was difficult to see her through the torrent of rain but once he did he was captivated.

She was smiling. He had never seen her smile like that before. Head tipped back, throat exposed, rivulets of water cascading down her skin. She licked her lips, tasting the rain on her tongue. Droplets caught on her long eyelashes and her kaftan clung to the curves of her body. When she caught sight of him watching her, she blinked the water out of her eyes and held his gaze. Amidst the deluge, the world seemed to hold its breath. Because nature's raw energy was awe-inspiring but it was nothing compared to the force that was building between them.

CHAPTER SEVENTEEN

MALIK

"I think Nasir's expecting us," Malik said as he surveyed the neat lines of soldiers stationed at the border.

No doubt the moment they left Henri's kingdom, Nasir's spies had informed him of their army's departure. It was pointless of him to send men to bolster his border defenses. In the face of such a large army, Nasir had sent these men to their deaths.

Malik sat calmly in the saddle as he assessed the situation, while beside him Henri's horse shifted restlessly. Behind them was an army of thousands, some soldiers on horseback, most traveling on foot, with wagons and supplies bringing up the rear. Ele was traveling in one such wagon, a compromise on Henri's part. He would allow Ele to join them but on the condition that he rested in the wagon. Ele had begrudgingly agreed, though Malik suspected the wagon would not contain him for long once they arrived in Nasir's kingdom and the fighting began.

It had been two days since they left Henri's kingdom and Malik had set a punishing pace. Time was just as much their enemy as Nasir. Though he had no way to confirm it, he suspected the water supply to Merovia had already been cut off. They had brought what water they could store and carry, but it would only last them one more day. The people of Merovia would be frightened and suffering. Their crops withering already beneath the punishing rays of the unforgiving sun god. If Nasir defeated them in this war, the consequences would be catastrophic. Malik refused to entertain it as a possibility. Victory was the only acceptable outcome.

But first they had to cross the border.

Henri signaled for his army to remain where they stood while he cantered ahead to position himself between two opposing forces. Malik followed on his heel and halted at his side. He could see that their approach unsettled the border soldiers. It was rare that two Merovian kings were seen together, let alone united in one cause. Still, the soldiers maintained their formation, their training holding them steady.

"Who is your captain?" Henri demanded.

"We have no captain," one of the soldiers replied.

There was a beat of quiet as Henri absorbed what that meant. Nasir had indeed sent these men to die. They were a weak show of resistance, not even enough to slow the combined army down, but more than that, they were a strategic move against Henri. A cheap emotional shot designed to cut open the first wound in this war. Nasir knew what it would do to Henri to take the lives of men that didn't need to die. Henri was not callous with life. He did everything in his power to preserve it, no matter whose life it was or the personal cost to him. This move was designed to taunt him, force him to go against his moralistic nature. Henri's face was hard and betrayed no emotion, but Malik knew him better than anyone. He was fighting an internal battle between his conscience and the demands of war.

"You are vastly outnumbered," Henri shouted, his voice carrying across the land. "If you surrender, I will spare your lives. You have my word. If you refuse, you will die here and now. Choose."

Malik's cock broadened involuntarily at Henri's savage, commanding words. He had always been a bold ruler, confident to the point of cocky in his decisions. His arrogance had once infuriated Malik, but now, seeing him at the head of a great army, it drew out a different response entirely. Raw desire. With every demand and ruthless order he issued, Malik felt his pulse quicken. It had been too long since he kissed his lips or felt Henri slide inside him. He ached with the need for it. His body felt hollow, deprived, and desperate. Every time Henri looked at him, even if it was just a fleeting glance, his blood heated. He was so quick to arousal he would probably come at the slightest touch.

"We serve our king," the soldier replied, while the others remained decisively silent.

"So be it."

Henri motioned for the soldiers on horseback to move forward. They aligned themselves on either side of Henri and Malik and awaited his order. Before Henri even drew his sword, Malik knew that he would join in the killing. He was not a man to have others do unpleasant work so that he didn't have to sully his own hands, but he was also not a king to send others into battle while he stayed safe on the fringes. He would bloody his blade and risk his life like every other man standing beside him. Malik drew his shamshir in solidarity and on Henri's command they attacked.

It was shameful how quickly the border soldiers died. It was not a battle, it was an execution, and it felt *wrong*. These loyal soldier's deaths were unnecessary. Wasteful. Nasir could have chosen to prepare his army and confront them at the border to defend his kingdom. Instead, he had decided to barricade himself inside his fortress, leaving his border soldiers to face a futile death. He was a coward and in the end it would not be enough to save him.

"We keep moving," Henri ordered.

The army resumed marching across the border into Nasir's kingdom. Malik hoped the men were being careful to step over the bodies of the fallen soldiers and not trample them under foot, but he didn't look behind him to check. He supposed the encounter and its bloody carnage had given everyone a taste of what was to come. While Henri's army had seen war under Heroux's leadership, the rest of the soldiers had no experience of the brutality of the battlefield. The things that men were capable of doing to each other when sanctioned under the banner of war.

These soldiers were used to patrolling borders and enforcing the king's law, not defending their homeland from conquest and their people from annihilation. What made it worse was that the enemy was not foreign. They were killing their own countrymen. No doubt these thoughts weighed heavy on the men as they marched, along with the sobering notion of their own mortality. Despite having the advantage of numbers, men would still die in the coming conflict. Some of these soldiers would never see their loved ones again.

Hours passed in reflective silence as the terrain began to change around them. The sandy earth gave way to rocky ground and mountain passes emerged in the distance. The air, usually dry and crisp, held a hint of moisture and brought with it the reprieve of a cooler temperature. Occasionally, Malik caught glimpses of sparse vegetation growing in the jagged cliffs; hardy shrubs and even some desert flowers, clinging to life within the rain shadow. But then he glimpsed something else entirely on the horizon.

"Halt!" Malik called and raised a closed fist to the sky.

The men heeded his command and the steady rhythm of marching ceased. Malik stared ahead into the distance as a large blur took shape against the shimmering heat.

An army.

Malik threw a sharp look at Henri whose features tightened in response, an entire conversation passing between them without a word. The horizon was flooded with a sea of soldiers advancing towards them. The battle was about to begin.

TAHLIA

"We're not going to reach them in time." Isa tossed the reminder over his shoulder.

Tahlia stared at the broad expanse of his shoulders as he sat in front of her, behind the first hump of their camel. No matter how many times she looked at him, his sheer size always astounded her. She was also astonished that he could wear so little under the harsh desert sun and not be roasted like a pepper. She was wearing a long sleeve full length kaftan with a headscarf wrapped around her neck and face, leaving only her emerald eyes visible and the back of her hands exposed. In contrast, Isa wore loose pants and a sleeveless shirt with no headscarf. His arms, neck and face were completely at the mercy of the sun's rays, yet they glowed with a healthy golden hue.

His tattoos had also returned to a turquoise blue soon after they left her kingdom. She had meant to ask him about their disturbing change in color but with everything that had happened there hadn't been time. Now she thought she had solved the mystery herself; the black sand of her kingdom had somehow infiltrated him when he had tried to wield it, causing his tattoos to turn the color of ink. She wondered if the dark sand had felt any different coursing beneath his skin or if the change had been purely cosmetic.

Tahlia didn't know why the sands of her kingdom were different from every other kingdom in Merovia. She assumed there was a natural explanation for it, like how Dahane's—now Malik's—kingdom was known as the salt plains because of its flat expanses covered with salt that shined white beneath the sun. Or how Nasir's kingdom captured all the rainwater because his mountainous region happened to fall in a rain shadow. Nature had curious ways of evolving and adapting that didn't always have an obvious explanation."

It was clear, though, that in the few short hours since they left her kingdom, the black sand had drained from Isa's system. Tahlia studied the back of him for a moment. His posture had changed. He seemed more at ease. Like the strain and exhaustion that had been weighing him down the past few days had dissipated. It was understandable. He no longer had to contend with keeping her alive whilst also safeguarding his men in a kingdom on the verge of rebellion. For the first time in what felt like a feverish nightmare, they were both safe.

Her idea of calling on the alliance with the water goddess to make it rain had won the people to her side and firmly established her as queen. She had the blessing of the gods, they answered her prayers, the people could not argue with that. It was ironic but Tahlia didn't have time to dwell on it. Following the performance, she had insisted that they leave for Nasir's kingdom at once. She knew Isa thought it was futile but he hadn't argued with her or tried to change her mind. Instead, he had assigned one of his men to oversee the kingdom in their absence and they both slipped away as discreetly as possible, which was difficult given the bright embroidered regalia and beads draped all over her camel.

"I know, but I can't just stay in my kingdom and do nothing," Tahlia replied. "If only I could move through sand like you, we could get there sooner."

"We'd still arrive too late for the battle. Sand moves fast but not that fast. The war might have already begun."

The words were like a punch to her stomach. Suddenly the air was too thin and she felt lightheaded, unsteady in the saddle. She gripped the frame to ground herself. She needed to talk about anything else, to distract her mind from the images of Henri and Malik covered in blood, their bodies mangled, their souls ascending to the stars.

Tahlia cleared her dry throat. "You never told me what price you paid for the goddess to change you."

"You never asked."

"Well, I'm asking now. She mentioned that warriors earn their sand wielding abilities through enduring a trial?"

A moment of silence stretched between them, enough for Tahlia to think Isa might not answer her question.

"When our forebears refused to submit to the Rouhan, they were exiled into the Idris desert and condemned to die. Great walls were erected to enforce their banishment. They wandered aimlessly in the desert without water, food, or shelter. Families with little ones and elderly ones, entire generations. Somehow, despite the harsh conditions, they survived. They found ways to adapt, to live. They persevered until they discovered a new home."

Tahlia knew the history, at least the one side of it that was passed down through generations. It was assumed those that had been banished had perished because there was no conceivable way they could have survived. The brutal lesson served as a warning to those who would consider rising up against the Rouhan and challenging their rule, they would be shown no mercy.

"When warriors choose to undergo the trial, we are sent out into the Idris desert with nothing more than ourselves. We have to endure eight days before we can return to the Citadel."

"Eight days!"

It was barbaric. The landscape was hard enough to survive with adequate provisions and shelter and camels for transport. She couldn't imagine walking the endless dunes for eight days with nothing to sustain or shelter her. She wouldn't last an hour.

"In those eight days, warriors face their darkest fears, their truest selves. The desert sends us visions and divinations."

Exposed to the extreme elements and suffering from dehydration, Tahlia could imagine that the hallucinations would be profoundly visceral. But there was something in the way he said it that pulled a question from her lips.

"What did you see in your visions?"

"You."

Tahlia didn't move, didn't dare breathe. It was like she had sensed his answer before he spoke. Knew the truth before it had revealed itself.

"What do you mean you saw me?" Her voice was like a whisper on the wind.

It was almost unbearable that he was so calm while she felt like she was dangling over the edge of a precipice.

"I saw you much like I see you now. The most beautiful woman I could ever see. I knew you were a goddess even then and that my fate would be tied to you."

"That's not possible."

Yet she believed him. She remembered how he had looked at her when he first saw her, a mix of obsession and reverence, as if he already knew her. As if he had been *waiting* for her.

He had called her goddess.

"When I returned to the Citadel after my trial, the water goddess knew what I had seen. She told me about you, that the gods hunted you, and that you had exposed yourself to save your king. Then I felt the vibrations when you and your king entered the Idris." He shook his head. "The gods and their games."

Tahlia's knuckles were white as she clenched the saddle frame. The idea of her appearing to him in some divine vision was unsettling, especially because she didn't know what it meant. Perhaps nothing. Or perhaps the water goddess was playing with them. She could have implanted the image of her face in Isa's mind and then manipulated him to derive meaning from it. Hadn't the goddess been interfering with mortals this entire time to serve her own agenda?

If it did mean something, if Isa's fate was tied to hers, he might have already fulfilled his role in her story. He had saved Henri and tried to rescue her. She was safe now. More than safe; she was queen. His purpose was accomplished. Their threads could unknot and Isa would be free to live his life however he chose. Prophecies only held power if people believed in them and she had never believed. She had been chosen by the gods but she had also chosen herself. She had chosen to live.

Suddenly, the air shifted around them, becoming heavy with sand. A sharp, hot breeze blew past them and Isa stiffened. He halted their camel. Tahlia watched as he scanned the endless desert surrounding them before casting his eyes back the way they had come. Tahlia looked over her shoulder to see an ominous haze building in the distance, transforming the usually sparse landscape into a chaotic surge of ferocious power. The sky above them, seconds ago a clear blue, was now morphing to the color of deep rust. The sun was being erased, lost beneath a dense vapor of dust. Soon there would be no line separating the land from the sky.

"The Naiab?" Tahlia yelled over the rumbling doom that was approaching them. Her voice was hopeful but even as she said it, she somehow knew that it wasn't.

"No. It's a red storm."

"A what?"

"We need to get down. Now!"

Isa urged the beast to the ground and the camel kneeled, folding its legs beneath itself, seemingly unconcerned about the storm approaching them. Tahlia quickly dismounted and tightened the scarf around her neck as the wind clawed at it, trying to whip it free. She stumbled toward Isa who had also dismounted, the sand shifting and sinking beneath her feet. He stood firm, as if rooted to the ground, staring at the wall of sand that was barreling toward them. It looked to be miles long and thousands of feet high. She could feel the pressure in the air fluctuate wildly, creating a strange heaviness in her ears and chest. Fear flooded her body. There was no way anyone could survive that.

It was odd to be able to reflect on her life in the seconds before death came for her. It made her feel like all of it had been for nothing. Like she was being robbed. She had fought and cried and loved and conquered and still this was how it ended.

How cruel the gods could be.

How magnificent this life was.

Isa wrenched her from her thoughts, enveloping her in a strong embrace, and holding her close to his chest as though his body could shield her. "Hold on to me."

She pressed herself against him, taking one last full breath, before closing her eyes to surrender herself. The storm hit with a fury, the roar of it filling her ears until it was the only thing she was aware of. She kept breathing. One breath, then two. She should be dead. The thought made Tahlia open her eyes and push back a little from Isa's chest. As they stood there, the storm raged around them like a swirling tempest. She could see thousands of particles churning and spinning but they never touched her. It was like they were standing in a pocket of air, invisible walls protecting them.

Tahlia glanced up at Isa to see that he was watching her intensely. That's when she realized he was controlling the sand, holding it at bay. She could see the slight tremor in his frame, the strained muscles in his jaw. She could only imagine how much power it would take to hold back the tide of sand. Isa's hand rose to softly cradle her cheek. Tahlia didn't know why but it made her want to cry. This man had only ever shown her respect and protected her since the moment they met. He hadn't cared that she was hunted by the gods. He didn't care that she belonged to a king. Everything he had done had been for her. To keep her alive. To honor her.

Isa's fingers were gentle as they pulled the headscarf down from her face. His gaze immediately dipped to her mouth but Tahlia couldn't tear her eyes away from him. As strands of her dark hair flew wildly about and the world erupted around them, Tahlia lifted her lips to his. Worlds collided and stars burst in the heavens, at least that's what it felt like. The kiss was slow and soft but more profound than the secrets of the universe. It stole her breath and banished her body. This was her only existence; this sacred kiss. His movements were tender and deliberate. Tahlia knew he had burned for her for the longest time but there was nothing urgent or demanding in the way he held her. One hand cupped her cheek as the other rested lightly on her hip, steadying her. When his tongue slid between her lips she melted, dissolving into him. With every touch, every taste, he worshiped her.

Tahlia didn't know when the storm passed over them. Time was no longer significant. When their mouths finally parted and their gazes locked inches away from each other, the world around them was quiet again. It was surreal. It almost felt like a dream except he was here, she could touch him, and the ghost of his kiss was still on her lips. He was hers. He always had been. She knew it as sure as she knew her own beating heart. There was nothing that would keep him away from her. The threads that had knotted together, tying them to each other, would never untangle.

"Isa." His name sounded different now, like a prayer, like hope. "There's something I have to tell you."

CHAPTER EIGHTEEN

MALIK

Their combined army had swiftly moved into formation, readying themselves for combat.

Henri narrowed his eyes to a squint. "Those aren't Nasir's men."

Malik frowned as he stared at the army marching toward them. They held no banners, no way to identify them, but as they drew closer, Malik saw that Henri was right. Nasir was not leading them. Malik should have known better. Nasir would never risk his safety by venturing beyond his walls and he would never leave himself unprotected by sending his soldiers away.

"You should go and take command of your army." A smirk danced on Henri's lips.

Malik exchanged a look with Henri. *His* army. Because he was a king and these men marching toward them were his to lead. He wasn't sure he would ever get used to that. At Malik's command, they had traveled to join Henri's forces. Malik had thought perhaps they would meet them closer to Nasir's city but they must have made good time.

Malik rode out to meet them and on seeing his approach, the men halted. They appeared to be well trained, strong, and disciplined, which almost made up for their inexperience on the battlefield.

"Which one of you is the captain?" Malik shouted.

"I am, Kafei."

An older man at the head of the army stood forward. His demeanor was confident but respectful as he gave a brief report of their journey, which was thankfully uneventful. By the time he was done, Henri's army had closed the distance and the two forces seamlessly combined. They continued on, moving with steady resolve and careful precision as they pressed forward through the harsh, rocky terrain.

Hours passed and every step became more challenging. The sight of the imposing mountains, with their craggy ridges and sheer cliff faces, provided a stark reminder of the ruthless nature of the land and the reason they were going to war. Because the desert was unforgiving and water was life. They would fight to live but also to reclaim this desolate untamed country that had birthed them.

"We should go over the battle plan one last time before tomorrow."

Henri's words jolted Malik from his thoughts and he nodded in rote agreement. "I'll come to your tent tonight."

They had already talked at length to devise the strategy, debating every detail, anticipating every blind spot. Having traveled to Nasir's kingdom several times as Heroux's emissary, Malik had firsthand knowledge of the kingdom and its defenses. He relayed the impressive fortress that was Nasir's palace, built several stories high on the top of a desert mountain. The city, he recalled, lay at the base of the mountain and on the other side of the mountain was a dam.

Malik did not know exact numbers of Nasir's army but it didn't matter. What troubled him more was being unable to predict how Nasir would react to their forces on his doorstep. Nasir had always plotted violence from a distance using spies and assassins, political maneuvering and alliances. He had never faced open war before. When cornered and confronted with little choice but to fight, what would he do? Surrender was unthinkable. Nasir's pride would not allow it. He could try to escape but they had planned for that already. Nasir was cunning. Perhaps he had laid a trap for them and they were marching right into it.

The road ascended sharply again and Malik was grateful to be on horseback. He would think even the nimble onyx would find these steep slopes challenging. Their pace grew slower with every mile but they were still on track. When the sun finally started to descend in the sky, Malik called for the army to make camp. The terrain was too dangerous to travel in diminishing light and the soldiers needed rest. It didn't take long before tents were erected and food was rationed out. Their water supply was dangerously low.

Like every other night, Malik's tent was erected in the middle of the camp, a spear throw away from Henri's. It made sense from a defensive standpoint but it had been torture last night, resisting the urge to walk over and enter Henri's tent. His mind had generated a dozen excuses to do so, but he knew Henri would see through all of them, and then he would tell him to leave. Malik didn't think he could endure the sting of blatant rejection. Doing nothing was easier. It kept the hope alive. He could still fantasize about how things might play out.

Now he really was walking the short distance to Henri's tent. Inhaling a deep, settling breath, he stepped inside. The tent was a generous size, much like his own, and furnished with some basic comforts. A thick rug had been laid out over the earth, adorned with an array of cushions, but Henri was not sitting on any of them. He sat on the carpet, leaning over a crude map, one that Malik had drawn days ago. Malik's attention drifted to Henri's bed, which was nearby. Next to it was another bedroll. Ele was curled up on it, already asleep, his shamshir lying beside him in case he had need of it in the night. It shouldn't have surprised Malik to find him there. It would take a while for Henri to let the boy out of his sight again. Still, he felt any residual hope of what might occur between them tonight vanish.

Henri lifted his gaze and Malik offered a shallow smile before making his way to sit opposite him on the rug. In the absence of water to wash, Henri had changed his clothes but his skin remained coated with a fine layer of sand. He smelled like sweat, horse, and man. Somehow, it was not unpleasant. In fact, it had Malik's cock twitching in arousal. The stubble along Henri's jawline had grown darker over the past few days. It still showed no signs of lengthening into a beard, though. Malik stared at it for longer than he should have.

"We will reach the city by mid-morning," Henri announced, as if to himself.

Henri went on to summarize the battle plan, referencing the map before him and setting the course of events straight in his mind. Malik simply watched him. The movement of his eyes as they traced across the map, the way his lips formed around words. They were both kings on the eve of their first battle but while Henri was sharp and focused, Malik was hopelessly distracted. What happened tomorrow would either kill them or define them. Yet he couldn't think about that. All he could think about was what would happen next. If they survived and power shifted and new territory lines were drawn, what did that mean for them?

It was never supposed to be like this. Malik had not expected to survive the summit. His only ambition had been to kill as many Merovian kings as he could before being cut down himself. He had tried to ensure that Henri would be the sole ruler of Merovia, but Henri's emotions had gotten in the way and Isa had interfered in his plan and now Malik was king. An outcome that still had his head reeling. Once, he would have accepted the crown without hesitation, to protect his people from rulers like Heroux. But then a foreign king had landed on Merovian shores and everything changed. Henri was the king the people needed, he was the king that could unite the entire country.

If they won this war, Merovia would be changed forever. Malik assumed Henri would claim Nasir's kingdom for himself and, though the victory would be shared, Malik had no interest in contesting that. Henri would then turn his attention to Kareem, if

Isa hadn't killed the bastard already and claimed his kingdom for the Naiab. Malik doubted Henri would care if he had, as long as Tahlia was returned safely. The walls would come down and the Idris desert would be recognized as a kingdom of Merovia. Dawn would rise on a new page in history.

It would be the beginning of an era and the end of them, because once the dust had settled, they would part ways. Henri would return to his kingdom, the ruler of an expanded empire, and Malik would govern his own realm. Their threads would no longer cross.

"I'm sorry."

Henri glanced up from the map, his brows furrowed slightly in confusion. "What for?"

"I should have told you about Tahlia. I should have told you about sending scorpions to the other Merovian kings. I should have been honest about my intentions for the summit."

"You shouldn't have done it in the first place," Henri growled.

"No, I'm not sorry for that. I told you, there is no line I am not willing to cross to save your life. If that makes me your hero or your villain, I don't care, as long as I'm yours."

"Malik—"

"I know you think I'm fighting your battles for you but I'm not. You have never needed anyone to fight your battles. You are a formidable king, a born ruler. I have only ever wanted to fight by your side."

"And you will. As a king. As my ally."

"Is that all I am to you now?"

They stared at each other, the air growing heavy between them.

"I would give up my claim to kingship, do anything you ask of me, if it meant being with you."

"Don't. You are a king of Merovia now."

"I would rather be king of your heart. You conquered mine a long time ago."

"Malik." Henri closed his eyes and shook his head as if he was exhausted from battling inner demons. "You don't understand. My closest friend sacrificed everything to save me and then I watched him die. I have to live with his choices and my failures every day of my life. The regret and the guilt and the pain, it never leaves me. I cannot—I will not—go through that again. I wouldn't survive it."

"So we can't be together, not because I ordered your assassination or because I was less than honest with you about the summit, but because you love me too much and you're afraid of losing me?" Malik let a moment of silence settle between them for emphasis. "Can you hear how ridiculous that sounds?"

"Says the man who has never lost anyone he loved," Henri retorted.

"I lost my brother," Malik reminded him bitterly, "and I have never forgotten him."

Henri's glare softened. "I'm sorry, Malik. I didn't mean—" He swore softly.

Malik released a patient sigh. "Henri, I promise from this day on to always be honest with you no matter the cost. So here is my first piece of honesty. I can't change the choices you and I have made in the past. We both have to live with them. But I can save us both from the regret and pain of the choice you are making now. Please don't let me go. The people we are willing to die for, are the same people we should live for. And I don't want to live without you."

Malik could see Henri's resolve weakening so he leaned across the map, cautiously closing the distance between them. Henri watched him but he didn't resist as Malik placed his hands either side of his face, bringing their lips dangerously close.

"Let me have you," Malik whispered. "Tonight and every night."

Their mouths brushed. The kiss was tentative at first but quickly turned desperate and starving. All the pent-up emotions and cravings rose to the surface, reducing him to one blind need; *him*. He wanted to feel every part of him, to taste him, and swallow him down. Henri's mouth opened under his, kissing him back but it was Malik who was dominating this. His fingers caressed Henri's stubbled jawline, holding him firm, as his tongue explored his mouth. It was his territory, after all. This mouth. This body. This king.

Henri was *his*.

Malik pushed forward and Henri gave ground, leaning back until he was laid out across the rug with Malik rearing over him. There were far too many clothes separating them. Malik could feel Henri hardening beneath him but he needed to see it with his own eyes, the proof that Henri still wanted him. Malik reached down to slide his hand inside Henri's pants and took him in a possessive grip. Henri jerked and his mouth broke away from the kiss to release a groan.

"Malik, we can't."

Ele.

Fuck. Malik cast a glance over his shoulder at the boy who was sleeping soundly a short distance away. He turned back to Henri who was looking at him with hungry eyes. It was impossible not to want him.

"Come to my tent," Malik whispered.

"Malik," Henri protested.

Malk stroked his cock in long, luxurious strides and watched Henri's face contort as his control weakened and pleasure edged his senses. It was heady to watch, to know the effect he had on him.

"I will make you come right here," Malik warned.

"Fine. We'll go to your tent."

Malik released him and they both stumbled to stand. Henri's hair was slightly tousled and Malik was sure his own attire looked less than orderly. With one last glance in Ele's direction, Henri stepped outside the tent and Malik followed. They made a concentrated effort to walk casually across to Malik's tent, nodding politely to the sentries on duty as they passed them. But once inside, they descended into craven beasts, clawing at each other, tearing clothes off and sinking their teeth into naked skin.

Breathing was difficult. Malik couldn't get enough air, couldn't get enough of him. It was too much and too little and he wanted more, now, all at once. They were pushing and pulling, each striving to lead the other, but they tripped on the corner of a rug and collapsed onto the floor. It didn't matter. They reached for each other, kissing and touching, their limbs tangling together. When they drew back, it was only far enough to gaze at one another, to savor this precious reunion, this moment of exquisite intimacy. It was like they both sensed how fleeting it was, that they needed to cherish it because tomorrow it could be gone, lost to blood and steel and the uncertain fate of battle.

Malik rolled on top of Henri and slid his hands up the length of Henri's defined arms, pushing them into an arc above his head. Catching his hands, Malik pressed their palms firmly into one another.

"I have been dreaming of this, of you, every night."

Malik's breath warmed the space between them. Henri didn't reply, he simply kissed him.

"It was torture not being able to touch you, to have you," Malik continued. "I never want anything to come between us again."

"You are a king now," Henri pointed out. "It changes things."

"It doesn't have to." Malik sat back to straddle him, the movement causing delicious friction between their cocks. "We can rule together, side by side."

"Are you trying to seduce me or negotiate with me?"

Malik arched an eyebrow as his lips curled into a devilish smile. "Both."

He leaned down to plant tantalizing kisses across Henri's chest and then lower to his stomach, following the line of dark hair that went beyond his abdomen. When he took him into his mouth, Henri groaned and Malik seized his hips to better feel his shifts and pushes against him. His own arousal was swollen and aching but he ignored it. Instead, he lapped his tongue over the head, sucked the glistening tip and then slid his mouth back down the shaft. Henri swore, his hands gripping fists of sand where normally they would grasp silken sheets. Malik could feel Henri's climax building. His thighs were tensing as he tried to hold himself off, extending his pleasure a little longer.

"I'm a very good negotiator, but I know you prefer a more direct approach," Malik said huskily.

Malik put his finger in his mouth and then slid it inside Henri. Henri tensed at the sudden intrusion, his muscles constricting tightly around Malik's finger, but then they began to relax as Malik moved it back and forward slowly.

"That was an unexpected move." Henri arched an eyebrow.

"Invasion is necessary sometimes."

Malik continued to move in and out of him and then returned his mouth to his cock, maintaining a rhythm that had Henri quickly losing control until he came undone completely. He was warm and salty and exquisite on Malik's tongue. Malik reared up to share his taste in a thorough kiss. Henri devoured his mouth greedily. Malik's erection pressed hard into Henri's torso, leaking onto his abs.

"Get the oil," Henri breathed.

"I don't need it."

"I know but I like it."

Malik chuckled and crawled over to his saddlebags to retrieve the vial of oil. When he turned back to Henri the sight of him stopped his heart. He lay sprawled out naked across the sandy floor, illuminated in the light of the oil lamp, all hard lines and muscles. His arms were interlocked beneath his head and he had hitched up a knee. He did not look like a king on the eve of battle. He looked like a man satiated, without a care in the world.

Malik crawled over to him and Henri smiled wolfishly. "A king crawling on his hands and knees to me."

"Just one of many things I will only ever do for you." Malik leaned across his chest and kissed him slow and deep. "Have I won you over? Will you rule by my side?"

Henri slid a hand through his hair, brushing it back as he contemplated the proposal. "We shouldn't be making plans until we have won the war."

That was not the response Malik had hoped for. There was still a shadow lingering in Henri's eyes, some kind of hesitancy. He wondered if Henri hadn't quite forgiven him yet, or maybe his love for him had diminished in the wake of his perceived betrayal.

Malik took Henri's hand and pressed the back of it to his lips. "We will win."

"You are a master of strategy." Henri sat up to devour the column of his neck, nipping it with his teeth.

Malik's thoughts scattered like dust. All he knew was this, Henri, his entire reason for drawing breath.

"Strategy is important," Malik agreed. "We wouldn't want to rely on our size alone."

Henri's eyes slid down to Malik's swollen erection. Malik followed his gaze. When their eyes met again, Henri's grin matched his own.

"I think I could outmaneuver you." Henri taunted as his hand lightly cupped Malik's balls, massaging them teasingly.

"I would surrender myself willingly."

Malik laid beneath him and allowed Henri to grip his hips as he positioned himself where he wanted him. Anticipation flooded Malik's body with aching need. He watched as Henri pressed his weight forward, the tip teasing his entrance, while Henri rubbed himself with oil in sweet simulation.

"What are you doing?" Malik asked, a little breathlessly.

"What does it feel like I'm doing?"

"Torturing me."

"You did surrender."

"Henri—"

The sudden push inside was brutal and erotic and made Malik cry out in ecstasy. He could feel the slide of oil as Henri pounded inside him, coaxing his body open with every thrust. Malik's senses flooded with euphoria. It was too much, too good. He never wanted it to stop.

"Open your eyes, my love."

Malik wasn't sure when he had closed them or that he had actually heard those words come from Henri's lips.

My love.

Henri groaned, rough and low with need and it was clear that he was barely controlling himself. Still, they held each other's gazes, drawing out their shared pleasure a little longer, marveling at how they fit together so perfectly as they moved as one. It was too deep but it felt right to have Henri pushing further than anyone else had ever dared. Never had Malik wanted someone so badly. Henri leaned down until his lips were at Malik's neck, his hand firm around his throat. A man who knows what he wants and what belongs to him.

"Henri." Malik ached inside and it was a delicious painful yearning, a sinful torment. But he longed for more than release. He longed for a future.

This was how it could be between them. Every night. Two kings. One kingdom. For the rest of their lives. Malik came to the thought of it, spilling himself over Henri like he had spilled his heart. He could feel Henri emptying himself inside him, warm and wet, as he shuddered above him. Then Henri collapsed on top of him, and despite the weight of him crushing his bones, Malik didn't push him off. He would suffocate before he ever asked Henri to put distance between them.

When Henri finally pulled out, Malik felt strangely hollow. Henri rolled off and stretched out beside him, pulling Malik's body with him. They lay there, their legs entwined, resting in the afterglow of their lovemaking, and tried to ignore the thought of tomorrow.

It was impossible to do.

A million words raced through Malik's head, speeches and arguments and pleas and reasons. He knew Henri didn't want to hear any of it, so instead he gave him simple truths.

"I don't want to know who we are without each other. I don't want to rule a kingdom alone and I don't want a different kind of love. Henri." Malik gripped his neck tenderly, forcing his eyes to meet his. "Tell me that whatever happens tomorrow, it won't change this. Us."

"I love you."

The words were unexpected. Malik searched his face, waiting for him to say more. He didn't. But perhaps that was all that needed to be said. Because Henri wasn't a man who fell in love easily, and his love was the kind Malik thought he would never find. Malik's expression eased a little, content to accept whatever Henri was willing to give him.

"Dead or alive, king or not, I love you." Henri took his hand and threaded their fingers together. "If we win the war tomorrow, I will rule by your side. If we lose, I will die by your side. Whatever the outcome, wherever we go, we will always find each other."

Malik brushed his lips with a tender kiss and committed every facet of this moment to memory. Tomorrow they would fight for their people, for their country, but they would also fight for this. The future they could have together. A lifetime shared. It would never be enough. It was all he could ever want.

KALA

Death, apparently, was very slow. Kala had expected to be dragged from the assembly room, taken to the city's entrance and strung up by her scrawny neck. It was always a possibility that they would cut off her head but that sounded like too much work and the mess was unnecessary. For all their stupidity, the guards didn't seem like men who would waste time making the extra effort.

Instead, Kala was taken to an iron cell, shoved inside, and left to rot. Days had since passed and the bruises from her beating had healed. The cell wasn't all that bad. The air was stuffy and it smelled like feet but the weathered stone was cool and dry. She was bored out of her mind but at least she was able to sleep. No screams of torture or cries for help kept her awake. In fact, she was pretty sure there was no one else there except for the old woman sleeping in the corner of her cell. Kala had thought her dead at first because she hadn't moved and she smelled like rotting flesh. But then, like a ghost, she had come to life in the middle of the night to pee down a hole in the floor. Kala had almost screamed in fright but instead she watched in petrified silence as the woman finished her business and returned to her corner.

The next morning Kala had waited for the old woman to move, to groan, to say something, but she only resumed her corpse-like state. Or perhaps she really had died in the night. Kala wasn't going to check. Instead, her thoughts turned to her own doom. She had decided that the guards meant to starve her to death. It was a surprising choice but one that didn't require much effort on their part. She supposed she should be grateful. It was a painful way to die but at least it was familiar.

Except that early in the morning on the third day, the guards delivered a plate of flatbread and dried apricots with a cup of water. Kala stared at the meal, confused. It didn't make any sense. Perhaps it was poisoned? That sounded too sophisticated for the guards. Her stomach gurgled in demand but she also felt a twinge of guilt. Everywhere else in Merovia people had no water but in a cell in the high mountain region she, a prisoner, had a cup filled to the brim. It only took a moment for the guilt to subside. It was unfair but when had life ever been fair? She wouldn't let guilt get in the way of her survival.

Kala ate the food and drank the water with relish. She thought about rationing half of it for her cellmate but that idea passed as quickly as it came. The old woman was clearly content to stop living whereas Kala was not. Having finished her meal, Kala sat back and waited. Minutes crawled into hours. She wondered if it was possible to die of boredom.

Part of her knew she should be frightened and perhaps crying at the thought of death, but she really couldn't be bothered. All she could think about was revenge. She replayed the moment she'd been caught over and over in her mind, thinking of what she could have done differently. She should have killed the guards before trying to turn the water back on. It played out so easily in her mind, though in reality she was unsure whether she would have been able to do it. But she should have at least tried. She should have murdered Nasir. If she had only fought harder, been smarter, none of this would have happened. If she could only break out of this cell, she swore she would find a way to bring this mountain down on top of Nasir's head.

"Stop thinking so loud. I can hear your vengeful thoughts from here."

Kala stiffened, her eyes wide as saucers. The old woman was alive. And she could hear her thoughts.

"I can't even hear you breathing," Kala stammered.

Perhaps she shouldn't have eaten all the food after all.

The woman didn't move, didn't even turn around to look at her. She stayed lying on her side, facing the stone wall, curled up within herself. She looked to be little more than bones.

"I like the quiet," the woman replied.

"How long have you been here for?"

It was probably impolite to ask but now that Kala had someone to talk to, she was desperate to break up the boredom.

"I've been imprisoned one way or another for a very long time. Why are you here? You're a bit young to have committed a crime worthy of death."

Kala tilted her head as she counted on her fingers. "Theft. Dishonesty. Trespass. Murder."

The woman's frail body shook but Kala knew that it wasn't from fear.

"Not such an innocent then. Tell me, if you were given a second chance at life, what would you do with it?"

"I'm not dead yet," Kala retorted, annoyed.

Just because they had caught her and imprisoned her didn't mean she had given up. She refused to let them win. As long as she was breathing, she would find a way to defeat them. If that meant doing bad things then so be it. That was the story of her life.

"If *you* had a second chance, what would *you* do with it?" Kala threw back at her.

Maybe the old woman was right and it was better to sit in silence. It was better than being judged by a rotting old hag. Kala refused to apologize for anything she had done in her life. Her choices, wrong or right, had kept her alive. They had led her to Ele, her chosen family, the only part of her life that had been good. And while she refused to be sad about her short life and bitter end, she could admit one disappointment; Ele would grow up without her. He would become a man, a warrior, perhaps a captain in Henri's army, and she wouldn't get to see it. She would never find out his full name.

"I wouldn't waste it thinking about boys," the old woman chided. "It is a privilege to be a creator and it is rare to find true love but it is rarer still to rule. Are you ready?"

Kala furrowed her brows at the lunatic. "Ready for what?"

"They're coming for you."

The next sound Kala heard was the jangling of brass keys, a whistling merry tune, and the slap of sandals against stone. She stood up slowly, though her stomach sunk to the ground, and she resisted the urge to back away from the iron bars. If they meant to kill her, she wouldn't give them the satisfaction of cowering from them. She would look them in the eye and dare them to lay their hands on her.

The guard appeared from around the corner and flashed her a sinister smile. It made Kala's skin turn to gooseflesh. She recognized him, the private guard with the stupid mouth that she had insulted.

Apparently, he still had a stupid mouth because he tsked at her as if she were a small child. "I warned you what would happen to you."

"I don't give warnings." She glared at him.

The guard unlocked the cell and stood in the door frame. "Time to die."

Kala stood her ground, challenging him to take her. The moment he took a step forward, she rammed into him, hoping to catch him off balance so that she could shove him aside and make a break for it. Instead, he seized her arms and hauled her off her feet as if she weighed nothing, which wasn't far from the truth. Holding her under his arm, she thought he might drop her, if only to break her bones, but she still fought. She kicked out at him, thrashing, trying to bite him, but he held her firm as he dragged her out, closing the cell door behind him. In that fleeting moment, Kala noticed that the old woman had turned around to watch. Her eyes were milky white, like sea foam.

Kala went momentarily limp. "You!"

"Yes, me. I volunteered for this, you know." The guard taunted and Kala tried to elbow him in the ribs. "Breaking your neck will be the best part of my day."

So she was to be hanged after all. The water goddess had deigned to pay her a visit and play with her mind in the last few moments of her life, but she couldn't bring herself to stop Kala's execution. Typical. Her death was probably nothing more than cheap entertainment. Such was the boredom of divinity.

"If you don't stop squirming, I'll break it here and now."

"Let me go, you son of a donkey!"

"Watch your mouth!"

"Curse your ancestors!"

Too far.

The guard dropped her to the stone floor and she instinctively braced her arms to ward off the blow she knew was coming, but then the muffled sound of horns blaring in the distance halted the assault. The guard looked around, uncertain, but Kala knew what the horns signaled; invasion.

Henri had come.

Kala launched herself up and snatched the dagger from the guard's belt before plunging the blade into his gut. She might have twisted it for good measure. He sagged to the ground, his face contorted in a mixture of pain and disbelief.

She smiled down at him. "Best part of my day."

Clutching the blade in her hand and stealing another from his belt for good measure, Kala took off down the corridor. She had no idea where she was in the palace, or if she was even still in the palace, but it didn't matter. While Henri stormed the kingdom and waged war against Nasir, she would find a way to the underground aqueduct and do whatever it took to turn the water back on. This was her second chance and she would not fail.

CHAPTER NINETEEN

HENRI

Henri tried to ignore the foreboding sickness in his stomach as he and Malik led their combined armies toward the city. The soldiers had taken up battle formation, spreading wide across the valley. He could only imagine how terrifying they looked from a distance. Dust clouds would be billowing behind them like an ominous veil. Before long, the blare of horns echoed from the city, alerting the inhabitants to the approaching invasion. Screams rang out, terror carrying on the dry wind. What unsettled Henri, though, was the fact that Nasir's army was not stationed outside the city to meet them. There appeared to be no resistance to Henri's forces entering the streets. There was no outer city wall. No defenses set up to repel them. It was as if Nasir was unaware of the pending threat. Or more likely, he couldn't conceive of a threat strong enough to come against him.

"Malik?" Henri's voice was steady but his eyes scanned the city's entrance, searching for an unseen danger.

Malik appeared to share Henri's sense of unease. His entire frame had gone rigid and from his expression, Henri could tell he was trying to decipher Nasir's plans.

"He could have positioned his army to defend the palace instead of the city," Malik thought aloud. "Or he could be luring us into a trap, having placed his soldiers throughout the city to take us by surprise as we move through the streets."

"It's a smart idea, breaking up our lines and forcing us to fight in tight spaces."

"We still outnumber him, though. What's his strategy for that?"

Henri didn't know. All he knew was that Nasir clearly wanted them to enter the city and they had no choice but to do so. He refused to wait outside out of fear or waste time negotiating terms of surrender. Nasir would never capitulate and his word couldn't be trusted, nor was there any time left to lose. No, this war started now. Henri wasn't sure what they were about to face, but he was confident that they would outlast whatever Nasir had schemed for them.

Despite the water supply drying up hours ago, the men stood firm beneath the blazing sun as they marched on, determined to defeat their enemy and save their people. Their loved one's lives depended on their victory. It gave the soldiers a singular focus. The men were clad in light material and headscarves, with some wearing mesh to shield their eyes from the sand and glare. At the head of the army, the Naiab stood ready for Henri to give them the order to unleash their sand wielding abilities. They hadn't had cause to yet, preferring to blend in with the other soldiers as much as possible in order to form a cohesive unit, but Henri was under no illusion that they were his biggest advantage in this war.

"We could send the Naiab ahead to scout," Henri suggested.

"There's no time."

Malik was right. Very soon they would be crossing the threshold into the city. There wasn't enough time for the Naiab to dissolve into sand, enter the city and spread out, make an assessment of threat and then return to inform him of it. Besides, he wasn't sure the information would change their strategy. They had limited options and no time to reassess.

Henri's mind raced with possibilities and contingencies, none of which were comforting. He wondered if the gods were watching them right now. Watching the battle unfold, a veritable theater of sand and steel and carnage. He wondered if they were placing bets on the outcome or simply observing it with cruel detachment. There was no doubt in his mind that the water goddess would be watching but he also knew she refused to interfere in the realms of other gods.

"Is there a war god?" Henri looked over at Malik curiously.

"The god of war and valor. Why?"

"Should we be praying to him for victory?"

"You put an end to human sacrifices and emptied the temples. I don't think any amount of praying will make the gods favor you any time soon."

Fair point.

Henri turned his attention back to the city but his thoughts drifted to Tahlia. He hoped she was safe. His instincts told him she was, that Isa had been true to his word and carried out their vengeance. Henri even dared to hope that she might be back in his kingdom, waiting for him and Malik to come home to her. She would be losing her mind worrying for them, but at least she would be out of harm's way.

Ele would also be out of harm's way if he simply stayed put in the wagon but Henri knew him better than that. No amount of stern words or warnings would be enough to override his sense of duty when the fighting began. It was why Malik had suggested that they give Ele a unique role in the battle plan. Henri only hoped it would keep him far away from the heart of the combat.

A low hum of anticipation filled the air as they grew closer to the city. Malik whistled a high, piercing signal and a squad of mounted soldiers broke off from the army, splitting in two directions to surround the city. Their orders were to cut off various exits that Malik thought Nasir might try to use if he sensed the tide was turning against him. The valley in which the city was built, surrounded by mountains, worked in their favor in this regard. It restricted Nasir's opportunities for escape.

"Prepare to engage!" Henri yelled, his voice carrying across the plane.

The sound of thousands of shamshirs being ripped from their sheaths made his blood thrum in his veins. They didn't charge, rather they filed into the city at a controlled pace, every man alert and prepared to respond to the first sign of threat. The streets were empty. Market stalls had been abandoned, their wares still on display, meat sizzling on hotplates. The people had likely fled at the sound of the horns, boarding themselves inside their homes, huddling with their families, hoping to be spared in the bloodshed. Henri shared their hope. He did not come here to kill innocents, he came here to save a country.

The quiet was unnerving. Malik silently signaled for the soldiers to spread out amidst the streets and then reconvene at the palace. If Nasir was hoarding his men for his own protection, then that would be where the battle would take place. If his plan was to funnel the army down a particular route so his men could ambush them, this response would lessen their losses. Henri nodded at Malik in silent agreement before they parted down different roads. He hated to lose sight of him, to not have him by his side, but they couldn't risk both of them falling prey to Nasir's trap.

Henri's eyes scanned the windows of the buildings as they passed beneath them. Most were closed or had heavy drapes pulled across them. From what he could see, there were no archers waiting for them with arrows lined up to pick them off one by one. Walking along the open streets unmolested felt too easy but perhaps the truth was simple; Nasir had no experience waging war or defending his kingdom. His arrogance likely prevented him from acknowledging the threat that Henri posed. Perhaps he hadn't expected the army to survive the journey without water. Now he was unprepared and cowering in his fortress, unsure how to respond to their presence on his doorstep.

Just then, small metal containers were hurled down onto the road around them. They exploded, filling the air with a heavy smoke and toxic fumes. Henri recognized the substance almost immediately. Sulfur. His horse reared in panic but Henri managed to cling on, trying to regain control of the beast. His eyes watered and his lungs burned as the chemical quickly filled his airways. He needed to get out of the smoke but he wasn't sure which direction they had come from and which way would lead him out. The smoke was so thick he couldn't see anything and his eyes stung every time he tried to open them. Then came the sounds of slaughter. Steel and groans and cries of pain. Nasir's soldiers were blocking off both escape routes, Henri realized, killing anyone trying to flee. His men would be unable to defend themselves, staggering blind and just trying to breathe. They wouldn't even see death coming before it cut them down.

"To the roofs!" Henri shouted before being overtaken by a violent coughing fit.

He was relieved to hear his order being repeated among the men. Hopefully, it carried across the streets. Henri couldn't breathe but he knew he had to keep moving. He slid from his horse, his sandals finding the ground beneath him. He slapped the beast on the rear to make it bolt and prayed no soldiers would be run down in its wake. Pulling the ends of his headscarf up over his mouth, Henri tried to get his bearings. The material did little to help filter the air. He was still breathing the sulfur in, pouring toxins down his throat. He stumbled forward, one hand outstretched, until it found a wall. His fingers searched its surface desperately, his feet shuffling sideways, until the wall ended. He kicked out with his foot and found what he was looking for; an exterior staircase.

It was something he had always admired about Merovian architecture. Most homes and buildings were single story or two stories at the most, but almost all of them had mud-brick exterior staircases to provide easy access to the roof. Since the roofs were flat, the people used them as another level of the house, to store items, to sleep in the cooler temperatures at night, or even to socialize during the day. It was easy to mingle when every building sat side by side and each roof practically ran on to the next.

Henri took the stairs fast and burst out onto the roof. His lungs filled with sweet, clean air. He spluttered, swallowing his own saliva to try to coat his scorched throat. Glancing around through watery vision, he was relieved to find that he was not the only one on the roof. His men had heard his order repeated among the several streets over and they were now spread out on rooftops across the city.

"Henri!"

Henri whipped around to see Malik standing on a rooftop a street over. His chest loosened at the sight of him, safe and whole. Clearly, Henri's men weren't the only ones who had been ambushed. His expression hardened in anger. Today would see the end of Nasir and his tricks. Henri walked over to the edge of the roof and peered down at the street below. It was barely visible through the fog of sulfur. He peered down both directions and saw Nasir's men waiting on either side, poised to execute anyone trying to flee. He knew it would be the same for every street his soldiers had gone down.

"Naiab," Henri shouted. The Naiab, dispersed across the rooftops of several streets, turned to him in anticipation. "Kill them all!"

The Naiab broke into a run, splitting in both directions and then hurtled themselves off the rooftops into the air. They instantly dissolved into sand which rained down on the soldiers below before they reformed into solid flesh to gut their enemy without mercy.

"Everyone else with me!" Malik bellowed and launched into a fierce sprint.

The men followed his lead, darting across the roofs with speed and agility. Some ran with their shamshirs at the ready while others pulled arrows from their quivers and knocked them up in preparation for their targets. With a direct line of sight from the roof, they would able to efficiently eliminate any of Nasir's men who lay in waiting up ahead. Henri ran too, pushing himself until he was matching Malik's speed, vaulting from one rooftop to the next, as if they were racing each other.

In the near distance, Henri could see their destination; the palace. It was just as Malik had described. A fortress built several stories high on the top of a desert mountain. At the base, he could see that an army stood waiting for them. Henri steeled himself in determination, satisfied to finally see the enemy gathered in front of him in plain sight. Nasir had delivered the first blow in this war and tried to thin their numbers but it wouldn't be enough to stop them. Smoke and retribution laced the air, fueling their every breath. As they flew across the last of the rooftops, a deafening battle cry tore from the throats of thousands of warriors. Death or victory awaited them as they leaped into the fray.

ELE

Ele tried to ignore the sudden screams that rang out as he raced along the outskirts of the city. Seconds later, a strange smell tinged the air, like rotten eggs left to bake in the hot sun. Something had gone wrong. Ele looked over toward the inner city, his instincts telling him that Henri was in danger, but he fought the urge to go to him. His king had given him an order and would not stray from it. Henri would survive whatever Nasir was throwing at him. He had already overcome impossible odds time and time again. His was the story of legends. He was a true warrior king. And he had Malik by his side.

Malik would never let him die.

Refocusing on the task at hand, Ele pushed forward, his legs propelling him to the desert mountain and the palace that sat on top of it. He needed to find the underground water system and turn the water back on. He had no idea where the system was but he had studied the map Malik had drawn and decided that the best place to start would be the dam. Thankfully, there were no soldiers on the outskirts of the city. From the sounds of it, they were all lying in wait within the city streets, ready to trap Henri's men. Nasir was crafty but Henri would still defeat him.

As he rounded the edge of the city, Ele skidded to a halt in a cloud of dust as he beheld Nasir's army positioned at the base of the mountain, their lines in perfect formation, their shamshirs raised ready to defend their king. His heart pounded in his chest as the soldier's collective attention fixed on him. Only a short distance separated them, he was within archers' range, and he had no cover at all should they decide to fire on him. He could run to the shelter of the streets behind him but that would be cowardly and he was no coward. Ele drew his shamshir and pointed it to the sky, the sunlight shimmering off the engraved Pelascene steel.

"Long live King Henri!"

An arrow whistled through the air. Ele waved his blade frantically in an effort to defend himself, praying the archer's aim was poor. To his shock, the arrow splintered at his feet. Ele blinked as he stared at the arrowhead buried in the sand, but he didn't have time to dwell on it as a thunderous battle cry split the air and thousands of soldiers surged out of the city streets behind him. Ele beamed at the sight of Henri leading the charge, his face a storm of fury. Malik ran parallel with him, matching his pace until they were running side by side. Ele raised his voice to join in the battle chorus then dashed out of the way, watching the forces collide in an explosion of metal, gore and destruction.

Ele desperately wished he could be one of the soldiers tearing through the enemy, burying his shamshir in their flesh, and protecting his king. But there would be more battles to come. Of that, he was certain. Ele spotted a path through the carnage and dashed for it. The ground was already slippery with blood and littered with bodies. He weaved around them, pushing past soldiers as they clashed and cut each other to pieces. A blade swung at his head and he ducked, but he fell to the ground as someone crashed into him from behind. Air whooshed from his lungs and a dull pain throbbed in his chest where his stitches had been. Ele gasped and clawed at the sand, trying to wriggle out from underneath the dead weight on top of him. It took him precious time but finally he was able to heave himself free. Ele rolled onto his back, panting from exhaustion. He stared up at the sky for a heartbeat and thought how odd that it could be such a beautiful, calm blue when the world beneath it was fiery chaos.

Scrambling to his feet, Ele took off at a pace. Neither army paid much attention to him weaving in and out, but he stayed low anyway and dodged the butchery until he was finally clear of the battle. Tilting his head back, he stared up at the palace that loomed over him. It was amazing how it had been built on top of the mountain but also somehow into the mountain. He looked to his right, his eyes following the mountain around until it disappeared. According to Malik's map, the dam was on the other side of the mountain.

Ele carefully began making his way around the base of the mountain. The hard ochre ground was steep and rocky. Occasionally he lost his footing, scattering pebbles and creating small clouds of dust which the wind swiftly carried away. He was moving slower than he would have liked but if he tried to go any faster, he knew he would slip and fall. He tried to distract himself from his growing frustration, even as he concentrated on where to place his feet next.

Once he found the underground system and turned the water back on, he would be able to search for Kala. She was here in Nasir's kingdom. He could feel her. Maybe she was spying on Nasir, waiting for the right moment to strike. Or perhaps she had already sabotaged him from within and was now watching her plan unfold with that smug smirk that always made him smile. One thing was for sure, she wouldn't be sitting waiting for Henri's army. Or him.

Ele couldn't wait to see Kala again. He had so much to tell her. Like how he had died and come back to life. She would be horrified. About him dying, yes, but more so about the fact that Henri had made a deal with the goddess of endings and beginnings to bring him back to life. Kala mistrusted the gods more than anyone. Even Malik was wary of the fact that he had been god-touched, as if it might change him somehow. Ele had to admit, there was a small part of him that found the idea exciting. What if he had been changed? Perhaps he would develop magic like Isa. But he didn't feel any different. Surely he would have noticed it by now if the goddess's touch had changed him.

As Ele made his way around the mountain, the dam came into view. It was larger than he had expected. He would need to get a better vantage point if he was going to see where the water was disappearing to. Ele glanced up at the steep surface of the mountain and sighed. Kala would have no problem climbing it. Scowling, he reluctantly started to climb. He felt like a newborn mountain goat, only half as graceful.

He knew he should probably climb higher for a better view but he gave up after only a few minutes. Looking out, Ele could see that the dam was huge. It was carved into the earth, surrounded on either side by sheer red cliff faces. The dark blue tint of the water told him it was very deep. He cast his gaze over the outline of it, trying to see where the water escaped, but it didn't.

Ele frowned. The dam looked like a snake that had its head chopped off. Perhaps the underground water system fed directly into the dam. He scanned the earth on either side of it as if he could see beneath its surface but of course he couldn't. Knowing Nasir, it was more likely that it was beneath the mountain itself. Maybe that was why his army was stationed to defend the mountain. He was protecting more than himself and his palace, he was guarding the underground water system.

If that were true, perhaps there was an entrance at the base of the mountain near the dam. It would make sense. Ele growled at himself for not paying closer attention as he trekked around it. He might have even walked straight passed it but he had been too busy concentrating on his feet. Ele looked back the way he came. He could retrace his steps or he could climb down and keep going further around the mountain. Grumbling, Ele started to climb back down. Once he reached the base, he kept walking ahead.

He knew he was probably wasting time. Maybe there was no entrance for him to find. Maybe the only way inside the underground water system was from within the mountain, beneath the palace. He hoped not. Even with a war going on, he had no idea how he would manage to slip inside the palace unnoticed. He wondered how Kala had managed it. He assumed that she had. She was clever like that. Kala would have so much to tell him. It would probably take them days to exchange all their stories.

They would have time. When Henri won the war, they would go back home and train together. His tutor would be keen to hear everything that had happened. He probably wouldn't be proud of Ele for losing the fight with Kareem, that was a shameful defeat, but he would be happy Ele remembered everything he'd taught him. Ele could show his tutor his new shamshir. He wondered if the man had ever seen Pelascene steel. Ele subconsciously ran his fingers through the short golden tassel that hung from the bone pommel.

Something glinted out of the corner of his eye, causing Ele to stop. Ahead of him was a small steel door in the side of the mountain. His heart leaped in hope but then he looked around, searching for the soldiers that were meant to be guarding it. There were none. Perhaps they were stationed inside. Or maybe the door was bolted shut. Ele approached it on quiet feet and then pressed his ear to the surface. Of course, he couldn't hear anything inside. It was a steel door. Rolling his eyes at himself, he gripped the metal ring in one hand and held his shamshir ready in the other as he pulled it with all his might.

To Ele's surprise, it actually opened. Inside was a dark, silent tunnel. Ele put his shamshir back in its sheath. He had no way of making a torch to light a path for himself, so he simply braced a hand on one of the walls and stepped inside. The ground sloped gently downward. The wall was rough, the jagged stone cutting at the flesh of his palm, but he didn't dare take his hand away. It was the only thing giving him any kind of reassurance. Navigating through darkness was scary. With every step he took his terror rose. It escalated even further when he looked behind him and realized that he could no longer see the light of the door he had come through. He froze in panic.

He was going to die. *Again.*

The darkness was going to swallow him whole. He would never find his way out. He would be buried beneath this cursed mountain.

"You stupid piece of camel dung!"

A girl's voice broke through his terror. It was faint as it carried through the tunnel but he recognized it like he recognized his own heartbeat.

Kala. It was Kala!

Ele stumbled ahead, his steps quick and sure now, his pulse racing for an entirely different reason. He hadn't thought to find her here, beneath the mountain. What was she doing? His mind pieced it together in seconds; she was trying to turn the water back on. Of course she was. The tunnel wound around but it was no longer terrifying because he knew who was at the end of it. When he finally saw a faint light up ahead, Ele sprinted.

He burst out into an open antechamber that was dimly lit by torches. There were several large clay pipes branching off into an impressive system of tunnels but his attention was immediately drawn to the girl whose face was pinched with effort as she tried to wind a lever around.

"Move, you old piece of worthless—"

"Kala!"

She jumped back, letting out a shrill shriek, but then her mouth fell open at the sight of him. "Ele?"

They closed the distance in seconds to crash into each other. Ele closed his eyes tight as he held her. She felt like home. But then, all too quickly, she pulled away.

"What are you doing here?" she asked.

"Henri and Malik are waging war on the kingdom."

"I know that. I meant how did you get down here?" Kala glanced around the chamber. "Where did you come from?"

"A secret tunnel that leads out to the dam. How did you get here?"

Kala looked away and Ele followed her gaze to see two slumped guards a short distance away at the entrance to a different tunnel.

"You killed them?"

She shrugged. "Easy to do when they can't see the blades being thrown at them in the dark."

Ele raised his brows, impressed.

"They had it coming," Kala said.

"Why?" Ele frowned. "What did they do?"

"It doesn't matter. They've paid for it now. Where's Tahlia?"

Ele couldn't hide the guilt from his face as he turned back to her. "Kareem took her. I couldn't stop him. But Isa went to get her back."

Kala nodded, satisfied. "Help me turn these levers. We have to open the gates to the conduits to let the water through."

Ele followed her over to the lever she had been trying to shift. They stood opposite each other, both gripping the lever at different sections, and counted down before putting their entire body weight into it.

The lever loosened a fraction.

"Again." Ele pushed harder against it as Kala pulled.

The lever gave way and Kala turned it, watching the gate slowly ascend at every turn. A gentle rushing sound filled the chamber. Water, he realized. Water was filling the pipe. They quickly moved to the next lever and took up position, pressing and pulling against it with all their strength. By the time they mastered the fourth lever, their palms were red and raw and their arms trembled from exertion, but they had opened all the gates and the rushing sound was now so loud they had to raise their voices to hear each other.

"That's all of them," Kala shouted, though they both glanced at other tunnels with pipes that led clearly somewhere. "What should we do now?"

Ele unsheathed his shamshir. "Find Nasir."

CHAPTER TWENTY

HENRI

War has its own rhythm. The sharp sing of the sword, the tear of flesh beneath metal, the stampede of a thousand feet, and the steady heartbeat of those left alive. Henri had fought enough battles in his life to recognize the pulse of war. It was strangely comforting. It gave a sense of order to otherwise brutal chaos.

All around him, the conflict roared in a frenzy of violence. Merovian against Merovian, countrymen against countrymen, but neither side held back from the slaughter. War simplified the most complex of moral dilemmas; there was only alive or dead. The Naiab morphed from solid flesh to fierce gusts of sand, scything through the enemy with the grace of a blade cutting through mist. Their comrades showed no fear of them, continuing to fight by their side undeterred. They had clearly decided that it was better to have magic on their side than against them. Especially when it could mean the difference between returning to their loved ones or being buried in a shallow grave.

Henri pulled his sword up in time to block a downward strike and then pushed back against the soldier, sending him stumbling.

Before he could recover his feet, Henri hacked through his stomach, casting his entrails across the sand. His sword arm felt heavy, worn down by the relentless impact of steel, but he kept fighting, embracing the familiar burn. He barely saw the faces of the men he killed. Young, old, scared, or courageous; it was enough to see that they were the enemy before he struck them down with brutal efficiency.

Blood soaked his clothes and dripped from Henri's face and arms. Most of it belonged to his enemy but some of it was his. A few opponents had managed to land surface cuts across his exposed flesh. It felt strange not to wear metal armor into battle but it did make his movements more agile and quick. It also made the enemy easier to kill. He didn't have to search for weak spots in their armor or deliver precise blows. He could slash erratically and it was effective. It was also cathartic. It felt good to finally release all the emotion that had been building up over the past few weeks. The anxiety. The rage. To focus every thought, every muscle, every movement on one single task; obliteration.

"Where is he?" Henri roared with fury, cleaving through each soldier who dared to stand in his way. "Where is your king?"

The soldiers didn't reply, not that they had any breath left to answer him. Henri's frustration sparked and surged like a brushfire. Nasir had not led his men into battle. From what Henri could tell, having carved a path through his forces, Nasir wasn't with them at all. He was a coward. Perhaps instead of facing Henri on the battlefield, Nasir had tried to escape. If that was true, the soldiers Malik sent out in anticipation of his desertion would intercept him and deliver him to Henri for justice. Or maybe, instead of trying to escape, Nasir had a different plan in mind.

"Where is he?" Henri bellowed.

His eyes scanned the killing field, knowing he wouldn't find Nasir, but needing to assess the situation. The momentum of the battle was strongly in his favor. Although he was sustaining losses, Nasir's men were being slaughtered at his feet. There were no reinforcements coming to hold their lines, no chance of recovering from their significant casualties. By midday the war would be won and Nasir's kingdom would be conquered.

Amid the massacre and ruin, Henri spotted Malik slicing through bone, guts, and sinew. He was beautiful, his movements swift and exact and merciless. Watching him now, no one would know that this was his first war, and his first as king. He fought without fear and he led his men like he was born to do it. Henri could still remember being unable to eat or sleep on the eve of his first battle. Once the killing was done, he had thrown his guts up all over the bodies. If Malik had spared a thought for his own mortality, or for the daunting responsibility of leading an army into war, Henri hadn't noticed. Perhaps he had been too distracted. They had spent the night lost in the pleasure of each other but when the sun awoke, they refocused on the battle ahead with calm, steady resolve.

As if sensing his stare from across the killing field, Malik's eyes found his. In that moment, Henri glimpsed a hundred years together ruling side by side. Facing every enemy as united kings of Merovia. Savoring every night buried inside each other, learning the language that their bodies made together. Years, a lifetime, spent loving him.

Malik dispatched his opponent with cruel proficiency before marching through the carnage toward Henri, his gaze never straying from his face. When he drew near, Malik gripped the back of Henri's neck and crushed his mouth with a rough, claiming kiss. It tasted of sweat and salt and blood. Henri met his kiss with a wild ferocity of his own. A need rose inside him, fierce and demanding, but now was not the time. It was just the adrenaline from battle taking over their senses. The near climax of victory addling their minds. It was so close they could taste it. It made them want to taste each other.

"What's wrong?" Malik asked as he searched Henri's face, his breath a little uneven. Whether from the battle or the kiss Henri wasn't sure.

"Nasir."

Henri didn't have to say anything more because Malik nodded in understanding. "I'll come with you."

Malik led the way as they moved through the thick of the fighting, slicing and stabbing where they could, without stopping or slowing down. Once they were on the other side of it, they stood staring up at the palace before them. At least the mountain wasn't too high or steep to climb. They moved quickly but carefully, ascending the path worn into the hard ochre ground. Henri's mind drifted back to all the times Malik had made him run up and down the stairs of the palace in the intense heat of the midday sun. It felt particularly poignant right now. His breaths drew in short and shallow but they weren't labored. He had somehow acclimated to exerting himself in the Merovian heat. A grin crept across his lips at the thought.

As they neared the doors of the palace, Henri noted that there were no guards standing watch at the entrance. Even so, they approached with caution, their senses on high alert. Stepping inside, the palace looked as abandoned as the city had been. Most likely, upon hearing the horns warning, the servants had scattered or taken shelter in their homes with their loved ones. Malik silently signaled for Henri to follow him and led the way to a nearby staircase. They began to climb.

It was fortunate that Malik knew the palace well. It was several stories high, a labyrinth of chambers and halls and endless staircases, all of it enclosed within solid stone walls. It felt claustrophobic. There was no view into the outside world. No windows, balconies, or open-air spaces. It was a fortress built with clean lines and a practical purpose, completely void of warmth, character, and beauty. Henri couldn't imagine Tahlia living in such a place. It was everything she was not.

"The next floor is the king's floor," Malik warned.

They stepped onto the landing and rounded the corner only to be attacked by a dozen private guards. Henri and Malik quickly closed in on each other to protect one another's backs while simultaneously defending against the onslaught. Henri unleashed a short sequence of strikes that wounded and maimed. He blocked counter attacks and dodged hidden blades. The soldiers were well trained but they had only ever been taught a Merovian style of fighting, against Merovian weaponry. They weren't accustomed to defending against a straight edged sword, the lack of resistance in it and the controlled depth of its thrusts. Henri could see the surprise in their eyes right before he speared them through.

Behind him, Malik was holding his own with effortless ease, attacking with eloquence and rigid concentration. His body moved naturally, as if driven by instinct rather than thought, except Henri knew that Malik did nothing without careful consideration. Nasir's men tried to breach his form but his technique was too refined and their mistakes ended in deadly consequences.

When it was done, bodies littered the ground, some of the men still groaning through their final breaths. Henri winced as he rotated his wrists and then his shoulders. He was beginning to tire. Malik noticed his movements but didn't say anything, he simply walked forward to stand between two doors. He glanced between them, as if trying to decide which one would lead them to Nasir. Or maybe he was tactfully giving Henri a moment to recover.

"How's your arm?"

Malik raised an eyebrow at Henri's concern. "How's your leg?"

Hurting less than the rest of him, if Henri was honest. The corner of Malik's mouth twitched, as if he knew the answer.

"I'll let you tend to my wounds later," Henri replied.

Malik smirked, even as he pointed to the door on his left. "Assembly room."

Henri shifted his grip on his sword with renewed fortitude. His palms were slick with sweat. He approached the door, and they exchanged a sobering look before Henri opened it. Nasir was standing across the room, leaning over a large table, studying a map laid out in front of him. Though his stance was casual, Henri didn't miss the fact that he was dressed in the thick fiber material Merovians wore into battle. He was expecting them. Or at least expecting that he may have to fight his way out of this.

As they walked into the room, Nasir looked up at them and flashed a cunning smile. Henri couldn't wait to slice it off his face.

"Heroux was right, you are a hard man to kill. Like a cockroach, you just refuse to die." Nasir's eyes danced between them, amused, as they both took up a defensive stance. "The foreign king and the lover who betrayed him. I see you have forgiven him already. He must be very good at sucking cock."

"Don't," Henri warned.

"Or perhaps this is purely an alliance of convenience. Love has no place in politics or war. Wouldn't you agree, Malik?"

Malik speared him with a deadly stare. "Enough talking. You've lost. Your army has been defeated. This kingdom is Henri's now."

Nasir scoffed indulgently as he moved out from behind the table to face them. "Not while I still live. You'll have to kill me, I'm afraid."

"I intend to," Henri growled and gripped his sword tighter.

"Two against one is hardly fair odds."

"Oh, I'm not fighting you. I just came to watch." Malik retreated, each step slow and deliberate, until his back was leaning against the wall, one foot casually crossed over the other.

His gaze flicked to Henri and the words hung in the air between them, unspoken. He didn't need Malik to fight his battles for him but Malik would always be there to fight by his side when he needed him. To defend his back. To help strategize his victory. Nasir was wrong. Love had a place in war, and Henri was stronger for it.

Nasir retrieved his shamshir and took several steps to the side, forcing Henri to mirror his movements in a half arc. "It's a shame it came to this. We could have ruled together, you and I."

"I already have a king by my side," Henri said.

The fling of the dagger was so fast Henri didn't see it until it shot past him and lodged itself into something hard with a sickening thud. Henri's heart jammed itself into his throat.

Malik.

Henri tried to glance behind him but the venomous look in Nasir's eyes was the only warning he got before Nasir swung at him with lethal force. Metal screamed against metal as they came together in a burst of violence. Henri had never seen Nasir fight before so he had no idea what to expect. He knew that Nasir didn't revel in bloodshed like Kareem or Dahane, he preferred manipulation and subtle tactics to brute force, but Henri also knew that he had challenged a Merovian king at the summit and won. Now he knew how. Nasir was fast, well trained, and unpredictable. There was no feeling each other out, no testing defenses or wearing each other down, he was going straight for the kill every time. His strikes were full-bodied and relentless. It was all Henri could do to defend himself against each blow but he knew he needed to break through his lines somehow and take control of the fight.

"Be careful! He's poisoned his blades."

Relief flooded his body at the sound of Malik's voice.

"Cheating bastard!" a girl's voice shrieked.

Kala?

Henri pivoted so he could glance over Nasir's shoulder. Malik was standing with his arms folded across his chest, a murderous look on his face and a dagger embedded in the wall a hair's breadth away from his head. Standing next to him was Kala, a look of indignant rage on her face, and Ele, his posture tense but observant. Ele's prediction had been right then; Kala had followed Nasir all the way into his kingdom. And despite a war waging around him, Ele had somehow managed to find her. It was enough to make Henri believe in fate. That the gods were somehow weaving their threads together in the great tapestry of life.

"The water?" Henri called out to them.

"Restored," Ele shouted back.

Nasir released a guttural sound of frustration as he pressed forward, lunging and slicing, forcing Henri to give ground. His movements were becoming more erratic now, driven by anger and desperation. In one way, it gave Henri an advantage because Nasir's footwork was less precise and he was leaving careless openings. But all Nasir had to do was slice his skin in a superficial wound and the fight would be over because poison would finish the kill. Henri couldn't afford to take any reckless chances. He needed to be patient and sure.

He swung his sword low, trying to force Nasir off balance, but Nasir rode his blade along the edge of Henri's sword and twisted, ripping it out of his hand. It clattered to the floor, out of reach.

That was not the outcome Henri had hoped for. Nasir lunged but Henri side-stepped and smashed his fist into Nasir's stomach. It caught him by surprise because he stumbled forward, and Henri took advantage of the moment by throwing him down to the ground.

Nasir's body landed hard enough to knock the wind out of him. Standing over him, Henri stomped his foot down on his wrist with crushing force, enjoying the primal scream that tore from Nasir's throat. His fingers reflexively opened and Henri kicked the shamshir clear across the room. He lifted his knee to deliver a savage blow to his face but Nasir caught it and slammed his fist down onto his thigh.

Henri cursed, his injury throbbing from the impact. He didn't know how Nasir knew of his wound but it shouldn't have surprised him. Nasir always knew his opponents' weaknesses. The danger of the right information in the wrong person's hands could turn the tide of wars. In an instant, Nasir was on his feet. He delivered a vicious punch to Henri's throat, crushing his windpipe, before slamming him into a wall. Dazed, Henri failed to brace himself against the impact and absorbed the full force of the collision as it vibrated his bones. He still couldn't breathe but survivors' instinct took over and he brought his arms up to deflect Nasir's rapid blows. Gasping for air, he caught one of Nasir's arms and locked it in his, twisting his body around and yanking it down until he heard the satisfying snap of bone.

Nasir's scream was chilling.

He staggered backward, clutching his useless arm, and Henri cleared his throat, trying to force air down his bruised windpipe. His focus never strayed from Nasir as he stalked toward him, though he could feel the rapt attention of his audience behind him. Nasir felt it too. Henri could see it in his eyes, the fear, the panic. He had no sword arm. He had no weapon. There was no cheating or escaping death. It was coming for him.

Nasir smiled suddenly, his laugh hollow. "Such is the fate of all kings."

Henri felt something press against his hand and he glanced down to see Ele offering him his shamshir. Their eyes met, the same memory passing between them of a time not so long ago when Ele had handed him an axe. The axe that had made Henri a king. Henri pulled the shamshir from its blue velvet scabbard. It felt odd, light and small in his hand, designed for a child, not a man. Ele retreated back to the wall and Henri turned his attention back to Nasir.

"Killing an unarmed opponent is dishonorable," Nasir pointed out. "I know you, Henri. You are a man of honor."

Henri gripped the shamshir in his hand as he drew closer. "I am. But I am also a king."

He whirled in a wide arc, the tip of the Pelascene steel slicing through the air to carve a delicate line across Nasir's throat. It was a lethal strike but not an instant death. Henri wanted to watch him suffer. His schemes for power, his indifference to the lives of the Merovian people, had caused so much pain. No amount of suffering would ever deliver justice for what he had done.

Suddenly a dagger struck Nasir's chest, buried to the hilt. Henri looked back to see Kala lifting her chin in satisfaction as she pointed a finger at Nasir. The dagger was Nasir's, retrieved from the wall. The recognition made Nasir's eyes widen in alarm. Henri supposed there was a poetic justice in the fact that his own poison was now spreading through his system, shutting down his organs as he choked on his own blood.

Nasir fell to his knees and Henri inhaled a full breath, perhaps for the first time in weeks. It was done. Nasir's body slumped to the ground, blood staining the tiles beneath him. Henri didn't move, he just stood over him, staring down at the last of the original kings of Merovia. They had each vowed to kill him and yet, against all odds, here he stood. Slick with sweat from battle, the rush of war thrumming in his veins. Alive and victorious.

At the sound of approaching footsteps, he turned to see Ele. His stare was trained on Nasir's corpse, his face pensive. Kala followed behind him, her expression cold and hard.

"Thank you." Henri handed Ele the shamshir and he accepted it with a sense of veneration, as if the sword had gained something from Nasir's death.

"Nasir's kingdom is yours. You are king of Merovia now," Ele said, as if he couldn't quite fathom it.

"One of them." Henri looked over at Malik who was standing back from the scene, allowing Henri a moment of space should he need it.

Henri reached his hand out to him and Malik stepped forward to take it. He pulled him in for a kiss, the promise of a lifetime of tomorrows on his lips. It was an oath just as binding as any words.

Pulling away slightly, Henri lowered his voice to a whisper. "I look forward to our future negotiations."

"Is this you inviting me to dinner?"

"Into my bed, actually."

Malik clicked his tongue disapprovingly. "Seducing me already."

"You admitted I conquered your heart a long time ago."

Malik smiled. "That you did, my love."

CHAPTER TWENTY-ONE

TAHLIA

The closer they drew to Nasir's kingdom, the tighter Tahlia's gut twisted. The days seemed endless as they traveled across the Idris desert, only stopping at night to rest for a few hours before continuing their journey with the rise of the sun. The war was surely over by now, yet they still didn't know who had been victorious. Part of her regretted not traveling across the borders through the kingdoms, at least that way they might have heard a rumor by now, but across the Idris desert was the most direct route to Nasir's kingdom and she needed to be with her family rather than hear of their fate secondhand.

They rode in companionable silence but Tahlia knew that Isa was eager for news as well. His men had joined Henri and Malik's army to fight in the war, he would want to know who had lived and who had fallen. He would be just as desperate to know if the aquifer had been restored. Without it, his people would not survive, much like the rest of the Merovia.

Tahlia had given no thought to what she would do if they arrived at the kingdom only to find Nasir alive and vengeful. It was simply not possible. If Nasir was alive, then Henri and Malik were dead and she refused to believe that. She would have felt it if they died. She would *know*. The connection between the three of them surpassed any earthly limits. They were tethered by something else, something infinite, and she would always feel them, no matter the distance between. As sure as she lived and breathed in this moment, Henri and Malik were alive. But until she saw them with her own eyes and felt their arms around her, her mind would not rest.

"Henri won."

"What?" Tahlia spluttered as she glanced over his shoulder and surveyed their barren surroundings, desperate for a sign.

"Look ahead."

Isa's eyesight was clearly better than hers but it didn't take long for her to see what he was referring to. The wall of Nasir's kingdom. It shimmered into view through a haze of burning heat, rising proudly from the golden sea of sand. It stretched endlessly across the distance and towered several meters high. Except it was no longer intact. The top of the wall was being dismantled, as were the watchtowers.

"Henri." His name from her lips was no more than a breath on the wind.

Tahlia released a whimper of relief as tears welled in her eyes. Gut wrenching fear drained from her body, leaving her feeling a little fragile but also elated. She wanted to weep, laugh, and scream all at the same time.

"Your king has kept his word. He's tearing the walls down."

Tahlia beamed at his back, even though he couldn't see her. "The Idris desert will be recognized as a kingdom of Merovia. Your people will be welcome to travel wherever they please."

Isa didn't reply. Tahlia knew better than most that there were no words that could adequately convey what it felt like to be free. It was the sensation of breathing in deeply and then letting go. It was seeing the world in vivid color for the first time. It was the wonder of choice.

Tahlia tugged at his elbow. "Look who's at the gate."

The sentries at the wall; they were Naiab. Isa clicked his tongue, urging their camel into a run. No one called out to them as they charged toward the wall. No one demanded that they halt their approach or identify themselves. In fact, the gate was already open. Isa slowed their pace as they passed beneath it. A Naiab warrior stood waiting just inside and Isa bent down to clasp forearms with him.

"Arsyn."

"Isa, my friend. You're late. You missed the war."

Isa glanced around pointedly at the wall that was being taken apart brick by brick. "Looks like you didn't need me. Besides, I had my own battles to fight."

Arsyn glanced at Tahlia, understanding settling on his features. "The others?"

"Holding the kingdom of the black sands for its queen."

The warriors' eyes went wide with surprise but Tahlia ignored them as she asked urgently, "The king? Where is he?"

"The kings are inside the city, Kafei, burying the last of the dead."

"Thank you, my friend," Isa replied, before spurring their camel ahead.

The city looked calm from a distance. It appeared as it always had; trapped within a rocky valley and eclipsed by a towering mountain. Tahlia had thought she would never come back here. It was hard to conceive that not too long ago she had been desperate to return. She had *missed* it. It was sick and twisted but it was also the truth. Sort of.

With time and distance, her perspective had shifted, and a new understanding formed. She tried to remember to gift herself some grace. She hadn't missed it. She hadn't missed feeling like a prisoner in a gilded cage. She hadn't missed her whole world, her very existence, shrinking down to the needs of one man. She hadn't missed the loneliness or the fear or the thoughts inside her mind telling her that everything was as it should be. That she was fortunate. That she should be grateful. No, she hadn't missed it. It was simply all she had known. For four years it had been her home, those years infinitely better and safer and happier than the years that had preceded them.

It felt like a lifetime ago. Even if the city hadn't changed, Tahlia certainly had. She was no longer the silk rose. She was queen of the black sands. Her world had expanded beyond the limits of Nasir's gaze and the confines of his palace walls and she would die before she ever allowed anyone to cage her again.

She certainly wasn't lonely anymore. With Henri and Malik she had found something she never knew was possible. A profound sense of belonging. Of knowing that wherever she was or whoever she was with, her heart would always be intertwined with theirs, and theirs with hers. It was why nothing further had happened between her and Isa. She had insisted that they wait until she could speak with Henri and Malik. She knew she didn't owe them anything and she certainly did not need their permission, but it didn't feel right to take another man into her bed without them knowing.

The past few days had been pure torture, the ultimate test in carnal restraint. Tahlia wasn't sure they would make it but they had managed to resist tearing each other's clothes off. Barely. Though Isa had maintained a respectful distance, she could see how much it killed him not to touch her. The kiss they had shared haunted them both. Sometimes she caught him staring at her and she knew he was remembering it, playing each second over in his mind, feeling the phantom taste of her on his lips. If she could feel this much from a single kiss, she wasn't sure she would survive more. She hadn't even allowed herself to fantasize about what it might be like to have all three men worship her. It was too much. Yet the possibility lingered on the edge of her thoughts, as if waiting for her to be brave enough to admit her deepest, darkest desire.

Isa slowed their approach as they entered the city. She was surprised to find the people going about their daily business, the markets filled with vendors and customers. One would never know that a war had ravaged this land mere days ago. The buildings had not been reduced to crumbling stone. The doors were not splintered, the brickwork was not scorched. Ash and smoke did not linger in the air, though there was a faint trace of decay on the wind. The people appeared to have resumed their lives, haggling amongst each other for a good price, and selling their wares to feed their families. Their faces were not haunted by the atrocities of war or the loss of their king. Tahlia knew Henri would have done everything in his power to keep the people safe and the city secure amidst the battle but it was still remarkable how unscathed everything appeared to be. It was a testament to resilience and a solemn reminder that life would always continue, no matter the adversity.

It wasn't until they came to a stop at the base of the mountain, within the shadow of the palace, that Tahlia saw any sign of the conflict that had taken place. Isa urged their camel to kneel and dismounted the beast before offering a hand to assist her. She took it, all the while staring at the ground in front of her. Stains of rustic red interspersed amongst the golden sand. The desert wind had not managed to paint over all the traces of blood just yet. The Naiab warrior had said the kings were still burying the last of the dead, men who had been slaughtered on this very ground. Tahlia wondered how many had fallen. She wondered exactly where they would be laid to rest.

"Tahlia!"

Her name sounded like a strangled cry ripped from a forgotten memory. She lifted her head to see Henri dashing out from the palace and racing down the mountain, kicking up clouds of sand as his feet slid precariously along the ground. She wanted to call out to him to slow down and be careful, but then she saw Malik, Ele and Kala emerge from the palace. Words failed her as her heart leaped with overflowing joy.

Henri threw himself at her, the force of him almost knocking her off her feet, but his large hand braced the back of her head while his arm wrapped around her waist, holding her steady and safe even as he clung to her. She couldn't help but close her eyes and breathe him in.

"Are you hurt?" His voice was muffled against her headscarf. "Did he—?"

"No." The word was all she could manage. She could hardly speak through the flood of emotion.

"I'm sorry. I'm so sorry." Henri sobbed into her neck. "I should have protected you."

Tahlia held him tighter, clutching at his body like she would never let him go. "Shhh. It wasn't your fault."

"It was."

"No, it was mine."

Tahlia pulled away slightly to find Ele standing beside them.

"Oh Ele!" Tahlia dropped to her knees, wrapping the boy in her arms.

Fresh tears escaped onto her cheeks but she smiled through them. It was hard to resist the urge to check his body over for wounds, to convince herself that he was indeed whole. Instead, she drew back to look at him and cupped his perfect face between her hands.

"My brave warrior. You are, and always will be, my hero."

He offered a shallow smile, as if he still hadn't forgiven himself, and never would despite her words. Tahlia's gaze drifted over his shoulder to Kala who was standing behind him. They exchanged a knowing look, one that acknowledged the ordeal they had both endured these past few weeks and the fact that they had both managed to survive.

A hand extended towards her and Tahlia glanced up to find Malik staring down at her, a warm, sweet smile on his face. She accepted his hand and he lifted her to her feet before tugging her into his arms.

"We would have come for you," Malik whispered, placing a gentle kiss on her cheek.

"I understand. Ele was injured."

"Henri was wounded too."

Tahlia's eyes widened with concern. "Is he all right?"

Malik gave an imperceptible nod as they released each other, though Tahlia slipped her hand in his, not read to let go just yet. He held it tight, as if he felt the same. She turned back to take in the sight of her family, alive and whole and within arm's reach. It was all she could have asked for.

"Thank you for bringing her home to us." Henri moved to wrap a hand possessively around her waist.

Isa remained beside the camel, a considerate distance away, watching Tahlia intently but also giving her space to reunite with her loved ones. Pressed between Henri and Malik, Tahlia instinctively nestled her head against Henri's shoulder, happy to be back where she belonged.

"I go where she commands," Isa replied simply.

Tahlia's eyes cut to his, the words igniting an instant warmth in her core. She wondered if Isa was jealous of Malik's fingers intertwined with her own and Henri's lips so close to her face. He must have read her thoughts because his gaze darkened and his posture stiffened, as if he were fighting against a primal instinct. Tahlia tilted her head ever so slightly, enjoying his discomfort far more than she should.

"Kareem?" This time Henri looked directly at Isa as he asked the question.

"Heartless. The queen of the black sands killed him."

"Queen?" Malik echoed.

Ele and Henri turned to her, aghast. "You killed Kareem?"

"Of course she did." Kala growled, insulted on Tahlia's behalf.

"Thanks to your tricks." Tahlia winked at Kala and the girl beamed proudly.

A knowing smile crept across Malik's face. "The dagger in your hair. Clever."

"You took his beard?" Henri pressed.

She had taken more than that but she didn't want to discuss the gruesome details in front of Ele and Kala. They would both likely relish in the story, especially Kala, but they were still children despite their innocence having been snuffed out a long time ago. Maybe now that the war was over, they would finally have a chance to be children. Wild. Naïve. Free.

Tahlia shrugged innocently. "Seemed like a good idea at the time. Besides, I couldn't let you two rule the entire country without me."

"We rule all of Merovia." Ele blew out his cheeks in awe.

"Except the Idris desert," Kala pointed out.

The Idris desert. In all the emotion, Tahlia had forgotten to ask about Isa's people. "Has the water been restored?"

"Kala and Ele turned it back on. The Merovian people now have equal access to water across the country," Malik replied. "We managed to restore the water to the Citadel aquifer this morning. It took us a little while to figure out which conduit was pumping the water from the underground reservoir."

"Kala killed the guards so we had to find the craftsmen," Ele explained.

"Orders have been sent out for the walls to be torn down in every kingdom," Henri added for Isa's benefit.

Tahlia shifted her gaze to Malik, watching him carefully for his reaction to the news, but he betrayed no signs that he was troubled by it. Perhaps the Naiab had won him over.

"Thank you," Isa said

"You kept your word. I will keep mine," Henri returned.

The world had changed around them in the time it took for them to cross the Idris desert. This was a new Merovia, not held ransom to the whims of kings or divided by past feuds or defined by brutal summits. The people would be united and protected under their reign. She didn't know how they would delineate the new territories, or where they would rule from, but as long as they remained together, that was all that really mattered.

It was the last thought she had.

MALIK

Malik jolted into action as Tahlia collapsed between them, both him and Henri instinctively catching her in their arms.

"Tahlia?" Malik searched her face as her head lolled back, exposing the delicate column of her throat.

One second she was smiling at them and the next she was unconscious.

"Somebody fetch some water!" Henri yelled and Malik was vaguely aware of Ele sprinting in the direction of the nearest well.

Henri kneeled, bringing Tahlia's body gently to the ground, but holding her head up to rest against his lap. He brushed errant strands of dark hair away from her face. She didn't look pale, there was still color in her cheeks.

"Has she fainted?" Kala leaned over to get a better look.

Malik shook his head, unable to answer her, but something made him glance over at Isa. He had gone unnaturally still, his expression carved from a violent aftershock and unbearable pain. Malik's heart splintered. He sank to his knees and pressed his fingers to Tahlia's throat where her pulse should have fluttered beneath her skin.

There was nothing.

"Here." Ele held out a wooden ladle filled with water and Kala tried to pour it between Tahlia's lips.

It dribbled down her cheek as her throat refused to swallow. Malik already knew the water wouldn't help her. Water could not bring back the dead. A small crowd started to form nearby of curious onlookers and faint murmurs of speculation.

"She's gone." The words were so soft Malik wasn't sure he had uttered them.

"What?" Henri demanded sharply. Malik's eyes drifted up to meet his gaze and the unspeakable truth passed between them. "No. No, she can't be."

Kala stepped back, dropping the ladle in the sand as if it had burned her. "The god took his revenge."

"No." Isa broke free from his stupor and approached them. He bent down over Tahlia and unclasped the brass vial from around her neck. "The god of beauty and fertility is trapped in here."

"Trapped?" Malik stared at the vial in alarm. "What do you mean trapped?"

"You trapped a god?" Kala echoed.

"The ending," Ele interrupted abruptly. "The goddess must have made her choice. Tahlia's ending for mine."

"No."

A voice clapped like thunder. It drew everyone's attention to Lunara who was standing a short distance away in front of the crowd that had formed. Her white long hair hung loose around her shoulders, amplified by the deep green salwar kameez she was wearing. Her feet were bare and her skin, darkened to leather from the sun, was pulled tight across her features. Within her eyes, storm clouds swirled like a tempestuous sky, promising rough seas.

She moved closer, dropping her voice to a hushed tone to ensure the crowd behind them could not overhear. "Tahlia's life is not the price that will be paid. That is yet to come to pass."

"What have you done?" Henri demanded.

"Not just me. The gods do not forgive, nor do we forget. Once Tahlia revealed herself to us, her fate was inevitable. She knew this. She used the time she had left wisely."

Isa held up the vial firmly grasped in his hand. "But if the god of beauty and fertility is trapped, her debt cannot be claimed."

The goddess stared at the vial for a moment, her expression heavy but unreadable. Malik wasn't sure if she pitied the god trapped within it or if she feared the fact that the same could happen to her.

"He chose her, but she incited the wrath of all the gods when she fled. And then she trapped one of us." Her eyes narrowed on Isa accusingly. "That alone would have signed her death."

"Bring her back." Henri clutched at Tahlia's lifeless body, as if he refused to let death take her. "Summon the goddess of endings and beginnings. *Now.*"

"What's done is done. It cannot be undone."

"Do it!" Henri roared and the crowd around them startled into silence.

Everything around them went still, like time had stopped. It should have. Gone. Tahlia was gone. The goddess of endings and beginnings was not going to bring her back. There was nothing Malik or Henri or anyone could do to save her. The gods had taken what she stole from them; her life. Her eternity.

Henri unleashed a gut-wrenching roar that reverberated across the sands. Malik reached out to him, tenderly resting his hand against his cheek. It was all the comfort he could offer as his other hand remained holding Tahlia's.

"So Tahlia's a ... goddess now?" Ele asked softly.

Kala shook her head. "She hasn't been sacrificed. The god of fire and ash can't receive her."

"She wouldn't want to be one. She never wanted that," Malik added solemnly.

"Our bargain remains," the water goddess interjected. "For what you have done, you will have my support throughout your reign."

Henri stared at her blankly as bitter tears filled his eyes. Malik knew it was the last thing he wanted. That he would trade it in a heartbeat if it brought Tahlia back to them.

"As will you," the water goddess turned her liquid orbs to Kala. "You restored the water table. For that, the Naiab and I will stand by you throughout your reign."

"My what?" Kala's eyes darted between them all, her brow furrowing in confusion.

"Tahlia named you as her heir." Isa's words were flat as he forced them from his throat. "You are now the queen of the black sands."

CHAPTER TWENTY-TWO

ISA

Isa carried her body in his arms, cradling her close to his chest. She was wrapped in soft white linen sheets, a death shroud. He couldn't see her face but even in death, he knew she would be beautiful. A beautiful, cold, empty shell where once there had been warmth and life and love. He knew that nothing really remained of her, just skin and bones, but he still held her with care and tenderness.

Isa had waited for the sun to melt from the sky before he stole her body away from where the healers had left it in preparation for burial. Tahlia would not want to be buried here in the kingdom that had caged her, and Isa refused for the god of earth and salt to claim her. She did not belong there. Isa had made his decision a heartbeat after Tahlia drew her last breath, though a small part of him continued to debate it quietly in the corner of his mind. He ignored the voice of dissent. Nothing could stop him or change his mind. He had come too far to turn back.

Last night he had mapped out a quiet route from the palace that would ensure he went unnoticed. He followed it now beyond the city and into the desert. The full moon made the soft velvet night sky look almost blue amidst the splatter of dazzling stars. He shivered as he walked beneath the luminous display, not because the air was cold, but because it felt like hundreds of thousands of celestial bodies were watching him, bearing witness to what he was about to do. Perhaps it stirred memories among the stars of their mortal existence before they joined the constellations.

Isa walked out into the desert, far enough to ensure that he wouldn't be seen from the city, then he laid her body down in the sand. It shifted beneath her, as though inviting her into its fold. A delicate breeze stirred the particles across the dunes. Isa retrieved a small vial of oil and poured its contents onto her. Then he took out two firestones and kneeled close to her body before he struck them. The spark ignited the cloth and the flames quickly spread from head to toe. Isa stood, his body suddenly feeling heavier than it had a moment ago.

Around him the desert was quiet and still, almost complicit, as he watched her burn. It was one of its tricks. Creating the illusion that he was the last soul remaining on earth. During his trial, he had almost come to believe it, but then he saw her face.

Tahlia.

His goddess.

She had never left him. He refused to let her go.

"What have you done?"

Isa couldn't bring himself to turn away from the flames. Even as the water goddess came to stand beside him, he maintained a watchful vigilance. He didn't need to see her face to know what it would convey; judgment. The favorite pastime of the gods.

"I can't just let her die. She can't just … not exist." His words were both broken and fortified, defending the choice he had made with every shred of strength he had left. "Forever is too long."

"That was not your decision to make. She never wanted to be one of us," the goddess reminded him.

A stubborn muscle feathered in Isa's jaw. The debate in the corner of his mind was growing louder now that it had been discovered. It didn't matter though. The flames crackled and the sky was illuminated with drifting embers.

"She might condemn me for it," Isa agreed and braced himself against the thought as if it were capable of wounding him to the bone. "I can live with that."

"So, it seems, must she."

If it worked.

The god of fire and ash may not accept her like this. She hadn't been sacrificed by a priest, amidst prayers and a ritual. There had been a delay between her breath leaving her body and her bones being burned. At least the god of beauty and fertility would not claim her. Isa reached for the brass vial around his neck, feeling assured by its presence against his chest. As long as he lived, he would never remove it. He would remain warden to her greatest enemy and ensure that the god of beauty and fertility never escaped from his prison. It was all Isa could do to keep Tahlia safe, in death or divinity.

"What will you do now?" The water goddess's question was soft, with an undertow of sadness.

"I promised Tahlia, should anything happen to her, I would pledge myself to Kala, the heir to the black sands."

The water goddess turned on him in an instant, her eyes flashing with a gale's sudden intensity. "You cannot go back there."

"Why?"

"You know why."

"The black sand," he said plainly and she gave a subtle nod of confirmation. "What is it?"

The raging seas in her orbs calmed a little as she considered her answer. "A curse."

"A curse on the land?"

"Partly." Her clipped tone indicated she was unwilling to reveal more but she leveled him with a penetrating warning. "You cannot return."

Isa knew the water goddess did not issue the warning lightly. In any other circumstances he would heed her words, but he had promised Tahlia he would serve her heir. Kala was still a child. She would need him if she was going to rule the black sands as queen. The prospect of returning to the black sands, of letting its obsidian poison seep beneath his skin, filled him with dread. In the short time he was there, he had fought every single second to maintain control over himself and not give in to the dark urges that were seeping into his soul. He had barely managed it. The relief he had felt upon leaving the kingdom was instant. The moment they had crossed into the Idris, the black sand drained from his system and his tattoos returned to their normal turquoise color. His emotions had steadied and he felt like he'd returned to himself.

That was after mere days. This would be years.

Isa didn't know how he was going to survive it or who he would be on the other side of it, but he had to find a way.

"I have no choice. I swore an oath to Tahlia and now I will swear one to Kala. My life belongs to her."

A weight settled on his heart as they both returned their gaze to observe the embers dancing up to the night sky.

"Then I can't save you," the goddess replied. "Either of you."

KALA

Kala stared blankly up at the ceiling as she laid in bed. Ele slept curled up beside her, their hands still clasped together, offering what little comfort they could to one another. They hadn't washed or changed clothes or turned down the sheets before collapsing on top of the bed. Exhaustion and grief made them crumble and disintegrate until there was nothing left.

Kala had never allowed herself to fall apart like that before. Not when she was taken to become a slave, not even when her family had tried to beat her to death. She knew she would have cried as a baby, but honestly, she didn't think she had cried since. Crying did nothing but waste precious water her body could not afford to lose. Breaking apart only made her more vulnerable to attack. Yet she couldn't help it, and neither could Ele, so they anchored each other as they both fragmented into a million pieces.

After crying herself to sleep, Kala had woken mere hours later, her body still numb but her mind overflowing with thoughts. The memory of Tahlia collapsing haunted her. The idea that she was now queen of the black sands was absurd. None of it felt real. She had wanted to go to sleep and wake up to find it had all been a vivid hallucination. Too much heat, perhaps. Or the belated effects of head trauma from the beating she'd endured. But she'd woken up in the same bed, holding Ele's hand, her tears dried and her heart heavy.

Tahlia could not be gone, and this could not be her life.

But it was.

In one way it was laughable. All her life she had fought to survive, scrounging enough food and water to sustain her for another day. She had hated courtiers and wealthy merchants and basically anyone who had been born to wealth and didn't know what it was like to suffer. To fear. To earn each breath. She had dreamed of one day being able to eat until her stomach no longer ached. Of finding a secret well of water that she could drink from whenever she liked, the water clean, cool, and bottomless. Her dreams had never extended beyond these things. Certainly not to living in a grand palace amongst kings and finding a family who would do anything for her, including naming her heir to a kingdom. It was more than she could have ever hoped for, far more than she would have ever asked for, and the price was too high. But Tahlia had paid it. There was no changing that now.

Muffled sounds filtered through her thoughts, drawing her attention to the door. It sounded like someone was arguing outside. She could barely make out their voices, but she thought she recognized Henri's. Then the muted voices turned to shouts, followed by a loud fracas. The moment Kala's hand slipped from Ele's, he jolted awake. She slid off the bed and crossed the room in an instant, running out into the hallway. She knew Ele would follow her, probably brandishing his shamshir, but it wasn't an enemy that greeted them. It was a brawl.

Except Isa wasn't fighting back as Henri stood over him, raining down blow after blow, each one more savage than the last. It made Kala's heart thump violently in her chest. The attack was vicious and unrestrained. Henri was going to kill him. Still, Isa made no attempt to defend himself. He didn't shift into sand or try to overpower Henri, which he could have easily done with his intimidating size. Isa simply surrendered himself to the punishment, as if he were willing to accept death without a fight. The Naiab warriors who had left their guard posts to investigate the commotion were now shifting on their feet anxiously, exchanging tense looks, and casting their eyes in Malik's direction, silently begging him to intervene. He didn't. He stood there watching the fight with a pained expression, but he did nothing.

Kala marched up to Malik. "What's going on?"

"Kala." Malik's features morphed to surprise at the sight of her. "You shouldn't be here."

"What happened?" Ele asked behind her.

"Neither of you should be here. Go back to bed," Malik urged.

"What's going on?" Kala's tone was firm as she directed the question to the Naiab warriors.

"Isa stole Tahlia's body and burned it," one of them replied.

Oh. No.

Frigid ice poured down her spine, stealing her breath, causing her head to pound in sudden urgency. Kala's gaze slowly returned to the fight and she knew, without a doubt, that Henri *was* going to kill him. Blood splattered across the floor, which was already smeared with crimson, and she was pretty sure she just heard a bone break. Yet she couldn't bring herself to move or even speak.

Isa had tried to offer Tahlia to the god of fire and ash. He had tried to make her ascend to divinity. It was unthinkable. Unforgivable. Tahlia never wanted to be a divine. She had fled the Hara and spent her life in hiding, trying to avoid that fate. The gods had finally got their revenge but the one comfort remained that in death, they could never reach her.

"Kala?" Ele's voice sounded far away but urgent. It sparked her to life somehow, bringing her to her senses.

It was instinct that made her mouth move when her mind couldn't. "Stop."

Henri didn't hear her or he didn't care because he certainly didn't stop.

"I am queen of the black sands and I order you to stop!"

Desperate, Kala turned to the Naiab and they responded in a heartbeat, several of them running to restrain Henri and pull him off. Henri thrashed and yelled, trying to break free, but the moment he saw Kala walk over to stand beside Isa he stilled. By the way he looked at her, she was pretty sure he had been unaware of her presence until that moment. He had been so focused on killing Isa, he didn't know his actions had drawn an audience. The Naiab released him but remained close, ready to intervene if he tried to attack Isa again.

Isa moaned at her feet, but Kala knew it wasn't from his injuries. It was because he was still alive. Barely. His face was a bloody pulp and his body was likely suffering through several broken bones. He would live, though. The Naiab were warriors. They commanded the sands and thrived in the harshest desert. He would survive a beating.

"Kala, step aside," Henri ordered. "I will kill him now or tomorrow but his sentence is death."

"He's not one of your people. He's Naiab. Only his Shahri can sentence him," she countered.

"They did it together! Him and the water goddess! His Shahri will not deliver justice!"

Kala stood firm as Henri bellowed at her. He had never raised his voice at her before but she wasn't frightened. She knew he wasn't angry at her. Not really. He was grief-stricken and heart-broken. They all were. Henri had reacted to Tahlia's death with rage. Malik with silent acceptance. Ele had fallen apart beside her. Isa had crossed a line. What he had done was not forgivable but it was understandable. The possibility of a loved one living on in whatever form would appeal to anyone. Except Tahlia had not wanted to live on, not as a goddess.

"I swear." Isa spluttered as he tried to move, drawing himself up to a kneeling position at her feet.

It was like seeing a mountain kneel.

"I swear my oath to you, as queen of the black sands. I made a promise and I will not break it."

A promise. To Tahlia, no doubt. Kala should have known.

Tahlia was no fool. She knew there was no chance the gods would let her live a mortal life. Trapping the god of beauty and fertility had not changed her fate. It had only bought her time. Time to get back to her family, to see her loved ones safe and reunited. Perhaps some part of her had embraced hope that she might have more, but another part of her had named an heir and made Isa swear an oath. She knew the gods did not forgive or forget.

"I accept." Kala stared down at Isa for a moment before turning her gaze on Henri and lifting her chin defiantly. "He is my subject now and I pardon him."

"You what?!" Henri howled.

Kala ignored him and turned her attention back to Isa. "We will travel to the black sands as soon as you are healed. Someone fetch a healer."

One of the Naiab left the group to carry out her order. It was strange to hear herself issue commands, to have her words carry weight.

"You can't leave," Ele stammered as he stumbled forward. His face was stark with disbelief.

"I have to. I'm queen now."

"You don't have to be queen just yet," Henri interrupted, his voice calmer now, though strained from the effort of leashing his emotions. "You are still young. Malik or I can rule as regent until you come of age. You should come back with us, with Ele. Enjoy being a child for once."

"Please." Ele stared at her, his wide eyes welling with tears.

It should have shattered her resolve in an instant but it didn't. Somehow, Kala knew where she needed to be and it wasn't with Ele. She loved them, they would always be her family, but she couldn't return to her old life. She had been gifted a new beginning, a chance to become something bigger than herself. Tahlia had died to give it to her. It was now her responsibility not to squander it.

"I'm sorry, I have to go."

Kala stepped forward until she was standing in front of Ele. He looked absolutely devastated. She knew she should feel the same, and perhaps she would later, but right now all she felt was determined.

"I will always be your friend. And you can come visit me whenever you like."

Ele didn't reply. He simply stared at her as if he couldn't believe he was losing someone else.

"At the very least, we will see each other on my twentieth birthday. You promised to tell me your full name, remember?"

Ele nodded mutely. Then he hugged her fiercely, as if he never wanted to let her go.

But eventually, he did.

EPILOGUE

HENRI

6 months later

Henri watched from the sidelines as Ele parried the strike and then lunged forward in a bold, lethal move. His tutor glided backward, his footwork light as a dancer, as he defended the charge with ease. To his credit, Ele didn't show any hint of frustration or tiredness, even though he had been practicing for over an hour. His concentration was unbreakable as he tried to feel out his opponent, watching and anticipating his next move, waiting for the chance to land a death blow. The boy's posture was tight, his grip on his shamshir near perfect. Henri couldn't help the pride that bloomed in his chest.

Ever since they returned from the war, Ele had insisted on having sword and sparring lessons with his tutor every day. Even after the lessons were over, he would remain in the open field and practice until he was exhausted. Henri knew the fire that fueled his single-minded dedication. Ele blamed himself for Tahlia's death, no matter how many times Henri tried to reason with him.

He could relate to that.

There was not a day that passed that Henri didn't think of her, guilt gnawing away at him like a cancer. Some days he felt hollowed out by grief, submerged in a sea of helplessness. Other days he raged; at the gods, at the world, at himself. He had sworn to Tahlia that he would protect her and he had failed. Twice.

It wasn't right. They had all survived against insurmountable odds and now they were living their lives, ruling over this great country. Yet without Tahlia, the significance of their victory felt dulled. She should be with them, standing beside him, watching Ele grow into a man. Her reflection should be in Henri's full-length mirror. Her warm body in his bed. Her laughter in his ear. Now every time he smelled jasmine or roses, he felt like he could hardly breathe.

The loss of Kala only added to their pain. Henri knew Ele felt her absence the deepest. Henri had hoped Kala would change her mind and travel back with them, but she hadn't. Not even Ele's pleas moved her. After Tahlia died, something changed in Kala. Overnight she became quiet and contemplative, no longer the reckless sassy girl they had met in the Thaka. It was as if she felt a fervent duty to accept the path laid out for her because Tahlia couldn't. Kala felt compelled to honor her memory and her gift. Even if it meant leaving everything and everyone she loved.

They hadn't heard from Kala since they parted ways after the war. Henri took comfort in knowing that he had established an extensive spy network across his lands, as well as the black sands, which would inform him of her welfare. It was all he could do.

He had no choice but to trust her to Isa's care, despite his better judgment.

Tahlia had trusted the Naiab warrior. She had made him swear to serve Kala should anything happen to her. It felt like a sharp wound to the heart, knowing Tahlia had chosen Isa over him. Henri didn't know why. He had dwelled on it for the entire journey back to his kingdom but even now, months later, he was none the wiser. Perhaps Isa had kept his word where Henri hadn't. He had come for her, when Henri couldn't. Maybe Tahlia's relationship with the warrior had deepened more than Henri knew. It was possible she had even fallen in love with him. Not knowing had almost driven Henri to madness, so he stopped allowing himself to think about it and forced himself to just accept it for what it was.

Tahlia's choice.

Everything had changed since that day. Merovia was not the same country it was before the war. The walls had been demolished in each of the kingdoms and new territory lines had been drawn. The people were now free to cross borders without their king's permission and the Naiab could travel wherever they wished. The Citadel, however, remained restricted to everyone except the Naiab. The water goddess did not want her sanctuary disturbed more than it already was. Truth be told, no one in Merovia wanted to risk their lives by entering the Idris desert, let alone traveling to the Citadel.

Since Tahlia's death, the water goddess had faded from their lives. Henri would have been grateful for it except that, after discovering what Isa had done, the unspoken question lingered in the back of his mind. For weeks afterward, Henri looked for signs in everything. A cool breeze on a scorching day. The unexpected scent of roses on the wind. A song playing in the city streets, the sound of tinkling bells. All of it confirmation. All of it mere coincidence. Finally, he had forced himself to reach a place of acceptance with that too. He had to believe that if Tahlia had ascended to become a divine, she would have found a way to show herself to him by now. Tahlia was gone, and a small part of Henri was relieved because the alternative was unthinkable.

The Merovians believed that when people died, they became stars, their souls burning bright for all eternity. Henri hoped that was true. In his dreams, he would always envision Tahlia soaring above the sky, her light infinitely brighter than all the other stars combined. And in his heart, he would always keep a place for her for the rest of his days.

An arm reached behind to encircle his waist as Malik placed a kiss on his neck. Henri smiled over his shoulder at him but it didn't quite meet his eyes.

"How is our little shadow?" Malik asked, casting his attention to Ele who was swinging his shamshir in a graceful, practiced arc.

"Getting stronger every day, and quick." Henri sighed. "A very dedicated student."

Malik made an impressed noise. "He might even best you one day."

"I have no doubt."

"But will he best *me*?"

Henri snorted. "I can't even best you."

"And you are very distracting so you have an advantage," Malik teased. "Do you want to go a round in the training field? Or we could have a bath?"

Henri grinned despite himself. Malik knew him too well. He knew that when Henri was in his head, he craved distraction from his thoughts and emotions. Fucking or fighting would usually do the trick. Sometimes both in quick succession.

Henri turned within Malik's arms and kissed him, thoroughly. Malik's mouth opened willingly for him and welcomed his tongue to explore his own. Henri had fought for his country, for his people, but he had also fought for this man. To spend a lifetime with him, ruling side by side. To raise Ele together into the man he was born to be. To grow old together, each line on their faces telling the story of a life well lived. A life they shared. A mortal life would never be long enough, but even after their bones were nothing more than sand, they would find each other amongst the stars.

KALA

Kala sat at a desk in her bedchamber, a quill in her hand and an oil lamp burning beside her. She was practicing her letters and words like she did every night, ensuring her grip on the quill was correct and her stokes were neat and elegant. She wanted her first letter to Ele to be perfect. A surprise. She wanted him see just how far she had come in only a matter of months.

Now that she was queen, she had tutors for everything. Reading and writing, languages and art, dance and weaponry. Her days had never been filled with so much purpose. It hurt her head sometimes, and it certainly hurt her body, but she preferred that kind of pain to the pain of hunger or thirst or violence. She never complained about her rigorous schedule. She was grateful for it. Each day she woke up eager to learn more.

There was so much about her new home she didn't know. The kingdom of the black sands was unusual. The ground was actually black sand. She wasn't sure why she had been so surprised to see it but she was. It wasn't like soot or ash, it didn't stain or leave a grimy residue, it was simply sand the color of midnight. According to one of her tutors, the black sand had been there for hundreds of years. It provided unique agricultural conditions where certain plants and herbs that couldn't be grown anywhere else grew to a flourish. The vegetation was rare and therefore high in demand and price, which in turn sustained her kingdom in trade.

Craftsmen also transformed the black sand into various unique wares such as obsidian glass, ebony ceramics, and onyx building materials. She recognized it in the mud bricks of every building in her city, between the windowpanes of her palace. More disturbingly, though, she saw it in the tattoos that flowed beneath Isa's skin. Gone was the turquoise blue that shifted and sparkled in the sunlight. His tattoos were now the color of ink. Kala had tried to ask him about it but he refused to talk about it. She hadn't asked again.

She hadn't asked about a lot of things. They hadn't spoken about the god of beauty and fertility that was trapped within a vial around his neck and they certainly hadn't spoken about what he had done to Tahlia in offering her up to the god of fire and ash. It didn't matter, though. Kala was pretty sure she could fill in the blanks on her own. Isa's fascination with Tahlia was obvious from the beginning and clearly something had happened between them when he went to rescue her from Kareem. Kala had seen it in the way they looked at each other, especially when Tahlia was reunited with Henri and Malik. Love made people do desperate things, become martyrs and murderers. It didn't make it right but it did make it understandable. Kala would not condemn Isa for it. Tahlia had trusted him enough to choose him to be Kala's guardian. She would not disrespect Tahlia's choice.

Selfishly, Kala was grateful to have Isa by her side. Despite their shared silence on certain matters, they had become quite close. She supposed it was inevitable when he was the only person she knew in the entirety of her kingdom but there was also just something about the man. His presence steadied her. He watched over her during her lessons and advised her on how to rule her kingdom and gain the support of her people. He never talked down to her or tried to stop her from doing what she wanted. He never treated her like a child. He treated her like a queen. It didn't take long for Kala to understand exactly why Tahlia had trusted him. He was a good man. A loyal man. Kala knew he would always serve her and keep her safe.

Isa's company was the only thing that eased her loneliness. Kala had been so confident in her decision to leave her family and travel to the black sands to start her new life as queen, she had given no thought to how lonely it would be. Some days the loneliness was unbearable. Other days it was easy to distract herself from noticing it too much, but it was always there. She missed her family. Most of all she missed Ele. Not a day passed when she didn't think about him and wonder what he was doing. She thought about all the times they had laughed together. The days he had brought her cake from the palace kitchen. She knew she had hurt him deeply by choosing not to go back with him, and maybe his hurt had turned to anger, but she hoped her letter would smooth things over between them. She hoped he would write back.

For the first few weeks after arriving in her kingdom, Kala had wondered if she made a mistake in her decision but now, months later, she was pretty certain she hadn't. Tahlia had given her a kingdom, a chance at an extraordinary life. Whether now or in ten years time Kala would have had to leave her family. Leave Ele. It was better this way, to do it sooner rather than later. She didn't want to grow too attached and then be heartbroken later when she had to leave everyone. Besides, she would see her family again someday. She hoped they would be proud of her.

Kala surveyed her writing with a critical eye and then, satisfied with her efforts, she placed the quill back in the inkpot. As she stood, she carried her oil lamp and glanced around at her bedchamber, admiring the expensive tapestries she had chosen to adorn her walls. She was slowly redecorating the entire palace to suit her tastes but these tapestries were her favorites. They featured patterns of lotus blossoms and leaves. It reminded her of Tahlia and the story of the lotus; each morning rising from the mud without stains to flower and then returning to the murky water each evening, folding in on itself to protect its inner beauty. A symbol of purity, strength and resilience. Kala would endeavor to be like the lotus, to be as strong as Tahlia had been.

Placing the oil lamp on her bedside table, Kala crawled beneath silk sheets in a bed that could easily have fit several people. It still felt strange sleeping alone. She had grown used to having Ele's body curled up beside her. Before that, she had always slept next to her siblings on the floor in a cramped room in a decrepit building in the Thaka. She wondered what her family would think of her if they could see her now, if they knew what she had become. The answer was plain in the memory of their twisted faces and hateful sneers as they tried to beat her to death. She didn't often allow herself to think of them and when she did, it always made her angry. It didn't matter what they thought of her. She was queen of the black sands now and she was going to learn all the knowledge of the world while they remained ignorant. Kala hated to admit it but the water goddess had been right about one thing; to rule was a rare privilege. She would not waste a moment of it by thinking about where she had come from or what could have been. Her life was going to be extraordinary and she couldn't wait for all the adventures to come.

REVIEW REQUEST AND BONUS SCENES

Thank you so much for reading this book! I hope you enjoyed it. It would mean the world to me if you could leave a review on Amazon, Goodreads, or BookBub. One of the most important keys to an indie author's success is book reviews. Book reviews give social proof to potential readers that it is highly likely they will enjoy the book. With so many options for books out there, book reviews are a must! Especially at launch time. By leaving a review, you are helping other like-minded readers to find my book and therefore are greatly assisting me in building my career as an indie author. So thank you!

If you enjoyed this series, you'll love the FREE bonus scenes which you can get by signing up to my monthly newsletter. It's easy, just go to my website at www.clairebutlerauthor.com and sign up!

You can also find a map of Merovia on my website. Check it out! Find me at:

https://www.instagram.com/clairebutlerauthor/

Clairebutlerauthor | Facebook

Clairebutlerauthor (@clairebutlerauthor) | TikTok

ALSO BY CLAIRE BUTLER

THE RED WOOD SERIES
To Reclaim A Kingdom
To Reforge A Destiny

THE DIVINE TAPESTRY SERIES
Of Sand & Silk

ABOUT THE AUTHOR

Claire wrote her first book before she knew how to write the alphabet. It consisted of scribbling on a page and having her sister illustrate the page next to it. She has since refined her books to include actual words. Claire has a background in Psychology. She loves writing fantasy romance books because it allows her to explore social themes in new worlds, intense emotions, the formation and shifting of identities, the power of first love, and the enduring bonds of friendship. Claire lives in Australia with her husband and two children. She is obsessed with beaches, picnics, and sunshine. Often in combination with a good book. Her favorite authors include Sarah J Maas, Renee Ahdieh, Carissa Broadbent, and Tahereh Mafi.

ACKNOWLEDGMENTS

As I sit here, I can't believe I have written my fourth book. This book was by far the hardest for me to write and I owe a lot of people endless thanks for keeping me motivated, focused, and for loving this story as much as I do.

To Menna my alpha reader, literary soul sister, work wife, soul mate and all-round hype woman - words cannot express how much your friendship means to me. When we both become stars in the night sky, I have no doubt we will find each other across the galaxy.

To my beta readers Elyse and Teresa, thank you so much for all of your insightful reflections and enthusiastic comments. This book is definitely better due to all of your feedback.

Endless thanks goes to Phoenix Rising Literary Services for proofreading this book! It was amazing to work with you and I look forward to doing it again in the future.

To my personal assistants Emma and Emily, you ladies are amazing! Thank you so much for all the work you have put in behind the scenes to support me and my books.

A HUGE thank you goes to Claire's Camels (aka my street team) for championing this series. Words are not enough to express how much you all mean to me.

To Emma and Isla, thank you for helping mummy sign books and pack orders. The cover of this book is our favorite color!

Lastly, thank you to you, dear reader. I hope you loved this book and that we will meet again soon.